D1353194

Diana Saville

Diana Saville has written seven books on gardens and their designs. She has also edited an anthology of poetry and paintings. After leaving Oxford University, she worked as a literary agent in London before moving to the West of England with her husband. Her previous novels are *The Marriage Bed* and *The Honey Makers*, and are available from Sceptre.

SCEPTRE

The Hawk Dancer

DIANA SAVILLE

SCEPTRE

Copyright © 1997 Diana Saville

First published in the UK in 1997 by Hodder and Stoughton
First published in paperback in 1998 by Hodder and Stoughton
A division of Hodder Headline PLC
A Sceptre Paperback

The right of Diana Saville to be identified as the Author of
the Work has been asserted by her in accordance with the
Copyright, Designs and Patents Act 1988.

10 9 8 7 6 5 4 3 2 1

A CIP catalogue record for this book is
available from the British Library

ISBN 0 340 67509 8

Typeset by Palimpsest Book Production Limited,
Polmont, Stirlingshire
Printed and bound in Great Britain by
Mackays of Chatham PLC, Chatham, Kent

Hodder and Stoughton
A division of Hodder Headline PLC
338 Euston Road
London NW1 3BH

For Michael with thanks

Acknowledgements ∫

I have learned a great deal from the following books which are essential reading for anyone who is interested in falconry: *Falconry: Art and Practice* by Emma Ford (Blandford, 1992); *A Manual of Falconry* by M.H. Woodford, including an inspirational chapter by J.G. Mavrogordato on rook-hawking (A. & C. Black, 4th Edition, 1987); *The Modern Falconer* by Diana Durman-Walters (Swan Hill Press, 1994); *Training Birds of Prey* by Jemima Parry-Jones (David & Charles, 1994); *Aspects of Killing Wild Animals in Britain* (Pamphlet; an investigation for the Hawk Board) by Dr N.C. Fox; and, for pure pleasure rather than instruction, that literary masterpiece, *The Goshawk*, by T. H. White (Longmans). I would like to thank too the many people who answered my questions, including Biff, Marie-Louise Leschallas, and Hayden and Maureen Roberts (and Phoebe). Falconers sometimes differ from one another in their procedures but any mistakes are my own.

Acknowledgements are due to The Society of Authors as the literary representative of the Estate of A. E. Housman for permission to quote the lines on page 123.

$\int$

A year or so later they were in agreement on one thing at least: that the change in their lives was traceable to that afternoon of the previous summer when she came out of the house and found James sitting near the pond in the garden with his eyes closed. He was making a good all-round show of being unavailable, which was infuriating in the light of his recent behaviour but not untypical since he would sometimes come home and sleep for the whole weekend.

'Are you coming or not?' asked Claire. 'You might support the annual show. And me,' she added. But he persisted in keeping his eyes and ears shut and did not answer.

She glared and tiptoed towards him.

'I'll be back in a couple of hours,' she yelled deafeningly in his ear.

As soon as he was sure that she had left, he stopped affecting to be deprived of all his senses and sat up and looked about him. It was a hot July afternoon and tranquil, so after a while he stripped off to his boxer shorts and walked over to the pool where he sat between the rushes with his legs dangling over the edge. He thought as always that it was a matter for regret that they had not bought a swimming-pool but she had not wished to maintain one and, besides, it being the 1990s, she had wanted what she called a pond with things, which was to say a large natural pond with frogs and birds and insects. Peering into its recesses now, he could see there was no doubt that she had not only a pond but plenty of things. They were moving.

He flicked the surface tension of the liquid with his toe to tease a water boatman, then, feeling drowsy, lay down again, his chest bared to the sun. A man is at his least defended lying on his back and dozing in the semi-nude, but then James was not actually anticipating the untoward this afternoon. Indeed he was at his most relaxed and peaceful, as usual after a row which had reached its climax, was purged and should now disperse. She had not quite forgiven him but would shortly and the days of huge fuss and heaving breasts would soon be over. He pillowed his head on the grass, watching a flock of cloud gliding slowly towards the sun. He smelt the scent of phloxes and felt pleasantly woozy, contentment being the best of all opiates.

He must have nodded off for half an hour or maybe even longer when, thinking he might have enjoyed a sufficiency of sun, he levered himself onto his elbows and then sat up. He was about to get up and toddle back to his pile of clothes and put his shirt on when he felt the bullet skim him.

At least his first bewildered thought was for a bullet, but this must be wrong, for he had heard a rasp, felt the sensation of strokes in the passage of this missile and then sensed a soft thud. Shocked, he raised a tremulous hand to his forehead. He had ducked by reflex; though too late, for the trajectory felt as if it had left a parting in his hair like a comb. The ballistic must have passed within an inch of his head. 'What the hell?' he muttered.

A sound beyond the pool made him inch round cautiously, so as not to draw attention to himself. Some twenty-five yards away, beyond the green reflections, he could see a large bird mantling a pigeon, crushing the pitiful creature in its talons. He could see even from his distance its yellow eye and rapacious beak stabbing and catching at its fluff. The sight stunned him. For a second he stood paralysed, then jumped to action.

'Off, you bastard,' he yelled and splashed his palms futilely on the ground.

The hawk looked up, clutched its prey and flapped for a vertical take-off.

'Off,' shouted James, getting up and starting to run towards the pair. Flustered, the bird shifted its foot and dropped its prey. The pigeon hit the ground with a thump. The hawk flew off to the overhanging branch of a Scots pine and lowered furiously.

James slowed his pace and walked towards the fallen victim.

To his initial relief and then immediate horror, for it must be suffering, he saw that the thing was still alive. He bent and peered at it. It was pink and grey, the colour of a diaphanous late sky, a stock-dove colour. It lay on the grass, its beak open, its breast poutered forwards, pounding bump, bump, bump, three beads of blood at the curve of its elbow where it had been punctured.

'You poor little bugger,' said James, who felt as though he had been raptored himself.

His legs felt a bit weak, so he sat down beside him, then continued to sit as a chaperon, and after that out of friendliness and also out of a loss to know what to do: for there was no doubt that a living dove posed more problems than a dead one. What indeed could he do? The creature was only a pigeon, but a man in all conscience could not leave a fellow-sufferer when he had himself almost shared in the near-mortal blow.

'Claire,' he called automatically, since Claire ought to know what to do, but Claire was not there and he recalled she would not return from the show until later.

He now felt uncertain and wondered whether he would have been better advised not to intervene. After all, the most he had achieved was to force the hawk to go hungry. He was reminded of the truth that in nature the purpose of existence is to find one's own dinner without providing someone else with his. Here he was now with half a dinner on his hands whilst the starving went hungry, which was no help to either. Still semi-naked, and distinctly chilly now that the dilemma had moved out of his body and into his mind, he cupped the stock dove in his hands, uttered a kind run of cooing noises and took it to the barn where the forlorn creature might rest on a bed of straw. As he gazed at it he felt again the air wave of the hawk skimming his head.

'Magnificent creature,' he muttered ambivalently.

As in most years the Longhill Summer Show was held in a large field only recently vacated by sheep. It was well attended for the organisers of the events always ensured there was something for everybody. There were tug-of-war contests and heaving of straw bales. There were sprints and rodeos. There were sack races and hawk displays and dog shows and even a collection of beautiful owls. Some of the young men, strong as tree trunks, rode the bucking bronco, a machine which spun them round. Others, more skilled and ambitious, entered the clay pigeon shoot. A larger, inert group of males, unable or unwilling to do either, would as usual spend the whole afternoon in the beer tent. The only unattended sideshow was the bright yellow kiosk which had been set up by a political group touting at all times for the odd floating voter.

In the marquee on the western side of the field, the afternoon was beginning to unravel now that the flowers and vegetables had been judged. The winners were triumphant while the losers, disgruntled, talked only of scab. Local people like the Bubbs and the Bevans and the Jefferies and the Powells were packing up and going home. A breeze blew in through the canvas flap but the air was hot and smelt of rhubarb wine, two bottles of which had exploded and fizzed over the ground. From time to time the river of noise rolling round the tent was swollen by tributaries from outside: keening sheep crammed into pens, or a passionate episode in the tug-of-war. Within the marquee an escaped parrot bludgeoned the congregation with his wings before he flew up from their heads and sat, a red-and-emerald cockade, on a brace in the apex of the tent.

Below him, a tall fair woman was making slow progress towards the exit. Clutching a cake and a piece of floral art driftwood, Claire Farley threaded her way through the throng of people. Now and then she paused to exchange a word or two.

'No James this weekend?' asked one.

'James away?' asked another.

'He's a bit busy,' Claire said brightly.

She stopped for longer beside another woman, also on her own, younger and of stockier build.

'Still no Stuart?' said Claire, taking her cue it would seem from her earlier encounters.

'Any time now. He'll ring at the last moment as usual,' replied the younger woman with an energy bred of hoping and waiting.

It was always like this, thought Claire. The gaiety when her SAS soldier husband was due home.

'It's been three months?'

'Nearly four. Not as long as sometimes.'

Claire felt her own problems diminished by those of Mary.

'Sam looked after you all right?' She referred to Mary's ten-year-old son.

'Yes,' said Mary doubtfully.

'There you are. You're an item now.'

'Not much of one. He spends all of his time watching telly.'

'Didn't I see him at the hawk demonstration?' Claire nodded in the direction of Mr Powell the birdman.

'He's started to help Wilf. But he'll be back in front of the box this evening.'

'Not if his dad gets home.'

'I expect his dad will join him. For the first few days he'll do anything for a quiet life and I'll do anything to give him one.'

'Well,' said Claire, making signs of forward movement. 'Give the returning hero my congratulations.'

'Oh yes,' said Mary. 'I think he's a hero. He doesn't, nor does Sam of course.'

'Nonsense. Every boy wants that kind of father for his dad.'

Mary nodded. 'Only joking you know.'

Claire gave an appropriate smile and moved on.

A stout, ebullient woman who was gesticulating to another couple turned round and seized her as she went past. It was apparent that she too had bought her fair share of driftwood.

'Snap,' she said.

'It's called doing one's local duty,' replied Claire.

'And we do more than most. We've had a necessarily expensive onslaught on the stalls. He's mad. Nearly £50 it's cost us.'

Claire regarded her friend with amusement. The wife of an MP, albeit for a neighbouring constituency, she was given to loud and subversive complaints on her husband's need to avoid public stinginess.

'Poor old Ellie. We all have our little problems.'

The two women exchanged a glance of sisterhood sympathy to cover all the irksome trivialities of domestic life.

'It's ages since we've seen you,' said Ellie. 'You've gone to ground. Where's James?'

Claire prepared to launch the usual reply that he was away or a bit busy or exhausted after a week's work and spending forty-eight hours asleep before leaving on Monday or absolutely anything except the truth that he was recuperating after a row about seeing the woman he had sworn he had given up months ago, but since it was her old friend Ellie, she at least gave herself the satisfaction of muttering, 'He's pretending to be asleep in the garden and I hate him.'

'Right,' said Ellie. 'Now we've got that one sorted out.'

'What sorted out?' said her husband, Anthony Milner, making an untimely interruption. 'Can I have your purse?'

'Christ. Not more.'

'Yup. Again.'

'As you very well know,' said Ellie as he disappeared again, 'I'd have got him to dump it years ago. All I wanted to do this afternoon was to catch up on some sleep in the deckchair just like your charming husband. But Tony comes from an honourable tradition. The show must always go on.'

'Believe me,' said Claire self-indulgently, 'the show must plod on for all of us.'

'Don't mope,' said Ellie, putting an affectionate hand on her arm. 'You must come over and have dinner with us sometime. We never see James in London. We'll get together and remind him of the more civilised little pleasures of country life.'

'How lovely. James could do with the odd reminder.'

Promising to meet up in the autumn after the summer holiday, the two women exchanged a few more words, then separated.

As Claire left by the main exit of the marquee, she saw Joseph Jenkins who was holding his box of failed vegetables. An annual competitor with the reputation of being a poor loser, he was talking to Mr Evans but glared about and raised his voice for anyone who would listen.

'What indeed, pray, can you expect from a judge who went to college?'

'What indeed?' agreed his companion and spat accurately through a hole in the tent.

'You were somewhat missed,' announced Claire, placing a walnut cake on the table and the driftwood floral arrangement in the pigbin. 'It was remarked upon by Ellie and a host of others.'

'I was busy.'

'Busy were you? It looked poor not to put in an appearance. Even a short one.'

'I intended to after my medicinal doze but I was waylaid.'

'The arms of sleep perhaps.'

'The wings of a dove actually.'

Claire paused in the act of cutting the cake and frowned.

'What do you mean?'

'A hawk took a pigeon.'

'A hawk?'

'When I was sitting by the pool. It must have been a hawk. Quite a bird. Yellow eyes. Hooked beak. It almost got me.'

'Really, James, don't be silly.'

'It was a damn near run thing. It nearly hit me anyway. It was a hundred mile an hour chase.' It was exciting even in retrospect.

'What happened?'

'I've just told you. It caught it by the pool. The pigeon's alive. I've put it in the barn. What do we do with it?'

'You took it away? It didn't kill it?'

'I stopped it.'

'Was that wise? It's wounded?'

James nodded. He felt irritated that she was calling his judgement into question. A good Samaritan, but chastised for being a creature of impulse. Any moment now, she would ask him whether he had thought through the implications.

Claire put down her knife which had been poised to cut a second slice of cake and looked at him. He rose to his feet, followed by old Jarvis, the overweight labrador, who was ordered straight back to the basket. Officiously she led her husband out of the large dark kitchen, through the lobby and dim back hall and then out into the warm ochre sunlight of the late summer afternoon which was dusty with seed heads and floating gnats. They crossed the stable yard where the cobbles formed an apron before the large open brick barn.

She is still angry with me, he thought, watching her tense, squared back and the jerky diagonal pull of her jeans as she strode. What the hell, let her leak her little irritations if she wants to. She'll get over it. It's always taken time before.

They entered the barn, one behind the other. The sweet hay

smell of the straw enveloped them and the spicy scent of the log store.

'I put it towards the back.' He looked round, puzzled that it was no longer there. 'Perhaps it's flown off. It must have recovered.'

She was standing in the far right-hand corner, looking down.

'It's here and it's dead.' She spoke accusingly. She was standing in front of him, blocking his view of the bird, taking charge by being obstructionist.

'It wasn't half an hour ago. Are you sure?'

He shifted over to the side and bent towards the pigeon. He touched it. There was no response, no shift of the eyelid, no gentle protesting grope of its feet. Both stared down at the wisp of departed life in the straw. Glazed eyes in death, beak open in rictus, yet, save for the three drops of dark blood, its feathers were still perfect, that immaculate miraculous formation, unruffled and still velvet soft around the hardening body.

'Shit,' he said sadly. 'I hoped it would have a chance.'

He feared she was glad he had been a failure which would give a weapon with which to browbeat him, but as they stared down shoulder to shoulder and united before this little death, he was relieved to sense that this had changed her mood to one of concession.

'It was awfully pretty,' she said. 'A stock dove perhaps. That pink, see? Well, there we are. We'd better bury it.'

'I'll get a spade,' he offered.

She turned round and nodded.

He was close enough to see the slight fair fuzz, like a gooseberry's, above her upper lip. The slope of her jaw and neck had retained a girlishness. He had always admired her clean, straightforward, honest looks.

'Claire. You are all right aren't you? Nothing went wrong this afternoon?'

'Not this afternoon. Tony and Ellie were there as I said, Ellie grumbling as usual about how much it costs them. Joe Jenkins was in a wretched humour about his cauliflowers and beetroots. Mary Cormack was there with her peaky little boy. The Sarwardine team won the tug-of-war. And that tiresome telly director was squatting on his heels and squinting through cupped hands.'

'Awful.'

'Pretentious anyway.'

They smiled, joined at the hip against this alien intruder.

'Nothing else?'

'Yes. All those people there asking where you were. Why is her husband so absent? Where is he? We never see him. It's humiliating. I don't doubt they've been having a mutter behind my back.'

'Nobody would think that. Even if they knew what happened which they don't. Please.' He saw she was suddenly on the brink of tears.

'Ellie did. I saw it in her eyes. Good old Claire, she was thinking, what a trooper.'

'So you are. There's no one better than you.' He put his arms about her and hugged her. 'You know that, don't you? You know there's only ever you.'

'Do I?'

'Forgive me, sweetheart. It meant nothing. It won't start up again.'

'Perhaps I'd be wrong to believe you. Stupid.'

'There is simply no way I could live without you.'

'Forgiveness is finite except in mothers.'

'Don't please bang on, my darling. I know I've been a rogue but at least it's an honest one and anyway it's over.'

'Is it?'

'You know.'

'For good. Never again.'

'Yes.'

They stood in silence, the pigeon forgotten, looking at one another in the ribbed light which had penetrated the arrow-slit windows of the barn. Swallows nesting in the rafters flashed to and fro, swooping for insects outside in flamboyant arcs and scoops.

'This hawk,' she asked, 'what was it like?'

James spaced out his hands. 'Medium big, pale front, I think some dark streaks but hard to say.' He remembered again the silence broken by the unfathomable rush. How naked and vulnerable he had felt in his little shorts.

'Just a common sparrowhawk, I suppose.'

He looked down at the pigeon, reminded that they had yet to bury it.

'That's it, is it? The very last question. Are we now entwined in mutual compatibility?'

She took his arm and hugged it.

When Herefordshire fields are ploughed in spring and autumn, the land turns red. This is because so much of the county lies on the old red sandstone, a seam of Jurassic origin which it shares with Devon. The earth is red and the rocks are red and many of the stone buildings are the same rich colour too, like terracotta. This was the case with the Farleys' house which seemed to have grown out of the soil. Coral in sunlight and mauve in evening shadow when it still exhaled the day's warmth, it had been quarried and built to the orderly and sensible rules of the eighteenth century. In its no-nonsense way it belonged comfortably to its landscape. Free of all architectural excess or doctrine, neither of which had penetrated to this remote part of England, it was simple rather than elegant. In front the face of the building was regulated by its rows of white sash windows and a central porch. At the back, the rear façade was equally plain. It overlooked a barn, a later addition built of brick and lying at right angles. Together, the pair formed a neat south-facing L.

It had until recent years been a working farm but its land which had been let to a tenant was then sold. Even so, it still looked over its fields and enjoyed a fine view. Someone at some time had planted trees here in this green valley – slow Herefordshire oaks and clusters of pines – not in park-like groupings to manage the landscape but for the purpose of sheltering his sheep and cattle from heat and storm. Though it was normal to fell trees in the course of modern agribusiness, these had escaped and the hedgerows too. It was this that gave the impression that the land here was put to a more leisurely use than was usual. In any case the up-and-down nature of the ground on this hilly western side of the county allowed a more traditional form of farming to survive. This was not a bereaved landscape like the plains.

The house was in that strange part of Britain that is still called The Marches. It is border country belonging to both Wales and England yet is neither, seeming to keep for itself a world and an other-worldliness of its own. It must be one of the last areas to have retained a Thomas Hardy quality with its green, remote and lonely countryside, for it is still possessed of a larger animal than human population. Over it and to the west broods the long dark spine of the Black Mountains and the dumpling hills and arrow-heads of the more northern promontories. Even the light here is special, due perhaps to the tricks it plays with the hills. This is border country and this is signified in its old name, The Marches: not a tribute to any season of the year; but a soft version of the Teutonic word *mark* which denoted the no-man's-land dividing one village community from its neighbours. The Marches: most people who have come to live here have been in search of a quiet life. They want the tranquil emptiness and know that it is the apartness of border country that keeps it quiet.

However, Claire and James Farley were not typical of such people. They had not sought a quiet life, but, rather, been bequeathed one, since the house had been left to James by a widowed and childless aunt. As legatees, they were not the most deserving. It had been many years since they had seen the aunt, not in fact since their marriage. It was scarcely surprising they had not been to see her: she was thought to be eccentric to the point of dottiness, and, besides, they were cocooned in London with two children of school age. In any case, this was the mid-1980s which was not a period when pioneer-type countryside tempted, the pendulum of the 1970s with its fancies of self-sufficiency having swung the other way. The 1980s form of country fantasies came swagged. Nonetheless, they woke up one morning to find themselves beneficiaries.

For a short while it looked as though they would be legatees in name only, for James proposed selling the house immediately and buying a more convenient substitute in Sussex. 'We would use it,' he explained, 'so much more often. And in any case, this farmhouse is probably unsuitable,' he added, having one faint but unpromising childhood memory. But attached to the will was a letter from the aunt, urging them to keep the home. 'You may not need it now,' she had written in her vigorous, undotty script, 'but you will come to realise that these things are rare and increasingly precious. Money is either spent or institutionalised.' The argument was persuasive enough to force a rethink.

The Farleys set off as a family group one May weekend, Claire, James and the two girls, Griselda and Katy, then fourteen and ten. They were doubtful but prepared to consider the house with an open mind. However, May is a fatal month in which to exercise critical judgement of the countryside. In the west of Herefordshire to which spring doesn't come very early, the verges are brassy with late cowslips and the big old oaks are gilded with the gauze of new leaf. Willing to be entranced, the grown-up Farleys looked about them as they drove along the lanes. There were dells pricked with purple from orchids and the furtive scent of the woods blew in through the window. At a clearing in the hedgerow they stopped the car and got out to gaze across the valley. They heard the loud sad curlews and watched the lapwings dance. Without realising, they had crossed into border country. They recognised it as different and knew for the first time that all this was theirs. They had about another two miles to go, so they returned to the car and drove on. The huge flank of the Black Mountains reared like an animal asleep in the distance.

In expectation, Katy hung out of the back window. Even Griselda who had affected a sulky boredom showed some interest.

'There's a pheasant,' said Katy, the younger, ready to be triggered by anything.

'No one's going to be *ébloui* by a pheasant,' said Griselda. 'Anyway it's a partridge with red legs.'

'What would you know?'

'That's enough. We're nearly there,' said James, paterfamilias.

They glimpsed the house through gaps in the hedgerow. It flashed pink amongst the green. Then the brambled opening to the drive, two columnar lines of hornbeams carpeted with ramsons; and the notice, a faded wooden nameplate crumbling at the edges. It was called Domain. They had of course known its name, but how different to see it and own it. *Demeine*, old French. *Dominicus* from *Dominus*, Latin: lord. Demesne: in Law, possession of property as one's own. Property, property, property. In direct speech, it is all mine, my land, me.

'I didn't realise how beautiful it was,' said James.

'It may be very pretty,' said Griselda. 'But honestly I just can't get excited by the countryside.'

'Only fourteen years old but her dissatisfaction with life runs so deep,' said Claire, craning forward.

Domain. They rolled along the leafy potholed drive and rattled over a grid.

'We don't think Squire Farley will be selling his inheritance,' said Claire.

'No,' said James as he reached the gate. 'But we'd better wait and see.'

Domain. He stopped the car. Claire got out and opened the metal gate. A rutted earth path continued for another hundred yards. A bowl of hills surrounded them, the emerald green of rising fields pressing in on all sides. At the entrance to the yard, a rusted tractor had come to rest from an earlier age. Its claws were spread out as though it had suffered a spasm, collapsed and then died. They entered the yard.

'Well,' said James after a moment. 'Better to travel in hope.'

There were two small buildings, shacked up in corrugated iron, and a brick barn which had lost its structure and was waterfalling down.

'Maybe,' said Claire 'the house is all right.'

Its stone was flaking and the ridge of the roof dipped in a saddle-back. They sent the children to what seemed to be the paddock and went inside. It had been uninhabited for a year. Untended for twenty years. An elder had seeded into the dining room. The sapling reached halfway up the wall. There was mould on the ceilings and curtains of ivy had penetrated two upstairs windows. The place was under invasion from species in relentless pursuit of their own life. They adhered like barnacles to the house. They owned it, these proprietors. They had moved in during the long human void.

'It's not on,' said James, rocking his feet on the floor. 'It's a tumbledown farm. It's going to be too bloody expensive.'

Claire went to the bedroom window and looked out.

'Yes,' she said. She did not seem to be listening.

From here you could overlook the concrete yard and rusty machinery and brick and stone collapsing like liquid, and reach out to the bowl of fields at the back. The emerald was intense. There were gold gauzy oaks and sea-green pines, then the hills rose up, then, behind, the navy blue spine of the mountain. It was sensible to resist anchoring it to a fantasy, but it was tethered, it could not break free.

'Let's go outside,' she said.

A flock of cawing jackdaws rose. A tumbledown farm. Outside the old working yard was a grassy vegetable patch with gooseberry bushes, gnarled and knobbly with fruit. Fans of rhubarb splayed and single bright peonies were blooming, persistent plants that enjoy peace long after the human beings have left them alone.

There was a sense of deep continuity. She sat down on the grass. There were wild strawberries with five-sided ivory flowers and the first of their unripe pointed fruits. Willowdown was falling and streaming across in the air. She looked round for James but he wasn't there. She got up, took out a pen and a pad of paper and walked on.

James too was exploring but had returned to the yard. He was standing in front of the half-dismantled brick barn. The amount of rubble made him feel a bit sick. Decay of this degree was not romantic. He had imagined a parallel universe to their house in Barnes and his imagination had handed him one in good order. He gave a last look round, then left the yard and turned right towards the remains of an orchard. He went to wait for his wife at the foot of an apple tree. He could hear his younger daughter calling in the distance. He closed his eyes. He had made up his mind. Half an hour later his wife arrived and sat down beside him. She was smiling and handed him a pad of paper. He noticed a sketch of the house and adjacent barn. There were notes. South-facing, she had written, afternoon light in shafts here and here. A weeping ash, wonderful tree, keep. Remove corrugated iron sheds, enclose yard after removal, open up terrific view. James put it down in irritation.

'For God's sake, Claire. This is not only expensive but a huge effort.'

His wife made a non-committal noise. She turned her head to look into the orchard, which was scabby and a bit gappy where gales must have toppled trees too old to defend themselves, but the apples were in blossom and frail cuckoo flowers were dotted about the grass in patches of rinsed-out mauve. Neither spoke, though in the silence there was no doubt that the house had become an interlocutor.

James felt the chill of responsibilities. He had owned the fiefdom of his domain for a few hours which on balance was quite long enough. It occurred to him that he was the one doing a favour to his aunt rather than the other way round. She had run the house down, written it off and required him to carry her burdens. What a neat exit. Odd, wasn't it, wrong even, that she should emerge as the beneficiary, posthumous moreover, rather than he, the living legatee? Surely the living should be given priority over the dead.

He said, 'I grant you it's charming but the problems rule it out. And as for my aunt, we agreed there's no real reason to respect the wishes of the dead. The dead are dead.'

A further silence. Claire made another jotting on the paper. 'We could sell the land,' she said. 'It would pay for the restoration.'

James stared across at the fields. A trio of curlews were curving across the dome of the sky. They exchanged high-pitched descending cries. They were an obscure reminder of his wife. He sighed. There was no question she had started to nest, was already gathering little bits of feathers and moss.

'This is mad.'

'Don't imagine all the troubles are on your side,' she added encouragingly. 'I'll have mine too.'

Not just the restoration, she thought, but afterwards. The running of a second home so far from London. Two miles from a village shop. Fifteen from the city. A mile from the nearest neighbour and he doesn't look your average communicable sort. Other troubles connected with a second home, like evacuee problems. Weekend parties, open house. All your foreign business contacts telling me more than I want to know about the tyre industry. Do

I really want this place? Absently she fumbled around the pocket of her trousers to find a handkerchief. Her fingers met instead the crumpled letter from James's aunt. *You may not need it now but you will come to realise that these things are rare and increasingly precious.*

'I think I should say now—' began James.

'I'll do it. You don't have to give it a thought.'

James felt exhausted. These intense emotions caused by a surfeit of adding up. He lay back in the grass.

'Katy wants it very badly. She has found a badger hair. She is going to bring a tent next time we come.'

'Children. So what?'

'I am sure I can do it. Give it a chance. Stage by stage. Selling the land. If the funds don't cover the costs we won't. I'll organise the sale and the restoration.'

If she had stopped she would have allowed in his hesitation. She held steady. There were old continuities here that must be preserved. The barn was falling down but eighty years ago there would have been strong plough horses coming out of there. Breath steaming on the icy air in winter.

'James.' She saw them as a family here, solid and enduring. She felt it would help keep them as a family.

'James.'

He stared at her. 'Why is it so important to you? It's not even yours.'

'It just is. It's important for us, not just me.'

He closed his eyes and retreated behind his lids. He calculated that in their present state the buildings wouldn't be worth anything even if they were sold. The money was in the land. But the price of property was beginning to move up. Maybe there was a case for letting her do it and then, when it was finished, they could take it to market.

He sighed. He had a flight to Detroit on Wednesday.

'We'll talk this over again tomorrow. When you're no longer under the influence.' He paused. 'You must realise,' he added, 'if we go ahead, all this will be your problem rather than mine.'

Right from the beginning it had always been accepted that Claire's department was problems or, rather, their opposite which is the smoothing of all obstacles. As you start, so you go on, and unwittingly she had begun in this way at their first meeting. It was a classic undergraduate encounter at Oxford, a formal party where she was the guest and he the gatecrasher. She in her neat black velvet suit, pearl earrings and a headband, and he tieless with a borrowed scarf. She had been stuck with a short man with a lisp when she was buttonholed by this fellow who was evidently a much sharper prospect. Slim-hipped with a bruised left-wing face and a large mouth, a lad made in the fashion of the day which she wasn't. At a period when the more modish girls moped round with moth eyes and fringes and ironed hair, she was not in the vanguard.

At the time she had read his sudden attachment to her as a compliment, though later he confessed she was simply the nearest and most expedient girl, a sure bunker against eviction.

'You didn't even find me attractive?'

'I saw a tall fair girl with sloping eyes, upright posture and friendly smile. Classy.'

'But attractive?'

'You were very attractive. You were a ticket-holder.'

'You were in me like a rat up a drainpipe,' she said crossly.

'As I said, you were classy.'

There was the nub of it, James wanting class as well as brass and, being definitely on the make, he had recognised in that instant his better. This was true morally as well as socially, for Claire who was the middle child of an eminent doctor had been raised in the school of service and trust. Even her face inspired instinctive trust. She had direct eyes, sloping downwards at the sides as James had remarked, a longish nose, wide mouth, clean jaw, that thoroughly English type of face that you would wish to take out on a good long walk.

To an outsider they had little in common – neither friends, nor background, nor tastes – Claire, though living in an age when everyone married dustmen, being accustomed to obedient public schoolboys. James was neither. He was a lad from the North, or so he had claimed, not as it turned out fashionable Mersey and not even very north, just poor old north of the East Midlands. He was at Oxford on a Midlands industrial scholarship, an achievement he had attained with much regret for it would return him to the world from which he wished to escape. However, as the son of a widowed mother to whom he felt an awful onus of responsibility, he had no option but to seek a fully funded place with the certainty of a job. Unfortunately the burden of responsibilities to his mother, on the one hand, and to the company funding his scholarship on the other, were more than enough for James. The result was that he had no wish to take on a third in the form of a permanent girlfriend however suitable she was.

This lack of commitment normally attracts more females than it puts off and Claire was not an exception. In fact, there is no greater aphrodisiac than nonchalance towards a nice-looking girl already used to male attention, and it was this that charmed Claire who had more than a streak of simple masochism.

When other men were out on the river or acquiring or discarding culture, James could be relied on to be oating around with the girls. Within a short period she had become hopelessly wrapped up in him however much she tried to conceal it. He would come and go, always leaving, not always returning, periods of sex and devotion followed by absence and on her part, though not she knew on his, abstinence or at best the odd despised affair. In this way the pattern of their relationship continued, for two years at university and then until after they had graduated. It was during a reunion after his latest two-month disappearance that they decided to marry. She was twenty-three and he was twenty-two and neither had considered marriage in the immediate future. But she had got pregnant.

She told him in the shabby bedsitting room that she rented in a flat she shared with two other girls. His reaction was one of dismay.

'You're a doctor's daughter,' he said.

'What's that meant to mean?' In any case she dreaded telling her father who she knew would be furious.

'You know what it means.'

'That it shouldn't have happened? Or that I'll be able to get rid of it?'

She saw in his eyes the answer to both.

'Do you really want me to go to one of those clinics in St John's Wood at dawn?'

She willed him to say no.

After an hour of turmoil and tears they agreed to marry.

In retrospect, that is much later, it occurred to Claire that James was not best suited to marriage, not surely because he lacked the capacity to love, but rather because he could never be sufficiently uxorious. Burdened in youth with the emotional duties and demands of his mother, he saw legal relationships rather in the light of restrictive practices. They were something to be endured rather than enjoyed. For him love was a more anarchic feeling which only flourished in spontaneity. Later Claire thought it was this as well as his early marriage which had made him prone to wander.

The first time she found out he was having an affair was about six years after they had married. When cornered, he had confessed and been penitent for his sins. The second time, a few years later, it had been a brief fling with a former flame. After that, although there were several times when she might have suspected, nothing ensued. They were companionable and affectionate as always, though this wasn't in itself a reliable sign. Indeed she had once thought dryly that he was never sweeter to her than when he was in the middle of an affair. However, she told herself that by now his work had become so demanding that he wouldn't have the time or energy to spend on pursuit. More recently, indeed in the last year, she had been given cause to change her mind and her suspicion had proved correct. It transpired that it had gone on for some while. The other party had been the divorced wife of a colleague, a woman in her thirties, by no means stupid, despite her volumised hairstyle and glistening starlet mouth which failed to close over her front teeth. It was not a great consolation to Claire that she wasn't much of a threat and that none of his affairs had ever been serious.

Claire had set her mind against leaving him. In the last case, she reasoned she was partly to blame because she had neglected him. As soon as the children were off her hands, they had exchanged the family house in London for a perch and she had started to spend much and then nearly all of her time in the country. An absentee landlord risks squatters, but at his age, she thought, the problem would diminish rather than increase.

Love without illusions is a fixed point. It was therefore her strength rather than weakness that she had stayed with him, but the battle against her instincts had in effect reduced her. Each of his affairs had robbed her of self-confidence. At her age a diminuendo was setting in. At one time she had considered taking on another man but had neither the desire nor the energy and in any case the idea appeared as unseemly as it was unwanted. But she felt that virtue had not proved its own reward and that a situation of her kind was by its nature unstable. This worry, though intermittent, had persisted. It would not go away.

3

Stuart Cormack stretched, stepped out of the car and shut the metallic blue door. The newish neighbours in the front garden across the road stared but did not recognise him.

'Who's that outside Mary's?' the mother asked her fat teenage son. 'She doesn't have many visitors.'

Stuart stood for a moment and looked around. The sapling cherry tree which stood in the middle of the lawn had failed to put on more leaf in his absence. They had been here three years but the garden still had the skimpy feel of new planting. He noticed two tiles missing on the slate roof before he relaxed and began to savour the afternoon's English sun. The deep, deep peace of a homecoming. His village, Toy Town, ribbon-development really to the south of Hereford with two black-and-white pubs, a church, and a round-the-clock grocery store at its heart. His home, Toy Town too, small, pin-neat, red-brick, pointed roof on the edge of a small estate. His garden, its central path flanked with two rows of marigolds and a blank expanse of grass. His dog kennel, neat as a doll's house and the netted rectangle of Gemma the Dobermann's run. The boy who would be in the back garden and his wife Mary waiting inside. The homecoming, a familiar experience but one that was also strange as he was the stranger.

She never came out to meet him on his return, but would stay in the house for privacy. The dog would bark her deep Dobermann voice, and the door would open whilst Mary would hide behind it. Sometimes after long months apart, she was shy due to worry and isolation and, perhaps, just shyness. The boy in the background would always be silent and look down. The homecoming when the professional was relieved to become an amateur.

He rat-a-tat-tatted on the wooden door, then added morse code as a hallelujah and peered through the spy hole. Behind him he felt the neighbours still looking and decided he'd have to plant some conifers. In his job, he had a reflex dislike of nosiness. The door opened silently with no sign of his wife, then she appeared in a man's white shirt and fawn shorts, her Dutch doll face laughing.

'You all right this time?'

He hugged her, crushing her with his muscles till she gasped.

'Feel all right, don't I?'

Last time he had come back with fever, but this time he was in good health and full heart. Closing his eyes he felt the comfort of her shape. She was his patch of safety, the hub of his stability. Wives and girlfriends walked out on his mates all the time, but Mary had stayed for eleven years. At the lonely moments, or the awful faltering night-before times on a tour or a job, he kept an ideal of her and the boy, which reality always failed to match. Yet if they were less than his dreams on returning, they were also more for they represented the normal world which could too easily be lost.

He released her and thrust his hand in his pocket.

'See what I've got for you.'

'Stu-art, I'm not a kid.'

'It's a girlie present.'

He brought out a gift-wrapped duty-free flask of Opium perfume, having flown back on a scheduled flight.

She hugged him. 'And what's this?' She pointed to a larger flat pack.

'Some flowers I picked and a couple of dead butterflies. Big exotics. Take them to school to find out what kind they are.'

'Won't the nature teacher guess where you've been?'

They exchanged glances and smiled.

'No. Anyway, he's not the gobby kind. Just tell him to shut up.'

He looked round the lounge: cream walls, three-piece floral suite, a fire in the grate which had never been lit, her old polished running cups on the wooden shelf on the wall, the utter neatness of a house lived in by one woman and a boy, and an absent soldier. Their neatness was in reality his neatness, which is to say obsessional. He was reminded of the child.

'Where is he?' He was still holding her by the hand.

'Out.'

'Didn't you tell him I was coming back when I rang?'

'Yes.' She didn't look at him, but picked at the wrapping of the scent bottle.

'Little bugger, what's he doing going out?'

'He's just a boy, Stuart. You can't expect him to hang around all afternoon.'

'You knew the time I'd be back.'

'I thought you'd be earlier.'

'I came as soon as I could.'

He hesitated, not wanting to ask the same question that he always did, but habit and need now drove him.

'Mary? You my best girl still?'

What he meant was, is there just me? Are you still mine? No mucking about? You won't ever leave me, will you?

'You my best girl still?' He asked it carelessly, but in that insecure second of waiting felt the pulse throb in his neck.

'I'm your best girl and always will be.'

For her it was true, even though being wed to a soldier meant marrying the military. And this was especially true in the Regiment where a man's first family were his mates on his four-man patrols which meant that in a way they were hers too. She knew them all, in some ways as closely as though she had grown up with them like brothers. Steve who slept like a baby, Jegs who prayed before fighting, Rob who had been adopted and whose father kept canaries. I am yours and you are mine and they are ours and we are theirs. After all you never knew if something horrible might happen and you might have need of your family too. This bogeyman was often there to haunt you. She couldn't always manage to forget him when Stuart went away.

At first she had been both proud and euphoric when he had joined the Regiment nearly ten years ago. But the joy had soon turned into panic, a state she took pains to conceal from Stuart since to him panic meant drama, which was alien both to his training and temperament. No drama then, just a pin-point of fear long since become an old familiar, blanked off in the daytime, squeezed out of existence by activities, but sometimes glimpsed in lightning strikes in the small hours of the night. This fear kept in step with his promotion, a *doppelgänger*, for the higher he rose in rank, the greater the daring and the danger. Quite simply, the best men were faced with the worst hazards, which meant that the best were most likely to be killed, so hers could get topped – when? She had once heard a grand term for this: 'the selection-destruction cycle'. The boneheads with their sodding abstractions. It was the wives who picked up the real pieces.

Thinking of all this now roused a conflict as always, that he should be only an instrument to be used which meant she was too, but then her usual daytime fatalism reasserted itself and the tension suddenly left her. It was summer, he was home, he was well, he was hers, the family safe and together again, live in the happy-go-lucky present.

'You're my best boy,' she said and put her arms around him and with pleasure because once this was said everything righted itself and ran smoothly. Tomorrow and for the next day she'd fuss over him and bring him breakfast in bed.

'Come on boy,' said old Mr Powell. 'Time you went home to your dad.'

'Don't like it when he gets back. Sh-she fusses over him.' Sam pushed out his bottom lip.

'None of those silly faces now.'

'Anyway he's not back yet.'

'Your mum said he's coming home this afternoon and you wasn't to be late.'

'I like it here.'

'You show respect for your dad. He's fought for his country.'

'I'm busy.'

'Your dad'll come and duff me up if he knows you're still here.'

'Nah. He don't care.'

Wilf Powell ignored the implication that Sam didn't care either.

'He does and all. You're his only boy. When you grow up you could be a real hero like him.'

'They call me moonie at school,' said Sam glumly.

'Hmm,' said Wilf. He knew this already, being caretaker at the school. He knew that none of the children dare bully the lad for awe of his father, but they mocked him instead.

'Well, you've got your glasses, boy,' he said, offering a reason. Through his own pebble lenses, he stared at Sam. It struck him how small he was for his age, ten years old, pale, peaky and with tufts of red hair, short-sighted with round spectacles hooked over his ears. Not, obviously speaking anyway, one for the military.

'Here' he said kindly, 'take Rowan's jesses.'

He passed him the pair of leather anklets. The bird watched as the child rubbed them with grease. Putting her head to one side, she shifted to the right of her turfed perch. A lanner falcon with a blue beak as hooked as her talons but breast feathers that were softer and plusher than a fur wrap.

'You my best girl then?' asked Wilf in his soft slow burr. He picked her up and slipped the hood up and over the bird in a dextrous rolling motion that echoed the dome of her head. Tapping it lightly into position, he did up the braces.

She was now blinkered but quiet, the leather scalloping over her eyes, whilst the fronds of the cap sprouted upwards in pineapple tufts. A hat for a barbaric and antique hunter, but no girl could have looked smarter after a visit to her milliner.

Sam took the bucket of disinfectant with which he had cleaned out the cages earlier in the day and poured it down the drain.

'I want to come with you,' he said separating each word for emphasis.

'You cannot, now.'

Thwarted, Sam looked round the familiar sanctuary that was Wilf and Aggie's garden. He liked it better than his own home. It wasn't of course a garden, or at least not like his parents' nor any other garden, which is to say that it wasn't a plant garden, for Wilf had neither flowers nor vegetables nor trees or even grass which were boring. Instead he had replaced all these with birds.

'It's a bird garden,' Sam had said when he had first seen it.

'Some folk call it a cage garden,' said Wilf.

'Not cages, they're palaces,' corrected Aggie. 'He takes more care of them than he do me, don't he?' She made a sign of dismissal with her hands. They were large in proportion to her body which was short and round like a friar's.

There were six palatial aviaries that loomed round the edge of the little yard. Wilf's neighbour, Mr Jefferies, an old widower who grew fuchsias, thought he was mad. Once a year they feuded over the chain-link fence.

'You'm bugger,' Mr Jefferies would say. 'You take the light from my fuchsias.'

'One more word from you, old man Jefferies, and my birds will eat your scrub-bred Jack Russell.'

Who would eat whom was in fact open to doubt since the terrier was a little tyke, so this was usually a gauntlet for a contest of strength which neither man could risk ever enacting.

In the distance Wilf could see Mr Jefferies' flat cap approaching now.

'Sh-shall I see you tomorrow?' asked Sam. As always, he stammered slightly on 'sh'.

'You spend some time with your dad,' said Aggie and she passed him a chocolate bar. 'Say thank you,' she added smartly.

A pout. Dopey old man and woman. Stupid. Boneheads, as his father would say. He scuffed with the toe of his shoe at the edge of the step, but took the bar and bit it. A mumble, the words not as shaped as thank you. Furious and dragging a little to show protest, he went round to the front of each cage which was the way he always said goodbye.

He stared at the Bengal eagle owl. Hoping that Mr Powell wasn't watching, he made little ears with his fingers at the top of his head and waggled them at the bird who stared back with his large luminous orange eyes. Goodbye to the snowy owl, bad-tempered but velvet-soft in its cage, then to the kestrel and the ferrets, so slim they could slip through a wedding ring, and each of the others till the last one, Chloe, a Harris hawk and the one he really loved. She saw him coming and screamed. A piercing screech, imperious and passionate. He was addicted to her voice.

'Chloe, Chloe,' he murmured.

Wilf had bred from her earlier in the year. The mate, though smaller and more vulnerable, had demonstrated his manliness by thumping her in the chest. Chloe, vanquished, had succumbed. When the chicks had hatched, they had quickly recognised Sam's presence by sight and sound. The best, called Bella, had grown attached to him and shrieked when she saw him.

'I sells her soon,' said Wilf, standing beside him. He indicated the young female. 'Sad, mind. She's a good 'un.'

Sam looked at him in horror then back at the twelve-week-old bird. Fully fledged, speckle-breasted and rufous, she sat with legs apart on her perch. She unfurled her great wings into an awning. Her opaque human-sized eye stared him out. Another screech.

'Sh-she,' he stammered again, 'sh-she don't wanna be sold. See? You musn't sell her.' Agitated, he pushed at his spectacles.

'Can't keep her,' said Wilf. 'Chock-a-block here.'

Sam dropped the remainder of the chocolate bar. Triggered by movement, Bella screamed, thinking it some prey.

'Where will sh-she go?'

'A good home.'

'Where?'

'Dunno, do we? We puts an ad in *Cage and Aviary Birds*.'

'You dunno who you sells her to.' He pushed at his specta-cles again.

'I take care, never you mind. It'll be a good home. Don't take on so.'

'I'll have her.'

'Silly, she'll fetch £750.'

Seven hundred and fifty pounds, the words stretched out like a piece of elastic. He had known it could happen yet not realised it. He had pored over the entries in the Bird of Prey column in the journal. At school, Mr Goring – boring Goring, as they called him – said he couldn't read properly, but he could read very well when he wanted to. He could remember, too, what he'd read. Goshawks – 1997 – large males. Baby barn owls, still fluffy. For sale female Harris hawk 1996 P/R – and that meant parent-reared – f/f which stood for fur and feather which told you that the bird had killed rabbit and fowl. Hateful that Bella should sit in a classified ad column. Didn't they understand? How could he get £750?

'Come on lad,' said Wilf.

'We were gonna train her.' Sam refused to meet his eyes.

'Not a tidy business, life,' said Aggie grimly. It was her opinion that there was too much money tied up in these birds.

Over the fence, in the six-inch gap between two cages, Wilf could see Mr Jefferies' face rising like the full moon under his flat cap. He didn't want old man Jefferies to witness a brewing scene.

'Now lad—' began Wilf, hoping to turn down the heat.

The little Jack Russell began yapping.

'Can you see the pretty bird,' said Mr Jefferies evilly.

'Barky-barky-barky-bark,' said the dog.

Wilf, goaded, advanced on the fence.

'Wilf,' said Aggie warningly.

Neither noticed Sam who had opened the gate and was slipping in silence away.

A shadow ran past the netted window and they glimpsed the top of the boy's red head. Then a door banged and the scuffle of feet transferred to the hall. 'Sam,' called Mary but the shoes were tap-tapping up the first few rungs of the open-plan stairway. She left Stuart and ran to the door.

'Sam? Come here, didn't you see the car? He's back, isn't he?'

Stuart moved beside her, a splitting father's grin for his son on his face. It looked fixed, which didn't stop it from fading.

'C'm' on kid. You all right? Where's a laugh for your old mate? Look what I've got for you.'

For a second the boy stood staring. He seemed paralysed midway up the staircase, unable to climb or descend. Then he turned and fled upwards, past the two photographs of himself above the stair rail, below the three of his father: his father with his squadron, his father landing after a parachute jump, his father posing with a deep tan, his father, his father, his father; his father, as powerful absent as present. The door of the bedroom banged.

'And what's all that about?' said Stuart. Dismayed he placed the gift he had chosen for his son carefully on the hall table – a model of a shiny black motorbike.

'Don't worry,' said Mary. 'I'll go up and sort it all out.'

Homecoming, she thought, meant as always that bleak no-man's-land that stretched between husband and son. She walked upstairs, pushed open the door of the bedroom and saw he had flung himself on the bed, head down in the pillow. She was worried. Was he ill?

'What's the matter?'

'He's selling her.'

'Who?'

'Bella.'

'I don't understand. Buck up, your dad's back.'

'The one I chose. Bella. The hawk.'

Mary stared at the stricken figure of her son. 'He's got others you know. Sam. Your dad.'

'Not the same.'

'Sam, your dad's just got home. Can't we talk about this later?'

'No.'

The noise was sullen. Mary weighed it and decided she would rather not complain. She looked at her watch and sighed. 'What's so special about Bella?'

'Sh-she's a Harris hawk.' The name was muffled in the pillow but detectable.

Mary looked at the walls. They were peculiar for a boy's bedroom. No guns, no football teams, no bikes, no racing-cars or pop stars: just birds, posters of owls, hawks, eagles.

'Sam, this is not the moment to be a pain.'

He made a small whiny noise into his pillow to define that he would make no effort not to be a pain.

Mary calculated that a row would not improve Stuart's home-coming.

'Well, I'd like to make it better but I don't see what we can do. If he wants to sell her we can't stop him.'

'Could buy her.'

A hawk. Mary recoiled. She was not sure she knew how much or why. 'I got you a gerbil, two gerbils,' she said, 'and they died.'

'Sh-she's not a gerbil.'

'Then there was that mouse and he got sick too.'

'I asked the vet what was wrong.'

He had indeed, an occasion which Mary remembered clearly. Sam had not visited the vet but had rung him instead. He had gripped the slippery little creature by its tail and whilst its feet pattered in the air he had made the mouse squeak down the telephone and asked the vet why was he ill. The vet claimed it was hard to tell.

'Well, it wasn't very successful anyway.' She suppressed a smile.

'Didn't want a mouse or a gerbil. You made me have them.'

This was true. She had hoped it would give him an interest. So it had, in a way, in that it had led to birds, and it now looked as if he wanted a hawk who would eat mice and gerbils.

'It's out of the question,' she said abruptly.

'I could pay you back.'

'How much?'

He sat up, flushed. His spectacles had been pushed off his nose by the pillow.

'£750.'

'£750? Come on. We'll hear no more of this.'

He flung himself back again.

'Pull yourself together and behave. Your dad'll be furious with you.' She got up, walked out in exasperation and clattered down the stairs towards the living room.

'What's up?' said Stuart.

'He's in an I want, can't have mood.' She added: 'Sorry about this. I like everything to be perfect for you.'

'Tell him no honking, no wanking.'

'Stu-art.'

'No wanking anyway.'

She didn't smile.

'Come on. It's not your fault. It's just kids.'

'He wants a hawk.'

'A hawk. What's he want a hawk for?'

'He's found a special one at Wilf Powell's. The birdman. He's selling her.'

'How much?'

'£750.'

'Shit. Not on, is it at that price?'

'It wouldn't be on if it were twenty quid. I don't want him to have a bird like that.'

'Why not? They're great, fantastic. All speed, surprise and aggression.'

'Exactly. One of you's enough.'

She wondered what she was going to do about the boy. He could push himself a bit harder, his teacher would say absent-mindedly at every parents' meeting. Then he would add that it was a shame that he didn't seem to have much self-confidence. Mary fretted about this too, not least because a solution seemed unlikely.

4

For some years Claire had earned a living by writing potted history, a form of work not too onerous for her to start when the children were still at home. The books to which she contributed sold in their thousands, fat, heavy, undemanding and highly coloured. Such tomes were designed for the mentally restless and she had not the slightest pretension or illusion about what was required. In her view her role was that of an outworker employed by a knitwear designer, for whom she would contribute her share of piecemeal work, in effect the equivalent of an arm in a jumper or the heel of a sock. The height of her ambition would be to knit the whole sock. Meanwhile she was part of a production row and the articles streamed out: a thousand words on Churchill or five hundred on Stalin, two pages on the making of America or three on the undoing of Soviet Russia. Modern pieces could be tricky, some falling out of favour almost as soon as they were published. *Royalty is no longer so exclusive, nor is it allowed to be*, she had written, *and it is remarkable that it has managed to survive this drive to make its members more accessible without loss of dignity or public esteem*. This was one text that would later become a matter for regret. Royal life had finished it off for ever.

Fortunately the task for today posed no such difficulty, but she was not in a writing mood. As it was a Tuesday, she was on her own, which was usual, with the dog and two cats and seated at the long scarred wooden table in the kitchen where she preferred to write when she was feeling costive, since it tricked her into the illusion that she was not actually working. On fine days in summer she could succumb to dreaming here and look out of the window from where she would sometimes see the SAS parachuting over the hills. It was a bizarre and carnival sight to watch the little circling and rising helicopter glinting in sunlight and each of the matchstick figures floating beneath the mushrooms of unfurled umbrellas. Today, however, being a dull day, there would be no such distractions. The only items to hand were an HB pencil, a child's exercise book, an old essay from which she could crib and a mind which would eventually prove willing to be focused. It was more difficult than it seemed, the business of composing a life in five hundred words or so. This morning the life in focus was that of Charles Darwin who had become a recycled object of fashion due no doubt to the millennial fascination with human origins.

She drifted for a moment in aimless thought. It was not entirely unproductive, this process; rather, part of a procedure that she recognised as orbiting. She wrote a couple of sentences in looping script. Her mind was not yet under control but still fluttering. The average adult has an attention span of fifteen seconds, she remembered. To focus was always hard. She moved the pepper mill to the left. Would she be better settled in the old study on the other side of the hall with its gloomy walls of books and out-of-date accounts? No, that felt too much like working. Here at the table she could just float into the subject and catch it unawares.

She noticed it had begun to rain outside, a warm and wet autumn downpour, with the leg of the rainbow descending into a bush of Mexican orange blossom on the far boundary. The rain blew tendrils of late honeysuckle gently against the window in a blur of orange and green and then slid behind to trickle down the panes. She doodled anything that came into her mind. *Western wind, when wilt thou blow, The small rain down can rain?* Henry VIII's favourite love poem. Pity she was not required to write something on Henry VIII with his piggy eyes and steroid jowls and virility problems. Or had she done him years ago? Probably. He was a first choice with publishers of this kind of book. They favoured turbulent times like his with lots of action. The Tudor and Stuart reigns when heads rolled in blood on the ground: of two kings, a couple of wives and a pair of archbishops. Pity that she must have done him already. He made good copy with his six wives destined for divorce or the axe. What would Mr Darwin have made of this excellent exponent of the survival of the fittest?

She now peered at a lithograph of the naturalist in question, a man with a Moses beard, seated in a wicker basket-chair. His face was turned sideways and his legs crossed at the knee. *Charles Darwin 1809–82*, she wrote as a heading and added a fistful of facts. *Darwin was born in Shrewsbury, the grandson of Josiah Wedgwood and Erasmus Darwin, the physician and poet. He studied medicine at Edinburgh* . . . She began to move at greater speed, touching the ground lightly. The art of this business was shallow coverage of the salient essentials. One had to compress decades without losing the coherence of a man's life. Within the space of several sentences she had covered his interest in zoology and geology, the encouragement by the botanist John Henslowe, his marriage to his cousin and his life in Kent, surrounded by his birds, conservatories and garden. She was beginning to maintain a rhythm. *Private means*, she wrote, *enabled him to concentrate on his work and perpetual poor health did not prevent its continuation.*

There was a knock at the door. She glanced up and decided to leave it unanswered. It was probably Jehovah's witnesses. She would meet two overweight hopefuls on the doorstep asking whether she ever thought about life, to which her chosen solution was to give a trenchant No. She carried on. *'The Origin of Species by Means of Natural Selection' provoked violent controversy and Darwin had to endure violent attacks on his book*— A second knock. They were persistent. Let them bugger off. —*but, out of the corpus of scientists who shared his views on evolution, he was the first to be granted wide expert credence for his views.*

There came a third knock, abrupt and impatient. No Jehovah's witnesses, these, with their soft beseeching smiles fending off blows. Perhaps it was the old lame tramp who would sometimes call to ask for a needle and thread. Casting an exasperated glance at the just-started work on the kitchen table, she scraped back the wooden chair, and marched across the room and into the dark hall. She caught a glimpse of herself wearing a pink cotton shirt in the tall thin mirror. She too was tall, but not slim enough to fit it. She noticed that the barometer beside the glass had fallen and that the paving under the door exuded a grey moisture, absorbed from the outside world. The outdoors still kept its old habit of creeping inside. Bad weather was set to stay.

She pulled at the thick wooden door which creaked open and found Mary standing there. The No she had prepared on her face began to fall apart.

'You've forgotten haven't you?'

It had been arranged that Mary who worked part time in a bank should come and help occasionally in the garden. Claire had indeed forgotten.

'Sorry,' she mumbled, 'but it's raining.'

'Doesn't worry me,' said Mary stoutly.

It's pouring, thought Claire but suppressed the protest. Standards of excellence had been laid down for Mary by her husband and Claire as employer had no wish to fail them.

'What do you want me to do?'

Claire made a vague gesture and then floundered. The typical product of a liberal education, her idea of employing people was to cosset them in the dry whilst she stood out in the rain. She sometimes wondered if this was why she had settled for self-employment. James who had come from a harsher background thought she was hopeless.

'Dig?' offered Mary helpfully.

'It'll make a puddle.'

Mary looked at her as though she were mad.

'Right. No puddles then. What about pruning? Last time we talked you said some trees were overgrown. Do any need a bit of lopping?'

Claire put her hand to her head. Mary had so much energy. Here she was offering a barrage of random activity whilst Claire was too feeble to harness it.

'No trees actually need lopping.'

This was not exactly true but she did not feel in a positively lopping mood. She had no wish to take surgical action. There was no doubt, she lacked the ruthlessness of the good gardener. No wonder the place was in a mess which could not be summarised as chaotic charm. She was reminded of her mother who had frightened off the tree surgeon at home by rushing out and quoting 'Woodman, woodman, spare that tree, touch not a single bough.' The man, startled, had left.

'Well, what then?'

Mary seemed expectant. She stood with legs braced and a drawhood over her round head, awaiting a task and instructions. In her world a good leader gives orders, a good leader is a good communicator. He instructs and he organises.

'I suppose,' said Claire, 'I suppose we could shift something.'

It was a shade vague to be an order but it was at least a selfless suggestion. Shifting things invariably involved two people. She cast a wistful mental glance back to Darwin who had lost his chance to be polished off until later. No good mentioning the work to Mary. Action alone would elicit respect at the moment, mental effort deserving of less. Thought, after all, came free, like air and sun: thought did not come out of the effort of thinking. She remembered that Mary had once referred to the military intelligence by the nickname of slime. How the active always hated the intellectual. How often they were right.

The two women walked over to the barn to fetch a pair of spades, Mary in her blue anorak, hood and trainers, Claire in an old wax coat topped with the only rainproof headgear she could find at short notice: the type of wide-brimmed hat that advertises Spanish sherry. It looked ridiculous. Two different uniforms for two ways of life, thought Claire. Mary who had glanced at her clothes would be justified in despising her. The effete intellectual with a big stylish hat covering a headful of notions. The other a woman of few words, but the ability to take competent action.

They crossed the main lawn, round the weeping ash (the good tree which Claire had noted on that first visit), through the wooden door in the stone wall and out into a secondary enclosure where the pigcote had once been. 'Open up the view' she had scribbled on that same day all those years ago. Even now in rain the view was indeed extensive, streaming away across green folded hills to the Black Mountains in the distance where the great mass of rock lay brooding. Nearer to hand the women squelched across the grass and converged on a tall pointed yellow conifer which looked frightful.

'I wondered about this,' said Claire faintly. She decided against explaining it was vulgar, when who knows? Mary might have one. She had brought it from Barnes where it was superfluous to requirements and the poor thing was even less necessary here. It should have been consigned to a bonfire years ago but Claire had kindly kept it in motion. This would be the fifth time it had been shifted.

'Where do you want it to go?' asked Mary, awaiting fresh instructions. She was finding it difficult to adapt to this woman. Stuart would give his commands not just once but twice which was standard mission procedure.

'I don't know.'

A tiny spasm of bewilderment crossed Mary's face. She put down her spade and waited. Her silence had the effect of making this seem ostentatious, though it wasn't.

'Umm,' said Claire.

'Shall we dig it out?'

'And then think?' This was not the way things were supposed to be done.

The two women set about the tree, Mary's blade slicing into the heavy wet earth like butter, Claire's pecking out chips of clay at the edge. Mud stuck to her boots and began to weigh her down as though she were rooted in concrete. She wallowed and struggled over her spade.

The rain increased in strength and volume, driving in thick horizontal ribbons through the air. The brim of Claire's hat caught the wind and blew off. Strands of sodden hair blew into her mouth and eyes increasing her incompetence.

'Easy does it,' said Mary.

Claire wondered: was she being sarcastic, but realised not. Mary was indeed working smoothly in a calm and steady tempo that was different from Claire's arrhythmic and erratic attacks.

Assailed with unequal force on both sides, the tree began to tilt towards Claire, then with a sudden jolt, its fifteen-foot length keeled over. It fell to the ground with a shudder.

'I'll barrow it to where you want it to go.'

Claire looked at the ugly thing, which was a monument to a previous misjudgement. She had never liked it which was the reason she continued to be sorry for it.

'Do you want it for your own garden?' It was a last attempt to keep it alive.

'Not really.'

'The trouble is it doesn't fit in anywhere here. It's yellow you see. Yellow isn't a good colour for trees in the country. Like purple.'

Mary looked puzzled. There was a polite silence whilst she navigated around this comment. Her neighbour had a front garden that he'd stuffed with pointy yellow fir trees and he was proud of them. He'd won prizes.

'Why don't you put it on the bonfire?'

'I don't like to kill it.'

This was becoming absurd. She knew killing was something Mary must have come to terms with. She would think she was barmy fussing about the life of a tree.

'We'll bring it over here.'

The two women wheelbarrowed the tree like an ambulance patient into the next-door part of the garden, or rather Mary drove whilst Claire supported the quivering tip of the fir. Claire looked round at the area they had just entered. There was a *mélange* of roses, late lilies and early asters, pink, mauve and white, a bit blurred and weedy but most tasteful. How Jekyll and tonal. No room for a yellow conifer in this section either. She had a faint memory that it had started life here on first entry. At any rate she had a definite sense of *déjà-vu*. She stood helpless, condemning them to more rain. Ridiculous, they could circle for half-an-hour simply because she lacked the guts to sentence any living creature to death. It was why she had become a vegetarian five years ago.

There was a deep rumble of thunder, echoing from hill to distant hill. The Black Mountains were now obscured by a blacker cloud, thick and tarry, that squatted over the top. There was no doubt that a storm was brewing. Exasperation with herself and the weather suddenly saved her.

'Oh God,' said Claire, 'let's chuck the damn thing.'

They despatched the tree to the rubbish tip and then returned to the house, coated in the characteristic red Plasticine mud of the district. They dumped their clothes, washed and walked into the kitchen. Claire cradled Darwin into a little pile at the edge of the table and walked to the cupboard to fetch and open a tin. She tipped its contents into a pan and put a stick of bread into the oven. The short-haired tabby was curled in a ball on the slats above the range. It purred as the rising waves of dry warmth floated through its fur.

'Not a great success, today,' she said, passing Mary a bowl of hot soup. They sat down at the table.

'I'll come back tomorrow afternoon when it's better.'

'You don't mind it?' She put down the little black cat which had jumped on her lap and was oozing up to her neck.

'Suits me. I like to keep busy. Stu says it keeps me more cheerful.'

'What do you do when he's away?'

'Work at the bank part-time. Run. Play squash.'

'You're terribly fit.'

'That's training. Stu calls it self-discipline.'

Claire went over to the oven and took out half a baguette. She broke it in two sections, buttered her own and passed the second to Mary.

'Eat up.' She watched her. She found this woman interesting. Though sturdily built she was pretty and feminine with her red flyaway hair, round face, round cheeks and snub nose, a face made up of circles. Yet she was different from the other women Claire knew. She was geared to accomplishing active tasks which was a masculine aptitude, according to students of human behaviour.

'He trained you, did he?'

'I train myself. You have to push yourself, see, if you're going to get anywhere.'

'Did he tell you this?'

Mary looked bewildered and then laughed. She pulled at the sleeve of her blue T-shirt. Her biceps were round, too, and strong. 'We talk about the mortgage, the broken window, how the dog's got a thorn in her paw. And of course about Sam.'

'Sam?'

'You know, how he's doing at school.' Or how he isn't, thought Mary. It pained both, Stuart especially. He had said the boy would end up a dosser. She opened her mouth but decided against speaking. She filled it instead with bread.

'How old is he?' asked Claire persisting.

'Ten.'

'He's a runner and jumper too is he?'

A sitter and a dreamer. 'Not exactly.'

'What's he want to be when he grows up?'

Nothing. 'He doesn't know.'

'Not follow in his father's footsteps?'

'Not likely,' said Mary, a bit too enthusiastically, then went on guard against any leakage.

'I'd have liked a boy. We just have the two daughters.'

This was true as far as it went, but was also a suppression of the truth. They had had a boy between the daughters.

'It might be easier to have girls. Less expectations, see?'

'Actually,' said Claire, 'we did have a boy between the girls but he was born very prematurely and he died.'

It was a long time since she had mentioned this to anyone, but it had happened half a lifetime ago and the anguish was fully purged. Still, it was hard for other people to gauge emotions so she rarely told them.

Mary put her spoon down and stared at her. Like all revelations it had caused a shift. An opportunity for intimacy opened up. The two women advanced and retreated before it.

'Sorry,' said Claire who was a great and inappropriate apologiser. 'Forget it. It was ages ago. But James would have loved a son.'

'Depends what they turn out like.' Mary looked down and chased one of the bits in her soup round and round with her spoon. 'Stu's got high standards, see?'

'I daresay, but ten's a bit young.'

'The trouble is he's not interested in anything.'

'Not nothing, surely?'

'Well, just this bird.'

'I don't understand.'

'You know Wilf Powell, the old caretaker at the school? Well, the boy wants me to get him his hawk.'

'What hawk?'

'A Harris hawk. It's £750 for a start and we're up to here with the mortgage. But it's not only that.'

Claire noticed that just thinking about it induced a rush of activity. Mary made little gestures with her fingers, flexed them, pushed back her chair and stood up.

'Mary. Are you all right?'

'You know what a hawk does?'

Claire paused. 'Well,' she said, taken by surprise. 'A hawk hawks. It flies, catches things. What do you mean? One caught a stock dove here a month ago.'

'There you are. What happened?'

Claire blinked at her.

'It killed it.'

'That's just it. They're killers.'

'It's natural. They're wild.'

'Sure. Fine. It's natural. But, if you keep one, you have to train it to kill.'

Claire noticed a flush of excitement on the right side of her neck. Her Dutch doll cheeks were azalea pink.

'That's still natural.'

'You don't see do you?'

'See what?'

'Look,' said Mary in a hoarse voice. 'I'm married to Stu. What's he do? He's a soldier, isn't he? What do soldiers do? They're trained to kill if necessary, aren't they? They have to be. They're the ones who do the business aren't they? He's a good bloke. He's a wonderful bloke, but one of the things he's trained to do is to kill. See? Look at it my way. Do I want a hawk too? In my back garden? I've never really wanted to know what Stuart does so I don't want to be reminded of it.'

Claire leant forward. And I was fussing about a yellow conifer, she thought. She felt ashamed. She ached with solicitude. 'Then you mustn't have one.' But the dilemma was evident even as she offered her little platitude.

'But don't you see? Sam's crazy about her. It could be the making of him. He's soft, he's not strong, he doesn't try, he doesn't try at anything.' Anxiety was sending her face slightly out of control. 'He's got no self-confidence. It's not Stu's fault. He loves him, aches for him to do better, but it grieves him and me too that he's a weakling. It—'

'I'll have it.'

'What?' Mary wiped her nose with an upward movement of the flat of the hand.

'I'll have the hawk here. Sam can come and train it here. I'll buy it and pay for its keep.'

There was an alarmed silence. Words which had tumbled out were pulled up short. They had become indiscretions.

'I can't let you do that. You're crazy.'

Perhaps I am, thought Claire, who was not given to wild offers and was somewhat surprised herself. She was aware that she was in the grip of conviction.

'You can give me some free help in the garden if you want,' she added more rationally. 'Or pay me back in any way that suits you, but I'll take the hawk.'

'Why?' asked Mary not without suspicion.

'I'm here. We've got loads of space. It's no sweat for me.'

Claire demonstrated with her hands, suddenly airborne with the middle-aged thrill of discovering a cause. 'I want to,' she added simply.

'I really don't know.' This was sudden. It was funny too that a woman so vague should now prove decisive.

'Don't make a big deal out of it. Imagine it's as if—' she hesitated, searching for a metaphor that might suit her audience, 'as if I had a piano for example and you didn't. So all he's doing is practising on my piano.' This parallel seemed a bit too artistic and unlikely for the occasion.

'You've no idea what you're letting yourself in for.'

'That's settled then.'

'I'll think about it.' Now Mary was back in control she wanted to scuttle away from the consequences.

'You can tell me tomorrow but it seems to me a perfectly sensible solution. So think it over in that light.' She added cannily: 'Common sense, that's all.'

After Mary had left, Claire went upstairs for an overview of the garden from the landing window. It was dark and the view was blurred by the rain but she opened the casement and looked out. The bird, she decided, could go in the far enclosure, or would it be better in the barn? Did they live in or out? What kind of bird was a Harris hawk? She realised how little she knew. There was no doubt that she had been rash. James would say she was rash. Never mind, old Mr Powell would knock up a nice home for it, she would pay whatever it cost and the boy would come and go independently. And if it didn't work out, at least she would have done her best to contribute. She felt slightly bewildered and a little worried too now that the flurry was over. Was this preparatory, she wondered, to entering a cooling-off period? But the expected chill of aftermath failed to come. The offer, though mad by any standards, had also been very satisfying. So profoundly satisfying that it must have arisen from her need as much as theirs, and made her wonder for a moment if hers was the need to be needed, but who cared?

5

'Somewhat rash of you to propose this, isn't it?'

'I don't see that it affects you.'

'Who would pay for it?'

'We would.'

'Then it does.'

'No. Not you and me. Mary and I.' She hesitated. 'She and me. Her and I.'

He was neither amused nor mollified. 'Hmm.'

'James, it's for a perfectly good reason.'

'All it's about is that you've had a bad attack of missionary spirits.'

'Something you wouldn't know about,' she said irritably.

'It doesn't seem sensible to me, that's all. It's simply impulse. And quixotic at that.'

'Leave me to make my own judgement. Anyway it may not go ahead.'

'All right but frankly, I just hope that it's a vegetarian hawk for your sake.'

At the other end of the line, there was the sound of a phone being replaced in a huff. James, who was in London, also put the phone down and raised his eyes to the ceiling. Leading his separate life during the week, he would not normally care too much what she got up to, but did he really want a village lad running into his garden every single day including each weekend? It was thoroughly irksome. In fact the more he thought about it, the more the whole thing seemed just stupid and when he got home this weekend he'd tell her again and put a stop to it, and too bad if they had another row which was more than likely.

He sat at his desk and brooded on how odd and irritable she had been of late, particularly since his last little adventure. Was he at all to blame? Was it not her fault too? Anyone objective would agree that she left him alone too much, spending nearly all her time now in the country. And whilst they still had a good marriage, wasn't it always true that long runs like theirs were based less on sex than companionship and that it was reasonable, even expected, for a man of his age to wander? In fact he felt less guilty about it now than in the past because by this stage he had at least earned the right to exercise a little discreet freedom. After all, no one could say that he had failed to look after his wife and love her, or that he had been less than protective of her feelings as well as fastidious about his own. He knew as well as the next man the need for an airlock between mistress and wife.

In a mood of rising self-justification and also out of mild curiosity, he took the back of a pamphlet on Pirelli and started to jot down some numbers on the left of the page. As far as he could remember – he began to count on the fingers of both hands – he had had eleven little adventures in the course of about thirty years, which worked out at the modest average of one every three years or a bit less.

As against that – he now drew a column on the opposite side of the page and began to fill it in – there was his pension, much of which would go to Claire since she was statistically destined to outlive him by four years; then £250,000 for life assurance. Next there was Domain, worth, what?, say £350,000 with its ten acres, plus his three-roomed nest in Chelsea, probably £200,000, no mortgage of course on either, but both had to be heated, to be lit, rates paid for, water rates too, together with the insurance for buildings and contents (he jotted down some more figures, ignoring the fact that Claire paid all bills on their Herefordshire home). There was also the cost of driving to and from one house to the other at, say, 63p a mile to allow for depreciation: which was £9,000 a year. Present-day expenses of course were less than they used to be since the girls were off their hands and the family holidays – formerly to Tuscany, or Alsace or the Dordogne or skiing at Courchevel in winter – were now fallen completely into abeyance, but his mother would at some time take this vacancy over. Arthritic, she might one day have to be moved into a home. Lord knows what that would cost. Cracked vessels last the longest. She was now seventy-eight; give her another ten years at £400 a week and that would amount to £208,000 at today's values which would far exceed the worth of her house. He sat back in his chair and shut his eyes. There was no doubt that he had been picked bare by his dependants.

He was annoyed to be interrupted in the middle of his wallow by the intercom which buzzed once and then again. He leant forwards. 'Give me a moment will you, Jilly?'

'The accounts you wanted are here.'

'One moment. I'm working on some other accounts.'

It had struck him that it would be interesting to work out the relationship between the brief column on the left side of the page and the longer one on the right, but the latter had caused some emotional disturbance. There was no doubt that modern commitments came with a huge price. He rose and walked round the room, completing a circle before he halted in front of a chart. He stood in meditation before it. It could normally be relied on to send him to sleep. From Michelin to Modi, Tokyo to Shanghai, Goodyear to Cheng Shin, no heroics or lyricism here. The pinnacle of invention would be to discover a 'run-flat' tyre. He gave an inward groan. A man in his position surely deserved the odd frolic he might find.

Feeling a little calmer and better satisfied with himself, he walked back to his chair and returned his mind to his sums. A lifetime's commitments: a total of more than a million pounds. Surely a few small peccadillos paled in relation to that. He leant forward, about to press the intercom for his secretary when Brewster, his younger partner, walked in.

'She says she's getting a hawk,' said James, amiably now.

'Who?'

'My wife.'

Brewster raised his eyebrows. 'Great,' he exclaimed but he wasn't in the least interested. He advanced and rested his spatulate fingers on the surface of the desk. 'Has Jilly brought you the accounts?'

'Not yet. I was busy.'

'I think one of the companies we've looked at is suitable. It's Crawley's. We could buy it at a knock-down price.'

James frowned. In their type of business there were few badly run companies nowadays that had retained enough basic value to merit a takeover. Almost all had been been forced to close during the recession.

'Look at it,' said Brewster, 'I'll be surprised if you don't agree.'

James nodded and pressed the intercom.

'Come up now will you, Jilly, and bring those accounts.'

He put his own private jottings aside to be fed into the shredder.

His secretary arrived: a short girl with long hair and thin legs who lived with her boyfriend in Ealing.

'What would you say Jilly, if I told you my wife had decided to keep a hawk?' He was quite amused by now. It had become a pretty diversion.

She thumped her armful of papers on the top of his partner's desk and regarded him through half-closed eyes. She smiled. He was an agreeable boss, generous and never a grinder.

'What would I say?' She began to laugh. 'What I'd say is watch out.'

Far better, realised Claire, to have presented James with a *fait accompli* rather than a warning. That way there would only be one row instead of two. She was undeterred but decided she would be in a stronger position if she were better informed.

She took the car and drove fifteen miles to the library. The weather was now dry and the lanes dusty again. Flocks of yellowhammers with less fear than a household sparrow flew over the hedgerows in front of her, fluting their high, liquid songs. To either side the cider orchards were stacked with bags of apples against the trunks. She smelt the usual autumn scent of fermenting fruit. A man passed in a pick-up truck with a collie sitting up like a wife beside him.

The librarian directed her to several books that were on the shelf. She glanced through the indices, found what she sought and returned home making a detour to pass the house of Mr Powell, the birdman, who lived on the straggling outskirts of the village just beyond the thirty-mile-an-hour sign. She crawled past a white bungalow with a red door, a wooden garage, and a cowshed with children kicking a piece of dried mud. Wilf Powell's cottage was isolated on the edge of the settlement, the right half of a semidetached prewar brick council house. It was normal in all respects but for the absence of flowers. The neighbouring garden, in contrast, on the other side of the chain-link fence was a fuchsia bower. There was no sign of human life about so she drove the remaining few miles home.

Parabuteo unicinctus, said the caption which referred to the Harris hawk. It was underneath a photograph of a large dark atavistic bird with yellow legs. *Parabuteo*: like a buzzard, though the creature was, it seemed, more of a hawk than a buzzard. A broadwing, native to the deserts of South America and the Southern states of the USA, Louisiana to Kansas, California and Texas. *Parabuteo unicinctus*, gregarious in its natural state where it hunted in packs. This cooperative instinct had made it a wonderful hunting animal for man. A lone trained hawk would bond with its master.

She read on, in thrall to a new and glamorous world. In Britain it had revolutionised hawking and was considered one of the best birds for beginnners. A beautiful, dark, reddish-brown creature, adaptable, highly intelligent and a rapacious hunter when well controlled and flown.

She began to turn the pages, seeking practicalities. How it lived, what it ate, how it exercised. She thought of the sparrow-hawk and the pigeon it had caught in the summer. A nice fat healthy pink stock dove. Diet was important. Did caged hunters eat doves? Did you trap and throw them a mouse? In which case this would be Sam's job and nothing to do with her. Or did you feed them hygienic plastic packs of frozen food like dog food? Were shins of beef an option? There was a large disturbing mystery here. She flicked through the book to the section on food. She read it with misgiving. Rats, quail, rabbits or chicks were the favoured food, with strips of beef for a lure.

She put the book down and went to the back door and looked out. To the west there was a buzzard at full stretch high in the sky. She watched it float on the thermals. The ground was cooling in autumn and lifts of hot air must be hard to find. Rats, quail, rabbits and chicks. Did they come tinned, in packages or individually wrapped? She recalled James's crack: I just hope it's a vegetarian hawk for your sake. She remembered Turgenev's poignant tale about a little quail. She set her face in the lines that reflected her determination not to be beaten. She smudged over the pictures her imagination made of rats. She blurred out their ears and tails. Her job was to be the boy's enabler, not the bird's feeder, or finder of prey. She would sit on the brink and watch.

6

'We'll try it again,' said Stuart patiently.

It was the same afternoon and as it was raining he had taken his son to the town swimming baths, a single-storey hangar of a building on the southern side of the city. They were standing at the shallow end where an aerobics class had just finished. The pool was as thronged and brightly coloured as a coral reef. The shouts of children boomed in the hollow water-filled space and shadows flickered like fish below a shoal of swimmers. Although the music had faded, everyone seemed to be enjoying themselves. Or everyone that is, thought Stuart, except him and his son. A man of quiet application, he reapplied himself to the simple problem in hand.

'Now look, Sam. No funking. There's nothing to be scared of. We're having a great time.'

Sam stared away. A current of shivering ran through him. The air was humid and the water tepid but his teeth were chattering in spasms. He cast a glance at the exit. How much longer would his father make this last?

'Please, dad, I can't do it,' he said plaintively. 'If you don't mind, I think we can go home now.'

'Course you can, Sam. Stop shaking like a leaf. I'm right here beside you.'

Yes, he could swim perfectly well in the shallow end. A nice steady crawl, his head turning rhythmically to the left to haul in the air, his feet thrashing like a mermaid's tail. Or breaststroke, both thin arms poking onwards and forwards together, knees splayed like a frog, his small head bobbing up and down on the surface. Yes, it was true, he was a champion swimmer, as good as a water baby in the shallow end, but put him in the deep end and he would drown, he knew it.

'I can't do it. Really.'

'You can. Just look at her.'

Both heads turned to watch a ten-year-old girl chugging like a tug up and down the central channel. Hateful, thought Sam. It was Tracy, the fat girl of his class. He felt a wave of despair and resentment.

'See? She's got no problems. You going to let yourself be beaten by that little tub of a girl? Now move it.'

For the eighth time man and boy launched themselves on a voyage that had so far defied completion, this journey from one end of the pool to the other. It had become a torment for both father and child.

'Come *on*, keep *going*, *don't* try and touch the floor.'

Push forward, arms out, feet together, then sideways, think of Tracy. The water opened and closed, blinding. Chlorine in his nose, slurps in his ears, his head like an echo-chamber.

'Don't try and touch the floor, forget about the floor.'

Where was the rail, where was his father, he couldn't feel the side of the bath, he couldn't see his father, he was drowning, he knew it. *'Keep going,'* but panic was making him flounder. He was falling, the water closing over his head. 'Push, push, carry on.'

He scrabbled blindly to the left, no rail, to his right, no father, where was his father? *'Keep going*. Don't stop. Don't look down.' Too late, he had found the rail and rigid with terror was trying to climb out, as his father's arms were pulling him back. It was his worst nightmare, the bad dream that came sometimes and woke him crying. *'Keep going. Don't stop. Push on.'* Just one more time, Tracy will see you, what will your mum think of you. *Don't look down.* Where was the bottom, his feet couldn't touch the bottom, he was out of his depth, he was drowning again. Choking, he reared up for the eighth time and shouted, 'No I can't!'

'What the bloody hell am I going to do with you?' said Stuart, holding his son who was crying.

He did a double-de-clutch with his feet under the water, turned round and supporting his child round his waist, swam back to the shallow end where the rest of the inmates were still splashing in fun. One or two watched as they clambered up the steps. A girl in a green swimsuit cast a covert glance at the man's muscled form and an eighty-year-old woman remarked on his trembling son.

Coughing, for he had swallowed a mouthful of water, Sam paddled in the footprints of his father across the wet floor. He wished he could speak but all he could see was the quelling expanse of his father's mute back. Still shivering a little but relieved to have escaped from the water, he followed him along the wet passage to the changing room. In silence, they showered then got dressed, pulling on jeans and, in Sam's case, his bendy spectacles and a red polo-shirt. 'OK mate?' asked his father. The child nodded but was wordless, locked into the shadow of his own failure.

Side by side they walked out of the building and into the street. Stuart glanced down at his son's profile and felt a pang. He also noticed his pallor. Like all the Regiment, he had received medical training.

'Here,' he said, stopping at a sweet shop to let the boy buy a pack of chocolate cream eggs.

'Better?' he asked and ruffled the tuft on his head. 'Don't worry,' he said. 'You tried really well.'

They carried on to Bridge Street and seated themselves opposite each other on blue plastic seats in a café. Stuart ordered two milk-shakes and a doughy bun and stared with quiet affection at his crushed son.

'You know what this is about, don't you?'

Sam looked at the girl bringing the milk-shakes and nodded.

Stuart waited tactfully till she had delivered and left. 'You know, don't you,' he said, 'that if you don't beat something it beats you.'

'Yes.'

'You know you've got to lick it.'

'Yes.'

'You know the only way to lick it is to do it.'

Sam nodded and blew on the froth.

'You know the best way of licking it is to do it again and again and again.'

A smaller nod. The boy and his responses seemed to be shrinking.

'You know you mustn't give up.'

Nothing this time.

'You know something? I'm scared of things too.'

Sam looked down at his grubby hands, as though embarrassed that his father should lie.

Stuart sighed and decided to come at the problem from a different direction.

'Do you want to be a mummy's boy? Want Tracy to call you a diddums?'

'Don't like Tracy.'

'But she can do it. And so can you.'

A wooden stalemate. As his blood sugar had risen, so had a will of his own.

Stuart gave another sigh and tried again. 'Shall we have one more go tomorrow? Face it together?'

'Don't know.' He failed to meet his father's eye. He sat in misery and prayed that his dad would go away again, to the other side of the world, to somewhere where he could be someone else's father. At the moment he wished he were no one's son.

'How did it go?' asked Mary when they got home.

'Don't worry,' said Stuart. 'We're going to crack it tomorrow.' He walked up to the dog and put his arms round her with pent-up relief and ardour. A no-problem area, she was great.

Oh-oh, thought Mary, there's been trouble as usual.

'You're a swimmer aren't you my lovely?' said Stuart.

The Dobermann who was anything but fierce slobbered over him and followed him to the table which was covered with a red-and-white gingham cloth. Mary set two platefuls of chicken, salad and a microwaved baked potato in front of her husband and son. Gemma, cuddling up to Stuart, put her silky muzzle on the table. He lifted the soft flap of her lip which was pink and shiny inside.

'You're gorgeous, aren't you?' he said.

The dog started breathing emotionally.

'I'm not hungry,' said Sam miserably, watching them drool at one another for a full half-minute. 'And I'm not here tomorrow. Wilf needs me.'

'You've got to eat,' said Mary automatically.

'Sh-shan't.'

'He's had a milk-shake and two chocolate cream eggs,' said Stuart. 'And a bun. He's bunged up with the stuff.'

'That's not proper food.'

'Let him be,' said Stuart who'd had more than enough of family life himself. He got up to pour out a lager, then turned on the video to watch a Tina Turner concert. She was wearing a frilly scrap of a dress and he stared in fascination at her sexy chicken-legged strut. Nearly twice his age but still gorgeous. 'You've got so much blood in you baby,' he exclaimed.

'Can you turn that thing down,' said Mary above the noise of her heated throb.

Stuart reduced it marginally. 'Don't you like the little lady's music?'

What do I do? thought Mary. Do I? She went to the phone which didn't ring often because, like all the members of the Regiment, they were ex-directory. She stood looking at it then turned away. 'Tomorrow I'll ask you to go to the supermarket,' she said.

'Oh?' His eyes were glued to the screen. 'When will you ask me?'

'Tomorrow.'

She turned back to the phone, picked it up and stamped in the numbers. She counted the rings.

'Hello?' answered Claire in her well-behaved telephone manner.

She strained to hear above the noise in the background.

'It's me, Mary,' she said quietly. 'I've rung to thank you.'

'What for exactly?'

'Your offer.' She leant sideways and shouted. 'Turn that thing down.'

Stuart pressed the remote and went to stand over the screen in protest.

'Sorry,' said Mary. She lowered her voice. 'You know, your offer about the bird.'

'Yes?'

'I've rung to thank you and to say if it's still all right, then we'll go ahead. I'll pay you back. Is it on?'

'Of course,' said Claire, thinking.

They agreed a few provisional arrangements and then rang off.

'It's on,' said Mary. She looked tense and her round Dutch cheeks were highly coloured and glowing against her red hair.

'What is?' said Stuart turning the volume up.

'You know,' she muttered. 'The bird.'

'Great.' He flooded the room with hot sound.

'I'll tell him,' she said. 'No. Why not you?'

7

On the telephone Mr Powell had explained to Claire that some people were squeamish. There were certain things she would have to understand. You mean feeding them rats and chicks and so forth, she had replied, but it was apparent this was not on his mind. 'It were best that you come out lamping,' he said.

'Lamping?' she asked. It sounded odd and she didn't understand.

'It's hunting by lamplight, see?' said Wilf Powell. 'We lamps the rabbits and lamps the bird. You wear only your very darkest clothes, mind.' She had dressed in funereal jacket and trousers and an ink-blue headscarf, and looked in the mirror with grave disbelief. A middle-aged woman and a vegetarian. Any queries?

By the time she had set out, night had fallen. She left the dog in the house and drove in solitude through the thin meandering lanes. The night was dark and beautiful, the fields smoke-black beneath a lighter sky. A horned moon rose on her right, pale and glistening against the navy and charcoal sea of the horizon. The air was cold and autumnal. Evening creatures were stirring and she felt attuned to the musical whirrs and snicks of their nighttime life.

A farmer had given the birdman his permission to hunt and they had arranged to meet by a gate on his land. She hoped that they would be waiting and when she approached from a distance it was with relief that she saw a single silhouette of the old man with the boy at his side. The smell of exhaust folding into the night air told her that their car had only just arrived. She drove onto the verge and stepped out.

She nodded at the two shadowed faces though only the man responded.

'Hush now. Whispering only,' he murmured. 'Wait here whilst I gets Chloe out.'

He opened his car door softly and bent deep inside. Over his head she saw a big box and was aware of a scuffling. He lifted it out and raised the lid. In the darkness she heard the gentle rustle of feathers and saw him smooth the hawk out before he shifted her onto his gauntletted left hand. The bird sat poised and alert, looking about her, adjusting to the freedom of the night. The bell on her leg gave an echoing muffled chime. In the sky above them, Claire noticed a star shoot and the distant diamond track of a satellite. The strangeness of this extraordinary moment gripped her. Unearthly, the old man, the young boy, the hunting bird, the pared moon and the diamonds in the ebony velvet sky.

'It will be a good night,' said Wilf. 'She is pie-hot.'

'You must keep quiet when we start,' whispered Sam.

'We're going to work up the slope to that field, see? Surrounded by copses. Then down again. The rabbits run slower downhill.'

He leant on the gate and pointed with his right hand. Then as quietly as an old poacher, he slid the gate open.

'The ground's bumpy, so watch where you walk. To stumble will cause you a jar. Follow me.'

'I've got boots,' she said.

He paused and surveyed her.

'One more thing, mind. I warn you. The rabbits do squeal.'

She halted. 'I suppose they do,' she said.

'Don't worry,' said Sam. 'Our Mr Powell's kind.'

She fell back a little.

The Indian file crossed the first field in darkness and silence. To an onlooker they would have seemed a strange and oddly assorted group. An old man leading calmly with the bird on his hand, next a small boy light-footed on the tufty ground and in the rear a woman stumbling over the tussocks in the pasture. Only their pale faces were visible in the thin moon-shadow of the night.

'When we gets to those trees over there, I shine the lamp

suddenly at the edge. You stop still then. Not a word or a movement, mind,' he whispered.

Five more minutes passed. In the distance there was a guttural screech, harsh and foreign, and then silence apart from the lonely shuffle of feet through tufts of grass. The hawk floated on his fist, a pie-hot hunting queen, ravenous and regal. Wilf stopped. He swung his free arm high with the lamp. It flashed. He kept the beam fixed. The brilliant searing blaze lit up the field and bush in its huge triangular shaft. The hawk on his left hand craned forward. The four stared with furious intensity at the focus of the beam; the bird, her master, his disciple and Claire. Nothing, not a thing stirred, no movement at its end: all that came into view were unevenly cropped grasses bleached by the searchlight and, beyond, the low skirt of the trees hemmed by the browsing line of the sheep.

He switched the light off abruptly. The quartet of hunters walked on, turning a right angle and then forking left. They stopped again. The same ritual. The light flashed again. Different this time. Instantly a pair of rabbits shone at the end of the beam. Chloe lifted herself in perfect gliding movement. Claire saw all this as though in slow motion. She held her breath. The bird's bells chimed. One on the tail and one on the leg, two different musical rings, echoing the melodic rowing rhythm of her flight. With the targeted precision of a bullet the magnificent dark bird burst along the beam of light towards a rabbit. As they touched, for a second, bird and rabbit seemed one, joined in the random passionate union. The bird caught the back leg, she tugged, she tried to lift, the rabbit gave a thump, a piston kick, the bird could not hold her. The rabbit escaped, bolting into the undergrowth. The prey had gone to ground. The light was switched off. Darkness again. The old man directed a torch beam onto his gauntlet as a signal for the hawk's return. She responded, floating downwards into the halo of milky light with soft exquisite grace, furling the great half-folded crinoline of her wings into her sides. She came to rest on his hand and stabbed at the bloody fragment of meat she was given in consolation. All that was visible in the cameo of albino light was the bird on the wrist, talons grasping the gauntlet, and the downward hook of the beak attacking the food. Two mouthfuls and it was gone.

Darkness again. They walked onwards against a line of rough hawthorn, through another gate, towards a spinney in the distance. It was hard to adjust the eyes from a daylike brilliance to night again. A few more minutes and he shone the lamp. A ghost grey bird flew silently across its alabaster shaft, trapped in the killing beam. 'No, no,' said Wilf, 'no,' but too late, her feet gripped and released, there was an urgent rustle and the hawk had gone. 'No.' He switched the beam off and plunged them in dungeon darkness again.

'What's happened?' the boy whispered.

'A little owl. I won't let her kill him.'

Focusing the small beam on his glove, he returned the huntress once more to his left hand.

'Sorry my lovely,' he told her, rewarding the hungry creature with a further scrap of meat.

A return to blackness. They pressed forward to the spinney, its hulk visible against the purple-black clouds. The curved moon had risen higher and swung like an ivory hammock in the sky. The stalking had become a slow stop-start business. Quietly they crept forwards and paused, single-minded for their quarry, the pulse of their breathing just audible on the quiet air. In the distance a pheasant flushed from his hiding-place gave an alarm call: cok-cok-cok-cok-cok, abrupt and bumpy. Another pause for the night to settle down. Then the beam flashed, its huge illuminating shaft. All saw the big rabbit at the same time. The bird blazed forth, death in her talons. The prey ran to the left, doubled back, twisted, turned, his cheeky but pitiful scut bobbing up and down. The hawk flew furiously low, adjusting her angle and speed at each trick and twist. If the prey was experienced then so was his predator. The rabbit was only a few yards before her, nearly at the boundary, nearly safe within a leap of his hedge, but within a second the bird was upon him, tumultuous and terrifying. Boiling with frustration, the assassin seized him. The two locked together as her talons closed round him. Gripped in her vice, the creature started to scream. It was a rending sound of torture: persistent, metallic yet human.

'Christ,' said Claire. 'Oh my God, why doesn't she just get on with it and kill him?'

'Stay here. It's cruel to let it suffer.'

She saw him running towards the noise, saw him reach them, bend over, jerk his arm and then the sound ended. The climax was silence and the shocked peace of death.

In the darkness, the man returned with the rabbit in his pouch and the bird on his fist.

Claire felt herself shaking. She sank down on the ground and buried her head in her hands.

'Dear God, I wasn't prepared for the cruelty.'

Beside her she sensed the boy too was shivering.

'Come now,' said Wilf. 'Let the four of us sit down an' talk.'

They huddled close to each other in the grass. For a moment he turned the torch onto the bird and passed her a couple more inches of beef.

'Why don't you let 'er have the rabbit?' asked Sam.

'She can eat it after she catches another.'

'I think I'll wait here,' said Claire.

The birdman pulled off his glove, put his free hand on her shoulder then thrust it into his pocket. He pulled out three chocolate bars and passed one to each of them.

'I'm not hungry,' she said.

'You eat. It's cold.'

It was indeed cold: a clear, still night, the temperature fallen near to freezing. The ground on which they sat had started to stiffen. An owl whooped, the hollow call of a tawny, and the crisp snaps of the chocolate bars pierced the air.

'I expected this sadness, see.'

'It's not sadness. Just pity.'

He stared at her in the darkness.

'Do you have a cat?' he asked slowly.

'Two.'

'Do you feed 'em?'

'Yes.'

'Do you feed 'em all they want?'

'Yes.' She wondered about the road he was travelling.

'Do they still catch mice?'

'Yes.'

'Rabbits?'

'Yes.' It was becoming obvious.

'Birds?'

'Yes.'

'What birds?' She was loath to follow where he led her.

'Sparrows. I don't know.' She had reluctant memories of a robin yesterday and a bluetit last week. Did that mean that a house sparrow, brown and dowdy, was dispensable? 'I try and stop them.'

'Do they obey?'

She shrugged in the darkness. If she had been younger and sillier it might have seemed petulant.

'How long do they takes to kill 'em?'

Nothing.

'Do they play with 'em?'

She did not answer. She would not aid him to pin her into a corner.

'I tells you this. A cat can take up to half an hour to kill its prey. My hawk takes at the most five minutes – if she's left to herself, mind. But it's cruel to let a creature suffer. I kills it at once.'

She shivered again. Beside her Sam had finished eating his chocolate bar. He folded the paper and put the litter into his pocket. Above them a star shot, like the burst of a rocket, a fragment of dust from a comet trail, less than a hundred miles away.

She leant forward. 'How do you kill it?'

'Break its neck. Instant.' His hands made dark expressive gestures.

'Why doesn't she kill them immediately?'

'She does sometimes – with luck. Depends where her feet go. A hawk kills with her talons, see? She crushes the middle of a rabbit like a vice, its vital organs, mind. One hook of her other talon squeezes its jaw and another pierces the eye. That way death comes at once.' He added with cunning, 'Not a slow torment like a cat, see?'

'Dreadful.'

'They tells me you're a doctor's daughter.'

'Yes.'

'You have a kind heart for a doctor's daughter,' said the school caretaker, 'but a lot to learn.'

She was silent.

'Hunt with a fair mind and a good heart, see?'

'You didn't let it kill the little owl.'

'A slow flyer and a fine bird of prey. Not vermin like your magpies.'

He looked down and stroked the bird's chest gently with his knuckle.

'Nor do I let her kill in the spring. Not even rabbits. Take a milky doe and a nestful of rabbits do die.' He added slyly, 'Do you stop your cats hunting in spring?'

She sighed deeply. 'It's all so difficult,' she said.

'Remember this. She's not a pet but a wild thing and you keeps her as close as can be to the wild. Remember. Respect the bird and never forget to respect the prey.'

He stood up and stretched. The boy, transfixed by his words and his movements, followed him.

'You too, Mrs Farley?'

She stood and hesitated. 'All right then, yes I'll come,' she said.

'Now then, we'll walk to the field by Quarrels Wood.'

It took another hour and three more thwarted attempts and forlorn returns to the fist before she made a second kill. This time it was a rabbit flushed from a bunch of stinging nettles in an empty field. He ran, bolting his way along a furrow.

'Go,' said Wilf, 'go.'

Again the huge dark red wings unleashed. There was a blurred dash along the beam. She flew low and hard, her head pushed forward like a snake, like a fossil bird. The rabbit pounded towards the sanctuary. The hawk flew too fast, hard to match so that for a second it looked as though the bird would overshoot him, then a manic frantic coupling. The scream, unearthly, but at least cut short.

'She's killed,' said Wilf. 'You see?'

The boy between them, they walked together to the bird and her prey. Ravished and lolling, the fur doll was pinned beneath her. She pecked three times, took three pinches of coiled guts, then lifted her haughty head and looked around. Her hooked beak glistened in the fractional moonlight with blood.

'Her talons will unlock now and I takes the rabbit and gives her a scrap of meat instead.'

The second dead rabbit rolled limply onto the first in his pouch. He patted the placket.

'She will have a feast tonight.'

The trio stood still, breathing heavily. It had been achingly hard work, watching, stumbling, hunting with hawk-eyes, as hard as climbing. Their breath vapour steamed in pants into the chill humid air. The woman felt sweat on her forehead.

'Time you were in bed, boy.'

'Please Mr Powell, let me see her eat him.'

'Time you were in bed, boy.'

Claire thought of the bird's speed and courage and aggression, the grace and wildness of her hunting. It occurred to her that at the beginning of the night she had been on the side of the prey. She had spent a lifetime on the side of the prey. But what now, when prey and predator were joined one to another?

8

'Everyone has to be a middle-class Whig nowadays,' said James. 'Even you,' and he stared at the bland, pink, jovial face of Anthony Milner MP.

It was two nights later, a Saturday evening, and the party of eight were seated at the Milners' dinner table. The candle flames flicked light over the circle of varnished faces.

'Don't look at me,' said Milner, who had long since mastered the art of side-stepping, 'when we have a real Whig here.'

He gestured to Hugh Stooke towards the far end of the opposite side, well away from him because he knew of old that his neighbour was a dull companion.

The younger brother to the heir of a long and landed lineage, Stooke flushed.

'The point,' said James, undeflected, 'is that everyone—'

'Absolutely no politics if you please,' said Ellie from the doorway. 'Not here anyway. This is our hideaway.'

Batting back and forth, she had cleared away a large blue-and-white platter of dismembered guinea fowls, their adornment of game chips, two cheese dishes with a patriotic assembly of local ewe's and goat's milk products (a reflex choice, there being a constituency vote even in cheese) and the last remnants of water biscuits. She was now bringing in eight wobbly little fruit jellies of dariole form, in the colours of cornelian, currant and caramel. The dinner had reached its fourth act and she was looking forward to sitting down and staying put, the replete stage when the hostess subsides. She beamed round and began to send the jellies forth to their destinations.

'No politics and no shop,' she repeated. 'I can't bear it as you are well aware.'

Alice Downton, another guest, took receipt of her jelly and held it trembling to the light.

'Well done, Ellie,' she murmured. 'Très splashe.'

'But I'm not political,' protested Stooke, a diffident soul who had passed his quiet life preferring to keep his head below his brother's eighteenth-century parapet. This was in fact the first time he had spoken, till now munching his way through everything including the napkin.

'That's because you're terrified of being either predator or preyed on come the Revolution,' said James.

Faced with the gentle inertia of the landed gentry, James became prone to the belligerence of the self-made man. His eyes flickered briefly across the shoulders of the girl, a stranger to the group, who was sitting on the opposite side of the table, and came to rest on Alice and her husband, with whom the girl was spending the weekend.

'Wouldn't you agree Alice?'

'One would not require or expect Hugh to be a street-fighter. Herefordshire is a feudal county, not a place for the Revolution.'

'England isn't a revolutionary country at all. Not like France.'

It was the unknown girl who had spoken. James looked at her with renewed interest. She was more simply dressed than the other women, as well she might be as she was considerably younger. She was wearing a cream silk shift with a scooped neck and a pattern of widely spaced maroon flowers. She looked an exotic specimen in this antique Anglo-Saxon setting. The girl had that specialised French form of beauty with high cheekbones and a big mouth pushed forward as though it was accustomed to saying 'tu' and 'vous'. 'Tu' most likely, thought Claire. She looked at her glumly and with a touch of foreboding. The girl had something about her: so very definitely foreign *fille*, that evident yet unflashy sexual attractiveness, despite her neat tightly cropped boyish head. Claire had been aware throughout the dinner that James had responded to her. It occurred to her that her alarm system had become a learnt mode of defence, a state of alert which never failed to register whom James spoke to and who spoke to him. I am like a rabbit, she thought, eyes set on either side of my head, not binocular but with all-round sight. I have evolved a special vision to survive. The thought revolted her.

She made a conscious decision to pre-empt.

'Such a pretty name, Chantal,' she said, laying claim to the girl's allegiance in advance of her husband. 'I've forgotten your surname.'

'Saintange.'

'Are you related to the Yorkshire Saintanges?' murmured Stooke automatically from the depths of his jelly. He was apt to play out his role.

'How very hard to live up to,' said James, ignoring the interruption. 'How come you don't have a French accent?'

'My mother was English.' Must be dead, thought Claire. Or divorced, thought James.

'I was brought up in both countries so I know which is the more revolutionary.'

'Oh, the French still strike at the drop of a hat,' offered Ellie. She pressed some more cream on her neighbour, Stooke. The slight, curly-haired bachelor accepted.

'A revolution takes manifold forms,' said Claire. 'If we lost our monarchy, I'd call it a revolution, wouldn't you?'

'That would be very dippy,' said Chantal. 'Brought down by adultery. Like your politicians too.'

Claire looked down, disconcerted that her neutral comment should have been spun round to point in a hazardous direction. She had a pressing wish not to discuss adultery, especially in public.

'Why don't you think it happens in France?' asked James. 'It doesn't, does it? Is it your privacy laws?'

He looked at her through slightly narrowed eyes. He savoured the good drink circulating inside him. He felt thirty years old; he knew he was still handsome if a touch portly, with brushed-back brown hair, blue eyes with black lashes and a dark red mouth.

'In France twenty per cent of men have mistresses. It is perfectly acceptable to many wives. It doesn't break marriages. It is why our marriages last.'

'Not our way,' said Ellie smugly which was dishonest. She had spent the last ten years up and down the motorways every week with her husband to and from London. She no longer trusted him to spend four days safely on his own.

The men leant forward with the exception of Stooke who took refuge in his jelly as the conversation moved out of his orbit. Milner and James looked like a pair of pointers who had sniffed something delicious and truffly on the breeze.

'You mean,' said Gerry Downton, Alice's husband, 'the way it used to be in the deep South. Every man has his darkie mistress.'

'All I mean is that the French have a mature attitude to all appetites. Food, drink, sex, the appetites are allowed for. A civilised person neither gorges, nor need he abstain.'

'No one's talking about abstention. The whole point of marriage is that it allows for the appetites as you so delicately call it,' said Ellie.

'Does it?' asked Gerry, daring his wife's wrath.

'I should have thought that's the point of it,' said Ellie.

'Presumably,' said Alice coldly.

'Better to marry than to burn, and all that.'

'What I would like to know,' said Claire, feeling she was better camouflaged by joining in, 'is why any normal man would want other women as well as his wife if he's happy.'

'Precisely,' said Ellie.

'Would anyone be so kind as to answer us that?' said Alice.

'A normal man,' said James, 'by which we mean *l'homme moyen sensuel*,' (he flicked his gaze towards Chantal at the moment of speaking in French), 'a normal man is driven by two engines.'

'Engines,' said Claire. 'You've never mentioned engines to me.'

'Two engines, as I said. They are both about self-betterment.'

'Different, I take it, from self-improvement,' said Alice.

'Clearly. Less moral,' said Ellie.

Anthony Milner leant back and rocked his chair on its two rear legs. 'Anyone mind if I have a smoke?'

'Cigarillos,' said Ellie. 'Would you like me to send him out in his own house?'

'Might I have one too?' asked James.

Claire looked at him sourly. This *bon viveur* she had married, with a big nose.

'Hurry up,' urged Alice. 'We can't wait. Engines.'

James leant forward, picked up the candelabra and lit the miniature cigar. All eyes were upon him and he paused a moment for effect. It was greatly enjoyable.

'Right. Engines. The first is to do with work. If this *homme moyen sensuel* sees another chap doing bloody well, he thinks: if that bugger can get there, so can I.'

'I don't see what that has to do with adultery.'

'Hang on. You will in a moment. This other engine, the second one, is to do with sex. If your regular guy sees a good-looking girl on someone else's arm, he then thinks: if that bugger deserves her, then so do I.'

James sat back, exhaled a smoke puff and looked challengingly round at the faces in the candlelight.

'These engines sound like one and the same motor to me,' said Alice.

'They sound like envy, pure and simple,' said Gerald Downton, a charming, honourable man who was commercially useless according to the gospel aired by his wife.

'It's more than envy,' said Milner. He screwed up his eyes which he sometimes did to suggest penetrating thought. 'It's something primitive, I grant you.'

'It's downright aggression,' said Alice.

'James is a very aggressive man,' said Claire.

'Not aggressive. Just honest,' corrected James. 'And if any of you lot were honest, you'd agree with me.'

'Well?' Ellie shouted to Milner at the other end of the table. 'Do you agree with him?'

'I think James is speaking for himself.'

'You can drop your public persona, if you want to,' said his wife sarcastically. 'No one is going to tell on you here.'

'He's not going to risk it,' said Alice. 'What about my dear husband?'

'Yes, Gerry? You're keeping rather quiet, too.'

Gerald looked at Claire who had spoken, then back to his wife. 'I'm too hen-pecked to be like that.'

James crushed his napkin in mock-disgust. 'What a pair of

lousy hypocrites,' he said. 'But then I couldn't have expected anything different. We've become a nation of hypocrites.'

'I would agree,' said Hugh Stooke abruptly as though affronted his opinion hadn't been sought. 'We are hypocrites.'

All eyes turned in surprise to him. He would normally in his fluffy way have shunned any contention. He blushed again but continued. 'What this is all about is territoriality, a basic animal instinct as we know, very ancient and very powerful. It's the instinct to get hold of or keep or defend the exclusive right to a property.'

'Exactly. Money, sex, or in your case, land,' said James.

There was a second's embarrassment. Stooke was commonly assumed to be non-sexual but it had never before been implied so overtly.

'Right. And in your case,' said Hugh, 'just money and sex.'

From his facial tension, it was obvious he was getting his own back.

There was a short but telling silence.

'My point,' said James, deciding to ignore it, 'is that these instincts, in whatever form, mark you, are basic and can't be eradicated.'

'Don't be ridiculous,' said Claire. 'We're not animals.'

'Aren't we?'

'We're civilised human beings and we don't just go around grabbing each other's possessions or trampling on people's feelings.'

'Of course we don't. Civilised people don't cause harm or hurt, said Alice.'

'They need not,' said Chantal.

'Such piety,' said Claire. 'Don't they?'

'Not if they're honest and play by the rules.'

'What if they're not honest?' Ellie thought back to that delicate period ten years ago when Anthony had formed a serious attachment to his secretary.

'Then the shit hits the fan,' said Anthony thinking of the same occasion and expressing himself in the language of that time. Neither, however, glanced at the other.

'Lack of honesty,' said Alice, 'means that things can get out of hand. Neither partner can step in and stop it.'

'You mean it's OK if it's above board.'

'Not OK but controllable.'

'It seems to me,' said Ellie who felt that the talk was nosing out of hand, 'that this conversation is inappropriate to people of our age. If we were ten years younger, say—'

'It should be inappropriate,' said Alice, 'but it isn't is it? Why do we women dye our hair? To seem younger? To act younger? To be younger. But why?'

'To compete?' offered Gerry. 'Or am I being too optimistic?'

'You are,' and she flashed him her gummy, toothy smile.

'To defend,' said Claire suddenly. 'Though please note that my hair is still naturally fair.' She avoided looking at Chantal, her intended audience.

'Very pretty too, sweetie,' said James.

'Youth comes out of a packet nowadays,' said Alice suspiciously.

'I think,' said Ellie making a second bid to close the conversation, 'that we should be looking forward to the sublime serenity of old age. I also think that it's time we had some coffee.'

She rose and showed her displeasure by scraping at the spilled wax on the table that had tumbled from the candelabra. She then walked to the dresser from which she fetched a little porcelain bowl of brown and white truffles which she placed on the table.

'I love truffles,' said Chantal. She stood up, leant over and took one. As she bent, the cavity of her scoop neck increased and the candle flames deepened the shadow of her slight cleavage. She put the truffle in her mouth and licked her fingers.

'Bon appetit,' she said and as she spoke, for the briefest of seconds, her brown eyes met those of James.

Oh-ho, thought James, if the ducks quack feed 'em.

9

Claire anticipated that in the days to come something strange and wonderful would enter her life and she planned for this with greater enthusiasm than she would ever have felt for a person. In the beginning there was a lot to prepare. The aviary was built into the south-facing open brick barn which lay at right angles to the house. The mews, as it was called, was a grand affair with two doors, a food tray that concealed the provider, a high perch covered with natural fibre carpet, a low perch near the front, a bath and a floor of sand. It took a week to complete, at the end of which they surveyed it and pronounced it to be a palace. It was light and airy but warm and dry and looked over the cobbled apron behind the house with its diamond insets of herb beds. The southernwood here had released clouds of resinous scent into the yard, as man and boy had brushed past in the to and fro of building.

Next, the three of them turned their attention to the shed which was emptied and cleaned and rededicated. A pair of scales was installed and a blackboard fixed to the wall on which they would chart the hawk's weight, crop and the weather. Already the place had begun to take on a world and smell of its own with the new, leathery scent of exotic equipment. At the back of the shed an old freezer was pushed into the corner to be filled with the food: a bulk order of dietary requirements. Not wishing to look, Claire dawdled before opening the crates. She took in their contents in a swift blurred glance. Frozen rats with their ears, tails and feet, three-year-old quail past their laying life and day-old cockerels, masses of frozen individuals with their golden fluff set rock solid.

Bella arrived at four o'clock on a Monday afternoon in early October. She came in a box and was already prettily caparisoned, wearing leg and tail bells and jesses which were the thongs on her feet. She looked gawky and adolescent with a chest too broad for her head and feet too big for her scaly legs. She was nervous and angry, but they managed to weigh her and as it was a nice, mild afternoon transferred her to the perch on the lawn and knotted her leash, which was normal procedure although it prompted a storm. To be tethered enraged her. Unnatural: she a wild thing, born to fly. Her bells chimed in discordant alarm and her white droppings sliced in fury across the grass. Claire and Sam sat in the shadows together and watched her thrashing in protest. It was only to be expected but they were dismayed to find that they had a frantic bird on their hands. Her eye was baleful, her tongue protruded and the inside of her mouth was pink like a crushed strawberry. She panted, she beat her wings, she threw herself upside down which exposed the paler softness of her armpits and she fought her jesses and the perch and even the ground. A wild thing, and at this moment it seemed inconceivable that they would ever train her.

'You've got to eat something,' said Claire at seven o'clock to the boy who had not moved from his original position on the grass. 'Come on. Aren't you hungry?'

'Shan't leave her.'

So she cooked up two platefuls of beans on toast and tomatoes and brought them with a pair of forks and they ate cross-legged and side-by-side on the ground. Then they waited until it was time to transfer her to the mews which they knew would be a turbulent moment. It proved an insult to hold her and she flung herself forward and hung like a trussed chicken upside-down from the fist, but Claire put her gently on her perch and Sam threw her a mouse, both kindnesses provoking a fresh round of fits.

This, then, was day one, embarkation one might say, and all they had done was not much, just a prelude to a lull followed by a period of intense training.

For the next week, under Wilf's surveillance, they fed her but left her alone to settle. By day four, Claire was giving the bird a diet of chicks and rats with all the nonchalance of peeling a banana. There was even some progress as now, after bating, the young hawk would sit on her perch and consent to eat. They could congratulate themselves that a level of peace had been obtained, though no contact.

No contact, yet within a short time this diva would have to be manned, to be tamed, to be coaxed to human touch, alien human smells and sounds. 'Not to worry,' said Wilf, as he outlined the three stages of training, of which the first, the foundation for the other stages, was this taming or manning. 'Not to worry. Be firm and patient, mind, and make sure she grows used to both of you.'

'She's Sam's bird,' protested Claire.

'Yours too, mind.'

'That was never part of the agreement.'

'Don't you want her?'

'I want Sam to feel she's all his.'

'He's gotta share her, like. She lives here. The bird belongs to both of you, mind.'

Large changes frequently take place gently and without effort; the hingeless door falls open as though in dreams. So it happened that Claire was no longer the distant patron and observer but the keeper and hunter, to be trained along with the bird.

It was a process, said Wilf, which he could accomplish in a couple of weeks. A novice, he added though without apparent vanity, could take forever. The method of training, to be pursued at all times with the utmost gentleness, was the management of the bird's instincts, her need for food. Here was the first rule of mastery. It was deprivation, harsh and naked. A trainer kept the hawk hungry, a desperate appetite inducing swift submission. An uneven contest, one might have thought, consisting of his will against her needs, but one which a raptor could successfully win by opting for sickness or even death rather than submission: hence the necessity for the scrupulous charting of weight loss.

Each day the little group rehearsed: picking her up, enduring her storms, weighing her, charting her weight on the blackboard, 1lb 12½oz today down from 1lb 13oz yesterday, tempting her with meat on the hand, not feeding her if she refused to eat on the fist, trying again and failing, trying and failing, cursing that failure, how could she resist the hand when she was hungry, look how the exasperating bird was licking her beak with her pink tongue, she must eat, but no, here it comes, failure again, and they were despairing. Until the fourth day when she suddenly weakened and succumbed and dipped her dark head to eat the meat on Claire's hand. That was a wonderful moment, reaching that point at which a wild thing starts to be manned, she trusts, yields herself to taming, the fossil bird made civilised.

'What a Bella,' said Claire. 'She's our best girl.'

And they sat together quietly talking to her for half-an-hour whilst she put her Persian head on one side and looked at the three of them with her dark liquid eyes, no longer mad but curious.

It was at this point that they decided to choose a few notes, the beginning of a melody, with which in time they might whistle her in to the fist.

'There's always a tin whistle we can use,' said Claire, 'but I'd quite like us to use our own voices too. Let's agree on a tune, so that if either of us is out separately, we call Bella in the same way.'

'I'm not very good at whistling, you know, and everything,' said Sam.

She led him into the dark intimidating house and placed him on a chair where he sat propped like a puppet with his little bony arms and legs dangling, 'Listen,' she said, and she put on a cassette and played a snatch once, twice and again, then isolated the first three notes: Pom-pom-pom, quizzical, strangely cadenced, part of a jogging rhythm, Beethoven's eighth symphony, the music that had run insistently through her father's head when he was pushed on long, foggy cross-country runs as a schoolboy.

'Try,' she urged.

He had a go at this alarming new world. Out came an embarrassed and inhibited small noise. Pom-pom-pom, more puff than melody.

'Oh,' she said not wanting to laugh. 'Maybe we'd better just use the old referee's whistle.'

'No.' He didn't look at her. 'I'll do it.' He stood up, turned his back on her which was bold for him and had another try.

'Well, don't worry. We'll keep the whistle in reserve. But practise.'

Within a week from the start of training, Bella had begun to jump to the fist, which was the next test, a major one since it marked the advent of the second stage of discipline when you put the bird on a creance, the long training line. Her task was now to fly to the fist for food. They stood in the paddock for these sessions, gradually feeding out further lengths of line so that she would have longer and longer distances to fly from where they placed her on different posts. This was one of the best of the early times for progress was visible and could be measured in yards. How ravishing to see her fly. Not only a good pupil but a dancer, a marvel of beauty, plumage and muscle. Her feathered shoulders lifted, her huge dark auburn wings spread in full stretch and her two bells called mockingly to one another with their differing chimes.

Each afternoon, after the school day had finished, the three of them would gather in the training-ground. The weather was kind, the sun still warm and the air soft for autumn with late clouds of floating gnats. To the rear of the paddock rose fields forming a grassy symmetrical bowl. It was a beautiful setting but the greenness was deceptive because the year was on the turn. In the hedgerows the field maples were mildewed and the blackberries starting to grit and rot. The trainers felt the pressure and the need for haste. The later they left it for hunting, the harder for the young bird to catch a fit and experienced quarry. But they dared not hasten except slowly. They fed out the creance to her, increasing its length – ten yards, then fifteen, thirty, forty and finally fifty. Fifty yards to fly to them. At fifty she was flying the full length of her creance. She was a marvel and a dancer and it would soon be time for her to meet the dummy bunny.

'A dummy bunny?' said James who was home on the middle weekend of the month. They were about to climb into bed.

'Fun isn't it?' said Claire.

She passed him the brown fur sausage with its white scut which she had brought up to show him.

'Where will this all end?'

'We tie meat over it and she learns to catch it.'

'You amaze me. All you think of is that bird. I've eaten out of tins this weekend.'

'Don't you think she's a beauty?'

'She hates me.'

It was true. Bella bated, flung herself off the perch whenever she saw him.

'She's not used to you. Go and talk to her gently and quietly tomorrow.'

'What shall I say to her?'

'You're not usually so short of sweet nothings.'

'Don't provoke.'

'Say Bella Musica, over and over again.'

'I could twitch the dummy rabbit.'

He put his hand beneath it and jumped it up and down. 'Quite realistic, isn't it?' he said.

She took it from him. 'How we teach her lamping is to put sequins on its eyes.'

'How eerie. What happens?'

'They glow in the lamplight and attract the bird.'

'Claire, put that dummy down.'

'Why? It's like going to bed with a teddy.'

'You know what? You seem happier than I've seen you for years.'

'I am happy. Bewitched you might say.'

'I love you when you're happy.'

'Not otherwise?'

'Better when you're happy.'

'People are always boring when they're unhappy. There've been times when you've made me boring.'

'Not making you boring now am I?'

'I thought you might when we met that girl at Ellie's.'

'What girl?'

'Don't affect ignorance. I know you too well. La part-foreign girl.'

'The boyish-looking one.'

'Chantal Saintange.'

'Ah. The saintly angel. Never my type, that kind.'

'I wondered at the time.'

He lifted himself on his elbow and looked down at her. She had three broad horizontal lines across her fair English forehead because she had a habit of raising her eyebrows when she asked a question.

'I'm getting old. Why should I want to risk a wife for a callow girl at my stage?'

'Because of your engine theory.'

'Oh that. That was just table talk. I'd drunk a bit much as I told you at the time.'

'Not that drunk.'

He nuzzled his face against her neck. The bunny which had slipped between the pillows tickled him and he removed it with a gesture of exasperation.

Of old, almost as automatically as driving, they fitted themselves into each other, nuts and bolts perfectly adjusted. She was the furniture of his life, stable and enduring and he felt her to be a dear and accustomed part of himself. The skin of her body had that soft powderiness that comes with age as though the human creature has begun its transition to dust.

'Does one assume that Ellie and Anthony still do this?'

'Of necessity. She wouldn't keep him otherwise.'

'And Alice and Gerry?'

'If he's unlucky.'

'No one would get lucky with Alice.'

'Who cares about other people? There's just us. You do love me don't you?'

'I must do, mustn't I? To be here at all. Still.'

'Touch me down there as you used to.'

'Is that the way you want it?'

'I could never bear it, you know, if you left me.'

'Dear James. Little James. You've always needed to be top of everyone's list.'

'Ssh. Don't talk. Just touch me again.'

Later, when they had separated, she said to him: 'Shall I tell you a story?'

'Might not stay awake.'

'It's a bedtime story. You're meant to go to sleep but not till afterwards. Promise?'

'What's it about?'

She put her hand up to the light cord, tugged and plunged them in darkness.

'How dramatic,' he said drowsily.

'It's from *The Arabian Nights*. It's about King Sindibad and his hawk.'

He smiled and shook his head in bemusement. 'Lead on, Scheherazade.'

He snuggled up to her, touching her full warm naked length as he usually did when they were in happy mood before sleeping. His left arm fell across and gathered her in. He shut his eyes. Chantal had felt different. Not powdery soft, but sealskin sleek with an oil slick at the centre.

'A king who was hunting with his hawk felt thirsty but the land was parched and dry. He searched the desert and found a tree dropping water like melted butter from its boughs. He let it fill a golden cup that was tied to his hawk's neck and told her to drink it. She refused. She struck it with her pounces—'

'Pounces?'

'—Talons. She upset the liquid. The king filled it a second time thinking she must be thirsty. She struck again and overturned it. King Sindibad was very angry. For the third time he filled the cup but instead he now offered it to his horse. The hawk struck it with a flirt of her wing. "Allah confound thee," said the king—'

'Quoth the king.'

'Quoth the king. "Thou unluckiest of flying things." He struck her with his sword and cut off her wing—'

'Darling Claire.' He kissed her shoulder. 'This is an unkind bedtime story. Not sleep inducing.'

'It's a story about loyalty, devotion and self-sacrifice, on the bird's part anyway. The hawk said to him in sign language, "Look at that which hangeth in the tree." The king looked and saw a brood of vipers whose poison drops he had mistaken for water. He repented deeply. She had protected him and he had struck her.'

'Is that the end?'

'The end is even sadder. The bird on his fist suddenly gasps and dies. The king cries out in sorrow and remorse for having slain the bird who saved his life.'

Having finished, she lay there in silence. There was a full

moon. It struck in shafts through the curtain folds, its sheen forming the pattern of the window against the wall on the opposite side of the room. It occurred to her it was a hunting night. Wilf Powell would be out with his pie-hot girl. Beside her James had fallen asleep. At some point he had doffed her and rolled onto his back. The night chemicals of sleep coursed through his body, leaving his breath slow, steady and untroubled. Bella too would be sleeping, her hooked beak sheathed in the quilt of her shoulder. It was a peaceful thought and made Claire drowse too.

They christened the dummy bunny Johnson after which he began to assume a furry and active life of his own as they pulled him around on a lead in front of Bella. At first she ignored him. But after a round of mis-trials – for the poor thing was young and still maladroit – she managed to grab him, her wing tips arching upwards, and discovered his meat. Then, as they pulled, she learnt to follow. The watching rooks screeched, the pigeons flocked in panic out of the trees and the dog wagged his tail at the edge of the paddock in wonder. The line murmured over the grass, Johnson jumped and Bella Musica threw herself downwards onto the rag beast. They were half tipsy with triumph but the job was not finished. Johnson must shortly be supplanted by a dead rabbit. And not just that. The biggest stage was yet to come. She was still on a creance and the real test was to let her fly loose.

But then it turned windy and gales bent the trees. Their hopes of setting her loose failed and the training was stalled. 'Not today,' warned the old caretaker. 'We wait till the wind falls, see?' On the third day when it settled, they started as usual, the normal ritual with the bird on the creance. She was called to the fist, she came, she fed, she bonded, but the novices were nervous.

The boy was the most fretful. 'We gonna lose her if we let her off the lead,' he muttered.

'I think we'd be happier if we kept her a bit longer on the lead, Wilf?'

'Let her go,' he replied doggedly.

It was a little try, that first time of letting her loose, only a toe in the water. They derobed, called and fed her, that was all, but at least she was free of the creance, a wild bird like her brothers and sisters in Chile or Kansas. Still frightened, they repeated the procedure, though not so often that all the feeding would blunt the edge of her appetite. She was learning not just to follow them, but to fly where they wanted, to a post, a perch, a particular branch on a little thorn tree, and still they had not lost her. They whistled and she came, she followed, a bondsman yet a free spirit ready to explore her surroundings which would become familiar to her: each tree, each clump of old nettles and a colony of anthills that rose like top hats in the hill to the right.

A few more days passed without mishap before they began to teach her to follow them on proper walks. One takes a dog for a walk, or a cat – which of us hasn't walked over the fields only to be followed independently by the faithful little kitchen cat – and it was just the same with Bella. Though not truly the same, for a flying bird on the loose has moved into a different medium where you can never follow her but must trust her. Because of this, they watched her with pride but also a latent sense of perturbation. With these first longer flights, the hawk had become a little more of a stranger again, *Parabuteo unicinctus*. And it wasn't just that. She had also reached that stage when human guidance is second best to the bird's self-education. It takes courage and confidence to move from Johnson or a dead rabbit to the real world where precision as well as power is needed for the kill. A bird of prey has so much to discover: air currents and thermals; wind speed and vantage points; crags, cliffs and the hiding-places in the undergrowth. She learns her living the hard way. The prey is not easy food when she meets the kick of a rabbit, the bite of a squirrel or the stab of a rook beak. It is only a mature bird and a brave one who can develop her assets of speed, surprise and aggression. These are the skills of the hunter and Bella would have to learn them patiently by herself.

If, at the age of fourteen, Griselda had cared little for the country and its awful solitudes, she cared no more for it now she was in her late twenties. As a result she visited her parents' home in Herefordshire rarely, spending most of her time in London where she worked in a literary agency.

The agency wasn't one of the large old grand ones but newer, smaller, younger and a little poorer as it lacked the revenues of a backlist. It had been going for twenty years and had been started by a woman in her mid-thirties who had devoted herself spiritedly to celibacy and her authors. A lively energetic soul, but a lifetime of battling was detectable in the lines of her weary professional face. The list of writers, or clients as they were known, was mixed. Made up of the poor, rich, gifted, hopeless and hopeful, this funny old beau monde was increasingly dominated by young toreadors and aspirant housewives. Now and then old men with red alcoholic noses arrived on the doorstep. They had made their reputations many years ago, since lost them, yet still arrived in search of a commission and a crust. Some of these unfortunate aged writers made more money when dead than alive, death inspiring a flurry of good publicity.

Griselda was responsible for looking after the work of fifty or more of these but she was also required – along with Guy Freke who worked in the room opposite – to sift through the daily quantity of new and unsolicited submissions. The vast majority of these were amateur and useless and not a few of the applicants were both mad and sad. 'Dear Sir, I have written sixteen novels and none of them has been published.' Or, 'Dear Sir, does it matter what colour paper I type my book on and should I use double spacing?' They would have made the hardest heart weep, though not for more than a second as time was money, as Griselda was so frequently admonished.

On this particular November day she was seated at her desk contemplating the rain spitting against her windowpane. It was four o'clock in the afternoon but it was gloomy enough to seem on the brink of a dark winter evening. Outside the golden lights in the offices had turned the sky to indigo. She considered the work piled up on her desk and sighed at the problems posed by the more worldly and demanding of her clients. Some of them could be both greedy and difficult. She sometimes wondered whether the novelists in particular were by definition mad, helpless before the fiction that came out of them and driven insane by the clamour of their imaginary worlds. She groaned, picked up her bag and went over to the coat stand from which she unhooked her long tweed cape. She shrugged it on, looked in the mirror and adjusted her dark strands to fall outside the collar. As she glanced round the room before leaving, she noticed her toy paper aeroplane on the floor. It lay where it had crashed this morning. A visiting editor, a man new to his job at Europress, had rashly admired it on her desk. She had aimed the little dart at the wall in demonstration and to her great embarrassment it had boomeranged between his eyebrows. His salesman's patter had flowed onwards, heedless and without change of tone. He had simply not noticed. But then publishers could be as awful as authors, she thought, as she negotiated her way through the traffic to her second editor's meeting of the day.

Jonathan Tor's welcome was effusive. A big man, he was well stomached and flaccid. He had a reputation for wining and dining to his personal satisfaction, and the results were apparent. Griselda settled into the maroon armchair opposite his desk beyond which he spread his bulk like a turtle. The room was intimately lit, but some expensive-looking squiggles on the wall had been individually focused. On top of the leather desk sat two photographs: the first of Jonathan's wife and the second of their three young children. She realised what she was meant to divine: that Jonathan was that rare spirit, a man with an unclouded family life.

'Tea, Griselda? Coffee? What can we get you?'

'An early whisky, please.' Really, he could afford to lunch me, she thought crossly.

He made his ponderous way to the drinks department which was immured behind a walnut door. An austere amber trickle was allowed to dribble into a cut glass which he handed to her before returning to his desk.

'All well?' he asked genially. 'Guy seems to be establishing himself.'

'He is.'

'And Myra is as lively as ever. The kind who never retires.'

'We certainly hope not.'

'No sign of flagging energy anyway, though one usually depends on the younger people for that commodity. How lucky she is to have you, if I may say so.'

'Thank you.'

They sipped quietly for a moment to mark the end of the overture. Then he shifted position and leant forward. 'Now, Griselda, to business. I am grateful for your visit on two counts. Shall we get the first over?' He put a finger to his temple. 'You look after Masha Guthrie, do you not?'

She nodded. Masha was an artist and film producer with a huge cult following. She was known to be very difficult but was the author of several ghosted celebrity books.

He rearranged the letters on his desk. 'We wondered whether she would do a vegetarian cookbook.'

Griselda stared at him in wonder. 'Masha has never been known to boil an egg. It is an open question whether she eats at all.'

'A minor difficulty. She will as usual be ghosted.'

'Of course. But I foresee a problem.'

'What?'

'What does she say if an interviewer asks her how she boils an egg?'

'I'm sure Masha can be suitably ontological.'

'Will you pay her ontologically?'

He frowned. It was clear he had become uncertain what ontological actually meant. He was now doubtful whether it meant anything at all.

'You will put it to her? If I make an offer in writing?'

Griselda thought. 'I'll raise it.'

'Good.'

'Is that all?'

'Not quite.'

He pulled open a drawer then thoughtfully reversed it. 'The second business is this. I wondered what you would say if I suggested we had an affair.'

Griselda stared at him. Her first thought was that she had heard incorrectly. 'Come again?'

'An affair. You and I.' His eyes had bulged a little.

This was stupefying. 'Me and you?'

He leant forward, his right cuff nudging the nearest of the family photos so that, unwittingly, he tilted its face towards Griselda. His wife looked at her enquiringly. She seemed perky to know the answer. She had a pageboy bob.

This is a difficult one, thought Griselda. If I'm tactless, Masha won't get the offer. Maybe as much as £50,000 down the drain. Masha will get to hear and will be very cross. Do I care? Not a jot. But then I might get the sack. Masha would be a big client to lose. Griselda glanced at the wife again. No doubt she had witnessed thirty propositions already that week.

'It is a charming thought, Jonathan, but look,' she picked up the photograph, 'she wouldn't be very happy would she?'

They both looked at this sprightly third party.

'You must understand she comes first.'

'Very commendable.' She put the photo back. 'But then I come second.'

His eyes had protruded yet more as he interpreted this to be progress. She was in play. The outcome was certain, subject only to negotiation.

He gave a plump little smile. 'First? Second? Perhaps we can discuss terms.'

'Then there are these.' She picked up the photograph of the children. 'Aren't they darlings? But they make three more clamouring to be near you.'

He put out a well-manicured hand to withdraw the picture. 'I think you misunderstand, Griselda.'

'I think not. You are a super bloke of course, and I'm very flattered, but my own view is that we should just concentrate on Masha. It would be too awful if I got wounded in the crush.'

She saw him scan her to check whether there was mockery or otherwise on her face, but none was detectable.

His eyes retracted and became opaque. He rose and, honour satisfied, gave a ritual bow of acceptance. 'One more thing. Do I have your assurance that this is just a little secret between us? Just you and me, Griselda? You won't tell anyone else?'

For the time being, she thought, though rely on me to splatter it all over London later. As she went out it occurred to her that this fat pompous ass was old enough to be her father.

'I must say, you know,' said James, 'I'm not looking for trouble.'

'Do I look like trouble?' She turned her small crop-haired head towards him. She had an expression of great purity.

He smiled. 'You don't look like your typical killer bimbo. In fact you look like innocence herself.'

Or within limits, he considered. She was seated at the end of the bed, cross-legged and naked. He wondered whether she had deliberately adopted such posed self-exposure. He wondered about a lot. He had no experience of the young and her simplicity and unselfconsciousness surprised him. So too did the situation in which he found himself. He had never before been the object of youthful fancy and he was both excited and alarmed. All the women in his previous affairs had been subordinates, former flames or divorcées which is to say that they were en route to being recruited. In contrast, Chantal was an outright volunteer.

It was one o'clock in the morning. The bedroom in which they talked was a large and spacious portion of her small two-roomed flat. It was simply furnished with polished wooden boards, a scattering of old faded kelims and some pewter lamp fittings. The degree of comfort differed greatly from that of Katy his younger daughter, he thought with unease, or even of Griselda whilst she was growing up. Both had lived in warrens inhabited by other young. Though he preferred to avert his eyes from thoughts of either daughter when he was with Chantal.

'I am just an affectionate ordinary girl,' she said.

'Does your affection always expend itself on—' He hesitated

over the phrase 'men of my age' and settled instead for 'older men' which had a statesmanlike ring to it. He pulled the sheet an inch higher to reach the top of his stomach.

'I like your—' She raised her hand, palm upwards for inspiration. '—I like your fruitiness, nicely *mûr* if you don't mind. You are married, no complications, established. Men of my age aren't too manly. They are wimps or lads. So it's quite simple you see.'

'Not so simple for me, I'm afraid. I hate to say this but my wife mustn't know.'

'How much simpler if she did.'

'It would be very hurtful.'

'You want me to look after her feelings rather than you.'

He had the feeling of being giggled at. If there had been another girl present as well, he would have no doubt of it. She and an unseen girl were giggling at him. Probably in response, the tip of his nose began to itch. He rubbed it. He took it as read that the young were not likely to defer to the feelings of the older generation. The decade in which the young had grown up, the so-called caring decade, did not bear examination. He felt like reiterating: I'm not looking for trouble.

He sighed instead. It seemed as if some sort of negotiation needed to take place. A compliment would not go amiss.

'I think you're a most beautiful and impressive girl. But you are also perfectly sensible and realise that my first duty is to my wife.'

It was not easy, he considered, to carry off this remark with dignity. He was in the anomalous position of lying naked, front upwards, in another girl's bed and one who was young enough to be his daughter.

He looked at her courageously. 'You may have been brought up amongst the free and easy ways of the French but I'm English and so is she. Very. More English than I am.'

'My mother was English.'

'So you said.'

'Do you want to see her?'

'You mean meet her?' James sat up in alarm.

'No. Her photo. She's dead.'

'I'm very sorry to hear that.' He lay back in relief.

'Look.'

She crawled on all fours over the bed to reach under the light on the cabinet and picked up a little cameo picture in a silver frame. She showed it to him. His middle-aged eyesight failed to adjust and he pushed it further away. The face was in the same mould as her own: pure, grave, with delicacy of feature and the large, pushed forward, full mouth.

'She's very beautiful. Very like you. What did she die of?'

'A car crash. Seven years ago.'

'You poor child. How dreadful for you. Why didn't you tell me before?'

He put his arms around her. She needs a father figure, he mused, or do I mean mother figure? I just don't want trouble, was the unworthy thought that reiterated itself.

'Can I speak to Katy Farley?'

'Who's speaking?'

'Her sister.'

There was the clatter of a dumped phone, a burst of male laughter in the background, communal and boisterous activity. It sounded more like a boozer, as Katy would now call it, than a hospital. Eventually Katy arrived.

'That you, Grisel?'

'You took ages.'

'I did my first operation last night. An appendix case. I've just run down to the end of the ward to see if he's still alive.'

'Oh Katy, what fun. Is he?'

'He is. Eighteen years old and I haven't polished him off.'

'Congratulations. You wouldn't like to do me next, would you?'

She could hear the snuffle of Katy's laughter at the other end. It was nice to hear her happy and relaxed.

'What do you want out?'

'My brain, dear. I'm suffering from cognitive overload.'

'Not an organic condition so far as I know. I'm old-fashioned. My kind only deals with the real thing.'

'What do you suggest?'

'Practise positive thinking. Say: you can; you must; you shall; you will.'

'It won't work.'

'How about: "Things are getting better and better in every way"?'

'Jesus, Katy. Listen to you. You'll be telling me this is the best of all possible worlds next.'

'I was about to.'

Griselda spluttered. 'OK. Enough of this neuro-linguistic programming. Are you off this weekend?'

'I am. I was thinking of getting a lift with Dad to the country.'

'Why don't you come with me instead? I haven't seen this hawk yet. Ma says she's started training it.'

'Great, isn't it? Well, better than bridge and golf anyway.'

'It sounds a bit more serious than that. She's obviously nuts about it.'

'About time. It's Dad who has all the fun.'

'What do you mean?'

'Only that he's always enjoyed himself more than she does.' Katy broke off to speak to another person, then turned back. 'Look, I can't talk now,' and she put the phone down, promising to make arrangements at the last moment.

Griselda also replaced the receiver, thinking that her sister might have made more of a point than she'd intended. It struck her that her father and Jonathan Tor were of an age, though at the same time she recognised that if there were the slightest parallel between them, which there wasn't, she and Katy would be the last to know about it. It was a horrible thought and yet she was surprised it had never occurred to her, given the abundance of cynicism with which she was prepared to dismiss the rest of the world. Her mother and father in contrast seemed sacrosanct. But then she was probably guilty of the offspring's usual inability to see its parents in the round. In her case they were simply fixtures to whom she had carved out unthinking portions of love. However, if her mother had stepped so far out of character as to acquire a hawk, then she might indeed have moved on and changed. And why not? In theory, it was probably an advantage. Her mother had always seemed too calm, too passive, reluctant to cudgel her way forward. If you're formed by another person at the age of twenty, wondered Griselda, are you held back and moulded for life?

Her thoughts returned to Jonathan Tor. His body seated behind his desk, his hand stealing out from the ramparts of family photos towards a piece of passing flotsam. It had probably seemed worth a try, no more than the minimum effort for the maximum possible return and nothing was at risk apart from *amour-propre*. She thought of him sitting and waiting then pouncing. Oh Dad, I do hope you've never been so crude as to let me down. Me in pigtails in a silver frame on your desk, unwittingly watching your florid advances.

'The boy's not gonna mind, is he, if I go along? Just stand at the side and watch the lesson?' asked Stuart. He was annoyed with himself for sounding diffident. But then it would be a bummer to be refused.

Mary put her head on one side which was what the Dobermann did when they held a conversation. He thought she must have copied the trick from his wife.

'Don't ask me. Ask him.'

'It's you I'm asking so why not answer?'

'Have a try. But don't take on if he objects.'

Stuart stared at her. 'You go there. He goes there. Have I got BO or something?'

'He's in awe of you. Afraid of you.'

'I can't think—'

'Shut it for a moment, will you. I sometimes think, Stuart, you're easier on the boys you teach than on Sam. You make him feel a dickhead.'

'That's not true.'

'He thinks you think he is.'

'Has he said so?'

'Not exactly.'

'Fuck it,' said Stuart. He sighed. 'I just want him to do well, that's all. Get a good trade, a million miles or so from a war zone. And the job of a coach, any coach, is to put strength into a kid. Strength and knowledge. More than some of those pansy teachers do at school.'

'You go on and on. It didn't work, did it, with the swimming?'

The swimming lessons had died a natural death, but Stuart decided to ignore this and move onwards.

'We agreed. OK? No mollycoddling. The way to learn is—'

'Not with him, it isn't. Let him go away and recover. He has to do the growing by himself. At his own pace.'

'So in the meantime he drowns does he?'

She smiled at him. 'Stop hamming it up.'

'Not,' said Stuart sulkily.

'Success means motivation. Remember who told me that?'

He grinned and looked at his hands. Success is the result of talent, motivation and confidence. He had forgotten but the reminder took him back. He had failed his first attempt at recruitment, suffered an agony of disappointment but encouraged by the staff, had been determined to have a second crack. On the day after his achievement, he had been told that success was talent, motivation and confidence – and then in the successive months of probation, he could have added attention to detail, practice and slog.

Mary watched the memories moving over his face. 'Don't ask him if he minds you turning up. Just go. Me, I'll be glad to get you out of the house.'

He was in truth driving her mad. These hours of waiting were always the worst strain. He had been hanging around with his bleeper stuck in his waistband, waiting for a summons and was meanwhile in search of a job. In the last two days he had planted a line of conifers against the picket fence, mended the gate and completed a couple of ten-mile runs with Gemma. His attention had now focused on smaller details which had included reassorting the lids on the jam and marmalade jars.

She looked at him expectantly. He was still mooning around, uncertain about going to see his son. She noticed he was staring at a patch of wood veneer that had peeled off the kitchen clock.

'This place is in a muck,' he said, pointing at a lump of dried Herefordshire mud on the otherwise immaculate tiled vinyl floor.

'Stuart. For Christ's sake, just get out.'

He glared at her, walked through the door out of the house, down to the end of the path, then promptly reversed direction.

Returning to the house he put his head round the door again. 'Sorry,' he said. 'You know what it's like waiting.'

'Yes. For both of us. But just go.'

He drove the Vauxhall out of the garage, waited at the T-junction for a milk lorry to pass and resigned himself to a slow blind drive in its wake along the B road. It was the route to the camp and he could have driven it in his sleep, indeed had practically done so on return trips at night when the ebb of adrenalin had left him drowsy. After ten minutes he took the thin lane to the right signalled by a finger-post which would be a short cut to Domain. As was usual in November, the road was clotted with farming mud, squeezed into giant ridges and furrows by tractor tyres. At this time of the year the landscape became an Indian earth-red, where the fields oozed into and merged with the roads. To his left, he could see the origin, a young ploughman setting about his dogged business of making parallel runs north to south and then south to north at five miles an hour, not much faster than a horse. A flock of white seagulls fluttered in his wake, lifting and settling like butterflies, they too compelled to traverse the same run, north to south, south to north. The wind blew their wintry mewing and the faint strains of pop music across the field, an escape from the glazed cabin of the tractor. An old Meat Loaf hit: 'Bat out of Hell'. The lonely ploughman was having a party on his own. Though not introspective, Stuart thought of his own life in relation to the ploughman's. The latter rooted to the spot and bound to routine and safety, himself in perpetual motion in face of unpredictable danger. He would not want to change positions.

He left the farm worker behind, passed a conifer estate awaiting its felling for timber, and drove carefully around a sharp bend. This was not a lane that had seemed known to him, yet its form was familiar. He had of course seen its pattern many times from the air – was this it? – though the explanation seemed scarcely sufficient. Then he suddenly remembered that he had been down here among the tree roots and grass stalks. The memory caused him to smile.

He glimpsed the pink house between the dour dry-leafed hedgerows and trunks, and turned the car into the drive and through the white gate which had been left to swing open.

As he passed the little orchard on his left, he sniffed the cidery scent of fallen apples. He parked the car and stepped out, noting with approval that the place looked well tended. Neat in all his movements, he walked lightly to the door and admired the grid formation of climbing stems against its stone façade. Everything was tied trimly into place and it occurred to him that this might well be the handiwork of his wife. In the yard, he caught sight of the metallic green bike they had given Sam for the previous Christmas. A black labrador was sniffing at one of its pedals. A lousy guard dog, it had failed to announce his presence. He wondered whether to go round the back but felt reluctant to present himself without warning. Even here, there was a minor obstacle. It was clear that the door was not designed to expect or encourage visitors. No bell, no knocker, no letter box, no invitation to the outside world. It was one of those old farmhouses that looked in upon itself. This isolation was congenial to him, however much he needed the laughter and slagging of his mates.

He shrugged, then rapped his knuckles against the top right panel of the door. No answer. He knocked again, then walked back along the paved path and peered through the window pane, lifting his hand to his forehead to form a visor. His own reflection stared back, his dark eyes, short haircut, navy parka, then, to the left, a blue sofa and on the right a rust armchair. He walked round the side of the house and shouted. A woman appeared, glaring at him as though he was a tinker come to offer a cowboy's restoration of her tarmac drive. He thought again of the door: no knocker, no bell, no hawkers here, wife and son welcomed, but not father.

'I'm Sam's dad,' he called. 'Come to see the the boy genius,' he added in a more uncertain tone.

She put down the box she was carrying and hurried towards him, showing extravagant signs of welcome. The dog chose this moment to announce his arrival, now that it was official.

'You're not coming to whisk him away, are you?'

'I've come to ask if I can watch the bird's training. Just stand on the sidelines,' he said, determined not to mumble. 'I won't be a nuisance, you know.'

She laughed, and it brought a warmth to her face. She wore

no make-up and looked lined and weathered and natural. 'Sam will be thrilled. And me too. So am I.'

He looked at her doubtfully. 'You don't recognise me, do you?'

She frowned. 'Should I? In any case, I'm not supposed to, am I? I know that getting famous is the last thing any of you lot want to do.'

'We've met. Sort of.'

She looked aside and made a strange retracting movement of her chin to express surprise, like a tortoise withdrawing its head.

'Do you remember?' he said. 'A small bunch of us coming here – oh, years ago, to look for an escaped prisoner? You remember? We felt like a right bunch of prats.'

The recollection sparked in her face. 'Oh no.' She put out a hand. 'Was it you? You were training?'

They stared at one another, remembering. It was customary for the Regiment to give advance warning to the local landowners when a bout of combat-survival training was planned. It took the form of a grim and realistic endurance test in which a soldier was forced to assume the role of a prisoner on the run. If caught he would be subjected to torture.

'You were the prisoner?' she asked wonderingly. 'I didn't see you.' She recalled the civility of that strange surreal visit: the platoon of soldiers dressed for combat wandering over the lawn on an English summer's day. Men with twigs all over their hats. 'Madam, we are looking for an escaped prisoner.' They had sought him on the ground and in the barn and had not found him.

'I wasn't the prisoner. On that occasion I was one of the hunters.'

He did not bother to add the obvious sequel that he too had been trained as a prisoner. For a fortnight at that time, he had been on the run, a simulacrum intended to give them a taste of a future terrifying reality. They were trained in elaborate techniques to elude capture and any local landowner who found them was expected to connive. They were under instructions never to feed them, but Stuart had found one who had relented. After three days of trapping rabbits, eating roots and sheltering under a hawthorn hedgerow, he had been discovered by the farmer's wife who had brought him a huge plate of eggs, field mushrooms and bacon. In this way and many others, the simulacrum diverged from real life.

An awareness of this real life passed through Claire's understanding at the same time as his. She looked at him for a moment without speaking, measuring the gulf between this man and herself, between him and all of her kind; between this member of a tiny elite minority willing to take imponderable risks on behalf of the huge majority, sedentary, fearful and careless of their debt. For a second the admiration within her gathered weight but remained unspoken. To do otherwise would have caused embarrassment and laughter. This man no doubt conformed to the benchmark SAS recruit: an achiever who was cheerful and unpretentious, as well as practical, intelligent, confident and stable. A hard benchmark for Sam, for any child, to live up to.

She stirred. 'Come and have a look,' she said and started to walk him across the cobbled yard. 'The light will go soon, so he's just giving her some exercise in the paddock. There's no time to take her out on a walk.'

'My granddad had a kestrel when he was young,' offered Stuart. 'I guess it's in the boy's blood.'

'Not yours?'

'Oh me, I was a bit of a town lad when I was young. I now wish I'd been born in the country.'

'He loves her,' she said simply. More than anyone or anything, she thought, but decided it would sound better unsaid.

Leaving the house behind them, he noticed with amusement the barn on the right in which they had searched for the prisoner – a trooper called Hogey if he remembered correctly – and walked on over the lawn. They then entered a corridor of hedging with some spent borders to either side, a fact that made him realise that his wife must have her work cut out. From now on, he'd be lucky to see a single plant grown in their own little garden. Then he forgot all this as they emerged into a field of rough-cut grass. In the middle of this arena stood the small whistling figure of his son. Stuart heard with amazement the precision of his clear three-note sound.

'He's never been able to whistle. He's one of those that puffs.'

She put a hand out to check his advance. 'You'd be surprised what he can do when he sets his mind to it.'

For a few minutes they stayed in the lea of an elder at the edge of the field and watched. The boy didn't notice them. He stood in his plaid wool reefer with his back to them, splay-legged to brace his frail body against the rocking movement as he swung the lure in deepening circles above his head. It was the fag end of a still grey day with a low blanket of cloud, the kind of November day that was normally filled with a windless silence. The only noise was the sound of the braided line whipping its spheres in the sky. It was moving at speed, the cord causing a rhythmical friction against the air.

'Where's the lady?' whispered Stuart.

Claire pointed quietly and covertly.

To the left, and some fifty yards away the bird sat poised and motionless on the branch of a small tree. She looked as still and quiet as though she were meditating. Meanwhile the lure, a pair of back-to-back pheasant wings with a bit of beef, whirled round and round, a plumb on a lead, circling to the left then a huge elliptical swirl to the right, as the boy, a ring master, played it like a fish on a line. Then without warning the hawk lifted. She neither fluttered nor fumbled but winnowed with huge unerring strokes towards the line. Her dual-tone bells chimed faster and faster. The two different speeds of bird and lure began to close and then met in perfect consummation.

Stuart shook his head in awe. A brief memory of watching a faultless meeting of missile and rocket flashed across his mind, but this technical exactitude was overshadowed, obliterated by the bird's beauty and power. No wonder the boy was obsessed by her. What a go-go girl.

'Can I meet her?' he asked.

They walked through the old bleached grass towards Sam who had his left arm crooked in a right angle, enabling her to feed from his fist. Alerted by the swivel of the bird's head, he glanced up and started at the sight of his father.

'Mum didn't say you was coming.'

'A bit spur of the moment, isn't it.'

'So, what do you think of her?' asked Claire, judging attention would be better passed swiftly to the bird.

'She's amazing,' said Stuart. 'Amazing.'

Sam's face softened as he looked with infinite pride at the bird pecking the last scrap of meat on his gauntlet. Claire noticed Stuart had looked with both tenderness and pride at him.

'Tell him about the bird,' she urged. She suddenly ached for the child to show his full paces. Only she and Wilf knew how much effort he had put into their small, secret world.

'The boy doesn't have to do a party piece,' said Stuart. 'Not if he doesn't want to.'

Claire ignored him. She started herself, knowing that the child would be unable to resist the temptation of taking over.

'This,' she said, pointing at the yellow flesh around the nostrils, 'this is the cere. And—'

'And this, Dad—' in the background she gave a tiny smirk of satisfaction as he interrupted '—this here is the mantle, see?' He indicated the rich sepia cape of scalloped feathers on the upper part of her wing. 'And these feathers are the middle coverts, the secondary coverts and the primary coverts.'

He stroked the vee-d tips of her deep mahogany primaries with a respectful gentleness, running his small grimy knuckle in the direction of their flow. She made warm soft settling noises, lifted her wings to spread like a bustle then refurled their span.

'These primaries, they're the longest wing feathers. Ten on each side.' He added, 'She can get up a speed of thirty miles an hour in a large cage and much more in the open.'

Stuart listened in silence. There was no trace of stammer, no sh-she, in this naming of parts. No sh-she when he talked of her. He realised the change that had taken place in his son.

'Show her off to me again,' he said. 'Go on. Work her with the lure. Take her round the field.'

'It's getting a bit dark,' said Claire. 'Don't you think it might be better if we took her in?'

'Oh well, OK,' said Stuart. 'There'll be another day.'

'Once more,' begged Sam. 'I'll take her round the field properly just one more time.' He felt an enormous pulse of pride in himself as well as the bird. It was the very best, the very very best, the greatest thing he had ever done.

Stuart looked enquiringly at Claire. 'Your orders, Madam?' he said.

'Just one more time, but mind out, be careful. Watch those rabbit holes on the far side. You can't see where you're going.'

With a child's impatience he had started to run off before she was halfway through. 'Slow down,' she yelled.

They watched him reduce his speed to a steadier pace as he took the bird back to her post. He was frowning with intense concentration. This made his face in profile look both comic and serious, with his snub nose, his glasses and the little scuffed tuft of hair that stood up on the crown of his head. He put out his hand and the bird stepped gracefully from the gauntlet onto her perch where she sat waiting. The light was fading fast and it was this perhaps that caused him to try and beat it by running to the other side of the paddock. Too dull a sky and she would fail to catch the lure.

From a distance the pair who were watching could see him travelling and then disappear, though it was very sudden for he was upright at one moment and then apparently down at the next. Only a cry warned them and its nature was such that they were already racing in panic towards him. It was the strangeness of the cry that put Claire in that iron grip of fear that paralyses inward muscles whilst enabling the legs to seem like separate appendages driving the body to its destination. As she ran, her heart drummed in her throat. The child was now visible, lying on the ground, his leg twisted under him, but useless, a puppet limb without a master. He was crying and moaning, his mouth moving in a latex shape of pain. His father, who had sprinted faster, was already crouched beside him.

'He's broken his leg,' he said grimly. 'A knee-break, I think.'

'It's my fault,' she cried in self-remorse. 'I should never have allowed him to carry on in that light.'

'Don't be dumb. No blame on you at all.'

He leant over the boy and began to lift him gingerly, stopping at each new angle for fear of causing damage.

'I'll run him to casualty,' he said.

As he started to walk back over the field, a small regular insistent sound made itself heard from his waistline.

'What on earth—?' began Claire.

'Christ.' He stopped still. 'That's all we need. Sorry. It's my bleeper. I'm on call.'

The sound pulsed, a methodical alarm in the dusk.

'Can you take him?' he asked helplessly above the sound of his son's sobbing. 'I've got to answer it. Can I use the telephone?'

She gave him directions to the hall, then held out her arms to receive the boy's body in their cradle. They sagged under his sprawling load. Like any sick animal, his tense muscles made him heavier than he seemed. Unable to walk with him she sank down in stages in the centre of the field. In the midst of this pandemonium, child moaning, father running to the house to commune with headquarters, it occurred to her to turn her head to check the bird. She now realised that the hawk was no longer there. She must have been frightened away by the commotion. I'll worry about it afterwards, she thought; she can't have gone far. She glanced up and saw Stuart with a look of resignation approaching her.

'I've got to go. It's a massive piss-off and couldn't come at a worse moment, but I've got to go straightaway.'

'Don't worry,' she said with the composure of one who at least knows what the job now requires. 'I'll take him to hospital and get him sorted out.'

'He's fainted. I hate to leave him.'

He took back his motionless son and carried him over the field and through the garden and they put him to lie flat in the back of her car. As they were lifting him in, Sam emerged from his brief loss of consciousness.

'Where's Bella?' he said.

Where indeed? From a second glance, still invisible. Not on the post, on none of the perches, nor the blackthorn, not the ash nor the oak on the boundary. The bird had not been insubordinate but frightened and the result could be worse.

'I'll go back and put her to bed in a moment,' said Claire reassuringly.

She closed the back car door, left to lock up the house and returned to climb into the driver's seat.

'Poor boy. Do you think he'll be all right?'

'It's nasty for him but I'm sure it's a clean break. He's only a lad and it'll heal. Will you be OK?'

She nodded. Would Bella? A grim and cussed catastrophe sequence seemed to have opened up. Anything could now happen. She had a sudden sickening thought that the boy might have put the wrong jesses on her, the leads on her feet. Inconceivable, he wouldn't have. He wouldn't fly her in the wrong ones. The old man had drilled them to check. A bird could hang herself, get caught in a tree, undetected, and starve to death. She had a sudden ugly vision of a disabled boy and a dead bird, all caused by her negligence. Even if he suffered no damage, he would never forgive her for the loss of the hawk, neither would she. She tried to dismiss it. No point in wallowing in a grisly scenario. When she returned later, she would see again that fierce face and hear the chink of the bells, that cool welcoming chime of her bells.

12

It was a false consolation and its comforts had faded by the early evening when she started the return drive to her home. By now she could not doubt that the bird might be lost if not threatened with death. Sam was safe with his mother beside him, but the hawk was in danger. She was young, still vulnerable and frighteningly on the free. Like Stuart, she too was learning to be a prisoner on the run in a world that was filled with enemies. The air was an unkind medium, open and without barricades. She could have flown over the rim of the hills and on down the valley and then anywhere and everywhere on an increasing gradient of danger. In nature, how easily the predator could become the prey. It was already dark and now, as she turned on the car radio, she heard that wind and rain were forecast for tomorrow. She gave a groan. Buffeted and waterlogged, for, compared with a falcon, she had little oil in her feathers, the hawk would struggle and shiver. And if she flew upland where the nights would be harsh and frozen later this week, there was a horrible danger of frostbite. She could lose the fingertips of her beautiful, auburn and silky wing-feathers. Winter could turn her into a morsel as fragile as glass.

It occurred to Claire that till now she had merely been playing. A captive bird – a bird born of captive parents – though not a toy, is as indulged and sheltered as any domestic. The element of risk and therefore suffering is reduced to nothing. The fact that the hawk had been kept in meant equally that the real world had been kept out. They had trained her to meet it – 'Remember,' Wilf had warned, 'she is not a pet but a wild thing' – but it was still no more than a simulacrum:

for life in the wild was no plaything but subject to a terrifying reality.

By the time Claire had arrived home, she was convinced that her one hope was to find her immediately. The longer the interval, the greater the chance diminished. She swung into the drive, her headlights picking out the pale columns of tree trunks, and halted the car abruptly outside the house without bothering to roll it along to the garage. She stepped out, walking with deliberate solidity, her shoes making a confident smack on the path, forcing herself not to run, knowing she must salvage her energy for a long and disheartening search. She anticipated a ghost of failure. She went to the telephone in search of the old man's advice but there was no answer. He had doubtless gone to the pub. She decided it would be a waste of essential time to track him down. Determined to stay calm, to think in order to plan, she put on two layers of woollen clothing, boots, and an old thick thornproof coat. In false optimism, she added her falconer's gauntlet and a spare pair of jesses. Armed with a packet of chocolate biscuits, some strips of raw meat in a plastic bag, a torch and a sturdy lamp, she and the dog walked over the lawn, through the hedges and out to the field at the back of the garden.

The night was full of snuffling noises and very dark, a purplish black, the clouded darkness of a bruise. It was difficult to see, yet she was reluctant to switch on the lamp at this stage, preferring to rely on the rods of her eyes to adapt to the darkness, a process that took about five minutes. Every time she illuminated the ground with the lamp, she would lose this facility and have to reaccustom herself from scratch. She walked slowly and carefully, negotiating the ground with her clumsy soles as delicately as though they were a showgirl's high heels. Only once did she switch on the lamp and that was to check the whereabouts of the line and the lure. She found it lying where it had been left on the uneven ground which had tumbled the child. Unchanged except that the beef had been pecked from the pheasant's wings. Not unexpected perhaps but disturbing. If Bella had eaten, she was unlikely to be very hungry. Not hungry enough to need her feeder, her flunkey, her keeper.

She drew the line in, picked up the lure and wove the device into its neat figure-of-eight coil. Flashing the lamp upwards, she rolled the beam slowly over the branches of the flanking trees to search. Pointless. No dozy bemused bird awaiting its dazzle, ready to toddle home. She turned it off, walked forward slowly, readjusting her eyes to the blackness and opened the gate on the far side of the field which led to the foothill. Jarvis, no partner, subsided in protest, exhibiting a reluctance to hunt in the dark. 'You are the original amoeba,' she snapped. 'Get up, you bloody wimp.' Hauled to his feet, he groaned his reproach but continued. Claire began now to whistle the three-pronged note of training. It was a quiet night and the sound floated clear and alien. An owl, fooled mysteriously, answered. She called again, and again it replied. She cursed that the harsh beloved screech of her own bird might be suppressed by the hoot of a foolish intruder but she carried on calling. For a moment the two-tone dialogue continued with its strange musical farce of mistaken identities. She felt despair. The owl was a reminder of the sheer huge hopelessness of her task. Hundreds of other birds out in the darkness, hundreds of trees, hundreds of hiding places and secrets and pathways whilst the whirlpool of rain, wind and winter moved urgently closer. In a futile gesture she shone the beam of the torch on her wrist. Absurd invitation. They had scarcely embarked on the night training. Oh Bella, she said out loud, you pretty thing, think of a nice warm perch, a good dinner in the oven, a fancy menu, rabbits, rats, quail, beef, chicks, whatever you fancy, better than any titbits you find on the hoof, oh Bella you sodding idiot, you stupid little pig-headed fool of a bird, come back my darling. How else, she wondered, could she communicate with the creature. Light, noise, movement, smell and voice.

Her lack of success oppressed her. She sat down on the turf and cursed the bird. There was only one other possibility and that was to return at first dawn. Claire sat hesitating, knowing there was no point in venturing further in the darkness but equally incapable of turning round and walking back to the house. There was still some brute hope in the blind act of moving forwards and only the surety of failure in returning home. She decided to advance just a little further. I shall walk round the copse, up to the top of the hill, shine the torch down the other side and if she's not there, leave and set out again before dawn.

Now her progress was slower. It was uphill on untended land, infested with dead clumps of bracken. Twigs and fallen branches from the spinney cracked underfoot. She was beginning to feel nervous on her own behalf as well as the hawk's. To be out at night alone, attracting attention, no doubt everyone could hear her except this infuriating bird. Not suspicious by nature, she shied at shadows and felt that the night breathings had begun to assume sinister human tones. The thought struck her that she could always use the torch as a weapon in case of an attack. She crept forward and then at the brow of the hill stood still and pressed the switch on her lamp. The triangular shaft pointed to the sky and then stroked down. It was beginning its trajectory from left to right when it hit an owl floating silently across. Though noiseless itself, simultaneously in the background there sounded a rasping cough. She froze, all senses converging to decode it. Not a fox voice which resembled the abrupt bark of a dog. Was it a sheep? A ewe could sound like an old man coughing up fags. There was a silence, then the rasp came again, breathing and human. A shuffling sound. The hope that it was a badger died immediately. This was no badger hump-backing his blind way in continuous contact with the ground. It came at long enough intervals to indicate strides, human again. She felt a chill of real female terror. She flashed the torch down and across, using it like an aggressor for shock and for dazzle, no longer seeking a bird nor even a man but an enemy.

In a night landscape, a beam of harsh light distorts and makes strange. It had stroked over and passed from the thing before she realised that it had found its object. The image it left was monstrous. In a silence that roared in her ears she swept the light back. Twenty or so yards away but only its head was visible above a stook of bracken. An elephant head with a long black proboscis extending over its nose. She opened and closed her mouth like a deaf-mute in a dream.

Then from this distance it spoke.

'What for God's sake are you doing? You've been making a hell of a clatter.'

The irritation introduced the most odd note of normality

into the extraordinary scene. There was no doubt that the emotions of a rapist or murderer were not usually expressed by such everyday tones of annoyance. The thing with the proboscis, contrary to appearances, was human rather than animal.

She at once grasped the explanation and regained control of her voice.

'Are you MoD?'

That must be it. The land bordered the hill which overlooked the army camp and was doubtless patrolled by the Ministry of Defence. A warm relief flowed through her.

'What did you say?'

'MoD. Are they goggles you're wearing?' His proboscis must simply be goggles.

'These? Oh God, yes. They're night-vision goggles. They turn night into day.'

He raised his hand and lifted them up to his forehead.

'You scared off my bird,' he said, not without testiness.

'What bird?' She leant forward. The torch shook.

'Put that flaming light out.'

She dimmed it. 'What bird?'

'My owl.'

Just the owl. She sighed, exasperated. 'I hoped it was my Harris hawk. You haven't seen her have you?'

'You won't find her, my dear woman, by making a racket like that in the undergrowth.'

Already distraught, she lurched into anger. 'I shall report you for rudeness.'

'Report? What on earth are you talking about?'

'You're MoD aren't you?'

'You're a lunatic. What gives you the idea I'm anything to do with the Ministry of Defence? I'm a bird photographer who was in the process of taking a picture of a flight line of that owl till you came along.'

She stared at his hulk which was all she could see in the darkness.

'I'm sorry,' she said. 'This is all a bit of a muddle. We're at cross purposes. My hawk flew off late this afternoon. She's young and inexperienced and I'm terrified I've lost her.'

'Well, let's not stand here arguing the relative merits of our two losses.'

'I don't think you understand. The hawk's not wild, she's a pet and not just mine. She belongs to a child.'

'Don't you have telemetry?'

It was a reasonable question and neutrally put but she felt the accusation. The thought had knocked at her head all the way to the hill top. She had ignored it but it had not given up and had now found an external way to insist on being heard. Why don't you have telemetry? Why not? It was the fitting of a device which would have enabled radio contact with the bird. Why not?

'We didn't think it necessary with a Harris hawk,' she replied stiffly. Who was this bastard anyway to sit in judgement upon her?

There was a silence during which she hoped he would digest the feeling of being unwanted. In the distance she could see the starry domestic lights of houses in the valley, and the occasional moving lamps of a car on the lonely road. No doubt bland conversations were taking place out there. 'Another sausage, Terry?' 'That was very tasty, Mother.' From far away there came the windy bellow of a cow.

'You are clearly in no mood to take advice so I'm not offering it. But all I would say is that your best bet is to go home now and have another try as soon as it's light in the morning.'

'I intended to do that anyway.'

'Where do you live?'

'Back there. Why?'

'So that I can let you know if I see her. All right?'

The bracken rustled. With every movement, hundreds of thousands of dry spores would be released into the air. The air must be full of invisible life like plankton. She wondered if an invisible Bella could see her.

'We live down the far side of the valley. A straight walk back. There's a copse, a field, our paddock and then the house. You'll recognise it. It's stone with a brick barn. Oh, and there's a weeping ash in the garden.'

'OK. If I see her I'll let you know.'

'Thank you.'

'Go back. You won't find her now. She's calm and quiet at night. All your *son et lumière* will be likely to frighten her.'

'I'm most grateful for your advice,' she said, hating it. 'Come on Jarvis.'

She decided to withhold her good wishes about his owl.

She stomped back down the hill, the anxiety of her outward journey replaced by anger on the return. The man thought her an idiot. She wasn't. Negligent. Nor that. Yet the result was the same and she tried not to anticipate being the messenger of sorrow and disaster.

She rang Wilf as soon as she got home but there was still no answer, and there seemed little point in trying the pubs. What would he say? Oh ay? Better to have dumped the boy and saved the bird? Not likely.

She hadn't eaten, wasn't hungry but forced herself to have a bowl of soup and some bread. Jarvis sat beside her, his paw on her foot, feeling unloved, abused and neglected. Claire pulled the dog against her, patting his side which felt solid like a bolster, stuffed full with his innards. 'You'd better leave room for a freezerful of day-old chicks,' she said and grimaced. Maybe not. No good fussing; if they'd lost her, they would just have to buy another bird, but the thought was sickening. The phone rang. She looked at it and hesitated. It might be Mary so she left it. The clock ticked, measuring a wasted evening at the end of a bad day. There was a scratch. The little mouse who lived in a hole in the kitchen had emerged, fooled by the stillness. It was busy and confident. It scuttled on clockwork legs along the back of the wooden surface and into the rearing shadows behind the kitchen sink taps. It was a fieldmouse with big eyes, saucer ears and a small body. It now discovered a bread crumb. The large dog and the tall human being watched it. It ate, and then sat up and rubbed its head with its tiny fists. 'You shouldn't be here,' said Claire. It froze and then flashed back along its tramlines and into its hole. The hope rose in her that if a mouse could take care of itself, and even bracken spores, then so would a well-equipped hawk.

Claire had not been expecting to sleep but must have done so for she was woken by a knocking at the front door. She staggered out of bed, across the corridor and stood at the landing window.

It was scarcely light, deep grey pearl with a maribou mist in the valley, and she realised she had overslept. The banging came again, recognisably peremptory. She peered forwards and beside the porch caught sight of a hand holding the black goggles. Last night's dream sequence continued. She rapped on the windowpane and the man stepped to his left. He was stocky with dark hair. He looked up and shouted something, a summons possibly.

'I can't hear,' she said. 'I'm coming down.'

As she threw on the same clothes which had been lying in a heap on the floor, she felt she was in a film which was running backwards. She raced down the staircase.

'I'm coming,' she said as she dragged open the door.

'I think I've found her. There are some rooks mobbing a hawk at the top of a tree.'

She gasped and went to fetch the glove and the meat.

'She's just over the crest of the first rise,' he called.

They walked through the garden, the paddock and the field as yesterday in the silence. Her tired legs jolted her. The air was thick and saturated with mist like a damp towel. At one point she stumbled and he put out a hand to support her. She did not look at him. Towards the crest of the hill, he stopped her and whispered.

'I'll wait here. Call me if you need but I think I could frighten her. She's at the top of the tall oak on the right. Or she was. Let's hope she's still there.'

'If she doesn't come down, is it climbable?'

He shook his head slowly.

At that moment they both understood that the bird's life would depend on her training.

She took the last hundred-yard haul alone. She was breathless. The bones of her ribcage felt see-through thin, on the verge of cracking. She stood for a moment to count her heartbeat down and continued more slowly. Her hair and the skin on her face were dripping with mist though, as she climbed, it grew more gauzy and the visibility lengthened.

At the top of the hill she stopped and looked to the right. There it was, a huge dry-leafed oak with right-angular branches. An oak but no rooks. The veteran oak but no rooks which meant no mobbing. No omens. A void. Her swollen heart contracted.

Her hawk had been mobbed and had therefore flown. Misery, heavy as a weight, filled her. She might be somewhere, she thought forlornly, I must try to whistle her in. Her lips were sluggish and cold. She pushed them to form their smoke-ring O but it was soundless. She re-formed and tried again. Then as she blew for a third time she heard the faint rescuing chime of a bell. She walked forward very slowly towards the tree, craning her neck up, scanning the height of the trunk streaming with mist-water, trying to trace the sound through the brown leaves on the branches. The dual chink came again of a bird rousing herself at dawn. Bella, she said. Volatile with joy, her lips changed like mercury: they could whistle. She gave the three-forked notes; held out her left hand, the leathered wrist, the perch. The symphonic notes offered their pledge of a cropful of meat. It was met by the exultant chimes of the bird lifting in flight, floating down through her freedom to the fist. She banked gently and landed, rapacious with hunger. As the hawk tore at the meat, Claire clasped her anklets and fitted the leash for safety.

They stood under the tree for five minutes, the bird preening, the keeper triumphal. Hearing a shuffling through the bracken, Claire turned round. She had quite forgotten the goggle-man.

'Thank you so much,' she said.

He came up to her. 'Is she all right? I was worried the rooks might harm her as she's young.'

'She's fine. Hasn't suffered any damage.'

He stood beside her and watched the hawk in admiration. 'I was going to say it before but it wasn't important on the way here. I'm sorry I was so bad tempered last night.'

She shook her head to mean that nothing mattered now. In any case she was only half listening.

'I must go. I'll photograph her some time if I may.'

'Where do you live?' She did not look at him, was enslaved to the hawk.

'The opposite direction from here. In a cottage on the Stooke estate. I'm going back now. Got to catch up on some sleep.'

She glanced up at him enquiringly. He must have been up all night.

He moved off a little and smiled. 'Glad it's had a happy ending.'

'I don't know your name.'

'Ravell. Peter Ravell.'

She was about to thank him again, self-engrossed she hadn't even asked about the owl or his photograph, when suddenly there was a rustle above them. It gathered into a soft crescendo which filtered down through the canopy of branches. The dry brown leaves of the oak began falling, fluttering in flakes around them, hundreds, then more, a thousand, onto their heads, their shoulders, on the bird and over the ground. The oak was losing its dead leaves all at once in a long drawn-out sigh.

'It looks like winter's come,' he said and left.

13

Ravell walked down the hill and across the common to where he had hidden his equipment, then followed the slip track to his car. It was seven o'clock in the morning and he was half asleep. Drowsily he laid the folded hide in the back of the Land Rover, then the high-voltage flash equipment and finally the night-vision goggles which had cost him £4,000. He hauled himself into the driver's seat and glanced in the mirror as he strapped on the belt. Shadowed with stubble, he thought he looked old and tired in the grey morning light. It occurred to him that the photography of nocturnal birds was best left to the young and severely needy, especially in winter.

He bounced the car gently over the rutted track and onto the lane which led to the main route. He passed the milk van and a truck of store sheep, their carved faces pressed hard against its horizontal slats. He thought with regret of last night's outburst of ill-temper. His apology, useless unless explained, had been disregarded. It had not been the moment to expand. To excuse himself on the grounds that it had taken a day to prepare the shot, to set up the hide with utmost unobtrusiveness and accustom a nervous bird to its existence, all in the hope of photographing the owl with a mouse in its mouth – only to have it ruined by this woman. He would have to repeat the procedure again tonight, this time in silence. It would have been better to shelve it until the spring and the nesting time when the downward flight bringing food to the young was predictable. Better still to copy the hard professionals who stayed in bed whilst the bird triggered the automatic flash in their absence. But then his passion lay in the bird rather than the product.

Of late, he knew he had shown a short fuse with idiocy. Yet perhaps he had misjudged her to be a fool. It was an error of judgement to search for the bird after dark, but she had been anxious rather than an ass. A lady with a falcon. He had a vague memory of a medieval tapestry at the Musée de Cluny. The details were lost to him but he thought it was indigo and showed a woman wearing a wimple and seated with a bird on her hand. A little merlin, was it, from the age of chivalry? He had been less than chivalrous to this modern variant of a woman with a falcon, for he had failed to give her the least benefit of the doubt.

He pulled into Hugh Stooke's drive and turned right along the perimeter track where he pulled up at the cottage. It was by the stables and a pretty bay mare who had grown used to him whinnied. He jumped out, unlocked the front door and then returned to the back of the jeep and transferred his equipment to the hall. The building, converted from a single-storey, stone-tiled barn, smelt fungoid and musty. He had been here for two months and had lacked the energy and direction to adapt it into even a temporary home.

When he had parted from Sabine, four years ago, the final severance had been hurried, odd after so extended a precursor. So all he had taken at the time was his picture, an oil painting of a field of sunflowers, his three-foot wide ammonite and his photographic equipment. His share of their spoils, which had been in storage all this while, would in due course follow when he had bought a permanent home, though the thought aroused little enthusiasm. He wondered, had he turned at forty-eight into a natural nomad? Take care, he told himself, be warned, the next step is to become one of that lonesome breed, the ageing traveller.

Rather than fling himself on the bed and sleep immediately, he went to the bathroom first to wash and shave, a small act of discipline. Standing before the mirror he brushed off an oak leaf that had slipped under his collar. That had been an odd moment, early this morning in the penumbra after the dawn. There had been no wind or earth tremor to trigger the loss of all foliage. Yet a message to detach had spread from leaf to leaf, from branch to branch as though the central nervous system had suddenly spoken. Strange how in that second it had passed from one season to another.

It was a pitiful thing, thought Mary, seeing his sense of failure. He had sobbed at the beginning, not for his leg but his failure. The bird had performed but he had fallen. As she watched him, she had to swallow the choke of her own tears.

Not much to say, she wrote to Stuart. *I took over from Claire in Casualty. We had to wait for hours, though Lofty's wife, Jenny, who's now a nurse there shoved us through. She said if it had been a sunny day it would have been crawling with ten-year-olds with broken legs. They agreed the break was his knee. He's ever so proud of his full-length plaster. They say that so long as he's careful he can go back to school. Good old Wilf cheered him up when he called by with the hawk who's the bird's mother.*

She put her pen down, wondering how best to describe his visit. She laughed at the memory and reflected it was probably a good thing that the old man had been blunt.

'Cocked it up, didn' you?'

'Not my fault,' he said grumpily.

'No it weren't but you see why I says you got to share the bird. Old Claire, see, can take over till you stops hobbling.'

Sam gave a wriggle of frustration but was weighed down by the ballast of his leg.

'I miss the best bit of Bella's training, don't I?'

'Buck up boy, you gets the best bit at the end.'

The three of them were sitting in the neat front room with the running cups freshly polished on the shelf. The hawk, Chloe, was transfixed by the fish tank in the corner. The fish wreathed their expressionless way through the foliage floating in the water. They looked bored, in need of livening up.

'Does she eat goldfish?' asked Sam, also bored.

'Don't you touch those fish.' Mary had a vision of the mischief that could result from a brooding boy.

'Er, probably bad for her digestion, like,' said the caretaker diplomatically.

'Why?' asked Sam. 'Birds were reptiles, eh? Snakes eat fish, don't they?' He looked longingly at the fish in the corner.

'Not a good idea,' said Wilf.

'Why not?'

'Because, boy.'

'That's enough of why.' Mary eyed the bird and the new beige carpet on the floor. Together they opened up the potential for fresh source of trouble.

'I hope, Wilfie, your bird is continent.'

'Eh?'

'What I mean is does she drop on the floor?'

'She's clean,' lied Sam, ripe for any diversion.

'That's as maybe.' Mary fetched a swatch of newspaper and laid a printed moat around the man and bird. She didn't always buy the newspapers when Stuart was away for there were times when she preferred to avoid the headlines.

'We knows when we're not wanted, don't we girl?'

'Don't go, Wilf.'

'Got to, son. Aggie and me are taking the snowy owl up the mountain.' This, a grievous mistake, provoked the biggest outburst.

'Oh Wilfie, let me come.'

'Patience, lad. When you gets to my age you knows that the whole world can wait.'

The currents of old and young which had touched, now diverged.

Mary continued her letter to Stuart: *I guess caretaker's a good name for him. It's true, isn't it? He's been like a granddad to Sam.* To me too, she thought. It was night and she went up to check that her son was sleeping. She opened his bedroom door. He was lying on his back, his leg flat on the bed like a felled tree, his head turned to the side with his right hand close to his cheek on the pillow. He must have been sucking his thumb, a habit that she believed she had broken. She thought: we're alone again as always. This year we'll be alone when we go back to Yorkshire for Christmas. She felt no self-pity. The Regiment wives were rocked in the same boat, the women were meshed together to form part of a single family. They played squash, they used the men's gym, they lived in the present and chatted. There were times when they tried not to think of their husbands. Their husbands had successfully left them behind. They set out on their missions 'sterile' as they termed it, without photos of girlfriends or wives.

Identification was dangerous, so it made sense for the wives also to strive to leave their husbands behind.

Could anyone outside their world ever begin to understand? For twelve years she had been an army wife. She was thirty-five. She had been young at the beginning in Wiltshire, grown up in the barracks of Germany and now here she was feeling prematurely old. Unlike some, she had never grown used to the waiting, though accepted that worrying was part of the life. She now looked in the bedroom mirror. She made no sign or movement but stared at her face with dispassion. At times like this she could see the effects of worry like toothmarks. Tomorrow she would finish her note to Stuart. *I think Sam's happy and doing pretty well. We're planning a really good Christmas and lots of fun with the gang.*

Broken arms in slings were commonplace but a plaster cast on the leg was a news event in the playground of Dilgate Primary School. A jealous group gathered on the edge beside Sam who was sitting down, crutches to hand and his limb stretched out like a flying buttress before him.

'You slipped did 'ee, Sammy?'

'He was abseilin' wasn't he? Shooting with 'is dad.'

'We live near the camp and my mam won't let us hear what your dad and the others say because of the soldiers' words.' Elspeth Evans was Welsh Chapel. Her parents were strict and tribal. They muttered about dirty books and dirty words. They had resurrected the notion of fornication and the word 'fuck' was hellfire.

'How did you do it Sammy?'

'I slipped like she said. I was running.'

''E can't swim,' said fat Tracy, triumphant to have found another butt. ''E can run but 'e can't swim. 'E's too thin. Thin people drown.'

'Thin's not yours is it Trace? My mum said you were a bladder of lard.' Debbie had flint eyes. She crackled her packet of chips.

'What's a bladder of lard?'

'Doan know.'

'Trace is a pig's bladder.'

A shapeless push-and-shove took place; the grunts of 'not'

and 'you are' issued from the scrum of bodies in red V-necked pullovers and grey skirts and trousers. A scruffy aimlessness marked these playground disputes. Children who didn't use words used their bodies instead but half-heartedly. No one got damaged. Amy and Rebecca, the offspring of two new middle-class entrants, looked on. Transported from Reigate and Purley, they were ill at ease with the physical world. They stayed together for comfort and observed. They wore headbands and the badges on their blazer pockets were sewn on all the way round, not left to flap loose at the bottom by mothers with five children who were faced with their fifteenth badge in seven years.

The shoving ran out of steam. There were still ten minutes to kill before they were gathered in by Mr Temper who was supposed to be having it off with one of the mothers, a harassed woman with a trim nose and a job at one of the fruit factories. She smelt of cider but the scent of sour ripeness failed to make her voluptuous. People in her road who had it off were rarely seductive. They were like wartimers: lonely, in need and dissatisfied.

They turned back to Sam. The plaster leg had mileage. It was virgin as snow; they could toboggan over its slopes, covering it with their pens: autographs and rhymes and graffiti and tattoos. 'Wham, bam, thank you Sam,' or 'Trace loves Jason,' or more daringly, 'Debbie loves Jen,' or when words ran out, just, 'Hereford United.'

'Leave it,' shouted Sam and tried to poke one of the girls with his crutch. 'Don't muck it about. My dad will come and get your dad if you do.'

'He's away isn't he? My dad says he's gone to Northern Ireland.'

'I don't know where he's gone. He never tells us.'

'Let him be.'

'You won't be able to fly your hawk will you Sammy?'

'I see her every day.'

Their heads were clustering like flies round his leg. Biroed names scrawled in unjoined-up writing appeared. The names of the Marches. Morgan and Jones. Preece, Griffith and Jenkins. Bevan and Williams and Davies. Many of these dynasties would unite in marriage and coalesce. The sons and daughters of hop-pickers and goosefarmers and cowmen and organists, the descendants of ancient Celts and medieval yeomen and stay-at-homes.

They talked modern. They no longer said nesh or yauling or costrel but the streams flowed on in the same place. The foliage sprouts from the mouth of the pagan green man over the church doorway. Theirs was a country childhood and most of them would stay though the job profile might change.

> Oh stay at home, my lad and plough
> The land . . .
> And all about the idle hill
> Shepherd your sheep with me.

14

'I'd like to see you tonight. Late probably.'

James did a little anticipatory swivel in the armchair at the desk. His gaze travelled over the charts on the wall to the window. From here he had an angle to a church spire. It had been damaged a few years ago and resurrected in glass fibre, a fabric which made it less aspirational than its original stone.

'I'm going out to dinner.'

'With whom?'

'None of your business.' This was delivered with the pretty imperiousness of the French female.

'Now, darling. None of that girlish snapping.'

'I don't see why I have to be pushed into the little spaces of your life.'

'Chantal, I'm working tonight.'

'Work or wife. It's always one or the other.'

This cross-patch passage was familiar. All his little affairs had foundered on resentment. Yielding changed to complaint which led to an ultimatum. The women's desire for freedom was so often sham. Underneath they found his lack of commitment an insult and he had received several quivering declarations to this effect. He had no wish to see Chantal follow this trend. He was obsessed with her to the point of taking risks and was in danger of being careless. Usually he checked his pockets before going home lest any stray tickets or mementoes gave grounds for suspicion, but of late he had forgotten to be so fastidious. Of late he had spent whole nights at her flat.

'I'll give you a call anyway. If you're back, wait up for me, can you?'

'I might not be back.'

'You might.'

He put the phone down and rang Brewster, his partner.

'Have you talked to him yet?'

'It's fixed.'

'They postponed it at the last moment before.'

'They'll stick with it this time. They have no option but to sell.'

'You know I prefer to do this long distance through the medium of the lawyers and bankers.'

'Crawley won't. He insists on meeting. He wants guarantees.'

'For what?'

'Protection of his staff.'

'He knows that's impossible.'

'He belongs to a previous era.'

'I don't look forward to this.'

'Nor I. He's beside himself that it's at a knock-down price.'

Why, thought James, do I do this? I could afford to sell out now. Yet the drive to press on, press on, was irresistible, the need to acquire companies a compulsion, and the reason came to him now. He had a teenage memory of his father spending the last five years of his life in the kitchen where he had sat and gazed in despair at the wall. Five years of certifiable mental illness whilst his mother bustled with life. He knew it was memory to be kept at bay lest it should teach him something about himself. This family memory was contagious and could gnaw away at the forehead. He could not bear to be like his father. Over-compensation for what he most feared was doubtless the way the theory would go. No matter. Anything rather than his father's drooping face, its wet wool folds. A man of no appetites ever, he had sat and looked at the wall. His aproned mother had been ashamed and all her energies and pride had gone into her son.

Now, thirty-five years later, he stood at the double-glazed window and eased the catch. Outside it looked cold and misty like floss but he felt the need for air. As he pushed it open, the oceanic murmur of winter traffic came to him. I am mad, he thought. I could retire now and sell up. I'll join her in Herefordshire. We have enough for a comfortable future. She can write her little history pieces, I can do what people do when they retire: pootle around with a mower, manage my pennies on the screen, get lightly pickled by lunchtime. This business with Chantal is dicey.

Yet he knew these were only signs of avoidance of what he faced in the evening ahead.

The meeting was to be held in one of the lawyers' offices. In theory it represented the mid-game, negotiation being divided into three stages like chess. The opening was marked by the offer. The second stage, as here, was the adversarial confrontation. The end-game would be the intense accelerated closure.

The table was arranged as though for dinner but each place setting consisted of sheets of paper, a glass of water and a pen neatly laid to the side in the same position as a knife. They could hear Crawley breathing heavily as he climbed the stairs. James would have preferred to avoid this sign of human frailty. Till now the man had been no more than a balance sheet. He entered, a short stocky fellow with small eyes and features crammed in the centre of a broad face. James knew this physical type, a fighter, a dog with a bone, in this case his empire, a hopeless out-of-date autocracy. Fowles, the lawyer, was the first to move forward and shake him by the hand. It struck James that he too was typical, a commercial lawyer, indifferent, perhaps even oblivious to the human subtleties of a deal. All that mattered was the contract rather than the deal. Even so, James would have preferred this representative to negotiate rather than himself. He shrank from striking the blow.

'Shall we sit down?' said Fowles pleasantly. Impervious to the atmosphere, his manner was nonetheless useful in blotting it up.

'We are all here now,' said Fowles.

'And which of you buggers is going to begin?' asked Crawley in his Sheffield accent.

James cleared his throat. 'We might as well get straight to the point.'

'We'll get straight to the point,' said Crawley, 'which is that I won't sell without guarantees.'

'We know that. You know too that it's impossible for us to give them.'

'That's very disappointing. I hoped you'd reconsider this before meeting. Very disappointing indeed. It puts the offer in a different light.'

'You wouldn't get guarantees from anyone.'

'I know your lot. You're just a bucket shop. I think we'd get a better price.'

'That too is doubtful. You're open to try, of course, but there's always the risk of being left at the altar.'

Crawley stared at him. His face was hot and red. 'Open the window, will you? London's a stuffy place.'

'I'll do it,' said Fowles. He pushed back his chair, walked round the shiny table and fiddled with a catch at the foot of the glass. 'Not much luck here. It needs a key. Anyone know where the key is?'

Those who felt co-operative shook their heads.

'Sorry, I can't do anything about this.'

Fowles returned to his seat. The activity effected a little transition.

'I know this is difficult,' said James shifting in his chair, 'but all I can say is that we would consider keeping on as many as possible, but you know we can't keep you nor Irving.' He was referring to the number two, the managing director. 'However, we will try and retain half the rest.'

Crawley went purple as though his face had been hit. His mouth seemed to have been pulled inwards as if on a leash.

'The figures aren't too good,' continued James. 'Yours is a cyclical industry and even in the good times your company hasn't been sufficiently expansionist. Not to put too neat a point on it, the decline has meant you've been almost at the point of—' he hesitated, the man must know it, have been told it by his accountants '—trading insolvently.'

He was looking at some point on the ceiling when he said this, to detach himself from his audience. What he needed to convey was that the truth, albeit painful, had the neutrality of fact. He continued to look upward. 'However, I must impress on you, we're neither a bunch of assassins nor vultures. In practice our operation is rather benign. Without it your company will go under. If we move in, it has a future. It's as—'

'James,' said Fowles.

James frowned at the interruption and turned his head a little sideways. 'In its niche market, we could establish it and develop it worldwide. We live in a culture where winner takes all. We—'

'Hang on,' said Fowles. 'Where's that damned key to the window? I don't think he's feeling too well.'

'Oh my God,' said Brewster. 'I think he's going to have a heart attack.'

James turned. He was in time to see Crawley listing sideways, his stocky physique reducing the speed of the seizure to that of slow motion. His face was contorted and twisted on one side. The vision clutched at James's innards, the image invading them with its awful power. He felt as though the four chambers of his own heart were under squeeze.

'Oh Jesus. Loosen his collar,' he said. 'Quick. I'll fetch an ambulance.'

Fowles, his back turned towards them, an act of evasion, was still fussing about the key.

He sat on a red plastic seat in the hospital waiting-room. It was linked by horizontal struts to a row of chairs on either side. Why? To prevent vandalism? Who would steal one of these horrible chairs that had supported so much private anxiety in a public place?

Still in his formal business attire, he sat in penance, offering himself as a hostage to abort a sacrifice. He had ordered a taxi at his expense to bring Crawley's wife from Sheffield to his bedside. It was no absolution but she had said that her husband had already suffered a previous heart attack in February and she had pleaded with him that morning not to go.

It was clear, thought James, that Crawley had not been fit to play the game. Here was a fact beyond denial. But Reason, disembodied like some eighteenth-century figment, seemed to have no effect on his Conscience. Manipulated by emotion, it multiplied out of control. It suffused him with guilt. It did not feel to him as though this background to Crawley's ill-health eliminated James from his role as unwitting cause.

Random thoughts began to swirl through his mind. He remembered the night his wife had recited the story from *The Arabian Nights*. Another story entered his head. He couldn't recall it exactly, he groped towards it through a fog. Was this it? A man sees Death threatening him in the marketplace. He recognises his face, takes horse, rides all day and collapses in the place of safety to which he has fled to escape him. As he lies exhausted, Death comes up to him and asks why he had raced all the way. The man says: I saw you in the marketplace, I thought you threatened me, I tried to escape. Death says: I did not threaten you, what you saw was merely an expression of surprise because I knew I had an appointment with you this evening eighty leagues away.

Poor old Crawley, thought James. Poor old me, cast as Death. But then it occurred to him that it could be seen as the other way round. Here he was in flight from the miserable mortality of his father and he comes face to face with it in another form. He brooded, keeping his eyes down, looking neither left nor right. In a hospital he would be likely to encounter death in all its manifold forms.

After about half an hour, he saw a pair of sensible shoes and slim ankles walking towards him.

'Are you the brother of Mr Crawley?'

'No,' he replied. 'I'm . . .'

'You're the friend?'

He stood and nodded. It seemed he had become so, no longer an adversary or even a stranger but almost kin.

'Your name is—?'

'James Farley. I was with him when it happened.'

She looked down at her list and frowned.

'How is he?'

'Don't worry. He's all right. It was a heart attack but slight. His wife, you said, is coming? Yes? We'll tell her what he'll require.'

At that moment James felt as though he had received a reprieve.

'Should I stay?' He knew he sounded like a child begging to be excused.

'No need.' The doctor, a young woman with curly fawn hair, shook her head. 'Not unless you want to. He's resting.'

So, leaving his telephone number, he escaped.

He ignored the passing taxis as he walked through the streets of Fulham. He tried to disperse the events of the evening through the rhythmic exercise of his limbs, but they clung to him, draperies he could not shake off. Worries teemed through his mind. He was conscious that in the next few days he would have to decide whether to acquire Crawley's company. The thought of going forward was dreadful, it filled him with abhorrence, but the truth was that if he didn't he would be faced with huge and fruitless service bills. However, it was also likely that the choice was no longer his to exercise. The man, so wounded, would doubtless opt to sell it to him. What else, for Christ's sake, could he do? This realisation reminded James of the old benign rules for negotiation: that you should leave something in the deal for the other fellow. Yet what indeed was in it for Crawley now? Not only sacked but flat on his back with a reduced life span. In all this, thought James, I believe I am blameless, but have been put in a culpable position. He knew he would have to deal with this feeling by the force of adult will.

When he arrived back at his little flat near Draycott Avenue, he poured a large whisky, looked at his watch which said after midnight, and decided to ring his wife. He had not spoken to her during the day and craved the cluck of her sympathy. The telephone rang five, six, seven times. He waited. She would be asleep, snoring perhaps. The telephone was on the other side of the bedroom. She would be turning on the light. Looking at the clock. It would take her time to reach it. She surfaced slowly.

The ringing stopped.

'You woke me,' she said croakily. 'Has something happened?'

'Listen,' he said and told her.

'Oh poor darling,' she exclaimed. 'Do you need me? Do you want me to drive up straightaway?'

'No,' he said. 'Don't do that. There's no need. It's just been pretty awful, that's all.'

'Are you sure you don't need me? Is there nothing I can do?'

'Don't come. Just be with me in spirit. As it were. I'll see you on Friday evening as usual. Claire, I do need you.'

He put the phone down, drank his whisky slowly and turned on the fire. He wandered around the flat, stood at the desk and picked up and put down a glass paperweight with a frog on a waterlily, one of his wife's knick-knacks. He did not feel like going to bed. He knew he would be unable to sleep. He looked at the captive frog and realised he did not wish to be alone. He drained his glass and returned to the phone.

'It's too late,' she said. 'Why imagine that—'

'Chantal, listen,' he said, and for the second time in ten minutes recounted the evening's events.

'Oh my God,' she exclaimed. 'Oh darling. How dreadful.'

'Can I come round? I do need you. Please.'

She hesitated. 'Yes.'

He was on the point of banging the door to his flat when he returned and detached the phone from the hook. Then he left and hailed a taxi to her flat on the other side of Albert Bridge. He buzzed the entry phone, spoke and climbed to the first floor. She opened the door, naked under her long muslin shift. He shut his eyes and put his arms about her, stroked her short hair, fine and velvet, the neat architecture of her face, ran his hand down her flank to the cleavage of her buttocks. The refreshment of a young body entered him. Revived, need for her rushed through him in an erotic torrent. He lifted her shift and pushed her up against the wall. The door was still half-open. He threw it shut then jammed her in the corner between its hinges and the side wall. He opened himself. 'You're hurting me,' she said. He did not answer, lifted her right leg and jacked it up around his waist. His fingers bit into her and explored. The wide wet softness gaped against him and received his surge. The sensation was violent. He ejaculated at once, then sank his head onto her shoulder. 'Sorry,' he muttered. She twisted her head sideways. 'Sorry,' he murmured again.

15

The middle of December was awful, the worst part of a swamp month. It was hard to remember the previous June when all the meadow herbs and grasses had been in flower, impossible to imagine that in half a year's time the world would roll round and allow all this to recur. In the meantime, the rain which had been forecast would not stop and for a week it was windy and stormy. The rivers burst their low banks and converted the flanks of the fields to marsh. The sheep were washed white like woollen jumpers. Pregnant ewes, not yet gathered inside for the birthings, huddled in the lea of hedges against the prevailing wind. Canada geese flew honking down at dawn, drawn by the mirage of standing water. Strange birds were blown inland off their course and frightened the locals. A paired colony of mallards fled from the devil shape of an ink-dark shag.

All night the trees groaned in the gales. Roosting pheasants forgot about guns whilst they were rocked in old apple trees as if in cockleshells on the waves of a sea-storm. Not all the trees managed to survive. A huge small-leafed lime was uprooted. It fell with a crack into the branches of its neighbour which held it up in its arms whilst its roots starfished from the ground.

The hawk who could not have endured this was safe and snug in her mews but Claire was still worried she would forget her training. She confessed this when Wilf arrived early one morning with a rabbit which the ferrets had killed.

He thumped it onto the table. 'One for the pot.'

She looked at his good-natured pink face and watery eyes with real affection. He was wearing his usual flat cap and a woolly waistcoat whose plains and purls had started to unfurl. He was eternally cheerful.

'Five rabbits,' he said. 'A bumper crop.'

'Who taught you?'

'My dad was a good poacher, mind. When we married Aggie was a town girl and looked down on me, a country boy.'

Claire gave a portion of the rabbit to Bella. Its fur would reappear in her castings, the oblong pelleted relics of her food that she threw up delicately after eating. A tiny fastidious world of feather and fur, coated in gleam.

'You keep her training going whenever you can,' said Wilf.

She was now on her own, for the sessions had to take place during the short light hours of the day when the old man and the boy were away at the school. Just me and my bird, she thought, but the hours spent on their own were giving both of them confidence. Whenever possible she was taking her for a walk across a long run of fields. She was no longer in doubt of the hawk's fidelity, but only her fitness. Vigorous exercise was the answer. No chance of catching a rabbit unless she was fit.

By now they both knew every detail of the routes. The old nettle grounds, the empty jar of Marmite in the hedge, the cluster of hilltop pines that came into view at the turn of a corner, a sign of welcome for the ancient traveller. As the days passed, other details changed. The first pre-Christmas lambs arrived, waifs in their oversized coats. The white ones huddled and shivered whilst the black babies grew strong, their dark skins wicking up the heat. When Claire walked through the fields, the bird would follow by flying from tree to tree, from bare ash to oak to larch to the wild wintry cherries. Claire was reminded of the way that the local children would give directions according to the trees rather than the roads: 'turn left at the big oak and right at the ash'.

On the twentieth day of December, she suddenly realised that she had scarcely prepared for Christmas. The automata of cards had been sent and received but the house was empty. No pine branches or holly berries, no varnished golden gourds or nuts and kernels with their sandalwood smells. No food either. Chastened by guilt, she got out the yellow earthenware bowl and mixed the dough for a large batch of mincepies. As she stretched and rolled the pastry, knowing by instinct how far she could tease its elasticity, it struck her that these days of walking and flying Bella, of tempting with Johnson or a dead rabbit or the swing-lure had become a form of procrastination. That the point of fitness had been reached and overlooked and pushed to the side. Stamina was not an end in itself but a goal on the way to another. The bird was now due a serious pitch at a rabbit or a pheasant. Her weight was tight, her appetite keen. Only she, her master, was the obstacle. And why? Because she was scared. Bella was young and inexperienced. What if she failed to kill the quarry immediately? The responsibility would fall on her keeper.

Claire looked down at her handiwork. Thirty little patterned pastry circles sat before her in their patty tins with thirty smaller hats to the side which would be the seal to each glistening syrupy dollop of mincemeat. Sixty little dinky pie-crust edges, home-made, mark you, not shop-bought, fed to you in this season of goodwill and human comfort as a pledge of my devotion and care. What next? I've got to let her try and catch a rabbit. Automatically she began to scoop up the mincemeat in the spoon and use her index finger to slide precise amounts of the spicy fruit into each cavity. I've got to let her try and catch a real rabbit. She put the pastry hats on the tarts and opened the oven. A blast of heat was flushed out which struck her in the face. She went to the window to look out. It confirmed what she already knew. That it was a fine day, a transparent winter light, it too rinsed clean by all the rain which had been blown south-eastwards. Outside she could see a thrush pulling a worm from the grass. More elastic than the pastry, its ringed length stretched to an improbably narrow girth and then snapped. The two halves concertinaed, the thrush swallowing the upper, whilst the lower contracted into the ground, only to be pecked in a repeat motion by the bird. What am I going to do? she thought. She realised that until now she had been sheltering behind an old man's skirts. She looked at her watch. The pies would take twenty minutes to cook in the oven. Already their cinnamon perfume, moist and warm, was filling the room. It was tempting to retreat into this fragrant and housewifely burrow. I shall wait until they've baked and then I'll think.

*　　*　　*

The clarity of the light also appealed to Peter Ravell and he decided he would dust off his photographic equipment. He had spent the first half of the morning writing up his notes from a week ago when he had been watching a little group of tufties on the nearby pool. Charming trilling drakes with formal black and white plumage, a pigtail and yellow Liquorice Allsorts eyes. Adept and specialist divers, they caught most of their food on the pond floor.

For as long as he could remember he had felt a passion for birds and he and a fireman's son would go scrambling together on the Cornish seabird cliffs during holidays when he was young. The interest, however, had fallen into abeyance as he had grown up. His father had been a maverick, always starting businesses which were destined to collapse, and the pressure had fallen on Peter, the elder son, to secure and succeed in a steady conformist job. At university he had succumbed to the careers officer and had ended up as a management trainee in one of the international drug companies. He was now confined to the pipeline of the upwards spiral, with a child, a Swiss wife whom he had married young and a salary to support. In later years he had come to believe that the only benefit here was that this life had moved him all over the world and allowed him to follow his first interest, which was his fascination for birds. This also meant that at some stage duty and escapism were bound to collide.

He was forty-one when this happened and he was due for promotion. He had reached that point when he would move from his position on a plateau of sixteen directors to that of eight in the advance towards the top of the pinnacle. In that year alone, his forty-second year, he had taken ninety flights. He had sat on the plane at Delhi airport thinking: do I want this, do I want this next step? He remembered the mynah birds yesterday evening, feeding on the hotel lawn. At that moment he had mulled over the possibility of his freedom. He knew that, within the company, immobility was not an option. The refusal to advance would mean he was doomed to sink down. He knew also that the decision to change, let alone abandon his prospects, would wreck his marriage. Yet on his return he had gone straight from Zürich airport to convert his wife.

It was March and she was watering the patrician cymbidium

and paphiopedilum in the shade of their heated, bourgeois conservatory. She was wearing a pink blouse, spotless; her head was shiningly coiffeured, almost 1940s in style. He spoke to her. 'I should have known that you would turn into your father,' she said. 'Try not to say things like that,' he replied. 'I shall continue to support you, but am I unreasonable to ask you to pull the ropes beside me?' She stared at him. She decided to be bewildered, uncomprehending. 'You want me to return to my old job of ten years ago? To be a dentist once more?' He looked down. Ten years had made a difference to her. The extent had been unnoticed till now. She had grown too grand, he had made her too grand to be willing to peer again into people's awful mouths.

He had refused the promotion. A year later he took a part-time consultancy post. He was now photographing birds in all his spare time. Sabine found a man with a house on one of the lakes. Her voice which had grown harsh became gay and purring again. Things which had seemed terrible had fallen into place once more. They could both say: it was all for the best really.

All his money went on equipment. A second-hand pair of night-goggles and optical detector unit, a complex control centre for the photographic machinery. It took a year before they started to pay for themselves. Then another year before he was making enough to support himself by his new work, though his needs were so few that he didn't want much. In any case he was gripped in the ardour of a vocation. The work was fraught, difficult and enthralling. There was so much to learn. Gently coaxing a windy bird to trust. Capturing the complexities of its flight, knowing its path, its predictable speed of deceleration. Filming the nest, the chicks lying on top of each other, the exquisite growing gradations of wing and tail. The sheer tantalising variety. The loud-voiced skulking wren, the grey scarecrow flight of the heron. The rosy spoonbills of Florida. The hawks in the dry southern states nesting in cactus. Buzzards locking feet and tumbling through the air in courtship. The migrations of flocks in autumn, so close that sometimes it almost seemed as though their wing-tips were touching. Birds were dancers in the sky. Hawks above all were dancers.

He thought now of the woman that night with the Harris hawk. Her name was Farley, according to Hugh, who had added that she had a pushy husband. He crossed the room, looked up her number in the phone book and lifted the receiver to dial. As he waited, he remembered his impatience but that she had agreed to let him photograph the bird. She answered and he spoke briefly. She hesitated, said she was thinking of going out now with the bird, she wasn't sure but on second thoughts, yes, she would be glad for him to come.

He put down the receiver, took his photographic vest with its flaps and pockets off the hook and slipped it on. He covered it with his old waxed coat, then picked up his equipment and two carrots. He left the cottage, pushed the door shut which required several attempts as usual because it was warped, and walked to the jeep. The mare hung her pretty head over the stable door. He stroked her velvet nose in the soft space between the scrolls of her nostrils. She took the carrots fastidiously, one by one, snuffling them up from his palm. 'Later. I'll take you out later, Dessie,' he promised. 'I've got an appointment.'

Even in the porch he could smell the mincepies. The scent, warm and delicious, evoked the pre-Stollen days of his youth and briefly made him feel in need of a family again. He had forgotten about Christmas.

She opened the door, saw him sniffing and smiled.

'Do you want one?'

'They smell awfully good.'

She disappeared and returned with two. They were small, sized for only a single bite, but to avoid a greedy appearance he broke each in half and ate it in flaky bits. They were hot and sweet and melting.

'Wonderful,' he said appreciatively.

She watched him. He was a strongly built man of medium height with thick, brown hair. His clean-shaven face was lively and full of purpose. She realised she had not assessed him adequately before. It had been dark then and her attention had been on the bird.

'You're not very hirsute for a naturalist.'

'What?' He was startled.

'Nothing.' She thought of explaining that beards seemed a tiresome part of the credentials. Maybe a Victorian hang-over.

'Anyway, officially, I'm a photographer.'

He finished off the last portion of pie and brushed the crumbs from his collar.

'You've called at an opportune moment,' she said. 'I've got a problem.'

'What kind of problem?' he said without much show of enthusiasm.

She hesitated. 'Perhaps I should tell you on the way.'

He recalled their last meeting. It occurred to him that if she was the kind of person who attracted problems, he would prefer to know this at once.

'Tell me now,' he said.

Her mouth started to form a word, stopped then moved again, fumbling and embarrassed.

He frowned. 'What is it?' He made a marginal shift away from her.

'Just a moment,' she said. 'The point is this. What do I do if my hawk catches her first rabbit and fails to kill it at once?'

He stared at her. 'Shouldn't you have thought of this before you took on the responsibility of the bird?'

She gave a tsk of irritation. 'It's too complicated to explain. What do I do?'

There was a moment's silence.

'Ah,' he said. 'You have found a use for me, haven't you? You want me to do it?'

She looked down. 'Is it necessary?'

'No. A hawk is one of the quickest killers around. Five minutes at most whilst a cat or a terrier can take up to half and hour.'

She remembered Wilf. 'I've been told that.'

'Sure. These catch-to-kill intervals have been carefully studied.'

'So I don't need to?'

'Of course not. There's no human intervention in the wild.' She looked relieved but he knew he could not let her off lightly. 'However, if you're in a position to save it pain – and you may not be – could you stand by and let it suffer?'

She put her head back against the wooden door jamb and for a moment closed her eyes. The winter sun, bleached and oblique, lit up the fair down on the cheeks.

'Look,' he said slowly, 'you mustn't be feeble. It's too easy to be feeble-minded, especially nowadays.'

She opened her eyes and looked at him. He had a wide honest forehead.

'Natural cruelties,' she said. 'What a minefield. I'm a vegetarian you know.'

He shook his head. 'One day you must explain that. Meanwhile I can't make up your mind for you.' He shrugged to express his detachment. He had come for a purpose and wanted to press on.

'You needn't worry,' she said. 'I've done so. Come in.'

He followed her into the hall which was dark but warm. She stopped to slip on her coat and boots, both muddy, in a state to rebuff the social niceties so he made no effort to help her. Instead he stood and looked at the large potted plants, succulents and blossoming pink striped amaryllis, stacked up on the thick windowsills. They were mature enough to have been nurtured for years and reminded him of Sabine and the orchids in their Zürich conservatory. Was she still watering them for her new man in her house on the lake? Or had they already served their home-making purpose and been dumped?

'My wife had a liking for fancy house plants,' he said.

'She doesn't like them any longer?'

'We divorced.'

He heard a murmur. It was muffled because she was bending down to adjust her trouser leg into her boot but it sounded like: too feeble-minded for you? If so, she was not looking for an answer nor did he offer one.

'We'll go out this way. Through the lobby.'

She whistled up the dog then led both of them out of the house and over the cobbles to the hawk's pen.

He stood at the entrance. The bird was long-legged and looked rangier and more glamorous than he remembered. She seemed restless and keen to be free. As he watched her, he suddenly realised that he too would prefer to be free. There was something about this occasion that made him reluctant to be saddled with his work. He was also aware that he might be required to do more than spectate.

'Could you wait a moment,' he asked. 'I'm going back to leave my gear in the house.'

She glanced up from adjusting the hawk's jesses. 'I thought you wanted to photograph her.'

'I know. It can wait.'

He walked back, dumped his equipment and returned.

The three of them set out in the same direction as before, through the garden, to get out onto the fields and up the hill. The moist earth smelt musty and herbal. To their left there came the small noise of running water in the brook which was full from recent rains.

It was only the beginning of the walk, not serious territory, so they talked but quietly.

'You know,' he said, 'in the middle ages, the lady's falcon was a merlin.'

'The little one.'

'Little perhaps but she would present you with a far bigger problem than the one you've got. Merlins catch larks. Two birds that everyone loves and admires but one eats the other.'

'You've seen that?'

'Once, yes. It's a spectacular contest for the lark rings up in the sky and the merlin spirals up with her. He needs to get higher to stoop. But in this case the lark got away. They're evenly matched but she was a plucky persevering little thing and she outflew him. She was wonderful. She sang as she went.' He stopped to remember. They had reached the start of the hill and he looked up at the route ahead and then down at the hawk carried on the fist.

'Don't kid yourself she'll get a bunny today. The prey often escapes. They're flight animals, evolved to escape. No point in psyching yourself up for something that's not likely to happen. She's young and my guess is she'll miss him. A young predator and an old prey are a poor match.'

'You don't know her,' said Claire stubbornly.

He made a concessionary shrug.

As they climbed the hill side by side they fell silent, with the quietness of fishermen waiting above their lines. There was a light wind and small clouds drifted from the southeast. Once they had crested the brow of the land, it would be easy to slip her into the wind and downhill. At the bottom there was a small spinney which Claire had always avoided until now. Here, gatherings of large rabbits bounded over the grass at its edge, experienced and confident in their natural territory, proper champions. What use the countless limp dummies that Claire had pulled out of the bushes during their walks together? What kind of encounters were these? Pseudo duels. Suddenly Claire realised that her ambivalence of the morning was gone. She yearned for the bird's first catch and kill, the culmination of all the training. She felt goaded by this man's know-all warning. The bird could strike and would.

They were now at the top of the hill. They stood and looked around. The light was wonderfully clear and exhilarating. Before them lay the wide scooped valley and the patchworked ridge. Fields of green pasture and purple earth; tumps and old burial mounds; low tufted hedgerows and medieval stone farmhouses sprawling amongst mistletoe orchards in the bowl of the valley. The scene was ancient and unstirring. The distance had stilled the movement of life. Even the browsing drift of sheep seemed to have slowed to a stop. Only the clouds moved, towing shadows across the land.

On the fist, the bird leant forward and roused her feathers. She looked round, waiting, watching. No movement in the whole panorama; it seemed instead centered and poised within her.

'The rabbits will be there,' said Claire, pointing towards a patch of hazels and some brambles near the foot of the hill.

He grimaced. They both knew it was difficult territory. The prey would have ample warning, they would pop into their burrows. She would have neither speed nor surprise on her side.

Then, at the edge of the canvas, all three saw him at once. Midway down the hill below a trio of hawthorns where the grass was uneven and tussocky. He was a large rabbit, a buck bigger than Johnson and a survivor doubtless of many encounters. Did he have sanctuary to hand? They could not see it. The decision had to be instantaneous.

'Go,' said Claire and swung her arm.

She felt the reflex of the bird's talons on her fist, an extraordinary feeling, like a pump of raw adrenalin shooting into her arm. Her bloodstream joined with the bird.

The hawk surged, lifted and burst forwards, arrowheading towards the buck. She was downhill racing. Surely she would have an advantage. The short front legs of the rabbit would cut his speed downhill, enabling her to overtake him. But the buck had bolted, ducked, turned right and then dipped suddenly out of sight. They ran forwards and saw the mouth of his burrow concealed in a ditch. Bella loomed over it, crushing a tussock of grass in frustration. Panting, she turned her head and looked at them, her expression one of bewilderment.

'Poor Bella,' said Claire. 'Not like a dummy is it?'

They picked her up again and continued cautiously downhill. Both knew that the spirit of a young bird could be broken by repeated failure. It was important to achieve success as soon as possible. The chase and the kill were instinctive, but a pattern of botched early attempts could make a caged bird lazy. Just like a human being, she could give up and accept the easy option. Success brought motivation and confidence.

Ravell knew that a professional would act as a beater, flushing the prey out of the brambles. He knew too this would flout her notion of fair play. Instead he suggested keeping closer to the hedge. That way they would be slightly less noticeable and might also cut off the quarry's line of escape.

They redirected their trail slightly to the west, towards the boundary line of trees which had been allowed to grow up.

'Ah no,' said Claire. The bird had seen it at the same instant. Her feet tightened on the glove. It was a squirrel at the foot of a hedgerow hazel. A squirrel could give a bird a bad bite, making her ill for months. The infection would rob her of any field experience before she was rested for the five sedentary months of moulting.

'No,' said Claire again. The squirrel deserted his larder of nuts and jerked into an immediate gallop up an overhanging branch of the tree to which he clung frozen like a chameleon.

They continued in stealth to follow the line of the hedge trees. Forwards but slowly, not noticing the eyestrain of peering on a bright day. The breeze had increased in strength and the grass tufts shimmered and rippled in the wind. They walked past a big old fruit tree with a burred bole, its carcases of rotten apples lying on the ground.

'Up there.' Ravell was looking in the western quarter of the sky. 'See? That won't help.'

She followed the direction of his stare. A buzzard was slope-soaring in the blue, the current filling his sails. Every rabbit and vole would have seen him and been alerted to the need to scuttle for shelter. They stood still and watched his wide impassive arc. Floating and faintly mewing, he made the hawk on the fist seem clumsy and tame. He represented the next stage, an evolution of power and mastery that she would one day attain. She too would learn to use the thermals like routes. Today she was tied to the land.

They stood with their faces uplifted, Bella's tilted to the side, admiring his marvellous use of freedom, till a trio of rooks mobbed him and he turned and sloped off to the right, fading and fading to a speck which vanished out of sight.

Claire blinked and looked down. She blinked again.

Bella, can you see?

There, a hundred yards to their right, beside a matted group of old nettles, she glimpsed a rabbit cropping the grass. For a second she made no movement, fearful of committing the bird to another awkward start. But Bella had seen. Her talons convulsed on the glove. Slowly Claire lifted her arm. The bird's wings burst out, like a sprung umbrella. At the same moment, the rabbit ran, not in a straight line for his burrow but desperately zig-zagging from side to side. She was twelve yards from him, the great wings drumming, she banked, twisting with him, her landing gear dropping, the talons ready to lock in a vice, but as she grasped at his leg, he kicked, broke free, streaked forwards, till she caught up with him, a flying fish, and seized him. He hunched. Then, as she penetrated, he began to squeal. Claire did not need to think but ran towards them, the automatic response to pain. His ears were laid back, his eyes bulging. She put her hands down, jerked his head back, felt the snap, there was a stretch and a tremor, then immediately the relaxation of death, the warm limp flop. Her breath was coming in great thickened gasps. Both she and Bella were panting. She looked at the hawk and thought of the buzzard in the sky. She thought: she is on her way. She sensed the man behind her. Together they watched her start to pluck at the soft belly. They would let her feed up a bit as a reward. Her first catch. Tonight they would let her stuff her crop. Her first and best triumph. She thought again of the high soaring buzzard. She thought: my beautiful girl, my American bird, my most beautiful Bella.

16

It was two days after Christmas. The house was still full but fragmenting. Claire's widowed father was reading the thin post-turkey newspaper in the conservatory to keep out of the way of James's widowed mother until she was safely despatched on a train. Claire was spending overtime with the bird to keep out of everyone's way. James had cleared off, no one knew where, leaving his wife to run his mother to the station. The two girls were in Griselda's old bedroom to be by themselves. They had just found a photo of her first lover in a drawer. His name had been Friedrich. A boy with a cylindrical head, he had been staying one summer at a school teaching English to foreigners. For months afterwards, he had plagued her with cards saying, 'Ich liebe Dich.'

'Jesus,' said Griselda. 'What one does as a kid. I didn't know this was still knocking around. Bin him quick.'

'You had such poor taste in boys,' said Katy 'You always did. You still do.'

'What choice do I get? They're all gay, broke or married. Or writers who can be all three. Very muddled anyway.'

'That Jonathan Tor business has made you really grumpy. You should have dumped him to his wife.'

'I'm not cruel enough. Nor sufficiently screwed up.'

'What will become of you?'

'I'll get old, disillusioned and cross-eyed. An old version of a young me. What becomes of anyone?'

'You were born bored. Do you remember the first time we came here? I was ten. We were sitting in the back of the car. You said "I don't like the country." Mum said: "Only fourteen years old but her dissatisfaction with life runs so deep." I've never forgotten that.'

'Sorry. We can't all be keen young doctors.'

'Oh, me I'm not keen. I'll switch to becoming a GP. I'll get bossy and withhold pills. I'll be tough and mercenary and switch on my answerphone at nine o'clock in the evening and refuse to receive calls until ten which is when you start getting paid call-out rates.'

'Katy. Really.' Griselda made an open-mouth face. 'Do they do that? No wonder I'm disillusioned.'

'I shall live in the country and be diverted by rose-cheeked country folk. Tim Benson, the Doctor Finlay of Lancashire, told me that one of his patients was so fat, they had to make him a special coffin when he died which they couldn't get through the church door for the funeral. They had to hold the service outside. It was very embarrassing.' Katy took off her navy wool jumper and pulled on a scallop-edged pink cotton top which her grandmother had given her for Christmas. She looked at herself in the mirror, shuddered and subsided onto the bed.

'Yuk,' said Griselda.

'Yuk indeed. Anyway, there's a lot to be said for country patients. They get fat because they eat lots of chips but it saves you doing cholesterol tests because there's no point because they won't give up eating chips.'

She took another look at her cotton top. 'Pink for a girl,' she said. 'Would you believe it? It probably gave grandpa his breakdown.'

'Grandpa, sweetheart, had a breakdown because of grandma. No more, no less.'

'What happened?'

'For five years he sat and looked at the wall. Or was it the Rayburn?'

'Then what happened?'

'He died.'

'You don't die of looking at the wall. It keeps you going for ever.'

'Maybe the Rayburn had fumes. Maybe it was his dicky heart. *I* think it was a lifetime's nagging. Ma always said she nagged Dad. Grandma had grand expectations. She still does. Age hasn't withered them nor arthritis shut her up.'

'Fancy stuff,' said Katy. 'Who's been reading a manuscript?'

'Grisel? Katy?' It was a shout from Claire downstairs. 'Your grandmother is going to catch the midday train. Can one of you run her to the station?'

They looked gloomily at one another.

'Do you notice,' said Griselda, 'how she always says "*your* grandmother"? And *your* mother to Dad?' She raised her voice. 'Coming,' she shouted, then turned to Katy. 'Who's going to do the business then? You? You're the baby.'

Katy unsnuggled herself from the duvet. 'You'll owe me,' she warned.

She clattered downstairs in her big black boots and pink top to the hall, followed by the wafting Griselda. Both Mrs Farleys were standing side by side, exchanging platitudes on the weather.

'You look very pretty, dear, in your little top,' said Mrs Farley senior.

Watched by her mother and sister, Katy gave a suitably pink simper and began to collect up the luggage. Kisses and promises were exchanged.

'I can't find James anywhere,' said Claire.

'If we're going, we've got to go now,' said Katy.

'It's very upsetting. He was going to go through a little financial problem with me.' Mrs Farley, who was as tough as an old boiling fowl, staggered publicly on her stick.

'Come on, grandma. We can't wait.'

Katy shepherded her out of the house and over the gravel to the car.

They watched from the porch.

'There she goes,' said Grisel. 'Back to her dwarf conifers and china thimbles and reading groups and name-dropping and manipulation of people by calling them dear. That's what happens when you finally make it out of Scrag End.'

'You've got very sour,' said Claire. 'Watch it. There's another view which is that she's a poor old woman who's been widowed for years. However I'm glad you're around to give vent to the things I think but don't dare say in public.'

The car engine coughed, stalled and ignited, then jerked over the light covering of snow towards the gate. A smooth ride would not be in prospect. A hand fluttered from its window. There were reciprocal waves from the porch. As always, contact would be strenuously maintained by both sides till the car disappeared from sight.

'Flop till you drop,' said Griselda.

The car noise chugged out of hearing. It was replaced by the sound of heavy footfall and the lobby door opening into the hall.

'Oh no,' said James. 'I haven't missed her have I? Oh God, has she actually gone? You should have called me. I was in the loo.'

Claire flashed him a look. 'Where's my father? Don't say he's hiding there with you.'

'It's Christmas. What do you expect?'

'He's in the conservatory.'

Claire walked through the house. She could tell that even her feet felt cross because they were hitting the floor with a rap. Christmas. When everyone took the chance to fall apart except her. She had to brace them and feed them and swim resolutely through their cross-currents. The unpopular members of the family wouldn't even get talked to if it weren't for her.

She peered round the door to the conservatory and found Douglas, her father, lying in the wicker chaise-longue with the paper over his face.

'It's all right. You can come out now.'

He pushed it aside. His white moustache looked puckish.

'She's gone?'

'Does she really merit this disappearing act?'

'I used to recognise her type in the surgery. You know what you learn to do? You evaporate.'

'You can always spend Christmas in Australia with Simon and Jenny. Or in LA with Caro.'

'Too far. And too much fuss.'

'I know my place. The nearest available child.'

'Claire. I've always been very fond of you. You were my favourite.'

'Oh I'm the dutiful one. Write it on my gravestone will you? She always did her duty.'

'I can go better than that. She always did her duty but with a frown. I had an assistant like that. Or how about this? She always did her duty but let everyone know.'

She laughed, delighted.

'Want a drinkie?' he suggested.

'Drinkie? Drinkie? That's not your kind of word.'

'You get like this when you're widowed and retired. You turn into a bit of an old woman. Even a bit of a young girl. Arch anyway.'

'No drinks yet. Wrap up. As soon as Katy's back we're going off for a picnic.'

'Claire. It's cold and there's snow on the ground.'

'It's cold but it's sunny. It'll be wonderful up the mountain. Besides I'm fed up at the thought of dishing out yet another lunch.'

'We guessed. Look. No filling.' Griselda who had walked in held up the uneaten half of an empty mincepie. 'I wasn't going to tell you but it's the third that I've found.'

'Oh God. Really? How feckless.' She laughed and found it so pleasing that she couldn't stop laughing. How lovely to have ballsed up so many mincepies. All that cooking. Bugger their expectations. 'You see, I had something on my mind.'

'Important?'

'Terribly.'

An hour later the five of them were sitting on two wetproof rugs in the snow. It was the plateau of a foothill beside the Black Mountains. They were under the long undulations of the white spine. It looked wonderfully animal, like the flank of Moby Dick. There was no one around. No hikers or hang-gliders, but far away on the top of the glistening ridge, they could see a trail of human ants, silently scaling the top of the scarp. James pulled the cork from a bottle of white wine. It popped gently in the clear soundless air. They dipped their hands into the hamper which was stuffed with bread, cold goose, apricot pickle, cheese and fruit. It tasted better, sharper, fresher in the open. Around them the sun sparkled on the snow grains, striking diamonds of light. Claire looked up in the sky for buzzards, birds of the uplands. No sign. Maybe it was too cold up there. Lapis blue but arctic. She had decided against taking Bella for a walk in the snow.

'Happy Christmas, grandpa,' said Katy, clinking her glass against his.

'Happy Christmas that's gone. Happy New Year to come.'

They all raised their glasses and fell to munching again.

'What an empty world,' said Katy. 'How perfect if it were always like this. If it belonged only to us.'

'It does today,' replied Claire.

'Where have they all gone to?'

'They're all scrummaging round at the sales.'

'Don't want to go back to London,' said Griselda. 'All those people. All those writers noting the flux of things. Middle-aged publishers saying can I grope you please in front of framed photographs of their wives.'

'What's this?' asked Claire.

'Oh nothing.' She regretted mentioning it. A spoiler like litter in a nice place. 'All I mean is that it's so lovely here I don't want to go back.'

James made little filling-up signs in the direction of his father-in-law's glass. I think, he decided, I think I'm really going to have to give her up.

17

As it was a cold miserable day in January, Mary was having a work-out in the regimental gym. The place was a bit of a moveable feast because on Remembrance Day in November it changed into a church for the event before reverting to type. The wives were allowed to use it though only at certain times and with deference to the men. Some of the latter were fitness fanatics and the keenest of these body-builders could be found pedalling away on their own at one o'clock in the morning.

Mary was sitting on the rowing machine, content to drift on the treadmill and let it drive her like a dog. It developed the heart, lungs, pectorals, biceps and not least the legs. She thought she would soon have the most powerful thighs in Herefordshire. It was true that only a fruit case would choose to do this, but it was a matter of pride to keep fit. It was amazing how many of the girls maintained a high standard. There were quite a few who kept up with each other, whether they were bank tellers or tax clerks, nurses or shop managers or airline pilots. Whether they said 'Can I help you, sir?' or 'This is your captain speaking.' The reason being that the self-respect of their mates was catching, and gave the wives a standard to live up to.

Mary had reason to be proud, married to a man who had proved himself capable of going somewhere. He had always been army barmy and although the ladder was long and arduous, he had already scaled the first four of its rungs. Trooper, lance corporal – or comical as they called it – corporal, and sergeant when the pay had improved, which was the point he had reached. Staff sergeant was next, in charge of the men in the troop, then WO1, meaning warrant officer, on to WO2, then the jump into the commissioned ranks. A very good man could go all the way, with honours and knighthoods and the lot. The other theory, of course, was that before this the selection-destruction cycle would start to operate.

On the gym machine to her right was Beverley Jones, a girl who had the potential to become something of a friend. She was the wife of a new trooper but, unlike a few of the other women, Mary was never one to stand upon rank. Not least because it was impossible not to be amused by this girl. A bit of a blowsy Brummie blonde, but fun, warm and immensely good-hearted.

''Ow's the budgie then?' asked Beverley, her arms pedalling away.

'Budgie's doing very well. Caught a bunny before Christmas.'

'Oooh. Just like our husbands, innit?'

Mary laughed. Linda Grainger, a nurse originally from south-east London and married to another sergeant, watched from the other side of the room and came over to join in the talk. Most of the wives knew each other, since all, no matter how different, had more in common with each other than with outsiders. It wasn't just the wives' club in operation, but a genuine recognition that they needed one another, especially those that came from distant parts of the country. It was these strangers who were always required to be strongest. In a crisis they lacked the comfort of local family support. In comparison the Hereford girls, who in fact formed the majority of wives, had it comparatively easy.

'Your John's squadron is due back tomorrow, isn't it?' asked Mary.

'Can't wait,' said Linda. 'Can't wait.' She had been working on dumbbells for the last six months and had acquired the newly fashionable bottle-topped shape with square shoulders. 'As soon as he gets through the door I'll cart him off to Tesco to push that trolley. I'll have two free hands. Bliss.'

'You should be so lucky,' said Bev. 'Squadron sergeant flies in, debriefs, hands in kit, comes home, straight off to the supermarket. 'Oo's a lucky girl. Is he a lamb then?'

'What I say,' said Mary, 'is that we're all lucky because the Regiment trains them. They do their own washing, ironing. That's more than my dad or brother does.'

'It's all right for you with a neat bloke who joined from the Guards,' replied Linda. 'Mine came in from the paras. They're a rough lot, those buggers. He took some licking into shape.'

Mary and Bev looked at her with some sympathy. She had walked out on him three years ago but returned within six months. To their credit the marriage had stuck. She claimed this was due to the time that they spent apart. January to December was a long time to live with a husband. Though not everyone was in agreement about that.

'It's been the third Christmas we've spent apart,' said Carol, a friend of Linda's and married to a lance corporal in another squadron. 'But he's the last one I can have a honk to. He came home for two days. Two days. What happens. The colonel turns up. Sorry Carol, he says. And my David's gone.'

'What a bunch of whingers,' said Bev. 'Let's go and have a party. I've had enough of machines.'

Linda put an arm out to admire her own biceps. 'I've got a welcome-back party when the squadron gets home. Welcome back with lots of curries.'

'Not a buffet. Let's have a proper party.'

'Come on, Bev. Here's four of us and we can't come up with a man between us.'

'I've got a bit of a bloke. He's a butcher. He's a laugh. He doosn't do his wooing with flowers but now and then he brings me a pair of lamb chops.'

'You don't, Bev, do you?'

'No, I don't. You should see him. No chance of him getting lucky.' She paused. 'Nor me either, come to that.'

I think I'll go to London, thought Claire. See what's going on. Four months since I've visited the flat.

The memory of her daughter's remark about middle-aged married gropers lingered.

She rang James late, then early the following morning and was not deterred by the lack of a reply. She caught the train which went through Oxford, a long loopy uncomfortable route but beautiful at any time of the year except January after a snow melt when the untilled fields of old rotting beans lay beaten and smelly in the thaw. The carriage rocked. Her plastic cup of tea slurped. Sorry, she said to a man beside her who was using a laptop. He was adding up or subtracting. He was interrupted by his mobile. He looked the sort who might have arranged for someone to call him simply for show.

Opposite were a pair of glum youngsters. Neither talked till one of them said to the other: 'Won't do the bugger again,' whereupon they both fell silent once more. Poor lads, had they just ploughed the Regiment's selection course? Mary had said the failures were slapped back to Hereford station at once. And where, for that matter, was Stuart? Mary seemed anxious, but never said. No question, she had guts. But in the old days it seemed it was yet harder for their wives, supposed to hide the fact that their men were even in the SAS. What had Mary told her? That a friend admitted she used to say her husband was an electrician and prayed that the lights didn't blow the story with a fuse.

At Paddington station there was a queue waiting for a taxi. She walked out to board a bus but the traffic was static. A bomb hoax, someone kindly said, which had brought the whole of W2 to a halt. She started walking, reached the Park where she found a cab to SW1, then SW3. In the early days after their marriage, they had lived for a few months in Sloane Avenue. A horrid furnished flat with thick white carpets and a red tapestry. James had been twenty-three. He had hated his job, been envious of friends in a position to grow Zapata moustaches.

The traffic was running freely but she decided to walk. She bought a bunch of irises, a piercing blue, in Sloane Square; improper for them to bloom so early. They were Dutch, doubtless; those Netherlanders had bought up all the English florists. She wandered into Peter Jones, such an old and familiar store. At the age of twenty-three she had been wheeling her crying baby through its ground floor. To its credit it had changed less over those years than Griselda. Even its fashions seemed the same. Thick heels, roomy toes, flared bottoms. Other former fashions had also returned. Pale pink politics, Darwin, the Beatles. In thirty years time no doubt they would be recycled again and she would witness a repeat. Dear God, we'll be over eighty then.

She turned off by Draycott Avenue and let herself into the side door that led to the flat. Up the stairs which James had once tumbled down naked when drunk, and into their small three-roomed apartment. She pushed her key into the door and went straight to the telephone and rang his office. He was in Sheffield for the day. Of course, poor love, he had Crawley's business to face in the aftermath of the heart attack. She put the phone down and walked round the flat. All was neat and in order, the bed made, a triangle of sheet at the corner turned back. Doubtless Mrs Palmer had tidied up.

As she looked round she realised that over the years the flat had quietly changed gender. Little by little she had withdrawn her presence and only traces remained. The paperweight of the frog on the waterlily. A grey opaline vase with a fluted rim. She would use that for the irises. A print of an oil painting: *The Arrival of the Jarrow Marchers in London* by Thomas Dugdale. Two beautiful people in evening dress and cigarette holders looking down from a Mayfair-type window at the dark jostling throng. It was a clever picture and she'd take this one back. And the photo of herself. Or was there? Where was it? She had last seen it to the right of the clock on the bedside cabinet. It had moved. Was it broken? Or had he switched it to the desk? After a thorough search she found it face-down under an old address book in the right-hand drawer. She picked it up and stared, puzzled rather than worried. The face in the frame was smiling, the sloping eyes closed in laughter, the straight fair hair blown back. It looked happy yet the mood did not seem to be infectious. She reinstated herself with a thump in the centre of the mahogany desk.

In Sheffield, James was sitting with Mrs Crawley and Howard Irving who was number two. He was tired, having spent the morning on the shop floor.

'He told me,' said Mrs Crawley. 'Alison, he said, I want it to go ahead.'

Poor devil, thought James. He has succumbed, given the only thing a sick man can bestow. His money and his blessing.

'How is he? Better?'

'I've persuaded him to retire. He's built it up, our business. He thought it would go on forever. Now it will. But he won't. Not at this rate.'

'He said it would mean sackings.' Howard Irving leant forward on his bendy chair. He was pale, his hair the colour of pâté. He was forty-nine, of an age to know that the old get knocked off first.

James shifted minutely. 'If it's to grow, it'll have to be more efficient. Cut the people at the centre by half and you step up efficiency and value. If we don't, it'll be dead in the water.'

Irving surmised he had nothing to lose. 'You buggers grow big by grabbing other people.'

'If you don't want to stay on board, then don't. I was going to suggest that you were among the half that remained. It was one of your boss's requests.'

'Howard,' said Mrs Crawley. 'It's not like you to be hasty. You've always been the slow sort. Bill wants you to stay. We want your old head on a new business.'

'I can't make a commitment exactly that you'll be number two,' said James, wondering what he had let himself in for with the 'slow sort'. 'There will be a degree of adjustment. But I'm sure your experience will be sought after.'

Irving looked at him wanly. 'A job's a job, isn't it? Number two or number three?'

If, thought James, you're even placed.

Lucky old me, thought Claire, looking at the photograph of herself. Free. I could go to an exhibition or a concert or a matinée. Women of my age go to matinées in pairs, don't they? *A Girl in my Soup*; *The Mousetrap*; a French farce; or are they a little more striving nowadays? *Uncle Vanya* or *The Provok'd Wife* perhaps. Or I could go to Kew and warm up in a hothouse. I could go to the zoo and sniff the smelly old lions. I could do all these things. Or I could open the wardrobe and look through the pockets of his suits. On balance it would be easier to do the latter. Only a few yards away and it costs nothing. What am I looking for? Theatre tickets? Restaurant bills for two? Addresses? All of them meaningless. The scent of scent? Billets doux in large childish handwriting? Knickers? Yes, any of these would have much more significance.

A welter of memories of past events clutched at her throat. It was degrading, humiliating that she had been here before and should therefore be used to it. She was passive, worse than passive: she was at one remove: it happened to him and so happened to her. A restoring voice reminded her that she had no reason to believe that anything had happened. She stood up and clutched at its sense of proportion. It was true. Maybe nothing had happened. She would simply tidy his pockets and empty his wastepaper basket in the interests of hygiene. Mrs Palmer was an old lady with bandages on her legs and could not be expected to do a thorough job.

She pulled open the wardrobe door, an ugly white panelled thing with a black button instead of a proper knob. She tried to ignore her fingers flitting away on an independent search among the pockets. Through the two navy pinstripes, worn to secure loans; the tweed jacket used in trendy mode for Friday dress, the olive moleskin waistcoat with an indelible dribble; cords, flannels, blue jeans for Saturday though he never spent them in town. Nothing yet. What would she prefer to find? Marbles? Bits of string? Conkers? That would be very cheering. My husband has turned back into being a little boy. Honest, he's no trouble any longer, not horny at all.

After ten minutes of frisking, she stood back. She had found nothing of interest. She blew a gust of held breath into the air. The wastepaper baskets still awaited but they caused her to feel squeamish. It was so terribly infra-dig to grovel. A scrummaging baglady on the floor. She walked round, peering at them, then set to. Most were empty. One had half an old cheese sandwich and a packet of crisps which she dumped in the bin. She left the fullest in the sitting room till last. Upended, it revealed a plug, a pebble, a luggage ticket, a light bulb with a broken circuit and a Klimt card, postmarked, addressed, but blank and unsigned. She stared at it, turned it back and forth. A portrait called *The Dancer*: gaudy, extravagant and gorgeous; sequinned with colour, with orange and rose and grass green. Girly stuff. Who would send this but a girl? Anon., and therefore so surely a girl. Who is it this time, Jim-boy? Who? Anon.

Carrying the card carefully since it had the aura of evidence, she placed it to the side of the photograph of herself in the frame. Then since she had no wish to sit here and stare at this strange and disruptive combination, she resolved to go out. She got as far as the door, opened it, then stood for a moment. On the other side of the wall she could hear the sound of a bath running, a very London uncountry sound at this odd time of day. The door to the shop opened and closed. Below, someone, a girl, called: 'Roberto.' Quick chatter. Brazilians, jewellery freaks. She stood still, thinking. Maybe this card means nothing; though I know him so well, it's something not nothing, of that I'm a 100% sure. If so, this time it will be different. Why? Because of me, I'm the one who's altered. In the past I'd have had it out with him. Tears, distress, promises, pretty meaningless, all they meant was acceptance of the status quo with the maximum fuss. He knew it and I did too. I've been the passive partner. This time it will be different.

She closed the door and walked back to the sitting room. To the unsympathetic eye as hers now was, it could do with a coat of paint. It had been allowed to go to seed, like her. She picked up the irises which she had left forgotten on the kitchen table, filled the opaline vase with water, inserted them to form a bare splayed arrangement and placed them on the desk to the right of the photo. She then picked up the card and wrote swiftly in her strong boarding-school script:

I wuz here. Rang you but your office says you're in Sheffield all day. Sorry about this gaudy card. All I can find to hand. Love. C.

She replaced the card in the frame and surveyed the cameo. Her presence was back, alive and speaking although nothing had been said. She thought of the bird. Together they had caught a bunny before Christmas. You watch and wait and move when there's no sanctuary to hand. A hawk spends most of its time waiting. This time she would arrange things in her own way. She went out and closed the door. As she stepped into the street, she bumped into the grey-head Roberto and his girl. Wearing a glowing cherry wool scarf, she was possessed of a wonderful silky olive skin. So beautiful, she thought: you can't blame him. She bought a nice check jacket with the proceeds from a piece she had written on the Belle Epoque, went to the Tate for an hour and then caught the train back to Hereford. Its catch-the-bunny rhythm rocked her satisfactorily to sleep.

18

In the normal course of events, James reflected, it is not natural for men to be dumpers but to be dumped, and in this respect he felt himself to be no different. In all his previous affairs it had been the women who had protested and left. As a result he had no facility for dumping but had grown accomplished at being left. Yet ever since he had found the conjunction of his wife's writing on his girlfriend's card, he had known he had no option but to tell the latter to go.

He was still recoiling from this discovery the other night. He had been tired when he returned from Sheffield, so it was a while before he had noticed the irises, and then in quick succession the photograph and the card. As intended, they had given him a profound shock. He had turned the latter over and stared in horror at the representation, as it seemed, of Chantal on the front and his wife on the back. Disparate faces of the same coin, they had induced in him a lightning flash that had seemed to him akin, almost, to schizophrenia. These two nicely separated compartments of his life had joined up and revealed the central split.

Such is the spirit of self-preservation that he had realised almost at once that the girl who was, so to speak, the front, would have to be made to leave. He was in no mental state to absorb stress on two levels. The business of Crawley had been and still was quite bad enough, and the thought of extra strain was abhorrent. Within five seconds, his obsession with Chantal vanished and left only an underlying dislike. However, after a couple of whiskies, he felt both guilty and sorry for her, though it remained true that only the method of her going rather than the fact of departure was in question. After another whisky he decided that the kindest way of parting would be to do it over a dinner.

Three nights later, they were sitting in the dark intimacy of their usual alcove in their usual restaurant. Lovers about to be disunited, though only one knew this secret and was having some difficulty with how to share it with the other. James had a pang as he looked at her. She was at her most beautiful tonight. She was wearing a large silver collar above the deep, deep swoop of a black boat-neck. He remembered her movements, her head thrown back: no one had ever been as exciting in bed. At the end of this, would there be room for just one more time?

She made beckoning signs with her fork. It was their custom to order different meals from the menu and feed each other a gamut of various delicacies.

'Open,' she said and popped a mussel inside.

He tried to chew and swallow but it stayed stubbornly solid and rubbery in his mouth.

'Chantal—'

'Open.'

A second mussel was reunited with the first. He was forced to do a dormouse and keep the most recent in his cheek-pouch meanwhile. It occurred to him that he would choke to death if he tried to say anything. He decided that it would be wiser to lie than to die.

In this way their eating of both the starter and main course was unblemished. In satisfaction she put her knife and fork together and pushed the plate aside. She had demolished a portion of mussels, half of James's crab soup, the breast of a wild duck, French beans and was awaiting a cute little sorbet which would help the pudding go down. He was always amazed by the amount that she, so slender, could tuck away.

'Darling James, not hungry?'

'Not really. The fact is, sweetheart, there's something I must tell you.'

'Jamesie, not serious.'

'It hurts me more than it does you.'

She looked at him and frowned.

'That old thing. That means the only one of us you think this will hurt is me.'

'No. It's not like that.'

'Do tell me. What is it like? Where will it hurt you? Here, or here?'

She reached under the table and immediately groped for his balls in quick succession.

He snapped his knees together. 'Chantal, stop it.'

'Not amused, are we?' She straightened up but left the table-cloth ruckled.

No, he thought, we are fucking not. He realised that her refusal to play by the rules could change very quickly from an asset into a liability.

'The fact is. The fact is . . .' He pushed a bit of leftover seaweed that had drifted onto his side plate over the edge. 'I feel I can't go on blocking your life. What we share is very special but it can't go anywhere.'

'I don't expect it to *go* anywhere, as you put it. Where should it *go*?'

'You're young. You ought to be married, having children . . .'

'You funny old anachronism. I don't need to be married to have a child.'

He felt he had driven blind into a perilous cul-de-sac. He wanted to reverse and get out fast.

'No, of course not. But you need a fellow your own age who can give you the total attention you deserve. Weekends. Christmas. With me, that's impossible.'

'I'd be happy staying with you during the week if you'd like.' She looked across at him coolly.

'Marvellous,' said James. 'Marvellous of course. But it's impossible. I've never fooled you about this. I've always told you my wife mustn't know.'

'But if she really loved you, she'd understand.'

The waiter, foreign and captivating though probably Cockney, appeared out of the gloom to offer a list of simple-life puddings.

'Rhubarb crumble for me,' said Chantal. 'I've already ordered it. You darling?'

'Nothing for me.'

'Oh James, you don't have much appetite tonight.'

'She does love me,' he said miserably. The dark restaurant and Chantal's face across the tablecloth dissolved out of focus into the moment when he had discovered his wife's photograph and the card. She had swooped down to the central position in his life, her absence become a presence which blurred out the surroundings. This hard-edged fact made him want to sweep all the other flotsam aside. But how did he tell the girl she was flotsam? That he wanted her a few months ago, well, last week, even as recently as four nights ago, an hour ago actually, but that all of a sudden she had become a bloody nuisance. There was something so horribly unchivalrous about it. He decided to start a new tack and set off towards the good old trick of self-deprecation.

In the distance he could hear Chantal saying, '. . . Of course, my aunt, on my father's side, you'll meet her if we can whisk over to Limoges . . .'

'Chantal. I am utterly unreliable. Irresponsible I know.' This was very difficult. Used only to defending himself, he found that pejoratives did not jump readily to mind. He tried to remember a few authentic nuggets of his wife's accusations. 'You cannot trust me,' he said with some conviction. He stopped short of calling himself a liar.

'But sweetheart, I know all this,' she said steadily. 'You are a cheat and a liar. It amuses me.'

His index finger moved up and rubbed his temple irritably. Surely she was deeply amoral. He was beginning to hate her.

'Do you remember that card you sent?'

'Klimt. Of course. Pretty wasn't it?'

'Blank. Unsigned.'

'Oh yes. Very discreet. Just as you wanted.'

'My wife found it.'

'And so? As you've just said, it was blank and unsigned.'

'She's not a fool, Chantal.'

'I don't take her for one.'

'She wrote on the back. An ordinary message as it happens. But still . . .'

'If she guesses and doesn't mind, then that's wonderful.'

'For Christ's sake. How can you be so obtuse?'

'James. What is this about?'

'What this is about is that I'm not going to see you any more. If you don't understand why, I can't help it.'

She put down the spoon which was half-filled with rhubarb crumble.

'Darling, I think all this work . . . this business of Crawley . . . it's made you overwrought.'

'It's nothing to do with that. It's you that's making me upset.'

He could have sworn that an expression of triumph almost gleamed in her eyes but thought this was probably his own paranoia.

'You always said how happy I've made you. You've said – let me quote you exactly – this is bliss. Remember? Do you remember?'

He wriggled at this female ability to repeat him back to himself.

'We've had wonderful times. I'll never forget you, but—'

'But now they're over.'

He nodded. He regretted the child's portion of dinner that he had eaten. Though little, it was still too much.

'You do understand, don't you?' he said pleadingly. 'We must part good friends.' He stretched out his hand across the table and lifted her ringless fingers.

'I understand.'

He kissed them lovingly.

'What I understand is that you'd like me to go quietly. Acquiescence is everything, isn't it James? She's such a good patient. Very quiet. Doesn't argue. Doesn't cause trouble—'

'Chantal, please. There are ways of parting. Don't be bitter.'

'—Doesn't talk out of turn. Doesn't tell your wife. Doesn't show herself in the office. Doesn't—'

'Chantal.' He thought of mentioning the word hysteria, but feared it might actually make her hysterical, which would be a pity since, so far, and this was a paradox, she had spoken softly and in a perfectly reasonable tone. Better, he decided, simply to restore her *amour-propre*.

'I'm terribly sorry. As I said at the beginning, I've got so much more to lose than you. You're a wonderful creature.'

'Am I?'

'The best.'

'Who'll be the next best?'

'Don't talk like that. No one.'

'What never?'

'I'm getting old, my darling. Too old for you, too old for myself. I shall look back on you as an icon in my youth.' Having crafted his part, he felt himself ageing into it by the minute.

'Poor you.'

'Poor me. In a month's time you'll have forgotten about me. I'll see you in the distance going about with an Olympian god on your arm and you'll introduce me disdainfully as a poor old friend of your father's. A poor old busted flush.'

'A friend of my father's certainly.' She looked at him reflectively.

'I know I'm pathetic. Can you forgive me?'

'Who knows? Let's see.'

He felt genuinely exhausted, walloped about the head now that the critical disclosure was over. Yet as these things go, it hadn't gone too badly. He thought he had reason to congratulate not only himself but her too. Indeed, despite all her cynical protestations, he felt he would soon be in a position to admire her. She was handling the breach with an unsuspected maturity. A clever girl but one who knew when it behoved her to be pliant. Perhaps after a while, they could meet in friendly fashion over lunch.

19

After its usual vagaries, spring reappeared in March when the lives of small things became busy and prominent again. Much of the fuss took place in the tops of newly budded trees where jackdaws snuggled in couples and rooks scolded over nests. Below them it was more tranquil. Violets and primroses bloomed in the hedgerows, and green hellebores faded in the woods, all fugitives from the fields where the crops grew in their traditional rotation of wheat, roots, barley and ley.

It was a nice morning and Peter Ravell left Wilf's house where he had taken some pictures of the barn owl and returned to the Stookes' estate. He did not go back to his own home but drove straight to the ramshackle and partly castellated house. He let himself in by the main door which was rarely locked in daytime and walked through the dark cool hall and up the stairs. Portraits of ancestors crowded the walls, some drawn as children before they reached adult status; but, though the hall and the corridors were fully peopled, Ravell thought that the house was now always empty. Hugh's elder brother and his family spent most of their time in London. Only Stooke the younger was to be found fluffing away here at all hours in his burrow whose walls were giving way around him. Here was a man who was in the passenger seat of his brother's inheritance and found it difficult to cope. As soon as Stooke major decided to re-exert his grip on the place, the days of Hugh's tenure, and his own for that matter, would be numbered.

He found his antiquarian landlord in his study with a map of the family tree.

'Wilf Powell tells me he wants to hunt rabbits on your land,' said Ravell. 'Pheasants too when they're in season. He has asked me to ask you.'

'What?' said Hugh.

'You heard.'

'Not now. Not when the rabbits have babies.'

'Not now. Course not. Later in the season.'

'Oh God,' Hugh muttered. 'It's all so complicated. So many conflicting interests. You see, my trouble is that I say yes to everyone.'

How little he had changed, thought Ravell, who had first come to know him thirty years before when they had lived on the same college staircase.

'You always did, Hugh. But this time it's only about bunnies so it doesn't matter.'

They stood facing one another in the middle of the study. Two middle-aged men who had the chance appearance of a pair of look-alikes, both dressed in denims and plimsolls. Tweedledum and Tweedledee. How come this uniform, although the inhabitants were so very different?

'I don't know,' said Hugh.

'What's your problem?'

'I'm no longer sure that I understand. Point one is that I'm a conservationist. I like the bunnies. I'm not like the local farmers who kill anything that moves on their land. Two. The hunt whom I still at the moment allow over my fields says that the fox population will shove off if the number of rabbits goes down. The snag here is that in saving bunnies, I'm killing foxes, but I think we'll ignore that one. Three. I like to say yes on principle to people like Wilf. Besides, point four, birds of prey must never die out. Point five? Oh yes, the shoot which perhaps I should ban. They need the pheasants. The gamekeepers think anything with half a tooth and a claw is inherently awful. What's six? Well, five's enough and where, might I ask, does this get me? All these sectional interests, and coming together to converge upon me. You see what a muddle I'm in. I no longer even know what I actually believe.'

Ravell felt a surge of not unsympathetic dismay. These were complicated issues and as a naturalist, even he too felt some conflict. He had never shot a healthy animal, nor wanted to, but he knew clearly that the countryside needed to be managed and could never be a bloodless and sentimental place. But if people like Hugh grew muddle-headed, the earth would one day fall victim to the lunacies of the animal rightists. There were times when he felt that the true natives like Powell were the only ones in tune with the land.

He sighed, but was reluctant to chastise him. 'I appreciate that as a gent you feel under pressure to oblige all sides here. There are few enough of you left around.'

'Redundant and superfluous. I shall continue to stay hid in my study.'

'Cheer up. You live in one of the last feudal parts of England. The mob isn't likely to find you here.'

'Don't be too sure.'

'Shall I tell Wilf OK? He wants it in writing. He doesn't want to be had for poaching.'

Hugh scribbled on a piece of paper and handed it to him. 'These days,' he said, 'I don't like to put anything on paper but I won't agonise about this one.'

'You weren't as indecisive as this when you were young.'

'It's a lifetime in the country that's done it. If I'd stayed on working in ICI, I'd have been different, but the land sucked me in and down. In the end it blows your mind. All I can do is play the buffoon nowadays.'

He looked so doleful that Ravell felt quite sorry for him.

'Oh don't you worry about me. How are you getting along in the stable cottage?'

'Pretty well. You know, Hugh, you should be charging me double the rent.'

'I shouldn't be charging you anything at all. But my elder brother insists that it brings in an income. I find life so complicated you see. Just sitting here and reconciling all the conflicting interests.'

Poor old gentle yielding Hugh, thought Ravell walking back to the cottage, or was it his consumption of all the 1960s LSD? Either way, it was the countryside that nourished the English eccentric. Am I, he wondered, witnessing the end of a species? The disappearance of two species, in fact, because the reduction of welfare meant that Dole Lane – the name given to a road in the village where only three of them were in work – was probably going the same way too. Maybe all that would be left to inherit these green acres of England were the smiley weekenders and thrusting newcomers in between.

Pondering the future, he walked round the gravel path towards the cottage. Ahead he saw Claire Farley about to step into her car.

'Hang on,' he called out. 'Don't be in a rush. Where are you off to?'

She paused, holding the door open. 'Just passing, you know. I've decided to put Bella down for the moult shortly. This week will be the last time I'll be able to take her for a walk. Do you want to come? To the valley beside the mountains?'

He sighed. 'I've got to go to London for the next five days.'

'Oh well. That's it then.'

'You're going to stop flying her now until August?'

She nodded.

He looked at her. He had got used to these twice-weekly outings. But of course. They were bound to finish. He had forgotten that it was normal to rest the bird during her annual moult which lasted about five or six months. She would have her food rations increased to promote the growth of new feathers. A couch potato for the next few months, she would be too podgy to want to fly.

'Of course,' he said. 'I'd forgotten.' So all this would come to an end. He would miss it.

'Well, if you can't come, there it is.'

They stared at one another. He saw that she had a smudge on her cheek.

'I could come today,' he offered.

She looked reluctant. She would have Sam with her this afternoon. For reasons she did not want to examine, she had begun to prefer to see Peter Ravell separately. The company of a dependent child was a distraction. It had its limitations. Beside this, Peter was a luxury.

'No,' she said. 'No good today.' She stood swinging the car door indecisively. The metal flashed back and forth in the light. 'You can still come and photograph her.'

'Everyone's desperate for me to take pictures of their birds, dead or alive.'

'Sorry. Am I one of a number? Just give me a place.'

'We could still go for walks together. For a change, you could come with me.'

She squinted at a lock of hair that had been blown forward. 'I could, couldn't I? That would make a big change.'

'Come in and have a coffee.'

She banged the car door shut and followed him mutely. It was the first time she had been inside his house.

'Keep out of the kitchen,' he ordered. 'It's too much of a mess.'

She peered in fastidiously and retreated from what was less than absolute mess, but still chaos. However, a spice rack and the scent of last night's cumin on the air suggested that he was not inclined to neglect himself.

'A lamb casserole,' he explained. 'A good one. I'd offer you some if you could stay for a bite but you don't eat meat.'

'I do now.'

He swivelled round.

'No need to look amused,' she said.

'Just surprised, that's all.'

She gave a small passing-off shrug. She had returned to meat a month ago. It had not been an effort of will but natural. The five years' abstinence had been an aberration, a blank phase, something to do with fading herself out, perhaps to do with James. She thought it funny that she now relished beef that others rejected.

'Why?' he asked.

'It was ridiculous.' She spoke summarily, indicating that the matter was closed.

She walked out of the kitchen and into the sitting room and looked round. It was sparsely furnished with a crimson carpet and two moss velvet chairs. There was a black iron range with an arm for a kettle to swing from and two garlanded doors on either side. It was the kind of thing that could have raised a family of twelve people. Now she doubted if it was ever lit. She walked round the room, mentally disentangling his personal belongings from the rented. On the far wall there was an oil painting, not a print, so presumably his own. It showed a field of sunflowers, all with staring faces, plants with no sides or backs. She stopped beside a table in the corner. A large whorled ammonite, three feet in diameter, lay curled up on its surface. She ran a hand over the rhythm of its flank. It was of course quite wonderful, yet it left her uncertain.

'This is a bit fashionable isn't it?' she said.

'What?' he called, then stuck his head temporarily round the door.

She pointed.

'Why?' He reappeared with the coffee.

'Because everyone has to buy a pet fossil nowadays. I shouldn't have thought you were one for the smart cliché.'

'Don't be nasty, Claire. I got it in the sixties. Is that better? Suppose I dug it up myself?'

'Ah. That would make it different.'

'Do you know something? You're such a fucking snob.'

'No.' She recoiled. 'No.'

'Oh yes. Of the ivory tower variety. Of the "only the best is good enough" sort. All women are snobs. Different kinds admittedly. There are subtle as well as coarse gradations. I should know. My wife was an outrageous snob.'

'Which variety?'

'The Swiss variety.'

'Money?'

He nodded. 'I was no longer willing to earn it.'

She stared at him. 'James wants to.'

'Lucky you.'

'Am I lucky?'

'Are you?'

She ignored this. 'I earn my own living anyway. I expect to pull my weight.'

He remembered saying to Sabine, 'Am I unreasonable to ask you to pull the ropes beside me?'

'Lucky James. Drink up. You haven't sipped your coffee.'

He watched her as she bent her head. Her briskness had gone. The droop of her neck looked pensive. After so bracing a start, she seemed to have wilted as though a shadow had fallen across her mind.

He stepped forward. The thought of brushing her hair back

from her face rustled in his fingers but the knowledge that this would be a false step made him refrain.

'Drink up. Don't look sad.'

She half-drained her cup, lifted her head and smiled. 'Thank you. I must be going.'

'Come and see me. Won't you?'

'Shall I?'

'Later. Or are you perhaps going to grow fat and moult too?' He was glad to have succeeded in making her laugh.

That afternoon she stood with Sam on the hillside and watched Bella slope-soaring in the sky, her primaries angled to the currents, wing-tips fanned out like fingers to catch the streams and save her from stalling. She floated at ease, moving across the sun, splintering the light, fading to smallness, gathering weight and size, then banking at her leisure into the topmost branches of a tree. How much this wonderful creature had learned. The boy watched beside Claire, his round face tilted upwards, into the space and silence.

'Will she remember her training?'

'Some of it, I imagine. Will you?'

'I won't forget. Never. What about you?'

'I won't forget. But you know what Mr Powell says. Within a month she'll revert to wildness.'

20

Griselda had learnt that a good office is obedient to routines, so it was normal for her to dictate letters to her secretary in the morning and to sign the finished copies in the afternoon. In the third week of March this practice began to fall apart since Sally had rung on Monday to say she was suffering from flu. A temp, or complementary worker as they liked to be called nowadays, was therefore ordered to fill the gap. However, Yasmin who came on Tuesday proved only temporary as her stamina had run out by Wednesday. Griselda ordered a second temp. 'Hi,' said Bonita, on Thursday morning when she arrived. By the afternoon of the same day she had completed five letters and put them on her temporary boss's desk.

Griselda read them but kept silent until the very last, when a degree of ill-temper managed to break through. 'Oh God,' she said 'Oh really. Honestly. Look. You've put commas all over the place. Between every subject and its verb. No full stops either. Not here. Or here. Or here.' Her finger jabbed. 'Didn't you listen when I gave the punctuation? I can't send these out. They're half-baked.'

'What's a comma?' asked Bonita who had a Spanish accent. 'And a stop?'

'Jesus.' Griselda surveyed her short pants and striped top. 'This is a literary agency, you know. I've got piles of letters and I'm supposed to be literate. Don't they teach you nowadays?'

'I've done a course.'

'In what?'

'English as a foreign language.'

'Christ. How old are you?'

'Eighteen,' said the girl sulkily.

Griselda, already more than ten years older, felt as though she had speedily acquired a further decade. At any rate this girl had shunted her into the stiff-backed ranks of the old traditionalist school. All pretence at free-and-easy manners disappeared.

'I'm awfully sorry but I'm going to have to ask you to do all these again. Well, these three anyway. They're important.'

'I just want to dance,' said Bonita.

Griselda took a look at her legs. They were long, undeniably, and had perfect thighs and calves. They made it hard to argue. If one were being a relativist, which one was not in a position to be, one would have to agree that legs like this were more important in life than commas.

'You shouldn't be doing a job of this sort. Typing isn't an all-singing, all-dancing kind of work.'

'It pays for the dancing.'

Griselda looked at her helplessly.

'Well, could you just type the one to Masha anyway.'

'What's a comma?' asked Bonita again.

'Oh forget it. I'll do it myself.'

'What shall I do for the rest of today?'

'There isn't much of it left. You can bugger off and go.'

'Now?'

'Yes. *Dansez maintenant.*'

'What?'

'It's from a fable by La Fontaine. It's called *La Cigale et La Fourmi*. It's all about the hardworking ant and the improvident grasshopper which is symbolic. In the last line the ant tells the grasshopper who has come to beg from her: *Eh bien! Dansez maintenant.*'

'What?'

'Oh God. Never mind.'

'I can just go can I?'

'Yes,' said Griselda, resigned to, even quite relieved to have a big gap in the temps for mañana.

She walked into the adjacent cubby-hole of a room where her secretary normally sat and settled herself at her desk to start typing the letter.

'Byesie-bye,' said Bonita, leaving. 'You take care.' She had wrapped a long emerald scarf around her throat and a naked thigh darted from her coat as she strode to the door with a dancer's gait, toe down before heel.

Probably find she's a star in a couple of years, thought Griselda. What do you need commas for? Quite right. It's things like commas that hold you back in life.

She typed the letter and an address label that went with Masha's contract and put it with the others in the tray for the post, then returned to her desk to check on the weekend's reading. There were two manuscripts and a synopsis with three chapters. The intercom buzzed.

'Hello,' she said.

It was Mandy in reception, a girl of random energy that was sometimes focused on the switchboard which was the actual job for which she was paid.

'There's someone here who says can she see you it's very important she says she has a synopsis and some chapters for you to read?'

No punctuation there either, thought Griselda.

'What's a comma, Mandy?'

'What?'

'Never mind, I'm busy. You know very well she can't just butt in. Tell her to leave them with a covering letter.'

There was the crackle of voices exchanging fire in the distance.

Mandy returned. 'She says she must she says it's essential.'

Griselda paused. 'Jesus, Mandy. You know the rules. Is she a nutter?' she added in a whisper.

Mandy snuffled. 'Who's normal here anyway?' she replied, getting her own back for the crack about her delivery.

Griselda hesitated. Here was an unsolicited person presenting one of the twenty unsolicited manuscripts that arrived every day, and under normal circumstances she would issue an inflexible 'no', time being money which she knew off by heart, but the day had managed to destroy all her resolve. She felt limp and exhausted, and wondered whether her shoulders were prematurely stooped.

'Griselda?' said Mandy plaintively, hanging onto the end of the line.

'Oh God. All right. Tell her just five minutes and that I'm terribly busy.' Who cares who it is? The aspirant, whoever she was, deserved to belong to and would remain amongst the ranks of the anonymous.

Mandy put down the intercom. 'She says only five minutes.' Fucking airs and graces, she muttered to herself.

Griselda got up, rolled the armchair back on its castors and brought the high-backed wooden seat to the other side of the desk to prevent the visitor settling into comfort. She guessed that the woman would have climbed her way to the first floor by now and faced a second staircase ahead. During this interval Griselda decided to arrange her face into the stern unyielding lines of the first barricade against getting published. As she did this, there was a knock at the door, though no sound of panting from which she deduced that the woman was young and fit. Most people, including herself, were a little short of breath after the climb. Another dancer, she thought to herself sourly.

'Come in.'

The door opened and a slender figure appeared, a girl of her own age, more or less. In silence the two young women reviewed one another; indeed a serious evaluation took place, which was unusual in these circumstances where it was the sought rather than the seeker who had rank.

Griselda was surprised and impressed. Though not pretty in a conformist way, the girl was swan-necked and graceful, beautiful even. Griselda, who did not consider herself to be provincial, remarked the full extent of her cosmopolitan air. She noted also that she had the confidence not to affect a smile.

She resisted the spontaneous temptation to rise to her feet. 'Sit down, won't you? What can I do for you?'

The girl, wrapped in a long navy coat, stepped lightly across the room. She looked solemn. She seated herself on the high-backed wooden chair and leant against its splat.

'I've brought a synopsis and a couple of chapters with me.'

'You can leave them with me. I'll give you a decision by the end of next week. You know there's really no need to see me.'

'I know all that. But I'd like you to read it whilst I'm here.'

Griselda frowned with impatience. Any credit earned by the

girl's grace disappeared. 'It doesn't work like that. I read material in rotation. There's a queue you know. You can't just—' she hesitated and decided to go ahead '—barge in and expect not only an audience but a reading. I've got lots of clients.'

'I'm sure you do and I respect that. But I think it would be in your own interest.'

What an amazing presumption. Well, thought Griselda, it's just one of those days. She cleared her throat. 'How very dramatic to think it's in my interest rather than yours.'

'Probably. Well, yes, really. I'd have sent it to you if I could but I knew it would be in your own interest if I saw you.'

'Why?'

'Because.' The girl looked back at her evenly. She was perfectly composed.

This prima donna with a child's answer was enough to cause in Griselda a fresh outbreak of annoyance. Lack of humility in a beginner invariably sealed an author's fate. There was no way she wanted to handle such a girl. Ten per cent, fifteen, twenty, whatever, would not cover the offence.

'Right. I think you should go to another agent. I'm terribly busy. I'm afraid I can't help,' she said crisply.

'Read it. Just read the synopsis and some passages.'

Oh God, thought Griselda. She decided to abandon her resistance. It would be easier and probably less fuss to agree.

'Here.' The girl passed the brown envelope over.

'A novel, is it?'

'Yes and no. Slightly more authentic than that.'

Griselda interpreted this partial agreement to mean a thinly disguised autobiography, self-therapy probably, the working out of a love affair, loss of some kind. She had the benefit of three years' experience at this job, enough to know that such a book was anything but unique.

'This is my second work,' said the girl. 'I've already written a novel two years ago.'

'Was it published?'

'No.'

'Did you send it to an agent?'

'No. I didn't think it good enough. I told myself to put it in a drawer.'

This was surprising self-discipline. The creature was a bit of a puzzle.

'You know,' said Griselda leaning forward to engage, 'if you want me to give serious consideration to the merits of this new one, you should leave it with me.'

'Please.'

'Suit yourself.' Griselda addressed her with frosty politeness. She opened the envelope and drew out a chunk of professionally typed sheets of paper. There was no name on the first page but she remarked a title which was *The Pattern*, more sober than expected.

'What does the title mean?'

'It reflects the fact that people in general, the characters in the book anyway, tend to conform to their own pattern of behaviour.'

Griselda picked up the synopsis and read it. It seemed that the work was written in the first person, in part diary and part narrative form. The narrator and the diarist, who were one and the same, had been witness in her youth to her father's persistent and ultimately tragic infidelity to her mother, which was to be referred to in flashbacks in the book.

This is doubtless autobiographical, thought Griselda. Her first assessment had been correct. She felt a little saddened and sorry for her visitor.

In contrast the diary sections of the book gave an account of the narrator's affair in her twenties with a middle-aged married man. There were parallels as well as contrasts to be drawn between her experience as the daughter and, later, lover of the same type of man.

Griselda put the synopsis aside, picked up the first few pages of the book and began to read without much expectation.

This is the still centre of my world, the diary where I never lie. I write my account in this simple room and trim away to the essentials. There are no falsities or façades here as there are in the outside world.

The intercom buzzed.

'I've told two callers you're busy,' said Mandy. 'Now here's Tom O'Rourke will you talk or not?'

'Tell him I'll call back.' She flicked the switch and turned back to the girl. 'Look. I can't concentrate. These things have to be read privately. Leave it with me.'

'Please.'

This was not being played in accordance with the rules. Griselda returned to the diary section, but now at random. She was too unsettled and irritated to absorb it properly.

I recall that first meeting. I recognised D.'s type at once and also his recognition of me. These things are invariably mutual. He is middle-aged and much married to a wary defensive wife. At dinner he began to show off. His eyes narrowed when he looked at me, though he is skilled enough to employ a measure of disguise. His voice deepened. His voice. It reminded me of my father's: gravelly, fruity and confident, though his way of expressing himself is more blunt.

Griselda turned the page and glanced up. She noticed the girl was watching her which made her self-conscious, but continued. She came to the end of a paragraph on the second page and, although she was reading with her attention under duress, something made her return to reread it.

'I hate to say this,' he told me one night, 'but my wife mustn't know.' I suggested it would be simpler if she did. It would be hurtful, was his response. In this, it is my experience that he is typical. Full of solicitude that is falsely applied. He can be easily tripped though I have no wish to do so, or not now. It is fascinating to be at the receiving end of this kind of behaviour.

Against her will and with a sense of voyeur's shame, Griselda had developed more than a passing interest. She turned the page.

He has two daughters as well as A., his wife. Sometimes I ask him about them, but he never replies. I have seen a photograph of the older, a girl of my own age, dark-haired wearing a check shirt and white trousers. I saw it the only time that I visited his flat, at the beginning. He secreted it in a drawer.

Griselda felt a shortness of breath. She began to flick over the sheets, not reading, waiting on alert for certain elements to jump out of the text. They had begun to assemble.

She put the page down and stood up, feeling trapped in a maze of someone else's imagination, which made her wonder whether it was her own. The girl sat watching her.

A slow burn started within Griselda. 'What is this?' She spoke very quietly. 'What is this about? Are you mad? What are you trying to do?'

'What have you recognised?'

'Nothing. There is nothing I recognise. Why have you given this stuff to me?'

'You and I have something in common.'

The weight of an awful foreboding forced Griselda to sink down again.

'I've no idea what you're talking about.'

'Haven't you? For the past few months your father has had an affair with me. I am, what? nearly half his age. Your age.'

Griselda felt terribly sick. She had a hideous puff of fear. She knew suddenly that this was far worse than anything she had imagined. This girl was spreading lies about the privacies and intimacies of her parents. The book was the product of a poisoned pen.

'How dare you,' she said.

'How dare I? Let me point out that you and I have a predicament in common. My father and yours are the same type. Persistent philanderers.'

'Get out.' Griselda picked up the sheaf of papers. 'Take this manipulative muck with you. I don't believe a word of it.' She stuffed it back in the envelope and thrust it with contempt towards her. She felt a huge bolt of hatred through her, a new feeling from which a life-long ennui had so far protected her. In that moment she realised just how much she loved her parents. 'Get out,' she repeated with contempt. 'You should see a shrink.'

'You would prefer me to work this into a full-length text and publish it without your knowledge, would you? Giving the correct names perhaps for the sake of accuracy? Think of your mother. Mine was killed in a car crash when she eventually found out.'

'You'd never get it published.'

'You can't afford to assume that.'

'Even if you did, no one would be interested.' She spoke vehemently but without inner conviction. This was not the point. Publication of such material would be utterly repugnant.

She put a hand momentarily over her eyes to try and think.

Hiding in the dark shadow of her palm, she was again over-whelmed by the temptation to sling the girl out, but she knew it would be an act of reckless self-indulgence.

She spoke slowly. 'This is akin to blackmail.'

'Not at all. There isn't the slightest gain to me. Shall I tell you what I'm doing? I'm forcing you to do something about it. Your father won't listen to me. He will you.'

'If this is true, which I don't accept, you were I assume a consenting party.'

'An initiating party, probably. In fairness to your father. And it's all over now. He dumped me because he said your mother would find out. But he'll repeat it with someone else. It's usually a pattern. I should know.'

Something, that saving doubt which is the last inner defence crumbled within Griselda. What she heard had the bare stamp of truth. He dumped me. This girl was speaking the truth.

For a moment she sat slumped in silence. When she finally stirred, the words she found were slurred. They were thick and swollen in her mouth.

'I don't understand. Why come to me? You could have told my mother. You could have if you'd wanted. Why not? Why involve me?'

'No.'

'Why?'

'I thought of it. But I didn't want to be responsible for her reaction. I judged it better if you stopped your father. Whatever you think I'm not harmful.'

Griselda's reactions were still slow. She was dazed, picking up one item after another in the sequel of an earthquake, reviewing them without much recognition. The familiar had become distorted and strange. She now turned her sluggish attention onto her father. He too seemed blurred. Why, she thought wonderingly, why him? Why had she chosen him? Was he so very special? She began to form the question. 'Why?' she started and then stopped. There was no need to ask for she had blundered into the answer. It was obvious. The girl had recognised him, she had said this in her diary, she had recognised her magnet. All people do. Perhaps over and over again.

This realisation shocked her back to life.

'Christ.'

The will to mount an inquisition rose and then choked within her. What had happened? How much had been changed in the scraps of diary and how much was true? Tell me all those minutiae that the diary is too discreet to cover. But the need to ask for circumstantial details faded, gave way to a horror of knowing them. She had been given too much knowledge anyway. To know intimacies would be to give her the same insight into her father as this girl. To make herself the knowing adult instead of the innocent child one needed to be all one's life.

'Oh Christ,' she said again.

Outside there was the sound of footfall. The light friendly chatter of a new arrival for Guy Freke in the office across the landing. The kiss on both cheeks, the opening and shutting of a door. Then a vacuum again.

'I suppose you'll try and take this . . . stuff to another agent to get it published. You'll write it.'

It would be unstoppable, oozing forth like an awful flow of bile, a contaminant.

'No. I was going to. I was full of vengeance against him. But I knew if I saw you I'd remove the need to exact it. I wouldn't need to write it if you acted on it.'

She has passed her vendetta onto me, realised Griselda.

'Do you always pass your vendettas onto other people?'

The girl was silent though her mouth moved as though she wished to find an answer.

'How do you know you can trust me?' asked Griselda. 'Me of all people.'

'I've worked it out. I know that you know that you've got to act on what I've told you. The responsibility for not doing so – for not telling your father – is too great. In any case I also know that in your position you are the trustworthy type.'

This degree of calculation left Griselda breathless. She felt as if she had been thrown across the room.

'A writer plays God with his characters. I grant you, you've gone one better.'

'You asked me if I always pass my vendettas onto other people.

The answer is no. And it's not a vendetta. Just an attempt to prevent further damage. What do you think it was like for me all those years ago? You of all people should know.'

There it came again, that insistent insinuation that they shared something. It was false and repugnant. The warped always believe they are normal, thought Griselda. She felt a violent desire to hurl her from the office, out of her life, a total erasure. She loathed her and feared her.

She stood up, the routine gesture for forcing the unwelcome visitor to go. 'I'll speak to my father.'

'When?'

'Tonight. Tomorrow. Will you give me the manuscript?'

'Here.' She passed it back.

'You know I'll destroy it.'

'Yes.'

'Do you have it on disk?'

'Yes.'

'Then what use is this manuscript to me? I destroy it but you still have the disk.'

'I'll send it to you when you let me know.' The girl scribbled down her name and address.

'What use is a disk? It could be on other disks or stored on your computer. At the very least, it's in your head isn't it?' Waiting to spill over, she thought.

The young woman looked at her with grim humour. 'What do you suggest? That I send my head to you on a platter?'

'That would be a solution certainly,' said Griselda evenly.

'Don't worry. You still don't understand, do you? I want to put things right now, not wrong. You'll have to trust me.'

I don't understand, thought Griselda. Except this perhaps, that what this girl seems to want most is power. Power over the past which she lacks, helpless in the grip of a situation. Power over other people's lives. Perhaps one day I'll feel pity for her, forgive her. Poor, dear old hopeless Dad.

'You'd better leave now,' she said. She looked down at the name and address on the note that the girl had passed to her with her long slim ringless fingers, and found it hard to suppress a small sound of derision. Chantal Saintange. Chantal. Can you believe it? Poor old Dad. What a schmuck. Not a Heather or a

Janice or a Wendy. A Chantal instead. What a schmuck. Poor hopeless old Dad.

'You'll do it?'

'Yes.'

She walked in advance of her to the door, opened it and held it whilst the girl walked through. She didn't look at her. She looked down to conceal her revulsion lest it have the effect of a goad.

When she had gone, she closed the door and sat down in the chair against the wall. It was instinctive, like an animal seeking shelter by a hedge. She put her head in her hands, sat there for a few minutes, then moved because she found she was shaking. She wanted to dissolve the shaking.

She went to the phone to get an outside line and rang her father's office though she knew it was unlikely he would be there. She left a message asking him to call her urgently. She put the receiver down and stared around, fighting an overwhelming desire to call Katy, a sister with whom she could share this terrible burden. She had lost something and needed her sister to replace it. Impossible, though, it must start and finish with her father. The need however remained. It was hateful, this need, recognisably part of the girl who too had hoped to treat her as a sister with her insinuation that they had something in common, the sisterhood of girls who had rampant fathers. My father isn't like that.

Wearily she collected her coat and scarf and the manuscript. She put her hand to her forehead which felt hot and wondered if it had brought on a small fever. Then she descended the stairs. It was late but Mandy, with a mug of coffee, was still at the switchboard. She handed her a list of calls. Familiar names and habitual routines. The rhythm of everyday life had returned: welcome, tonic and sane.

'They'll have to wait,' said Griselda.

'You were a long time with her pretty wasn't she well was she a nutter then?'

Griselda rested her gaze on one of the office cabinets in the hope that, inanimate, it would offer relief. She felt numb and exhausted. She thought of the tunnel-visioned introversion of the insane. By that definition, the girl was indeed a nutter. 'I suppose it would be fair to say she was a bit mixed-up. A horrible person really. Don't let her in again will you?'

'Don't you worry,' said Mandy. 'Count on me to give her the bum's rush. See you tomorrow.'

Griselda left through the swing door. Poor old Dad, she thought again. Poor darling Mother. Families. She read about them daily, but always as liabilities, not assets like her own, picture-book mummies and daddies. Now normal life seemed to have over-turned. She dreaded what was in prospect for the evening. As she sat on the Tube going home, a funny mix of nursery rhymes entered her head and repeated itself in confusion. Baby baby bunting, Daddy's gone a-hunting, A-tishoo, A-tishoo, We all fall down.

21

Griselda lived in Putney in a tiny house with a large mortgage although purchased on favourable terms. Part of a back-street terrace, it was reclusively positioned which did not seclude it from the throb of overhead aircraft or the drum of the main road, though neither of these two sounds disturbed her as she awaited a third which was the ring of the telephone. But several hours passed and it was not until a quarter past nine that her father returned her call. It was unusual for her to contact him and there was anxiety in his voice. He had just got in and received her urgent message twice on the answerphone. He asked what had happened. There hadn't been an accident had there?

She reassured him, damped his alarm, but begged him not to speak to her mother until she had seen him. She then picked up the manuscript and went out on this wintry spring evening to drive to his flat.

There seemed to be a traffic jam in the high street so she decided to keep to the route that ran south of the river, through Putney and Wandsworth, before turning north over one of the bridges. As she drove she realised she had no idea how she would cope with this meeting. What she dreaded most was her inability to control her own feelings. Since the afternoon, she had experienced a growing fear that she would change, indeed had already changed her father into an unknown and repugnant stranger. Her early pity had become, with delay, an anger. She felt that he had betrayed not only her mother but herself and also Katy. She hated the girl for having infected her with this sisterhood feeling. Then, as she drove north between the bright necklace of lights of the Albert Bridge, it occurred to her that she must have passed very near her flat. Somewhere out there in the darkness, this woman was also watching and waiting, just as she had watched and waited all winter.

The thought caused her to panic. Sweating, she crossed the main road and turned into a side street where she pulled the car into the kerb and stopped to regain control. For the first time she glimpsed a series of facts that she had so far managed to suppress. Griselda realised the dreadful enormity of her task. If she mishandled this evening, she could be responsible for the break-up of her family. She could be the channel through which the poison could spread. It came to her that to enrage herself with feelings of betrayal was disastrous. If she indulged in hate, he would return it. If she treated him as either a contemptible fool or an unpardonable knave, he would never forgive her and, knowing she was watching, might enact his resentment on her mother.

Griselda sat at the wheel under the sulphurous light of a street lamp and made a noise of self-pity and despair. I'm too young for this, she thought.

As the sweating eased, a great sadness engulfed her. With it, a flood of remembrance rushed in. He had been a good father and, though not one of nature's carers, he had always provided for and supported his little brood. Once, when she was small and her mother had been ill, she remembered him taking her to and collecting her from school. How proud she had been of him then, of his youth, energy and good looks. No other men took their children to school in those days unless they were house-husbands, androgynous and emasculated, tools for feminists and not real men. Another time when she was still little, she'd had a row with a friend and he had taken her aside and said never mind, when you've quarrelled with everyone, there's always old Mummy and Daddy and Katy to come home to. Later still she had loved him enough to be jealous. She remembered an occasion on a summer holiday in a friend's villa near Siena – she must have been ten perhaps – when he had paid more attention to the friend's child one day. Serafina, eight years old with brown arms, and round, peach cheeks and a fair fuzz on her back like a gooseberry. How jealous she had been. Perhaps she was still jealous. She had always felt that she was closer to him in some ways than any of them, nearer in temperament, sharing his wish to be aloof from the unreasoning and emotional demands of other people's lives. They had understood one another. Perhaps, Griselda thought sadly, I am tormented by jealousy now. She leant her left elbow on the wheel of the car and rested her head on her hand. She felt like howling for her lost childhood. A man passing looked curiously at the bent head in the empty car and faltered. His shadow, falling across the lamplight, aroused her. She lifted her head, turned the key in the engine, engaged gear and swung out.

The street where her father lived was lined with shops but they were sufficiently small and specialist to keep it quiet and sober. Only obsessives had the concentration to buy here. She parked the car and walked past the little brass signs for the dressmaker, the dry-cleaner with a warrant for fragile fabrics, the discreetly blacked-out restaurant and the jewellers to the side of the door that led to her father's upstairs flat. Glossy but itinerant, these traders were like flowers that bloomed for a while then died out.

She rang the bell and waited, the envelope tucked under her arm. She thought she must look like a lawyer about to serve a subpoena. Almost immediately there was the descending gallop of feet. He opened the door. The sight of him was in a strange way reassuring. The same slightly podgy face, the old jut of his chin, the ram-like maleness. Whatever he had done and concealed, this bloody fool, he was still recognisably the same, and still her father.

'I was worried,' he said. 'Are you all right?'

He leant forward and kissed her, rubbed her arm affectionately, and led the way up the stairs and into the flat.

In the corner the television was on. An advertisement for woodstain was finishing, to be followed by the usual brassy fanfare announcing the news. The camera made its nightly global swoop over the lights of the world and London.

He moved his dinner plate, a stir-fry packet, soy-sauced and over-cooked to judge by the volcanic smell and residue, then walked over to turn down the sound. There was a foghorn of a woman reporting an item. He watched for a second – 'What do you expect with Bosnia?' – and pressed the knob of the remote.

'OK. What's up?'

'Daddy.' She had not called him this since childhood. When she was three, she had followed him around one day: daddy, daddy, daddy.

She could not look at him. 'Here.'

She gave him the manuscript in the envelope. He took it, giving her a glance of enquiry. She looked for somewhere to sit down and went to the seat beside the desk. On her right she saw the picture of her mother gazing at her from its classic silver frame. It was smiling and happy, her fair hair blown back from her outdoors face. She felt terribly uncomfortable. She could not continue to sit there. She got up again and hovered.

'What is this?' he said. 'These papers.'

'This afternoon a girl came to see me. Chantal Saintange. She told me everything.'

His face showed no change but his body suddenly went heavy and stubborn. She could see him solidifying before her gaze.

'I don't know what—'

'Don't muck me about. I know everything.'

'I've no idea what you mean. What on earth she's said?'

'Dad, please. This is very difficult for me. She told me you had had an affair with her.'

'She's a liar.'

'Is she? She was honest enough to say you dumped her.'

He paused long enough to evaluate this. He said finally: 'I may have had a short fling but that's all.'

'You are saying what she says isn't actually true?'

'What is this? The Spanish Inquisition?'

'Please will you take it seriously. She gave me these papers.' Griselda pointed to the envelope. 'If you need circumstantial evidence.'

'This is . . . what you call evidence?' He began to leaf rapidly through the sheets. 'What is this junk? What is this?'

'It belongs to a novel she's going to write.'

'A novel eh? High drama. Well, there you are. You've lost your head. You deal in fiction.'

'Don't say that to me.'

'For all I know she may try this on everybody. Whatever she's said, that is.'

'Listen, Daddy, listen.'

She felt a moment's terror that, as a father, he would simply pull rank and forbid discussion – *amour-propre* would dictate nothing less. But oddly her instinct to beg him as a daughter proved right. The child's word 'Daddy', born of their old, immemorial relationship, lapped against him, entered him and drew them together and he quietened down as step by step she gave him an account of the afternoon.

At one point she said, not looking at him, not wanting to defrock him, 'I don't know the intimate details. She was discreet. I don't want to know them. Ever.'

'There are no details.'

A blank canvas without detail. The imagination feeds on detail. It devours it and breeds more. For each other's sake they had erased it. There would be no shape or colour.

When she had finished she said, 'Do you understand?'

James stared at her, inert. It was as though the air had gone out of him. He had been pumped up with denial but a slow puncture had set in. Bluster had given way to silence.

'I understand she played me like a fish on a line.'

For a moment he did indeed look like a big carp, his mouth working, drawing in water.

She looked at him sorrowfully. There had been something simple-minded about his confidence that he could get away with it.

'Forget the past. Do you understand what will happen? If I didn't speak to you, stop you, she said she would try and publish it.'

'She couldn't.'

'It's not impossible. Mummy could find out. Is that the way you want to risk her finding out? Can you imagine?'

His head whipped round.

'You'll never tell her will you?'

'No.'

'The bitch. The poisonous little bitch. Where's the guarantee that she won't try to publish it anyway?'

'I don't think she will. She promised me.'

'You trust a creature like her?'

Griselda's one certainty faded. 'Who knows. You don't think you should tell Mummy do you? Isn't honesty the best way?'

He did not appear enthusiastic. 'No. I don't think so. No.'

'Oh Dad.'

'The bitch.'

'You bloody fool.'

'Don't give me lessons, missy.'

'Why not? Aren't I entitled to? Look what you've done. Oh Dad, caveat emptor.'

With that phrase both he and she knew that he knew that she had moved over to his side. She had chosen to speak his language.

He stood up. 'Jesus. I could do with a drink.'

He went over to the wall cupboard and fetched the bottle and two tumblers, filled them almost to the halfway mark and passed her one.

He took hold of her left hand and led her to a chair by the fire.

'Listen,' he said. 'It's a shock to you. But you're grown up. You know how these things happen. I'm left alone too much. It's my fault, not your mother's but these things happen.'

'She said it was part of a pattern. It's happened before and would happen again.'

She found to her dismay that she had begun to cry. A silent tear dripped down the side of her nose.

He hesitated. 'It was a one-off.' Then he looked at her tears. They were more distressing, his daughter's, than any woman's. 'Oh Grisel. Please don't cry. Try not to judge me.'

'I wish it hadn't happened.'

'You don't think the less of me, do you?'

'Can't think the more of you.'

James swilled the drink round in his glass and watched the swirl of the pattern. 'I'm so sorry. I'm a fool. I've been a complete mug.'

Her pity for him returned. This must have been terrible for him. He was winded and with reason. He had belly-flopped into concrete in full view of his elder daughter. But, thought Griselda, it was awful for her too. The tears spouted afresh.

'How do you think I feel at being the one who had to tell you?' she sobbed piteously.

He reacted with briskness. 'Come on, little chicken. Don't wallow. Dry your eyes.'

She pulled out a tissue from her bag and blew her nose.

He said in a matter-of-fact, wrapping-up voice, 'One more thing. No telling Katy either. Right? It's between us, only us and it's over and done with.'

'Of course.'

In truth, she felt some relief that he had regained control and that the old understanding between them had been restored and affirmed once more. If anything this had made it stronger. He looked minutely embarrassed again. 'What will you do with the manuscript?'

'I'll shred it.'

'Give it to me. I'll do it in the office tomorrow.'

'In that case, I'll deal with the disk.'

'Peculiar practical side to this, isn't there?' he said half-smiling.

She smiled in return but the po-faced thought crossed her mind that this was no laughing matter. She wondered if she had made him take this seriously enough. Of the two, she had been and still was the more distressed. She hesitated but knew that they had passed the stage when she could raise it again. The episode and its sequel were over. The girl was in effect dead, though it was undeniable that she had achieved what she had wanted.

Griselda stuffed the tissue up her sleeve and rose to go. Feeling the need to escape the claustrophobia of the scene, James suggested going out for a bite to eat despite the fact that he could still taste the residue of his horrible takeaway earlier in the evening. Though no more hungry than he, she agreed. It was a long time since they had shared a meal as father and daughter. Later, as she sat across the table from him in a late-night café in the neighbouring road, she forked her pasta and blamed her mother for having neglected him. She had been self-indulgent. No middle-aged woman would be honest enough to agree, but there was a case that she had been served her just deserts, though of this she would have to remain ignorant.

22

The last two months had been contented for Mary which meant that they had been domestic and uneventful. Comparatively little had been going on for the Regiment and Stuart who had returned in February had been almost continuously home. Another squadron had been involved in anti-narcotic activities whilst his had remained at the base.

He continued to train as always, not only at the squadron lines but also on his own. One Sunday as she and Sam were driving into Hereford, she had passed him running along the main A465 road, dressed in his dark singlet and shorts. As the car overtook him, she had looked at him in the mirror. His pace showed no effort and his action was oiled and smooth. He found it so easy, he was even breathing through his nose. For a second she saw him as a stranger: a bloke with short brown hair, past his first youth, dedicated, immensely strong, someone else's husband. Here was a man who could kill a snake, stem a blood flow, stalk a terrorist, wield a 9mm Browning, free-fall from 12,000 feet, and also mend the loose brick in the chimney stack this evening, because he was her husband.

As he ran, he waved at Sam, pointing at him from the back of the Fiat.

Mary pulled the car into the kerb. Proud of their connection, she half wanted people to notice.

'Fancy a lift, you plonker?'

During the week he trained with his mates, organising routines that they practised over and over again, exchanging roles so that no detail could escape attention, no event ever come as a surprise. All locations must be familiar and every type of situation an old acquaintance. No crash and bang must ever find them unprepared. Detail, detail, detail; it was vital, literally so, for it could make the difference between living and dying. They used a phrase to sum it up which was: 'Train hard, fight easy'. It was indeed hard training, for even in lulls, especially in lulls, they had to keep up their strength, physical courage, and stamina. In the course of a day he might get through twenty-five rounds, all of it live ammunition and all of it shot to kill. At the end of the afternoon, and even after a shower, he would sometimes come home smelling of the lead fumes. She would sense it on his breath, in the pores of his skin. Some men smelt of garlic, he smelt of lead shot. Once she had imagined she could smell it on the pillow on which his head rested. He had told her that more than 5,000 rounds might have been fired in the single-storey house that day. No wonder it permeated his body.

'What did you do today, dear?'

What did ordinary men answer to that?

At other times they did what they had always promised each other they would do when they had the time. As the weather improved they toured round the old churches and castles of The Marches. One day he would be killing his targets with live bullets, the next he would be pacing some nave and chancel. She guessed that he relished the contrast. Her life, the wife's life, had always maintained its unremarkable even tenor, whilst his had always been hurled to extremes.

One late April afternoon when Sam was with Wilf, they drove across the county following the work of a master craftsman and his team whose medieval carving was renowned as the Herefordshire School. It was a brisk day of small clouds and showers. The fields were ploughed red and the wild cherries were white with blossom amongst the new green of larches. They went to the churches of Brinsop and Fownhope to see the tympanum, then to Kilpeck to study the famous twelfth-century sculpture on the door. The carving was still crisp and sharp. He pointed to the soldiers on its jamb, the one armed with a javelin and the other a sword. They stood under the corbel table and gazed at the tableau of medieval figures and fancies: the falcon, the wrestlers, and the gaping belly of the sheila-na-gig, a female fertility monster. Then, when they had seen enough churches, they embarked on a tour of the motte and bailey castles. There were more than ninety in the county to visit, most of them on the levelled tops of hillocks and spurs, but as Mary said, when you've seen one you've seen them all.

It was a period that she never wanted to end, though the part of her that she always buried and stilled knew that it could finish tomorrow. She had at last mastered the art of living like a dog: for ever in the present. At the beginning of May, when they had seen seven of the castles which meant there were eighty-plus to go, the squadron received the summons to go abroad. The time for indulgence was over.

'What will you do tomorrow, dear?'

What did an ordinary man answer to that?

The summons was expected but there was the usual intense rush to check weapons, kit, himself, always in that order. Mary had never expected Sam and herself to be on that list. Rather than spend the last few hours in strained silence, she drove him early to the squadron lines. It was the first time Sam had accompanied them, sitting next to Gemma hanging her tongue out in the back, a snail's trail of dribble dripping onto the seat.

'Giving me a real send-off, are you?'

She thought how happy and relieved Stuart looked to be pushed into proper action again rather than confined to the routine of training. The frustration of waiting was wiped.

'Be good,' he said. 'Don't go on the piss.' She made an outraged *moue*: as if I should. Only jokin'. Take a tease. He leant forward, kissed her on the cheek and squeezed her hand. Ruffled the boy's head: 'All right, mate?' Rubbed the dog's ear. 'OK, gorjus?' He was smiling. How wonderful to be in business again.

Vehicles were piling up all around them, delivering men and equipment. The noise was deafening, the movement exhilarating, some men sauntering, others running, the place a firecracker, gassing at a million revs, a billion decibels. In the last couple of months she had forgotten what it was like.

In the days that followed, life returned to its organised, sterile routine. The remaining eighty-five motte and bailey castles went unvisited and would probably always do so. Mary didn't want to stand all alone by some pile of stone on the antique ground. She did not want to feel historic, nor would Stuart when he returned.

She visualised him as always coming back through the door. For this reason she avoided, as she had for a long time, the church that they had not included on their itinerary. It was the church in Hereford that contained the Regiment's cemetery.

Yet one day after work, she suddenly felt the need to visit. She had always accepted, if not welcomed, the practical side of death. That Stuart had given her power of attorney. That he kept his personal stuff in a separate bag from his military kit to cause less distress to herself and his child in the case of death. That his personal effects would be checked before they were forwarded to filter anything that might upset her. A military intermediary would come between him and herself at the end for the best of reasons. What else? Maybe, too, he had already written a letter to her and to Sam to be passed to them after his death. Had he? Who knows? If he'd written, he had never said. And if the worst happened – 'drama', 'topped', 'slotted', 'ending up on the slab', all those phoney flip terms – she knew the routines as well: the visit from the family officer, the padre, the colonel's wife, they were very good, they looked after you. Good too if he was crippled, for the Regiment looked after their maimed. Men with bits missing, organs, eyes, limbs, were kept in service as long as they could. The Regiment kept its cripples, but then so too did the wife. Yes, she knew every detail of this.

And if he weren't slotted? She knew too from others the guilt if someone else's husband were crippled or killed instead. All this she knew, but it stayed on deposit and she knew that a visit to the cemetery would bring it piercingly to life, for its ghosts were their brothers. Yet, still, she needed to visit, not with the others or on Remembrance Day, but now, unofficially, and all on her own.

So Mary left the bank at four o'clock and drove straight to the cemetery which was on her route home. When she entered, she was relieved to see that the place was empty. Yet, although she was alone, she felt immediately an enveloping friendliness, a sense of family. She stood and stared quietly about her in the afternoon sunshine. It was as orderly as a vegetable garden, with headstones and graves growing in organised rows. At the side there was a separate section shaded with birches, their leaves casting lizard-skin patterns upon the grass below. Here, at the back, beside the modest entrance, was the Regiment's special plot. There was a notice on a raised slab, carved with the sign of the winged dagger and its legend: Who Dares Wins. It said simply:

22 Special Air Service Regiment
'God rest their souls.'

Outside the plot she saw an old man had appeared. He was leaning against the wall. He had a push mower, so thin and little that in the modern world it could serve no other purpose than probing the grassy nooks between graves. He had turned his back towards her and waited respectfully. His patience spoke of tact. He is waiting for me to grieve, she thought. She wanted to tell him to mow, that she was not grieving, she was learning, but she carried on looking. There were squares of stone on the wall, dedicated to the dead of the Falklands War. A wall of Falklands deaths. 19 May 1982. Twenty had been wiped out on that dreadful day when a helicopter had crashed into the sea. It was thought it had hit an albatross. Fate in the form of an albatross. Death comes not on the battlefield but in the shape of a bird. There was a slab to each of the dead, bearing the soldier's number and then below it his rank and name; and also, often, their nicknames. Name, rank, serial number, the soldier's enduring essence.

Slowly she walked round the simple plot. Almost every year someone had been killed in service. Several were killed very young: at the age of twenty-two or less. Others, also admired and since famous, had died in the Gulf War. Some of the older plaques had worn a little with the passage of time and the weather. Most were filled with flowers, but one headstone was as freshly furnished as a florist's bower; it must have been an anniversary, of his birth perhaps, or was it his death? The flowers, red and yellow, the colours of life and cheerfulness, obscured it. She remembered Stuart saying that you look at the names and say thank God, yet feel guilty that you're not on the list. The church plot was quite full, but there was empty grass where there was room for more. Who would fill it? You always visualise your husband coming through the door.

She sat on the seat under a pollarded tree which had resprouted and leaned against the plaque. It had been presented by the Hereford Branch of the SAS Association. The man with the mower felt he had waited as long as tact and understanding must require. He came forward quietly and pushed his old machine between the graves. The noise of the blades rippled backwards and forwards in a soothing engineless rhythm. It had the rocking cadence of a lullaby. All around her were messages of love and admiration, the testimony of fathers and mothers, brothers and sisters, wives and children. The next of kin gave the pledges of the living, paying tribute to the idealism of the dead.

Mary stayed until the old man had finished mowing, and then left.

Throughout these months Bella was left alone to moult. It was a long holiday of peace and plenty and indulgence during which she sat and ate and slept. No Christmas goose was ever better stuffed, for she was fed as much as she wanted and grew fat and lazy and overweight. Apart from the need to clean out her cage, no one even disturbed her. They avoided picking her up for fear of causing distress which would show in her feathers. Anxiety in a moulting hawk usually takes physical expression. Her new lengthening feathers would have fret marks, a bar or a slash of fright. Weak feathers meant impaired flight. She would be like an aeroplane with a damaged wing; a poor broken bedraggled thing with bad steerage and no useful life.

Like most hawks, she shed her plumage in matching pairs, dropping her flight feathers, the primaries and secondaries, in advance of her tail. Brown, overlapping petals, they fell in sequence upon the ground. At night, occasionally, Claire would creep past the dark cage with its roosting odorous presence and promise to gather them up on the following day. The discarded trophies were quills with fronded ends. One might be needed to replace a broken stub at some future date, a skill that was still known by the ancient term of imping. The young new feathers that the bird sprouted were tender and delicate, they grew in a sheath that was filled with blue blood. Freshly born, they were at their most vulnerable and a touch could cause them to weep or bleed. It took a while for them to become stiff and tough.

Beforehand Claire had imagined the moult would resemble a tree shedding and growing new leaves. The easy-come-easy-go of the season, decay drifting away on the wind like the senile oak leaves in winter, to be succeeded by the sap of spring. But this, this slow progression of the old and the new, was a much more effortful process. It was touchy and protracted. It was also a rite of passage for at the end of this first moult, the hawk would be declared mature. A growing-up and not just a growing would have taken place.

Liberation from the need to fly the bird gave Claire greater personal freedom too. Griselda had complained that she neglected them and she promised she would spend more of her time in London. She now went for several days or longer quite often. She organised the redecoration of the flat in whites and oyster greys. She changed the pictures on the walls. She took away the old curtains and made new hangings, sewing their sides and hems lightly by hand so that the material, a cream cotton with fleur de lys, hung in airy folds rather than with the bulk of a body bag.

Once in the evening, she saw James watching her as her needle dipped in shallow scallops along the edge.

'Why are you smiling?' she mumbled, her mouth bristling with pins.

'You cannot imagine how nice it is to see you here.'

'You see me most weekends at home.' She always called it home.

'You are part of the furniture there. Not here.'

Claire reflected afterwards that this was true. She had become a stranger to the place. So, too, she thought, had the unknown unseen woman who had sent the card. No more Klimt. No more presence. She had waved her good fairy's wand and the witch had disappeared. Of that she was certain. She had spot-checked him with telephone calls at odd times and had found him innocent. Easy, wasn't it, to have made her vanish? And yet, she wondered, how long would this interlude last? It remained in her mind merely that: an interval. She could not see it as a significant renewal. Rather that she was covering over old paint, as she had the flat. She had the feeling of marking time.

Griselda and James were not the only ones to complain of neglect. Early one evening Peter Ravell rang. Claire was sitting by the pool with Jarvis, watching the newly hatched moorchicks. They looked like tarantulas, their long skinny legs supporting bodies of black fluff. They were light enough to walk over the waterlily pads.

'I always think they're weird,' she said to Ravell.

'A bit evil, sometimes. I once saw them kill a jackdaw. It fell in the pool and they drowned it. Held it under water.'

'You and your traveller's tales.'

'I never see you now to tell you any!' he exclaimed.

She thought that he sounded lonely. With that sentence he had tried to take a step closer. She wondered whether to withdraw. 'I'm sorry, Peter. I've been in and out of London all spring. I've had the flat there to organise.'

'I know what two lives are like to manage. I had them. Remember?'

Jarvis, excluded from the conversation, wandered off. He hung his head over the edge of the water, fascinated. She saw his tail wag. How inefficient of the brain to send its impulses to the opposite end. What was he thinking? His tail quivered again. Could he get to eat them? They would be oily, rich and bony. There was a squawk of alarm from the mother. The brood scuttled like spiders to her side.

'I heard that,' said Ravell. 'What are you doing to them?'

'Nothing. I'm doing nothing. Drifting. As you warned me, I've gone into moult. Letting the days drift by.'

It was true. She felt sleepy these days. A thick seaweed smell rose from the water. It had been the first hot afternoon of the year. Algae covered the surface of the pool, cliffs of it rearing like green stalagmites from the floor.

'Or is it stalactites?' she asked.

'I don't think so. No. I think those are the ones that grow down.'

There was another silence. Not only because she felt sleepy but also unyielding.

'You're very quiet.'

'Sorry. Does that matter?'

'No. Most people, women certainly, talk too much.'

'Human beings are supposed to talk. It's the difference between us and animals.'

'I don't mean that. I mean that those who talk can't express themselves in any other way. Only by talking. Claire, look, this is a waste of time. I hate the telephone. Come and see me.'

She thought it was characteristic of him to put the receiver down abruptly. He could be an abrupt and bumpy person. He had lost the smooth lubricating patter of those who practise on each other's society, but at least the bumps were genuine.

Snatches of their old conversations came back to her, information she had gleaned during their walks earlier in the year with the bird. He was of Polish extraction. The pasts of people were often boring, of interest only to themselves, geneticists and genealogists – but not his. His great-grandmother, he had told her, had been renowned for pouring Tokay wine on the white starched tablecloth in advance of dining, so that a clumsy guest would not feel discomfited if he spilt his later. His grandfather had come to England, yet there were times when Claire had noticed that Ravell spoke as an immigrant. 'I feel at home here,' he had once said. 'Herefordshire is a twin soul to Poland.' He had explained that the farmers here were buying up the land there to run huge potato farms. Commerce had brought contact, of the lumpen and earthy sort, though he spoke of the connection as one of spirit rather than money. But then she knew as well as he that the tie with the land was not simply one of cash.

She had avoided asking him any of the important questions, the things that mattered, to do with love or money, though she supposed he did not have a great deal of either at the moment. All she knew about his ex-wife was that he had not seen her for four years. And his daughter? A will-o'-the-wisp, was what he had said. It was the only description he had given and Claire had not pressed him for more. The result was that she knew very little about his recent past. He had talked about his forebears but kept her at bay about the living. She had been willing to be fobbed off. There had been no reason to search out any greater intimacy.

Yet the thought now arose that he was pluckable, that she could do the taking and that she wanted to. She saw the way his body filled his clothes, and felt his square-backed hands and long subtle fingers. She knew by instinct the way he would touch a woman and how she would loosen to that touch. Claire was surprised at herself. Absurd, but for a moment it seemed as though she had accommodated the instincts of another person, perhaps acquired the characteristics of James's alien nature. Yet was it so odd when she considered just what she had been doing? For the last nine months she had been looking through the vision of a raptor.

She got to her feet quickly and diverted herself in the direction of the dog.

'Jarvis. Hurry up. We're going in.'

The dog, relieved from frustrated action, looked up and ran ahead of her. She saw his busy bottom disappear through the open archway of the garden door.

Griselda felt that she had taken over the role of her mother. Nothing wrong there except that she was uncomfortable about behaving like her father's wife. Once a week she had set aside an evening to see him and cook a meal at the flat. It was an odd departure since in previous years they had rarely encountered one another in London. Superimposed upon this empty background, the change of practice seemed false, but with time she assumed that like everything it would weather into custom.

This evening, as in recent weeks, she arrived laden with food which had been selected for their regular dinner.

'I'm late. Sorry.'

She started to unload her bag in the wrong order onto the wooden surface. An apricot tart, a small pot of crème fraiche, two salmon cutlets, watercress, a handful of new potatoes, one of which rolled onto the floor, a bottle of Chardonnay and a pair of avocado jellies. She had a moment's doubt about her choice. It was not the stuff of leftovers which were more appropriate for members of the same family. It was as always a very carefully chosen *diner à deux*.

James stood beside her, watching, his expression non-committal. At one point he lifted a hand which she thought must mean that he was about to join in, but he dropped it.

Finally he said; 'Don't think I'm not appreciative. You're a very good girl. But I feel as though I've acquired a chaperon.'

She went pink. 'I don't know what you mean.'

'Cream. Fraiche, too. How jolly nice. Only the kindest and most thoughtful of chaperons.'

She threw the bag in the bin. Not looking at him, she turned on the oven and ran water in the saucepan. 'If you don't want me to come, you only have to say.'

'Grisel. I enjoy these evenings enormously. I'm only sorry we didn't do more things together in the old days.'

'But.'

'There's no but. No. Well, only a small one that needs to be said.'

She applied herself to buttering the salmon cutlets and screwed the pepper and salt mills over their bland farmed flanks. She then started to peel the potatoes. She felt the need to fuss on.

'What?' she said after a silence.

'I'm waiting for your full attention.'

She turned round and stared at him. She felt shamefaced, eight years old.

'I'll say this once and once only. There's no need to do this, you know. For any other reason at all than that it's fun. What happened back in March with—' he paused to glance away, then rolled his eyes upwards in exasperation '—with her is over. It'll never happen again. I don't need to be electronically tagged. I'm sure you're old enough to know it's silly and demeaning.'

She looked as if she were about to cry. 'I'm not. It isn't,' she added incoherently.

He overlooked the negatives. 'Are we agreed?'

'Yes.'

He went over to examine the meal and could not suppress a small sigh. He felt claustrophobic and would have preferred to go out.

'Don't you want it now?' she asked tearfully.

'It couldn't be better, missy. It's terrific. Here, I'll lay the table.'

But he felt as if he'd had enough farmed salmon and emotion. He felt indeed as though he had a surfeit for the rest of his life of women and their agitations. All he needed was the deep vegetable peace of his marriage.

Exchanging the outdoors for indoors did not help. If anything it made matters worse. Claire had intended to do an hour's invigorating work but sank instead onto the settle in the darkened room where the blinds had been pulled to keep out the sun.

It was as though the curtains had been drawn against the world to allow her to close down on her thoughts.

It occurred to her that in the whole course of her marriage, she had failed to mature. The business with the card and the photograph had not been the stuff of action so much as defence. Resurrecting the flat in London was also nothing more than resistance, restoring the fortifications against attack. That was all she had ever done. Assemble her defences on all fronts. Had she ever managed to control him? Not once. What had she learned these last months? Plenty. Yet what had she done with this knowledge? Nothing. She had confined its potency to a box. She had separated it from the rest of her life. How do you train and master a hawk? You give her what she needs but also deprive her of what she wants. A perfect polar balance. Had she ever deprived James? Never. She had never controlled James because she had never threatened him with loss. And why not? Because she had been too frightened that if she threatened to leave him, she must be prepared to go.

It was not simply that loss would involve repercussions. It was also that she knew herself to be a careful and serious woman, who had been brought up in the notion of service and trust. How does one lightly withdraw from such a contract? How painful to shed old notions and acquire the new? She stood up from the wooden settle which in other circumstances was too hard to offer more than a perch, and thought of Bella. Jarvis came and pushed his blunt head against her knees. I am moulting, she thought. The old feathers are falling and the new ones hurt. They are sheathed in blood.

Ravell was making a feeble attempt to answer his correspondence. A query from his bank manager, a bill for a bulk order of film, a request from an Italian magazine requiring a self-portrait. They would feature his work in a few months' time. Unable to settle, he pushed them aside and looked round in search of a fiddly and engrossing task. He could, he supposed, mend the faulty light in the freezer where he stored his trannies. But that would fail to mop up his restlessness. Would she come? He doubted it. Too busy. She had defended herself with an agenda. He picked up the photo of himself that he intended to send to L'Airone and stared at it in embarrassment. Author's preferred self-image and it looked somewhat grim. He put the photograph down. The wish to see Claire had not left him and it made him discontented. He missed their small shared triumphs about the bird, and, even more, the sharing of private thoughts. He remembered the feel of her stumbling against him once. Last night he had dreamed fleetingly of her with desire. The reality of it still hung about him.

Although it was only the early evening, he felt prematurely tired. It would revive him to take the bay mare, Dessie, for an hour's hack through the grounds. He walked out of his cottage into the fresh new summer air. The face of the sky was cloudless, which promised a cool night, and there was already dew on the blades of the grass. He crossed to the stable to fetch her bridle and saddle and she blew him her welcome as he strode past. The tack room, which was the size of a pantry, smelt mucky and sweet, of leather and limestone, the fungoid scent of old mortar. The place was crumbling, for there was not much cash about. It was illiquid, in hock to the house and the fields and the trees. It occurred to Ravell that he could do this pantry a service by giving it a whitewash. Hugh had a generous spirit and deserved a return. I might also, he thought idly looking at the door to the rear, open up the space behind.

Thinking that even his best intentions tended to join the debris of his past, he reached forward to ease the saddle off its hook, but as he touched it, he became aware of a collective cheeping on the other side of the wall. It was faint and he could not be certain, but it appeared to be the murmurings of a family nest. He pressed his ear against the door and frowned. How on earth had they got into this windowless and in effect doorless room? It then struck him that the parents must have flown down the old broken chimney. He squeezed his shoulders past the shelves and gave the door a shove but couldn't move it. First thing tomorrow, he resolved, he would borrow a hammer and wedge. It was likely that the nestlings would need a human signpost to get out.

Dessie whinnied. 'Coming,' he called and, carrying her tack, opened the paddock gate and nuzzled the bit back against the sides of her soft mouth. Her toes chimed on the cobbles as she was led out.

*   *   *

She thought that Ravell might not be there, that he might have risen and left at dawn, but when she arrived, his Land Rover was still stationed in the barn. Claire knocked on the cottage door, once and again, then insistently. Only when she stopped did she realise that her own knocking had obscured a hammering that was coming from the stable at the far side of the courtyard.

He was breaking down the second of two doors, one behind the other with a space in between, when she traced him.

'Sssh,' he said, which was puzzling since it was he who was making the racket.

'What?'

'There's a nest here. The young are blocked up. It will be hard for them to make their initial flight through the broken chimney.'

The door suddenly hurtled back under the pressure of the wedge. There was an exhaling as though pent air had been released and a fizz of powdery distemper flakes showered downwards in small avalanches of snow. He beckoned and led her through, then propped open the door.

The nest was in an alcove halfway up the wall where two missing stones had provided a convenient hollow. Built like a skep it hung on the wall, pieced together with fragments of mud, pecks of dirt like tiny clay bricks. Three of the five chicks were perched on the rim of this doll's house, brownish with white breasts and forked tails. They fluttered but kept silent. They showed no sign of fear.

'Martins,' she exclaimed. 'How early.'

'Early but look, these ones are ready to fly.'

'I'll open the door.'

'No, wait.'

'Why?'

'They'll blunder. We've got to help them.'

He went over to the nest and held his index finger against the rim of the cup, beside their scaly toes. They appeared to debate the pros and cons. Then the leader, perhaps the first to hatch, probably the greediest, doubtless the family bully, put out his bold balletic foot. The long journey starting with a single step. A little hop and both feet were together. The chick stood there for a second, sizing up his funny new perch. His head clockworked up and down at different angles as he took his bearings, then he held still and very tight as Ravell crossed the room with him into the daylight. He moved his hand up and away to establish a travelling line into the sky. The little character suddenly unfolded his wings, tipped forward as if threatening to fall into a drunken dip, then lifted off on the same trajectory.

In turn they carried out the other two that were ready to go. The third was the smallest. Claire felt the featherweight of him settle into her hand as she walked to the door. His brothers were already swooping and arching with twittering cries in the sky. Come on in, the water's lovely. She saw the runt lift his head, his feet exerted their momentary grip as he teetered on the brink. He fanned his flying quills once, then twice and suddenly flew the nest of her hand. As she looked up and watched it join the pretty things wheeling in the sky, their freedom and gaiety entered her. She started to laugh. There was something crazily comic in their discovery of life.

'Terrific isn't it?'

'Amazing. Aren't they clever?'

There was a silence whilst both continued to look up at the pattern-making in the sky.

Finally he turned round and said, 'It was nice of you to come. Albeit at a rum hour.'

She looked confused and then brightened. 'I wanted to catch you in.'

'Well, here I am,' he said evenly. He somewhat regretted his lamentations yesterday. There must be some hormone that made one keener in the evening than in the morning after battering down two doors.

She took a breath, deep enough to be visible.

'The reason I came was to ask you if we could spend the day together and, if so, what would you like to do, but if it's inconvenient or you don't want to, say so and we'll forget it.'

My God, she thought, I am standing here humbly spouting this utter tosh because thirty years of James has brought me to this moment and I don't know how to deal with it. What does James say? Let's fuck?

There was no immediate reply because Ravell was nonplussed.

His first thought was what was he going to do with her all day? It must have shown on his face because he saw her gather herself in as a prelude to departure, although she had no hat or coat to pick up.

'Stop. Please. That would be very welcome.' Such a pursy word. He strove to correct it. 'Great, I mean.'

Claire looked doubtful, as well she might.

'We could go somewhere. Over the Cambrians. To Powis Castle. To—'

'Or we could just stay here. At any rate, I need a shave. A shower, too, after all that heaving around.

'You know,' he added, looking at her aslant, 'that little show this morning will be a hard act to follow.'

By the time he had cleaned himself up, she was sitting in the long meadow grass in the sunshine. He went over to join her. He had not intended it but he had taken care with his appearance. He was wearing a baggy shirt with a thin olive stripe, and cotton trousers.

'I thought we might go for a short ride round the estate.'

She sat up, startled. 'It's all of ten years since I've got on a horse.'

'It'll only be a humble hack.'

'I don't have a hat.'

'Pretty feeble. I'll lend you mine.'

James leafed through the brochures and read their twaddle about Zambian lions, Indian temples and Kashmir flowers. In the holiday world it seemed that the globe was divided into theme parks which were animal, vegetable and mineral – to these one made safaris, or plant treks, or trips to old stone ruins. On the last page of the pamphlet there was a picture of some people lined up by the rail of a cruise ship. A woman in a red dress with a Vee front was laughing and showing off the wrinkles of her expat neck. Unfortunately she was not someone with whom his wife would readily identify, which inhibited him from booking anything. He fretted on in search of the ultimate gesture.

He bent and picked up a few of the other pamphlets which were stacked on the floor. Their paper was art-weight and glossy. Page & Moy. Swan Travel. Abercrombie & Kent. Fine old names with which to cement a thirty-year-old marriage. Surely one of them would do?

'Jilly,' he said to his secretary who had just opened the door. 'I want to take Claire on holiday. Where do you think we should go?'

'Outward-bound or honeymoon?'

'Oh.' He rubbed his lip, a little surprised that it should be put in such stark terms. 'A bit of both, I suppose. No. Why not the latter?'

'It would be reeelly nice to try the Orient Express.' Jilly had always wanted to lean across a Pullman table decked with lampshades.

'Um,' he said weakly. 'It's not quite her style.'

'What is, then?' she asked, offended.

James thought. 'Oh God. In her present state of mind, probably Murmansk in January.'

She wasn't sure where Murmansk was, but could hazard a guess.

'How contrary,' she said.

In the grass, the hooves of the horses made a rhythmic and interlacing series of muffled plods. Sometimes together and sometimes in single file they rode along the bridle path that marked the perimeter of the estate. It was defined by a dilapidated old stone wall, but even without such a boundary, it was clear that the Stookes of Herefordshire had never looked out at the world. Instead they had stared inwards at their closed estates, their past surrounding them in tangible form. The Park had two castles, one an ivy-covered ruin, the other, within gun shot, which they still inhabited. It was in fact no castle at all, but an eighteenth century small brick building which had been subsequently upgraded with castellations and the usual stone casing. It made a snug retreat in a snug part of England which had for a long time sheltered its members against the fiercer world outside. Against the industrial agitation which had been to some extent held at bay by the Napoleonic Wars. Against the 1830s ructions and riots for Reform. And, to all appearances, thought Claire, against everything that was nasty even now.

'Merrie old England,' she said. 'You've found a pretty nice burrow.'

'One that confirms your view of me as a drop-out?'

'What?'

'Or to be precise, some monomaniac drop-out.'

'I don't—'

'A drop-out in a rented cottage?'

'It never occurred to me.'

'No? That would be the conventional view.'

'No. I think you've got courage.'

There was a silence during which the horses' hooves rustled through the grass.

'Claire. Just why did you come?'

She thought of various answers. For a moment she was tempted to prevaricate, but could not. Eventually she said, 'You know perfectly well why.'

'Do you know what you're doing?' he asked slowly.

She felt the rebuff and without talking they completed the rest of the circuit. She held herself in as they reached the stables. Ravell watched her swing down from the pony. He wished he had not spoken and now could not think of anything else to say. Yet the question had been needed. He saw before them either a mess or a fantasy that would fizzle out. Didn't she?

'You'll be a bit stiff tomorrow as you're not used to it,' he said kindly, holding the bridles of both horses in his hand.

'I am stiff and I'm not used to it,' she replied, 'and perhaps I've made a bit of a mistake too.' Backing off, she added like a polite child, 'I'd better go now but thank you for a very nice ride.'

It would be preferable, thought James, for the holiday or, at least, its destination to be a complete surprise but the wrong choice would be likely to backfire. He looked down at the options he had starred. Egypt, Siberia and the Indian Ocean. One hot, one cold and one wet.

He picked up the telephone for the third time that morning and let it ring again, but still got no reply. Frustrated, he banged it down. There was no real hurry but once something was on the agenda, he was keen to cross it off. He'd have to wait now and ring Claire at the end of the evening. He was having an impromptu dinner with Mr Aalmo, a rubber-lipped Finn who was in the tyre industry. How often, he had found, that men were prone to resemble their products.

Rather than go home Claire had spent the rest of the day researching in the public libary. Thanks to Griselda's intervention she had received a commission to knit a whole sock, namely a tome on the nineteenth-century naturalists. When at six o'clock she rose to leave, she was tired, though this was not caused by the effort of study so much as the aftermath of an aborted morning. I've made a bit of a fool of myself, she thought. Fancy exercising what little initiative I've shown, only to throw it away in the end. Well, who cares? It's only pride and pride is even sillier than folly.

So she went back and took Jarvis for a run. As she crossed the fields, she reorganised her universe into the same that it always was. Passive, enclosed and virtuous, though admittedly the latter by default. Never mind. To think in terms of a change had been a blunder and she had earned a rebuff.

By the time she returned to the house, she had manipulated herself into feeling positively relieved that he had removed a hurdle. Indeed she felt cheerful enough to celebrate what she already had. Her marriage had lasted for thirty years, nearly two-thirds of her lifetime. Shouldn't they give a party, or go on holiday or stick a milestone in the ground, showing how far they had come, and that there was only the same amount to go? She would raise it with James this evening. He had assured her he would be in tonight. Yet when she rang and rang in the evening and received no answer, the sequence of feeling began mysteriously to reverse.

'Do you know what you are doing?' Peter had asked this morning. The question had rankled. But why? The query had been more reasonable than her response. In fact, to judge by her vacillations, it was a question that demanded to be raised and not only for her sake but for his. Indeed, more for his. Only then did it strike her that in all her offended self-engrossed ramblings, she had left him out of the equation. Yet he was as stiff and encumbered as she was, not with a troublesome marriage, but with the pains of solitude. Both were walls of different kinds. He would be no more confident than she.

Claire picked up the telephone yet again and stabbed in the numbers. When he answered, she apologised and spoke simply. She asked him if he would come over but if he preferred not, she'd understand. She then took the phone off the hook and waited to see him for the second time in the same day.

Claire opened the door as soon as she heard the sound of his engine and walked over to speak to him in the car. Moths were making blurred movements in the air. It was already on the edge of darkness and she could not see his expression clearly in the fading light.

'I have to put it this way,' Ravell said simply. 'You didn't realise this morning that I was asking for reassurance. I ask you again, do you know what you're doing?'

'I can't blame you for thinking I'm barmy.'

A mixture of protest and amusement gathered on his face.

'Well,' she said, 'I didn't this morning, but I do now.'

She stood back as he stepped out and walked unhurriedly beside him towards the house. They seemed almost at ease, like an old married couple after an evening out. Instead of using the front entrance, she led him round the back of the building. A Hindu smell, thick and sweet, caught in his throat as he passed the outstretched doors of the glasshouse.

'Moonflowers,' she said. 'Calonyction.'

He looked at their blank white faces turning outwards.

'They only open at night.'

She saw his face, mocking and resigned.

'It's true,' she said.

He sighed and she put her arms round him.

'I won't ask you any questions,' she said. 'You know my situation. I don't know yours.'

He thought of saying that there were always women if necessary, but no one who mattered enough to give her a moment's worry. He left it unsaid. His was an unequal position and he would not relinquish his only defence.

They kissed each other with forgiveness, cancelling the muddle of the morning and the childish to and fro of the day. Her mouth was wide and powdery soft, her whole body laxer than expected, warmer than in his dream. He followed her upstairs, the wooden steps creaking which caused the dog to bark, and into the bedroom. Its windows were open and the scent of the moonflower had filled the air from outside.

She put a sidelight on and it shone on the washed-out, patchwork coverlet with a depression at the bottom.

'Jarvis usually sleeps here.'

He walked round, picking up her little bottles, opening the wardrobe on her side.

'What are you doing?'

He came over to her. 'Learning to see in the dark.'

He sat down on her bed, unbuttoned her shirt, and stroked her head, her full breasts and her arms. 'I still picture you in this tapestry as the lady with the falcon.'

Kindly they took off each other's clothes and pushed them onto the ground. She gasped as she felt the weight of him between her legs.

'Do I hurt you darling?' he said.

'That horse this morning. How comic. What a day to go riding.'

'Let me kiss you instead.'

He shifted down.

She leant on her elbows to watch him but the sensation was so intense that she was forced to close her eyes. For the splinter of a second she sensed the times that James must have made love to her with the mucus of another woman upon him, and the thought filled her with savagery. She drew up the man beside her in her husband's bed. As he entered her, neither spoke. The only sound their indrawn breath.

They lay transformed and entangled, not wishing to move. She rested against him.

'Do you know what you are doing?' She might have replied this morning, 'I am doing as I have been done to.' But what she felt now was a profound gratitude and affection. She stroked him with a drowsy gentleness before drifting to sleep.

Wilf was in the pub with Aggie, Joseph Jenkins and his wife and Tracy Powell's grandparents. The pub dog lay upside-down at their feet presenting its stomach for attention. Most of the pubs in the area had been gentrified with hops and menus, but not The Scully Arms which hung on grimly to its communal seat round the edge, its freehouse beer and its darts board. It was a warm July evening and the wives were drinking fruit juice, apart from Aggie who was nesting with a gin. Neither she nor the other women said much. They left talk to the men, though occasionally a sentence would erupt from one like an air bubble. For the rest they sat slumped in torpor.

''Ow's yer onions then Joe?' asked Wilf.

'Neck rot.' He shook his grizzled head. 'These things come in waves. The lettuces was bad last year, now's it's onions.'

'It's like a family, mind,' said Wilf. 'When one's up, another's down.'

'That means there's always a silver lining around,' said Tracy Powell's grandfather.

'I dunno about that,' said Jenkins who was not known for his optimism.

'True for some,' said the pub landlord who'd been listening. 'That bugger Williams has sold a parcel of his land to the builders.'

'No.'

As a collective they put down their drinks. The wives looked up. The dog, sensing attention had moved on, struggled onto its paws and walked away.

'How much?'

'Two million pounds.'

'Two million.'

'Yup.'

There was a shocked hush.

'Bugger me. I was at school with him. We sat next door to each other in class. He couldn't do his numbers then.'

'He can do 'em all right now.'

'A lottery innit?' said Aggie sadly into her gin. She had lain with Eric Williams at the age of sixteen under a hedge and, look now, how she'd ended up with Wilfie.

'None of that, girl,' warned her husband. 'No talking like that. You've had a square deal.'

'Don't you forget I was at school with him too,' said old John Powell who was a tiler.

His wife, also, looked at him wistfully.

'So near and yet so far, eh?' said Aggie to her.

The silence of mourning fell upon the women for a moment.

'Mind you,' said Wilf, 'he's not a bad sort. He's good in the pub. Some buggers won't part with it when they get it.'

'He'll part with it all right. I remember when we's young, he would go to the pub on Friday, play pontoon all weekend and come out on Monday and go to work.'

'I remember too,' said the old tiler. 'Him and me got two shillings one morning for thirty rabbits from our ferrets. *Thirty* rabbits. We never gets a better crop since for a worse return.'

They drank to their reminiscences of a time before housing estates and agri-business had taken up millionaire occupancy of their land.

'To the old days,' said Wilf.

'To the future,' said Mr Jenkins who couldn't wait to exchange his cottage in the picturesque style for a modern bungalow.

'Is J Mellors, gamekeeper, there?' Hugh Stooke shouted and knocked on the door.

Ravell got up and looked out.

'Hugh, how nice to see you. What's all this stuff about?' He screwed up his eyes. 'Hugh, isn't J Mel—'

'He is! My little joke.'

Ravell decided to ignore the reference to the enthusiastic hero of *Lady Chatterley's Lover*. It was not impossible that Hugh had seen Claire's car here recently overnight, but if so, it was cheap form to mention it. It was also surprising, but then Hugh could be unpredictable.

'What's up?' he asked.

'It's a nice evening and I thought I would take a stroll to this part of my world. Ponies have been getting a lot of exercise recently, haven't they?'

'Yes. Anything wrong? You said they needed it.'

'They do. My nieces have got bored with them. Nice of you too to put a coat of paint on the tack rooms.'

'Not at all,' said Ravell as pleasantly as he could. He felt wary. He could sense circuits were being made.

'You haven't got a drink, have you? A nice little drink. Fat one, actually.'

'Whisky?'

'It'll do.'

Ravell went back into the house and brought out the bottle from the kitchen cupboard and emptied it into two glasses. He did not invite Hugh in because Claire had left her jacket and a pair of riding boots in the hall. Instead he joined him outside and led him to a low stone wall where they seated themselves side by side. Its surface had retained the warmth of the day. In the sky he noticed a mock sun, its iridescent orange glow caused by the reflection of sunlight on ice crystals in the cloud. It was, as Hugh had said, a nice evening.

'Glug, glug,' said Hugh.

'What's up?'

'Problems.'

'What?'

'Bleeding money as always.'

'Oh,' said Ravell into his glass. It was ignominious at his age to have to expect a rent rise but then he had half suggested it several months ago.

'What do we do? Throw the house open for conferences? Hold weddings here? Turn it into a hotel? I tell you the roof's falling off. I fear the bank manager might withdraw his support.'

'I'm very sorry to hear this,' said Ravell, knowing that somehow, somewhere he would be the coda to this lament.

Hugh finished his glass.

'I don't know what they expect. We can't sell it for a housing estate or ribbon development. Not that we would even if we could, of course, hung round the neck as we are with three centuries of *noblesse oblige*.'

'It's very sad to hear this,' said Ravell, feeling his perch on the stone wall slipping away from him. Dispossessed himself, his sympathy for Hugh did not extend all the way to embrace his predicament.

'You know what?' said Hugh. 'In the old days there was a framework. The class system may have been feudal, but it worked. On the one side there was a sense of responsibility and on the other side gratitude. You see? Matching pairs. No longer of course.'

'No,' said Ravell, not really wanting to be cast in the grateful half.

'Anyway, the fact, old mate, is this. My brother says we've got no option but to sell this cottage so we can pitch the money at the bank.'

'I see. How long have I got?'

'Perhaps a couple of months. I'm dreadfully sorry.'

Ravell regretted the coat of paint that he had put on the tack room. It was petty of him, he knew, but he didn't care.

'Aggie, now don't you go playin' the lady of the manor. You had your chance and you missed it.'

'I says nothing.'

It was true. Aggie had not uttered a word since leaving the pub. They were now driving home in the bright blue Hillman Imp. She sat looking out of the window, her large hands folded in the lap of her flowery frock.

'You says nothing in a big way. Anyone can see it, you got the hump.'

She pushed forward her lips into a tight little bud of disapproval. 'I always liked a big an' hairy man, didn't I? Nothing new about that.'

'I tell you something, mind,' said Wilf. 'I may be short an' bald, but I saved you from sprout-picker's wrist or have you forgotten about that.'

'What?'

'You think you was such a grand town girl from Evesham, but what did your family do? They picked the sprouts in the fields. Very grand, I'm sure. You told me. They all had trouble with their wrists.'

Aggie looked at her hands. 'Don't you say anything about my family.'

'I'm not. I'm talking about you. You're a whingin' old nag. Could 'ave been rich. Grass is greener, eh? Just like sheep, wimmin, always wanting to find a hole into the next field. No better than Claire Farley.'

'And what's Claire Farley done?'

There was a short pause.

'Nothing most probably.'

'Why you mention her then?'

'I wasn't going to mention her.'

'Well you have.'

'So I have.'

'Well then.'

'Well, nothing.' He looked momentarily flustered. He was aware her eyes were skewering a pair of holes in the side of his face.

'Wilf.'

'Olright then. She's having a dance with Peter Ravell.'

The fresh air of gossip blew away the sulks. Aggie brightened up visibly.

'Who told you that?'

'I sees her car there all night when I went with the ferrets.'

'Where?'

'Outside of his home.'

Aggie reflected for a moment. They passed a troupe of guinea fowl pecking in the verges beside the house on the corner. She gave a little wave to Charlie Jenkins who was scything the grass. It diverted his attention and he nicked one of the chequered tail feathers with his blade.

'Oops,' said Aggie, wagging a ginny finger out of the window.

'I shouldn't have told you,' said Wilf, frowning.

'I'm your wife.'

'You won't say anything.'

Aggie sighed. 'Don't you trust me?'

'No,' said Wilf doggedly. 'Not in your cups. You shouldn't drink gin.'

'Well I promise. She's a good sort. I don't want to do her harm.'

'These things come and go,' replied her husband. 'When you're a caretaker you sees a lot of it about.'

'A bit philosophical innit of you, like?'

'That's me, Aggie. You didn't marry a rich man or a sprout-picker. You married a philosopher.'

They had reached home and he turned left into the concrete apron of the passage beside their house. As he switched the engine off, Aggie pushed her car door open as far as it would go beside the chain-link fencing to their garden. As always there was only about a foot's space for her to squeeze by. The alternative would have been for her to get out before he turned and help him push the car in. She sighed again. The news this evening about Eric's fortune had put these indignities of everyday life into a different perspective. It had made them prominent and offensive.

She looked across to Mr Jefferies' half of the house. She could see his flat cap above this summer's wall of fuchsias. He was training the largest into an agonised standard. He avoided catching her eye but the little Jack Russell was staring at them with its usual belligerence, its legs planted at the corners of its body like struts.

'Not long enough to run around on,' said Wilf contemptuously.

''Ow much do you think we could get for old man Jefferies' house and his garden?'

'We don't own it Aggie.'

'But if we did.'

'But we don't. We don' even own ours. And even if we did, he's not gonna drop down to please you and just die.'

25 ∫

They were not due to pick the hawk up for flying until mid-August. Meanwhile the early days of the month were the quiet time of summer in the countryside, the lull between spraying at the beginning and reaping at the end. The big yellow combines crouched at the entrance to the fields, awaiting their turn at the grinding round. In the stillness, the acres of corn exhaled a harvest smell of dry and seasoned ripeness. Pigeons flew down to peck at the seeds and here and there the stalks parted, mice or rabbits perhaps foraging at their base. But their days of feasting were numbered. By the end of the month, most of the crops would be culled, leaving a stubble carpet over the land.

James came home for a holiday. The honeymoon abroad had been deferred; in any case the destination had not even been chosen. He remarked on his wife's absent-mindedness, to which she replied with suitable vagueness. She resented this fortnight he had stolen from Ravell, especially since the days of convenient loving would soon be over. After he moved, it might not be so easy. 'When do I see you again?' he had asked. 'Be patient,' was all she could reply.

Once they had bumped into him at a lunch party.

'And who was he?' asked James on the way home. 'I had the impression he was following you around the garden.'

'Who do you mean?'

'The stocky dark chap with the lop-sided grin. You were talking to him at the beginning.'

'In the striped shirt?' Claire said skilfully.

'Yes.'

'The bird photographer. Remember?'

'Oh, him,' and he ceased to take any further interest.

This dismissal was a relief but also an insult. It provoked a ferocious rebellion. The following afternoon Claire slipped out for two hours which she spent at the cottage.

Ravell watched her dressing and said: 'I hate all this furtiveness. What would happen if you told him?'

'Please, Peter, be patient,' she said again.

'I can't hang on his comings and goings.'

'I know.'

'Look. There's something I want to show you.'

'I can't stay.'

'I've found the picture. Wait a moment.'

He pulled on his shirt and jeans and walked out of the bedroom. When he returned he was holding a book.

'Here,' he said, jabbing at one of the pages with his finger. She went and stood beside him, examining the reproduction of the medieval Arras tapestry that he had often mentioned, *The Lady with the Falcon*. Indigo, buff and russet, it showed an embroidered universe of trees, flowers and rabbits. A sad-faced, seated lady on the left with the hunting bird on her gauntlet and a little dog jumping up at her feet. On the right, a stern nobleman with something in his hand.

'It's not called *The Lady with the Falcon*,' she said. 'See? It's called *Offering of the Heart*.'

'That's irrelevant,' he said, and closed the book.

'What did he have in his hand?'

'Did he?'

She prised the book from him and leafed back to the picture. 'Oh,' she said, both pleased and horrified. 'He's holding a little red heart.'

'Is he?'

She looked up, slightly flushed.

'Claire.'

'I know why you shut it. You're afraid I'll get carried away by this, aren't you?'

He sat down on the bed and put his head in his hands. 'You always think of yourself. I'm not in a very pretty position, you know. No house, and on the edge of your life.'

She put the book down and folded her arms around him,

pulling his head against her breasts. Neither had oppressed the other with the word 'love'. At the end of the twentieth century its presence was too suspect and disruptive. But in the five-hundred-year-old tapestry, it was shown – albeit in courtly fashion – naked and without subterfuge. A small red heart held in the right hand: simple and childishly open.

'I shouldn't have shown it to you,' he said.

'What difference does it make whether you show it or not?'

For the last couple of weeks, the fat lady, as they called Bella, had been put on a slimmer's diet to bring her into hunting form. Delicately, with quarter of an ounce precision, her quantity of food was reduced. It was fit for rope-walkers, this anxious and skilled operation. If they failed, she would not realise her potential. If they overshot, she could go sick and even die. They knew too that even when bonny and slim, she would be unfit, and also, as Wilf had predicted, pretty wild. Picking her up was a replay of the first time. The torrential tantrums, flying upside down from the glove, open-beaked to bite, wings spread in tense flight, talons slashing at the end of her powerful shanks.

'Bit chopsy, ain't she,' said Sam.

'Isn't she,' said Claire, correcting rather than expressing agreement. She did not in fact know what he meant. 'Means she talks a lot,' said Wilf. 'Another whingeing old nag.' Though this left Claire none the wiser.

Yet the temper was not as bad as it seemed. For like all repeat frenzies encountered for the second time, it failed to convince and it would only be a matter of days before Bella, too, recognised it as a fancy pretence.

Knowing this, Claire savoured her new slim beauty the more for its wildness. They had brought her successfully through the moult and her fresh quills were strong and true with no fret marks or traces of hunger or anguish. Indeed, there were fantastical moments when the hawk hunched her feathered shoulders high, pressing their musky softness back to back, so that she seemed to have grown angel's wings.

When she was used to them again, they coped her, filing her beak and talons. It was as lapidary a job as a jeweller's. The boy placed a cushion under her breast whilst Claire applied herself to the detail. The clipping and filing, the cutting and buffing of gems. She moistened her finger tips and polished the scimitar bone of her beak. From close to, there were little hair feathers around her lower mandible whilst the festoon on the upper was curved. The bird's nostrils were flared and her large hunting eyes watched them, dark and liquid. How exquisite this detail. A work of art, infinitesimally evolved in all its stages, part of the long endless stream to perfection. Detail that endorsed the mindless powers of natural selection. Later she looked up what Darwin had written in *Origin of Species*; 'I can see no limit to this power, in slowly and beautifully adapting each form to the most complex relations of life.'

Johnson was dug out of the attic and they repeated the dummy bunny and the dead-rabbit training. At one point it seemed as though they were going nowhere, then suddenly Bella began to remember. When Johnson jerked she pounced. As the pheasant lure swung, she met it in the air. She went to the post in the paddock, then her favourite branch on the little hawthorn. Then the ash, then the old oak. She remembered the walks, and when they called, she came: the three-pronged whistle, and the chime of her dual bells in reponse. The two sides had renegotiated to trust one another again. All that remained was to make her fully fit through a tight diet and exercise. She was in her second season, her voice had broken, and she was luxuriantly feathered but firm; she deserved to be flown in peak condition to show off her matured powers.

A month after they had picked her up, they drove her to the foothills of the mountains. It was a perfect autumn day, golden, and the air was stinging and clean and so clear that the gilded sheep at several miles distance could be seen speckling the pastures of the green lower slopes. They lifted the bird out of her travelling box and Sam carried her on the fist as they walked up the slope. Far away beneath them, they could see a few brave farmsteads, outriders from the last small settlement, but there were no other human beings around. This spacious world belonged to themselves.

As they climbed the hill, they released her, casting her into the breeze. Her great wings spread and she rose forwards at speed. They watched her climb on the ropes of the thermals, then soar, quartering the land in sublime mastery of the air. For a little while she cruised, then stopped. There was a west wind and they saw her facing into its gentle resistance, hanging in lazy stillness as though she had found a perch in the sky. Her finger and tail tips would be adjusting with delicacy to the currents: fanning its streams to allow her to rest motionless in the air, setting about her patient and calm business. She waited in the huge blue dome as if on the branch of a tree whilst she scoured the baked furlongs of the land. No rabbit or bird could flee her searching high-altitude eye.

They had intended to work the ground, hoping to flush her prey from cover. Instead they watched helpless, in the spell of a trance, held in suspense by the floating ease of her display. Then suddenly, without warning, they saw her crank over and jet earthwards, wings pressed against her body, hurtling down with the thrust and speed of an arrowhead. Her watchers looked at one another without speaking, then, called by her chimes, picked their way over the grass to where she had dived into cover. They found her, a Tartar over her limp dead rabbit, one talon pinning him down, a few beads from the bracelet of entrails drooping from her beak. She turned her head to look at them with her impassive, indifferent eye. Again Claire was awed at how perfectly the predator had been adapted to her prey.

Later that evening, she leafed through her *Origin of Species* again: 'Thus the grand fact in natural history of the subordination of group under group which, from its familiarity, does not always sufficiently strike us, is in my judgement fully explained.'

The cottage which Ravell had rented had not yet been sold, though the builders had moved in. They were doing it up. Most days he rose at dawn and was out a lot to escape them. He was spending much of his free time and several nights during the week at Claire's. They were being sucked into one another's lives, which was making her jumpy and nervous. On one weekend James found an old blue shirt belonging to Ravell in his wardrobe.

'What's this?' he said. 'Not one of mine.'

'Oh,' she replied. She paused. 'Sorry. I bought it ages ago. I must have stuck it in your wardrobe after doing the washing.'

'Size 42 chest? Menopausal fatty are we?'

'I like something cool and roomy when I go out with Bella.'

Afterwards, Claire thought she was a pathetic and cowardly liar. Stupid too. Where was the point of depriving him if he didn't know it? He had every reason to think he was still in possession of what he had lost. Yet in another sense, he was so even-tempered and equable at the moment, so husbandly, that she was the one who felt threatened with loss. She hovered between two needs, wanting both of them. She now knew exactly how James must have thought. Say nothing and avoid the consequence. The bird uses the thermals, hovers motionless in the sky, making feathery adjustments.

She gave the shirt back to Ravell. It was evening and she found him packing. Clothes, photographic equipment, tent, riding gear.

'I'm off for a fortnight.'

'Why didn't you tell me?'

'What's the point?'

She felt a choke gathering in her throat. 'What do you mean?'

'I mean, what's the point in telling you I'm going away on a trip when I'm going to have to move, as it is. Probably out of the district. We'll fizzle out anyway.'

'No.'

'What do you suggest? That we grow old together?'

She filled her lungs with a breath. 'We agreed to live in the present.'

'We did but the present is drawing to a close. I can't see you driving miles to meet me.'

'I need you.'

'Do you? Doesn't this thrive on convenience? I was to hand, wasn't I? In affairs, the race is not to the swift but to those who live within a radius of ten miles.'

She felt weak, robbed by his cynicism. 'Why are you saying these things?'

'Because my moving isn't the only reason things are coming to an end.' He was folding a shirt with great deliberation.

'What else is?'

'Don't imagine our little encounters have gone unnoticed. Hugh made a reference to your visits to me' – he avoided

Hugh's boisterous analogy with Lawrence's gamekeeper – 'so too did Wilf yesterday about mine to you.'

'Wilf? He's said nothing to me.'

'Wilf is one of nature's gentlemen. He said to me, delicate like, as he would put it, that it might be a good idea if I put my car behind a bush at your place. Better not to give people things to talk about.'

Ravell snapped the clips of the case shut and threaded the buckle.

She flushed. 'It's no one else's business.'

'You're naive.' He picked up the case and took it to the door. 'The fact is this. If you don't tell James, someone else will. So you see, it's coming to an end.' He looked at her, testing.

She went to the window and stared out. On the road beyond the drive, straw had spilled from a lorry. Straw, grass, people who grassed. She saw the long poisonous trail.

'I'll tell him.'

'Do you know what you're doing?'

Claire said sullenly, 'You're in the habit of asking me that at key moments.'

'Do you?'

'I was going to tell him anyway.'

He said nothing.

'Where are you going?' She spoke so as not to remain on the same spot.

'About a hundred miles north west. To the big fields and the moors. To a friend. Horseback hawking at rooks. I'm photographing.'

He heard her draw breath. 'Let me come for a few days. I must come. Please.'

'You like me very much now, do you?'

'Why do you use a word like "like"?'

'Claire, what other word should I use?'

They arranged that she should drive north to join him the following week, but the weather turned bad. An equinoctial storm blew in and carried a mist that reduced visibility for days. It was not until Thursday that it cleared. She left at once and arrived in the evening.

It was a solitary huddle of crofters cottages of spare comfort for human beings and luxury for the falcons. Claire was given an ardent welcome from two pointers and a cordial one from their owner, a big loose-limbed falconer called Stubbs. Before supper he took her to see the birds. They were tethered in the evening sunlight outside their cages surrounding the four sides of a yard. One screamed and the rest looked up with their intelligent intense eyes. Stubbs pointed to the one they would take hawking, a large long-shanked falcon, a cross between the peregrine and the saker, favoured by the Arabs.

The following day they saddled their horses and left. She had been given Hopkin, a sturdy bay cob of equable temperament, and was riding on the offside of her host. To her right the bird stood poised on Stubbs's fist, her small cranium shrouded in the tufted exotic hood from which her nostrils and the scimitar of her beak jutted out. She had won a reputation for skill, tenacity and acrobatic power. It was a clear light as they rode quietly along into the slight but steady breeze. After about half an hour the country began to change shape and colour. This was land marked by the upheavals of a pre-human age, where fields became a vast moor of leaning irregularities. Its terrain of faded ling and tufts of spent turf offered no cover. There were few trees, no hedges, no buildings. They rode in isolated silence. Just the scuffle of hooves in the thrifty grass, the odd jangling of the bit and, once, the rush of cold water through a thin runnel. All three of them scanned the sky.

She queried a pair of black birds on the ground. 'Crows,' said Stubbs. 'They'll pickaxe her.' Then a few minutes later he raised his field glasses to his eyes. 'Do you see?' he said quietly. She followed the line of his hand. All she could see to the west was a quartet of black pock marks in the sky. Immediately he drew on the horse's bridle to change their direction of approach. It was apparent they would be coming from the east so that the falcon could head into the wind. In doing this they passed a couple of rooks within range on the ground but the hood remained on the bird and the bird on the fist. They began to approach with stealth. The horses conveyed an expectation, their ears pricking back and forth. Then – they were about a hundred or more yards from the rooks – he slipped the hood off the bird. Unveiled and dazzled, she paused for a moment, saw as they saw, reflexed, lifted and hung, then bulleted herself forward into the breeze.

The quartet of rooks bursts forwards and upwards. The falcon starts to overtake, she climbs the air, the rooks in panic begin to lose touch and splinter one from another. She singles one out. Ringing upwards, her great wings row her higher, reaching for the point from which she can make her brilliant deadly vertical stoop. The black bird twists and surfs beneath her, weaving on the wind as it has never done for its life. It rises, she rises too in a higher spiral, they ring up together, pushing into the remote wall of the sky. They are yoked on a single vertical leash. She mirrors its movements, then stoops. It is a feint. She stoops again, another feint. She can yo-yo him as she likes. The rook bobs, a cork in the air and begins to plunge round in confusion. The others are too terrified to mob. She rises again and there it is, the moment of the final killing stoop. She hurtles down, hits him with her feet. He plummets beneath her, struggles level as she rises and like the head of a mallet plunges back. The crack of their meeting explodes over the moorland as they spin in a final somersault down to the ground. The dead in the arms of the living, but hunter and hunted perfectly matched in fair flight. Seconds later the other rooks are zooming in screaming circles around.

It was by means of these cries that the cantering riders found her. The chase had taken the birds over a distance of more than a quarter of a mile. The falcon had the rook pinned on the turf. A little pitcher of black feathers spread out in a stellar burst on the ground. Only its sword head and its long feet, elegantly drooping in death, were intact. The falcon was standing in a blanket of plucked down. She was already feeding up on her kill, its blood scarlet on the black feathers stuck to her bill. Reining in their ponies, they stood a little way off and quietly watched her going matter-of-factly about her ancient Babylonian way of life.

26

James had come home late on Friday evening to an empty house and a note on the kitchen table. 'Will be back some time on Saturday. There is half a lamb casserole in the fridge plus veg. *Don't* eat plum tart. Use fresh fruit in dining room for pudding. C. P.S. Sam is feeding bird and dog, but give J. four biscuits in morning.' He read these instructions with displeasure, then some anxiety at their irksome deviation from the norm. No explanation, no wifely regrets for her absence, no sending of love in recompense. Disgruntled, he cooked his meal and helped himself to half the plum tart.

The following morning he rang Griselda, his father-in-law and Mary but no one knew where or why Claire had gone. He was puzzled. In the course of their marriage he could not recall a single occasion when she was missing without reason. Like a mother, her place was always there, for he could rely on the fact that she was as much of a mother to him as a wife. In a bad temper he went out and looked at the hawk. 'Ruffled feathers?' he asked. 'Me too.' He could visualise a whole day just wasted in hanging around. He would have liked to play a round of golf but there was no answer from the Milners and he didn't fancy a snap unplanned match with anyone else. In the end he took out the tractor mower and chugged up and down, which is what he would have done anyway if his wife was present but somehow her absence had robbed it of heart – though it was a mystery that these activities should be about people as much as grass.

For lunch he opened a tin of tuna and ate the remainder of the plum tart. Then, feeling guilty that he had rejected the healthier option of fruit, he took Jarvis out in the fields for a walk, though neither of them wanted to go. They escaped back to the house with relief. James looked round for the next thing to do. He realised with surprise that he had lost the simple rules of domestic conduct without her. At this point he decided to give up trying and went upstairs to fall asleep.

He was woken by the noise of rapturous dog. He looked at his watch which showed a quarter past five. Christ, he had slept for over two hours. Slightly jet-lagged, as always after the abnormality of an afternoon sleep, he called croakily; 'Is that you, Claire? I'm in the bedroom.'

He heard a couple of doors bang, then the creak of the wooden stairs. Jarvis crashed in and jumped on the bed. He went at once to the asylum of his allotted nightly patch. Claire appeared at the door. She looked tired and her hair was tangled. She stared at the pair of them without welcome, as though they were strangers.

'What are you doing here?' she said.

'Me? I've just had a snooze. Where on earth have you been?'

'I've been away.'

'I know that. No one knows where.' He swung his legs over the side of the bed as the adrenalin of a justified grievance reached them.

'I've been on a trip to Wales.'

'Doing what?'

'Rook hawking.'

He was bewildered. He was not quite sure what she meant, but this was not of great importance. She had got up to some funny things this year and he had the feeling that she had turned into a person he did not know.

Finally he said, 'On your own?'

'Actually, no. We were taken by a man called Stubbs.'

She came to sit at the foot of the bed beside Jarvis. She put a hand on his monumental flank, seeking stability. She was intensely sober.

They were now sitting on opposite sides of the bed, their bodies facing away from one another. James had to swivel round to look at her. Her demeanour made some small unnamed part keel over within him.

'Who's we?'

'I was going to tell you. Peter Ravell. The photographer.'

He sat very tensely. Then stood and walked round to her side of the bed so that he faced her. She did not look at him.

'You were going to tell me what?'

'I've been seeing him for some while now.'

He stopped breathing. A stone had entered him. His lungs were too rigid to breathe.

'You've been seeing him. You mean you've been fucking him?'

He heard him say the ugliness in someone else's voice. He wondered if he was dreaming almost, still the afternoon sleep.

'If you want to put it that way,' she said.

'It's impossible.'

'Why?' Claire looked up at him for the first time. He recognised defiance. It was undoubtedly true.

'Because you don't do these things.' He was shouting in his own voice as his lungs suddenly began to beat again.

'I don't and you do, you mean.'

'What I mean is, you can't. If you did, if you do, it would be serious.'

She looked stunned, then broke from her leash. 'You bastard, you fucking bastard. All these years. You supposing that I'd sit and take it for ever. I've waited it out and now it is serious.'

His mouth opened, began to form a circle as if to say no, then stopped. He sat down abruptly to support himself against this tide of fury.

'It's not, you know, really serious is it?' He could hear the word please in his voice.

She said nothing.

His head trembled. He resolved to hang onto himself. 'How long exactly has it been going on?'

'We met before Christmas.'

'But it?'

'A few months.'

'Where do you see him?' He did not want to know but the probe was compulsive.

'At his place. Sometimes.'

'Here? Sometimes?' He did not want to know this either.

She paused. 'Sometimes.' She saw his Adam's apple bob as he swallowed.

'In this house?'

'Yes.'

'In this bed?'

She did not answer.

James rebounded off the bed as though it were poisoned. His hands lunged and she thought for a moment that he might strike her but he contained the violence by grabbing her right wrist in a strangling grasp.

'Is that a substitute for my neck?' she asked piteously.

His grasp loosened. He groaned. He removed his hands and put them over his face. 'How could you,' he said again and again.

'I could because you did. You showed me the way.'

'Not like this. Never like this. You left me alone in London.'

'How many has it been, James? How many over the years?'

'A few. Nothing to speak of.'

'Ten?'

'No. Never.'

'More?'

'No. No one who ever meant anything. I've been lonely and bored.'

'You were treacherous.'

'Not like this.'

'This? I've told you. Voluntarily. More than you ever did me.'

'You lied. *Suppressio veri*. It's the same thing. Worse. You set up a camouflage. How clever. How you must have smirked.' He remembered her description after the lunch party: you mean the one 'in the striped shirt?' He wanted to kill her again. He wanted her to tell him it was all over.

She was still talking. 'And how many lies have you fed me over the years?'

'It's finished now.'

'Yes? I was a fool ever to believe you.'

'It's true. It's because—' but he realised he could never explain to her how his spells of philandering had ended. That business with the girl had been too awful.

'It's over,' he said sadly.

They sat in silence. A fleeting pain squeezed a muscle in his upper arm. Jarvis who had opened an eye once or twice at the turbulence caused to his mattress began to snore.

'I'm so sorry.'

'For what?'

'For what I've done.'

'Too late isn't it?'

'It's not too late.'

'It is, James. I've had the sinner and the prodigal son once too often.' She felt no pity for him nor wished to. A splinter of cruelty that she had never known to be within her allowed her to watch and relish his pain.

He stood up, compelled to action. 'I'm going to see him.'

'He's away.'

'Oh sure,' he cried out at being baulked. 'Heroic, isn't he? Lover runs away before husband. How fucking heroic.' But the look on her face warned him at once of his mistake. Her nature was dogged and loyal to a degree. If he insulted him, he would force even those basic loyalties that remained at home to make their final switch.

'Claire,' he said eventually in more subdued fashion. 'Just, please, don't do anything rash. We'll talk this over.'

The remainder of the weekend continued grimly. They did not talk it over. They ate at different times and slept in different beds.

'We can't go on like this,' James said on Sunday, but she walked out of the room. He asked her to describe his rival but she would not do that either. She would not talk to him about anything. It seemed she had clammed up utterly. In this way they passed the day in silence. Later, in the afternoon, he said to her; 'This place is a void, a shell, if we don't talk to one another.' 'I know,' Claire replied, 'but not now.' It was meagre comfort but the knowledge that this was finite was enough to steady him a little. Some of his equilibrium returned. It struck him that perhaps this whole business was an inflated gesture on her part, a mere feint. It was her 'turn', as it were, and she had taken it with a vengeance. In time he could not believe other than that it would all blow over. It had with him, so surely must with her. Their relative positions would then be judged by her to be squared.

Yet his spontaneous first reaction returned to haunt him. With Claire, it must be serious. As the time came for him to depart, he grew nervous and fearful again. He would be leaving her alone, beyond all control. One man's influence over her would ebb with the other's flow. A sort of panic returned. On Sunday night he decided to ring Griselda.

'I don't believe this,' she said when he explained. 'My wayward parents,' but he did not laugh and she didn't find it funny either.

'For God's sake, come and talk to her. She won't listen to me. Cancel whatever you've got tomorrow. For pity's sake, Grisel. You know how stubborn she is.'

Griselda arrived early on Monday morning having left soon after dawn. She found her mother hosing fresh water into the hawk's bath.

'Oh Mummy.' She remembered going to see her father on that cold dark night in the spring. To her horror she burst into tears. It struck her that she was always the one who cried whilst her parents remained dry-eyed.

Claire put her arms round her. 'He shouldn't have asked you to come. It's a wasted journey. No one else can interfere.'

'He's terrified you'll leave him. You mustn't go. I don't think you realise how much he needs you.'

'Don't I?'

'He depends on you completely.'

'He needs a bunker. We all do.'

'You've been together for thirty years. It's your bunker too.'

'Dearest Grisel, you really don't understand what's going on but I know you mean well to try.'

'You got married because of me. I can't let you drift apart.'

Claire looked at her elder daughter's face. She remembered her as she had first appeared. A little black wet thing. Now a grown-up single professional, though not as secure as she seemed. She and Griselda had never had much in common, but here she was, fighting to keep her parents together.

'Oh God,' she said. 'Oh God. If you could only understand.'

'But I do understand. That you're willing to threaten Daddy and us because you have fantasies over some crackpot man.'

Claire surveyed Griselda with much sadness. Her daughter's face looked drawn and wintry. 'Does that sound like me?'

'No. I don't understand, as you keep reminding me.'

'I'll tell you.'

She took her into the kitchen where she made two mugs of coffee and then walked to the back of the house and they sat down on the seat overlooking the cobbles.

'We got married, as you say, because of you. Thirty years ago. I was twenty-three, he was twenty-two. Very young, wasn't it?'

'By today's standards. For people like you.'

'By yesterday's too. For our sort of people. It's worked in its fashion. But all the way along he's had other women. We've only ever talked – rowed, that is – about a few of them, but I suspect there's been a number of others. Ten, maybe more. He denies them. Who knows? Thirty years is a long while.'

She got up and started pacing around. She didn't look at Griselda. 'There was one after Christmas, I know. It'll only be a matter of time before there's another. For years I told myself it was his little weakness. Like a gammy leg or something even more fundamental, a bad ticker, say. Wives learn to live with their husbands' frailties, wonky legs or whatever. But over the years it's crushing. The accumulation is crushing.'

Claire put her head back, inhaled deeply and then blew her breath out like a smoke ring towards the sky. 'I still care about him, you know, which is not uncommon in these situations because one does because one has always done so. You're too young to realise that caring is very much a matter of habit. The years, shared things, memories and plans, the fact that we've formed one another, you, Katy, they act like cement. Besides, he's a decent man, generous and basically kind. I recognise that. I'm just not sure I can take it any longer. This other man has given me happiness and self-respect.'

She stood up as if to stretch but instead of raising her arms upwards, she reached outwards. 'There it is,' she said. 'It's all out there. Life. I don't want to lose it.'

She turned round and stared at her daughter whose head was bent down. 'Grisel,' she said, 'Grisel. What is it? That was a long speech. Have I sent you to sleep? Do you blame me?'

There was a wait. A hazel branch quivered on the boundary. A squirrel grappled, in search of nuts.

Griselda spoke in the voice of a sleep-walker. The words came, drip-fed. 'He told me the girl at Christmas was a one-off. I remember those words. "A one-off." "Try not to judge me" he said.'

'What? You knew about her! How did you know about her? Who was she?'

'Chantal Saintange.'

A paralysis seemed to have set into both of them. The ability to move had been frozen. Only James was in motion and in each of their minds. He had begun a transition on the back of hard, shared facts. New, hitherto unsuspected truths were changing him. Shocks can be momentary or cause structural shifts. This was both.

After a few moments Claire spoke. 'He said to me that my affair must be serious because it was me. In a way this worried me because I didn't want it to be serious and it made it so when it might not have been. But now, now it is, now that I know her identity.' Each detail of their meeting at dinner returned. Each kindled a new pain at her humiliation.

'I'll not forgive him,' said Griselda. 'He betrayed me.'

'You're talking like his wife, not his daughter.'

They looked at one another startled.

'I see,' said Claire. 'She's the same age as you, isn't she?'

She sat motionless. The memory of the girl at the dinner party burnt into her, a thin line moving inwards like a hot fuse. That he had done this in her presence. So profound, the lack of respect. In her presence, to treat her presence as absence. As though she did not exist.

'Let me tell you what happened,' said Griselda.

As she told it she was haunted by the girl's insistence that they had a situation in common, a claim which till now she had been able to deny. They were the daughters of philandering fathers. My father isn't like that, she had thought at the time.

27

The glass room, no more than a cubby hole, was designated the foreign exchange unit at the bank. Mary had shared it for a month now with Sarah Dunns, or the Avon lady as she called her privately. She was the outward face of the cubby hole, her cosmetic perfection being a matter for wonder; whilst Mary did notation within and wondered how wise a move it would be to wear mascara. Sarah's spectacular rise must have been due to her expertise in festooning her eyes. It always encouraged their boss, a bald little creep named Harvey, to hover.

Today, however, he did not try to ingratiate himself with talk of business links or trade missions, nor did he address himself to Sarah but to her.

'Forgive me for asking, but your husband is in the SAS, isn't he?'

Mary, feeling too introverted to utter, inclined her head with caution.

'Well, the bank is thinking of sending some of its staff and clients on a Who Dares Wins operation.'

'What?'

'It's a conference in a very, um, relaxed environment.' He looked distinctly uneasy. 'Events are staged by former members of the SAS – you know, mine clearance, building bridges, tank driving, that sort of thing. It gives us a chance to network with our guests and to show team spirit.'

'Oh,' said Sarah Dunns. 'Will I be going?'

'We'll see what we can do.' Harvey stroked his hand over his bald pate purringly.

'Not me,' said Mary firmly.

'Not you.'

'I think,' said Sarah, fluttering, 'you have to be one of the linchpins of this organisation before you're required to attend.'

'A circus really, isn't it?'

'Come again,' said Harvey.

'What I think is this. That it's all very well for you to sham but my husband's in it for real.'

They looked at her with horror and exchanged glances. What she had pronounced was bad corporate form.

Mary too was distressed at what she had untypically said. It's because I'm upset, she thought, and pressed the fingers of her left hand to the upper part of her right breast.

'Mary,' said Harvey, 'it's only a business jolly.'

'With a serious purpose of course,' said the Avon lady.

'One day your husband might find it fun to do these things. You know, when he's left the Regiment of course.' He looked at her with curiosity. 'What will he do then? I mean it's not like working in a bank, is it?'

'No,' said Mary, 'and forget what I said. I'm not myself today,' and her hand returned compulsively to her upper breast.

'Well,' said Harvey, 'perhaps you'd like to know that the University of California has carried out research that proves the memory functions much better when people are actually enjoying themselves. So you see, go on a jolly – it's the best way to improve performance.' He gave a covert eye to Sarah and left.

I shall be marked down for lack of company spirit, thought Mary. Shouldn't have opened my mouth. He's the kind who'll never forgive a reproof. Through the glass she watched Harvey strut his balding bespectacled way across the open floor among the ranks of women in service livery. A turkey cock, his maleness boosted by the barnyard of female attendants.

'Mary, aren't you well?' asked Sarah. 'You seem a bit pale. Do you want to go home?'

'I'm fine. Just had a lot to do. I'll have to go early though.'

She had made an appointment at the surgery before picking Sam up from school. It's nothing, most probably. Ninety per cent of these things turn out to be nothing. A waste of time even to go. Everyone seems to be obsessed with their health nowadays. I think I'll cancel.

* * *

Mary waited at the gate of the school, looking with impatience at her watch. They would be taking the register, an event which had started the morning when she was a child but ended the afternoon for her son, in order to cut the rate of truancy. Eventually the children emerged in bursts and straggles. She searched for him amongst the younger ones who had reached those awkward years that bridge the bubblegum and brawling stage. She found him and waved. He ran towards her eating a packet of crisps he had saved from the canteen. Still undersized for his age and his dependence on her gave her a pang. He was in effect the child of a one-parent family, which meant that his wellbeing depended entirely on hers.

'Hurry up,' she said.

'Where're we gonna go?'

'To the doctor.'

'Why're we gonna go to the doctor's?'

'I wish they'd teach you to speak properly. Because I want to see him.'

'But why d'you wanna see him?'

'Hurry up and stop asking questions.'

Her right breast slithered about under the pressure of Dr Milsom's fingers. X marks the spot. Her brain could place it with arithmetical exactness, there, three millimetres to the northeast of his hand. It was an Everest, so couldn't he find it?

'That it?' he asked, as his fingers came to a halt.

'Yes.'

He probed a little further. A lock of his straight grey hair fell forward. His mouth pursed, thinking.

Mary had been staring with rigidity at the ceiling, neutral, but when she glanced at him she thought he looked very tired.

'I really don't think it's anything. You can get lumps, bumps, cysts the whole time. The tissue thickens. However, just to be on the absolutely safe side, I think we'll send you off for a mammogram.'

She sat up, swung her legs off the couch and put her under-wear and green jumper on again. She picked up the jacket of her little banking suit.

'Sit down,' he said. He began to leaf through her file. As it had been a while since he had seen her, he decided to throw her a confessional rope.

'Everything else all right?'

'Oh yes,' she said through the metallic taste of fear.

Dr Milsom stared at her intently. Throughout his professional life in this farming community, he had also had a number of the Regiment's families on his books. It was by no means uncommon for these files to be exceptionally full. Many of the wives, though resourceful and silent copers, were stressed. It was inevitable that some left, but how he admired the resilience of the survivors and their ability to battle it out. More than in most marriages they needed to be loyal and tenacious for they were likely to encounter the extremes of the usual ups and downs. Once he had said to his own impatient wife, 'You have nothing to complain of. Just compare yourself to those wives who have husbands with such dangerous and irregular duties.' He couldn't say this too often because repetition led to a row, but as a little reminder it had been effective in shutting her up.

The patrol had been tasked to locate and blow up the plant. For weeks now it seemed to Stuart as though they had been handcuffed to the claustrophobic interior of the jungle. They were covered in mozzie rep but still afflicted with insects and flies. They took care to drink continuously from a bottle of water for the heat and humidity were making them pour with sweat which would cause the onset of dehydration.

Waiting for the recce patrol to come back, his thoughts drifted to Sam and the effect of the bird. He had received a letter from him a couple of weeks ago looking forward to his return. If things went well he could be back home in not much more than a week. He ached for his wife and the boy. He would make sure when the lad grew up that he'd get him a job a thousand miles from a military base. His mind wandered to other tiny irrelevant things. Somehow it was consoling to concentrate on things that didn't matter. He remembered he had forgotten last time to lift a tree in the front garden because the roots had infested a drain. As he rested with his weapon and leaned against the bergen, he thought that when you were waiting you thought of everything and anything. Outrageous and incongruous. But part of a soldier's life was this endless frustration of boredom and waiting. He put his hand up to his face and touched his cam cream which he knew by now was encrusted in the crevices and hair growth. They checked each other's faces in case of telltale skin shine.

After about a couple of hours they heard noises. Experience as well as instinct caused them to categorise all noises, smells too, but this one aroused no concern as they recognised the sound of the recce patrol's return.

'Well?' said Stuart sitting up.

'Pack your gear, boys. We can chuck in an explosive.'

They agreed on their entry point and settled down for the rest of the afternoon and the night. More waiting and this would be the worst time, waiting and thinking about the operation ahead. The weapon, the explosive, would they do the business? Well before dawn they would reapply the cam cream and set out.

Most days at this time she would take Gemma for a run but Mary had no taste for her own company so took Sam to Claire's. She was not suitably dressed for action and therefore refused when Claire suggested they took the bird out. In the end they settled on watching the boy exercise Bella in the paddock. Mary watched him with a fierce and touching protectiveness.

'I owe you,' she said to Claire.

'It's turned out better than you expected, hasn't it?'

'We all owe you.'

'I owe you too. In a peculiar way, keeping this bird has changed me.'

'What do you mean?'

Claire sighed. 'More than it seems. I don't want to go into this but something's happened. I mightn't be able to go on looking after Bella. If I weren't here, could you take her over instead?'

Mary looked at the bird and the child. He was swinging the lure in its huge looping round. The hawk lifted off her perch and scooted to meet it. She closed on the feathers with their piece of meat. Mary remembered her dread of this trained killer a year ago and found it dispersed. Her hand moved over the top of her right breast. A new fear had now come from nowhere and invaded the old one's space.

She said: 'I think she's a wonderful creature. But something's come up. I'll know for sure in a week.' She turned her head to look at her companion and thought she looked strained. 'You're not ill are you?'

'No,' said Claire. She felt ashamed to admit that relinquishing her duties would not be a necessity, merely voluntary.

'I don't want to pry.'

'No.'

'Do you mean you're moving?'

'Possibly.'

'I see.'

The hawk had returned to her post. Sam walked back and forth in the paddock, revolving the line. The bird and her auxiliary showed off their masterful nonchalance. They were unaware of any threat to their co-existence.

It was a sublime injustice that death should spare old Mr Jefferies but snatch Aggie, though it managed it as expeditiously as possible. She had been waiting alone at the bus-stop where two passing witnesses had seen her fall suddenly to the ground. By the time they had summoned an ambulance, she could not be revived. The funeral took place in the village church which was overshadowed by a group of pastoral yews. It was attended by Eric Williams, by all of Wilf's family which accounted for about a hundred, and also by a colony of Aggie's. One by one the sprout-picking dynasty of Evesham and its fields filed in and stood to attention, stiffly attired in unfamiliar clothes. 'In the midst of life we are in death,' said the priest. 'Lord have mercy upon us.' 'Christ have mercy upon us,' they replied.

After the wake, it was commonly expected that poor old Wilf would break down and possibly collapse, but his orderly habits remained defiantly composed. His friends surmised that his daily routine must sustain him. Yet this didn't explain the fact that he seemed if anything a little brighter. As the days went by they were forced to conclude that throughout forty-five years, Aggie had remained peripheral, perhaps even an interference, to his real life which consisted of feeding and exercising the birds.

At the same time another shift and improvement became apparent when the two old widowed neighbours found themselves either side of the garden fence, tending their respective plants and flocks. 'Sorry about your wife,' said Mr Jefferies who had not been asked to the funeral.

'Not to worry,' replied Wilf.

And that was all that was ever said, though it was enough for both of them to understand, being men of few words.

It was a time for widowers. Immediately after the funeral Claire left to see Douglas, her father. At seventy-eight he lived in a white house with a pine-filled garden overlooking the sea at Lyme Regis. As she drove up the road she thought it was typical that he should have retired to a house on a hill, steep enough to make even her breathless. A lifetime of discipline had encouraged him to impose on himself the eternity of daily slog. She decided this attitude had probably finished her mother who had tried and failed to keep up.

She knocked on his door and looked round as she waited. White seaside houses that spoke of quiet respectable retirements in a port that was still sanctified by Jane Austen. She remembered she had brought the children to the beach here to look for fossils. She thought of Peter and his lonely ammonite. She had not heard from him. No doubt it was wise that he should stay away.

The door was opened by her father. His demeanour seemed almost flirtatious. Visitors no doubt were comparatively rare.

'Come to pay your respects to the ageing mandarin?'

'You flatter yourself.'

'Don't forget her either.'

He indicated the little black-and-tan mongrel, a companion who had managed to arouse his entire and concealed devotion. She lay down on the floor and uncurled herself like a hedgehog. Claire bent down to stroke her. She had retained her soft puppy fur and tip-tilted eyes. In private he called her the little lost boat person. In private he smoothed open her long ears and spoke gentlenesses into their folds.

Claire straightened up and surveyed her father. She complimented him on how spry and spruce he remained.

'I've a cataract in one eye, false teeth, no long sight, no short sight.'

'Has the equipment gone rubbishy then?' She smiled, admiring his undaunted attack.

'Ageing *is* rubbish, Claire.'

'I bet you didn't tell them that when you were younger.'

'No need then. My generation could be counted on to be a stoical lot.'

She followed him upstairs to the balcony on the first floor where they settled side by side on two sun-warmed wicker chairs to look out over the sea and the sky. The view was, as always, calming with its space and the absence of too much human clutter. Claire's mind drifted aimlessly with a toy boat that was sailing a line parallel to the horizon.

'I am thinking,' said her father 'of writing a monograph on Anthony Powell's use of the comparative.' He indicated his copy of the latest volume of the writer's diaries which was lying on the table beside him. 'Listen to this list of his words. "Goodish", "not intolerable", "less unprofitable", "quite impressive", "to some extent true"' – he looked up to stimulate a response – '"fairly elaborate and the reverse of cheap". There. What do you think of that?'

'That is his style, not excessive. It is the world of the relative.'

'Relativity. Quite so,'

'Life's all Einstein really,' she said sadly. 'Listen to me Daddy. I am thinking of leaving, I'm going to leave James.'

Her father put down his illegible notes. 'That is indeed excessive. Nothing moderate there. Or are you only thinking of it?'

'I'm about to see a solicitor.' She had been about to for days.

'About to. Not terminal, this, yet. Have you come to me for treatment or a diagnosis?'

She thought the old war horse looked pleased with his elegant challenge. He was always ready to assume his former role.

'Not for a cure anyway.'

'There are none. What's the problem?'

She smiled. 'It's like this, doctor. You see, he's had other women on and off all his life.'

Her father looked out to the sea. Light rocked on the water.

'Is that so very important? I did, you know, in middle age. Your mother got tired of what she called "the unnecessaries". So she shut up shop. I had to help myself liberally to such necessities elsewhere.'

Startled, she asked: 'Did she know?'

'I think so. Though neither of us said anything. We were less open about these things than you lot. There was a great deal of under-the-carpet Edwardian guilt.'

'Who were they, these women? What were they like?'

'Three of them. Ordinary women. Not the kind you drop fistfuls of diamonds or red roses on. Two are dead. One of a myocardial infarction. The other of a lymphoma, a very nasty thing. But I still correspond with the youngest and best of the three.' His face muscles relaxed, softened by memory. 'When she got cross, she used to refer to herself as the meat. Your mother of course being the milk.'

In bewilderment Claire watched the little sailing boat go about and turn back. It had the gaiety of a red sail, puffed out like the cup of a bikini.

'James has helped himself to a young piece of meat, whom he met at a dinner party with me.'

'I see. That must rankle.'

'Yes.'

'Turn the old milk sour?'

'Don't joke. It's intolerable.'

'Baddish certainly. Is it still on or over?'

'Over. He chucked her. She's a scribbler. She went to see Griselda and threatened to dump on us.' She elaborated briefly.

He listened. He said, 'Nutters confuse things for other people. Neurotics always suck others in.'

'He's been caught this time and he swears it will never happen again. A line that he's used before.'

'Probably true after this experience. Aversion therapy. Anyway, don't let her mess up the general picture.'

'What is this picture?'

'I like James. I start from this point. He's a bit weak on commitment and a bit self-indulgent but then he's been trapped. All his life he's been trapped. By his awful mother, by you getting pregnant so young, by his work and by you.'

'Not by me. I've made the mistake of allowing him too much freedom.'

'I'm not talking about now. You were both trapped, far too young when you married. You came together to fulfil a biological function, to look after the baby, solely for that reason at that time, no other. That was completed years ago. Nature no longer had any purpose for the two of you to stay together. However it had trapped him at a very young age. He had to give support to his mother, support you and two children. And, crucially, by work he didn't much like.'

'I paid my own way. Still do.'

'I know, but it's not the same. My sympathies lie with him. Especially since he's been stuck on his own in London. What on earth do you expect?'

'You can't see the philandering in my way. You're a man.'

'All right, let's say you've decided to break free now. Nature has tossed the pair of you aside. You can follow your own individual destinies. What are you going to do with this freedom? Take care, Claire. You're at an age when women lose everything. Sans teeth, sans eggs, sans husband. Sans everything.'

'I've found someone else.' She mumbled a little, knowing her father would use this to catch her out. He would do this when she was a child.

'Ah,' Douglas exclaimed. 'I should have guessed. In the surgery, the patient will offer any number of decoy ailments before getting to the point. You have found someone else, eh? All this posturing and you've been feathering another nest.'

'It's not like that at all.'

'No? Who is he, then, this answer to a married lady's prayer? What's he do?'

'He's a bird photographer and a naturalist,' she said, knowing that such ways of life sounded too fuzzy at the edges to recommend themselves to a professional.

He had stopped gazing out to sea, in order to look at her more intently. 'You're doing a book on naturalists?'

She nodded.

'A bird photographer too. I suppose you met him through your hawk. He sounds very flavour of the month.'

'You're distorting everything.'

'*You* are distorting everything. You took him on as an act of revenge and power.'

She rose to her feet and grasped the balcony rail for support.

'I took him on because I was fond of him, we had common

interests and I admire him and need him. He's modest and pure. He has all that James lacks.'

'He's a monomaniac, you mean.'

She remembered his description. A monomaniac living in a rented cottage. No, she had said: I admire your courage.

'You distort everything,' she repeated. 'James has broken up the family. Katy weeps on the telephone. And Griselda is so bitter she won't talk to him. She says she'll never forgive her father for having betrayed her and lied and done a run-around.'

'She's shocked – and jealous because the girl's young. Sit down, Claire. Let me tell you that the queen of my trio – the only one who's alive – is merely five years older than you. So you see you're in the same position as Griselda. Is it so very dreadful?'

She didn't answer.

'Is it?' he repeated.

'You're an old man now,' she said irritably. 'Old enough to present all this with tranquillity. Old enough for it not to seem the same at all.'

The wicker creaked as he stood up.

'Come with me.' He reached for her hand. 'I'll remind you of something to put it all in perspective.'

She followed him downstairs, where he put the little dog on a lead. Then they walked out of the house and to the end of the road which curved round to face the sea. They left the chaste white buildings behind and came to green fields whose slopes were knobbly with the polite droppings of sheep. The gush and suck of the sea was growing louder. Further ahead, the pasture gave way to exuberant copses and undergrowth whilst all the while the land led downwards. She gave him her hand to negotiate the bumpy descent of earth steps, which then turned into concrete that signalled the unsightly formalities of the beach. In the distance ahead lay the curling harbour called the Cobb with its strange snake formation.

'Is that where we're going?'

'Yes,' he said.

When they reached it, they started to walk side by side along its wide pavement, only partly sheltered by its stone shoulder crudely hunched against the sea. Gusts of stiff wind made the sunlight jump brassily in flashes on the waves. There was that rancid smell when the sea exhausts the same piece of land in its continuous ebb and flow.

'Wait,' said her father.

As he stopped her, she saw they had reached the first of the ammonites bedded in the Cobb's shoulder. She stared at the dark segmented circles of the fossil.

'Lovely geometry. It's like the unfurled tip of fern frond isn't it?' he said.

'Why are we stopping?'

'Because of this. I come here as I'm no longer nimble enough to scamper about at the foot of the Black Ven cliffs where the ammonites and belemnites are. So this tame one's become a bit of a friend instead. Do you see it, Claire? 140 million years old. Doesn't that put all your pother in perspective? I've enjoyed my life and long may it live but I'll join my friend very shortly. You too. Your mother already has.'

She looked at him and thought how special he was and dear to her, this old self-confessed reprobate, dearer to her in his own way than her mother or husband and even her children. It would be very sad when the time came to lose him.

She folded his arm in hers and hugged it, then walked him to the end of the Cobb, pushing her face into the wind. They stood, braced and linked, looking out to the sea. The soft floppy ears of the dog standing beside them were streaming backwards like pennants in the air.

'What was it like, losing her?'

He raised his eyebrows, thinking.

Finally he said: 'One feels a bit like an amputee. The tissues and connections still seem alive though there's some numbness. Then you get used to it. Then it's a little as though you've never had a leg at all. One gets the hang of being a widower like one gets the hang of being retired.'

'Dear Dad.'

'Life goes very fast but the way you travel is so important. Don't go off in the wrong direction for the sake of it.'

They turned and walked slowly back in silence.

'I think we'll take the road,' he said. 'I'm tired now. Don't want to fall and break a hip.'

Claire bought a fruit cake in the high street bakery and they climbed haltingly up the hill.

'Did I give you a satisfactory diagnosis and treatment if not a cure?'

'It was very satisfactory but I'm not sure whether it will work.'

They climbed a little further and he stopped again.

'You see that house?' he said pointing to a large white ice-cream confection on the right. 'They have an atrium, a jacuzzi and a gym. Awful isn't it?'

'Oh Lord, if you say so. Very vulgar.'

'And nine very white statues in the garden.'

'Ugh.'

'Baddish certainly but not intolerable.'

29

In recent days James had fallen subject to spells of panic. He was also furious and felt himself misunderstood. It was his wife who had erred yet the family's resentment had fastened exclusively on him. He had thought it would all blow over but it showed no sign of settling down. He was drinking heavily and there were times when he felt quite ill. He agreed with his partner, Brewster, that he would take a few days off. Common sense told him that the more time he spent with Claire, the better.

On the same day that she went to see her father, he drove home to Herefordshire. When he arrived at lunchtime the house was empty, of course, but he anticipated her return. The dog was asleep in the kitchen and the hawk was on her perch on the lawn. She screeched once as he passed. 'Shut up, you trout,' he said. 'You're responsible for all this.' He thought, with self-pity, that he was surrounded by the enemy in manifold forms. He went inside and sat in a chair but the frustration of lonely waiting only fomented his anger. Used to moving at speed towards a destination, it wasn't long before he felt the need to take some precipitate action. He decided he would reconnoitre his rival's den. He found it infuriating that, according to his wife, the fellow was still away.

He jumped in the car and drove over straightaway to the Stooke estate. As he turned sideways over the potholed surface to the stable cottage, he saw with shock that a Land Rover was parked outside. He deduced from this that Ravell must have returned. Or could Claire have lied about his absence? Perhaps he had not been away. The heat boiled up inside him and he felt like lobbing a grenade. He parked the car and sat for a moment to try and regain control. Then stood up, walked over and knocked at the door. He was trembling slightly. To suppress it, he tried to clench his muscles but this only made it worse. His whole body was shaking and he realised his arms had jumped akimbo. Thinking he must look like a two-handled jug, he brought them down and held them tightly by his sides. He heard a quick step, then the door opened to reveal Peter Ravell.

The two men faced one another. There was a silence, clotted with unspoken words. It continued as James found himself choking, genuinely unable to speak. Unforewarned, he had prepared nothing to say. All he could think was: this fucker has been in my bed. All the anger that had been shielded from his wife converged in a violent rush on the true target. This man, threatening his wife, his children, way of life, money, everything he had quarried in a lifetime. He thought again of his violation of the sanctum of his bed. He felt like felling him with the jawbone of an ass.

'You fucking bastard,' was all he could eventually get out.

Ravell flinched. In the end he said: 'I suppose you'd better come inside.'

James entered. He was still trembling but the release of the expletive had expelled a great gobbet of feeling which allowed him to start regaining control. He was determined to grab the ascendancy, but as he followed Ravell through the newly painted but almost empty house, his emotions took a fresh turn. He realised that this man seemed to have few, if any, material possessions. To some husbands in James's position, this demotion of an adversary might have brought relief. Instead it served only to feed his anger. The man's lack was an insult. A potentate would have made a worthier rival.

'My wife must have been mad,' he said contemptuously.

'I think she had better be the judge of that.'

'I don't intend to stay long.'

'Quite. What have you come to say?'

James had prepared nothing to say but his brain was now sufficiently obedient to stop hurling words and give him a strategy. Fully evolved it arose in his cuckolded mind.

'Well?' said Ravell.

'No pleasantries, as you might imagine. You may not know it but she's been using you.'

'I don't think I want to discuss her behind her back.'

'I'm not asking for your opinion. I'm telling you.'

'Then I don't wish to listen.'

'She has used you to get her own back at me. You're a convenient answer to a spot of jealousy. A pawn. I'm telling you this for your own sake. She'll toss you aside.'

'I think you should leave.'

'I'll leave when I choose to leave,' shouted James.

'You'll leave when I push you out and I'm pushing you out now.'

He put out a hand and for a moment it looked as though they were about to wrestle. But, too old and too inhibited, too horrified perhaps, they broke apart.

'You bloody fool,' said James. He turned and strode out. He realised he was still shaking.

On the way home, James regretted having held himself back. The anger had not lessened within him and drops of sweat collected in his brows. He noticed that all his movements were jerky and strove to bring them under control. Like a drunk he started to drive more slowly, and negotiated the bends with exaggerated care. He was relieved to arrive home without mishap, relieved too this time that Claire was not back.

He walked round to the side of the house and passed the hawk on her perch again. When she called, he went over to her. She was no longer the enemy, but another living tethered creature who might offer him solace. He felt he had acquired enough enemies without her too. She, however, did not share his viewpoint. She had never grown used to him and at his approach she now bated away, straining against the leash, her great wings winnowing the air. As he bent down towards her, she lashed out and one of her long curved talons that tipped her scaly yellow toes struck him on the cheek. Shocked, he started back and put his fingers to the cut. It was not, fortunately, a deep wound, but the physical injury proved the final straw. A burst of fury attacked him. He almost heard it like the flame spurt of a blow torch. 'You're vicious,' he said, 'a harpy,' and he reached forward and loosened the vital falconer's knot of her leash attached to the tethering ring. 'Just go,' he yelled and jumped back. 'I never want to see you again.' He retreated to a safe distance and flapped his arms. Bella, alarmed, hopped to the side and collided foolishly with her bath. She cocked her head, considering him with her opaque implacable eye. Then suddenly sensing release, she bounded forward and took off. Below and still attached to her, the long tethering tackle streamed backwards in the air, forming a dangerous trail.

He watched her disappear down the valley and out of sight. Then he turned and, fingering the rope of blood on his cheek, walked slowly back inside the house.

After James had left, Ravell had sat for a time with his head in his hands. Then, trying to regain everyday normality, he started to organise his equipment into bags, but his fingers were too unsteady to continue. He was furious and shaky and the description of himself as a pawn kept coming back. It had been hurled in vengeance, but was it possible that it was actually true? The word was tormenting. He combed through the memories of their shared recent past. He recalled the smell of the moonflowers through the window before they had first made love. 'They only open at night,' she had said. He had mocked at the time but, had he not also passionately succumbed? He remembered the occasion he had shown her the tapestried woman with the falcon. The red heart held in the man's courtly hand. 'I shouldn't have shown it to you,' he had said. 'What difference does it make whether you show it or not?' Throughout he had tried to hide his feelings, but wasn't she right? What difference did it make whether he showed them or not when she knew they were there? He had tried to defend himself but still allowed himself to succumb. Had he not simply fallen dupe to the phenomenon of romantic love?

And if this was the case, what indeed did it say about her? She had seemed so grateful and tender but, underneath, was it for her, then, no more and no less than as James had said? An eye for an eye, a tooth for a tooth, a fuck for a fuck. He felt his face wince as he looked at the unpalatable truth. 'Do you know what you are doing?' he had asked her. Had she? Had she not in truth known better than he? Had she just used him? The more he pondered, the more his fear began to take shape and become fact. Perhaps, to give her the benefit of the doubt, she had thought she had loved him but he had failed to see it in context.

He remembered her seated beside him only a few weeks ago, entranced by the falcon's pursuit of the rook. He thought now he had looked at the scene in miniature, ignoring the harsh framework to which the cameo belonged. If one looked at it in context, what it showed you was how easily in nature the predator becomes the prey. How could he have forgotten this? And what an innocent fool he had been to consider himself, poor old *homo sapiens*, an exception. He was reminded of the saying that in the natural world, the purpose of existence is to find one's own dinner without providing someone else with his. He reflected bitterly on his own position. It was partly his own fault but it was still a mess. I am a bloody fool, he thought: I have ended well and truly in the cooking pot.

He sat for a while, then took charge of himself and finished his packing. He was steadier now and calmer. Leave them to sort out their own mess, he decided. Tomorrow he had a flight to catch and work to do which was always a salvation.

At half past four Sam bicycled to the old farmhouse. Noticing that the gate to the drive was open, he pedalled in without stopping, scattering the gravel in a satisfyingly wide-sprayed arc. He propped up the metallic green cycle against the side of an outbuilding and went to the jam jar hidden under a rhubarb behind to fish out the keys to the back door and Bella's shed. It had been arranged that in Claire's absence today he would look after both dog and bird.

He walked round the side of the house, munching a noisy packet of crisps. The dog barked at the intrusion and levered himself onto the window seat of the kitchen. Recognising his old friend he waved his tail. But instead of letting him out, Sam made first for the hawk's weathering lawn. When he arrived, he found it puzzling that her bow perch was empty. He stuffed the crisp packet into his pocket and ran to the cage. There had been a change of plan perhaps. The discovery that the cage as well as the perch was empty drove him into a panic. She had gone. Had she been taken, stolen? He crossed and recrossed the lawn, breathless, whilst Jarvis wagged from the window. He ran back to the shed and confirmed that the leash was also missing. Terrified, he let himself into the house and searched blindly for a note. Jarvis came to him, pleading for attention with his pink open mouth. The kitchen door opened and James came puffily in.

'What's this noise? Oh, it's you, Sam. What are you doing?' He thought his wife wrong to give a boy this age the keys to the house.

'Bella, where is she?' He was on the brink of tears, his cheeks mottled red.

'She's gone. I don't know. She flew that way.' James threw out a wobbly arm in the direction of the valley.

'How did she escape?'

James was silent.

'She's wearin' her leash and her mews jesses. She'll hang herself on a tree and die.'

He spun round and ran out through the garden in the direction of the valley. Jarvis followed and fell into a slow lope behind.

Claire drove over the Severn bridge and up the Wye Valley, in the shelter of its lush overhanging cliffs. She thought she had probably worn out her father but that, unequally, he had helped her revive. During the whole of the journey, she had reflected on his advice. Should she do as he said: endure it, just sweat it out? Did she truly want to break up the marriage? Durable things were beautiful because they had shown a fitness for their purpose.

As she turned into the drive through the column of old trees, she thought how fiercely she loved the place and didn't want to lose it, to break the continuity with its past. Then, as she parked the Rover, she noticed that James's car was also there, and Sam's green bicycle. He was staying later than usual. She walked round the side to the lawn. The bow perch was empty but she assumed that he and Bella were together. She opened the back door of the silent house and called. No answer but a mug and plate on the table indicated that someone had been there.

'James?'

Still no answer. Was he also out with the bird?

She climbed the stairs to the bedroom to change. As she walked straight to the wardrobe, she didn't notice him at first, then saw him propped up on the bed, unshared for days, a whisky bottle and tumbler in his hands.

'What's happened?' She went closer to peer. 'And what the hell have you done to your face?'

'She did it. Your oh-so beautiful girl.'

'Not Bella?'

James nodded. 'The cow. I talked to her. I've talked to all your pets today. Including Ravell.'

'You did *what*?'

'I told him you'd taken him on as a swipe at me. Well it's true, isn't it?'

He poured himself another whisky.

'How dare you!'

She thought of her father who had said the same thing. All yielding left her. Claire hated them both. Who were they to meddle and assume? She went to the side of the bed and thought about striking him for stating this element of truth which poisoned the whole.

She said coldly, 'You just wanted to wound. You're a child. You get gratification from hurting. Even Sam's more grown up than that.' She looked round. 'Where is he?'

'Hah. Looking for Bella.'

'What do you mean?' She felt apprehensive.

'She flew away from the perch.'

He flapped his arm. It was uncoordinated. She realised he was considerably pissed.

'She couldn't have.' Mentally she checked the safety of her tethering knot. She always checked them obsessively.

'With her lead on?'

'Seems so.'

She panicked, put her hand to her head, but was also suddenly suspicious. 'Why did she scratch you?'

He sat up, defensive. 'Ask her. You always talk to her.'

'That knot couldn't have given. The leash couldn't have broken. It's Terylene. She scratched you and you undid her, didn't you? I know you. You let her go.'

'Look at this. It could have been my eye. Don't you care about this?'

'You let her go. And Sam's out there looking for her. Has he told you she can hang herself and die?'

He flapped a hand down in drunken dismissal. 'Ever since she came, you've cared more for her than for me.'

'If he climbs a tree to get her and falls, you'll have his death on your conscience as well as hers.'

'You'd like that scenario, wouldn't you? Very harrowing. So that you can thrash me over the head with it, again and again and again and again.'

Grimly Claire walked out of the room to the continuum of his shouting 'again and again'. Then she let herself out of the house. She fetched a rope from the barn and, like the dog and the boy, hurried through the paddock and beyond.

He had run all the way over two fields, but the slope of the hill had forced him to slow down. By now he was very tired and starting to stumble. His ability to whistle had also dried up. When he pursed his lips, only a puff of shrivelled air blew out. He tried to spit but couldn't muster enough saliva. He wished he hadn't eaten the whole packet of salt crisps. He should have drunk a glass of water like his dad always said. Forlorn, Sam sat down beside Jarvis and thrust his hand in his pocket, seeking his referee's whistle. At the bottom, beneath the string and the penknife and the sweet cellophanes, he found the good old Acme Thunderer. If he couldn't do it himself, he would have to use this instead. He rubbed the grit off and put it to his lips. The shrill scream bounced round the valley. If she couldn't hear that, she was deaf. Deaf. Or dead. The awful thought made him jump up again, his heart thudding like an alien thing. He scanned the valley, thinking. He had patrolled this ground so often that he could visualise every detail of the land and knew its rhythmic cries. But the land was less use to him now than the sky. He was looking into a western sun and had to squeeze up his eyes behind his glasses to decipher the light. It was autumn and large flocks of small migratory birds were already on the move, practising for the imminent marathons of flight. But for Sam these were no more than confusion. What he looked for were the telltale mobs of rooks, blackbirds and magpies. Yet at this distance shapes were so simplified that it was hard to read one silhouette from another.

Then, as he peered myopically, he thought he could spy activity around the dense head of a far oak tree.

He began to run again over the grass and into a stand of rustling bracken. At this point the dog decided to give up. He plodded in his sensible way to stand guard over the place where the pair of them had sat. Sam sprinted forward, tripping over the stones and roots, tangling with brambles. The barbs of a stem rent the leg of his trousers. He was scratched and breathless but also convinced, as he began to distinguish more clearly the individual bird's cries. He started to call out that he was coming, but as in a nightmare only a whimper came out. He was pounding more and more slowly as he reached the tree. Looking up at the rooks by its branches, he missed his step on the ground and fell on a bed of soft tussocks.

For a moment he lay there, winded. The lull was filled with the deafening heave of his own breath, but also further away and outside him, there was something more subtle. The mocking and delicate sound of twin chimes. 'Bella,' he said. He pushed his glasses back onto his nose, picked himself up and limped to the tree. He stood by its bole and stared up through the tabular layers of its wavy leaves. There was nothing. He shifted his position to alter his angle. Still nothing. Then some leaves fluttered. There she was. It was the tip of her wing. As he saw her, his heart bumped. The bird was alive. He moved to the left and called her again. She looked down, then reflexed and jumped but was pinioned. Her leash must have tangled and caught in a branch.

He stood back to think, then walked round the tree to assess its pattern of branches. She was tied to a lateral stem about two-thirds up of the big oak's height, but he thought if he inched his way with the help of the creance, he could climb its ladder of boughs. Just take it slowly and calmly, his dad always said. So, after a pause, he took the creance with great deliberation out of his pocket and tried to lassoo the lowest of the branches. It took several attempts but the third one held. With one hand over the other, he pulled himself up amongst the leaves and green acorns, smooth and swollen in their scaly cups. There was a long way to go.

Mary arrived to find Stuart sitting on the concrete step in front of the open door. He looked weak and when he stood up became wobbly.

'Oh love,' she said. 'Why didn't you go inside?'

'Doesn't matter about me,' he protested. 'It's you I'm screwed up about.'

'Can't you tell? Wake up, you plonker. Can't you see I'm alive?'

'Oh Mary.' He looked at her transparently honest, sturdy face.

He didn't care about the nosy neighbours or inadequate conifer hedge or anything, but folded his arms about her and leant on her. She felt as solid and dependable as a bollard.

'Just a cyst,' she said. 'A little cyst that got me over-excited.'

'What a pair we are. Me as well as you, up the creek with fever.'

'You look awful. The colour of a turnip under that tan. And those spots.'

'Better a bug than what happened to Mannie.'

She drew back and stared at him.

'Poor Linda.'

'Poor old fucking Mannie.'

'Invalided out.'

She looked at his drawn face. You all start at the peak of hope and fitness, she thought. Then bits gets chipped away. Bits of nerve and body get shattered. One way or another, over the years each one of you has changed.

'When the three years of this tour is up, you know,' she said evenly, not watching him, relying on information that she knew would be carried in his voice, 'will you stay? Do another?'

'Or will I return to unit, you mean?'

'I suppose I do.'

'What do you think?'

'You'll stay.' She expected the momentary bleakness; then corked it down, where it belonged.

'I can hack it, you see. Some of them can't.'

'And when you're forty,' she said, 'or thereabouts?'

'When I'm no good to them, I'll—'

'Jump out of a cake at business conferences.'

'Sure. Fun. Why not? And become a minder or a bodyguard or run a security service and use the skills I've learnt.'

She was silent for a moment, anticipating. She knew that the change of occupation from an SAS soldier to your regular ordinary married bloke was one of the most difficult times. The lion lies down with the lamb but it can be a rotten partnership. You stop making a fuss of him. He expects it. You get on each other's nerves and walk apart. You've got used to a split with one partner abroad. You're realistic enough to have perfected a marriage that works best in bursts.

'Don't think ahead,' he said wearily. 'Take it as it comes.'

'But I do. I'm an army wife.'

'You know what you always say about visualising me coming through the door?'

'Yes?'

'Sitting on the step just now, waiting, I realised it's true too the other way round. I always see you opening this stupid front door. I never really think you'll be ill, that you might not always be here. Not really.'

She inspected him. 'Don't take me for granted. Ever. Will you? Nor Sam.' She frowned. 'That reminds me. He should be home. He was going to check on Claire's dog and bird and then come straight home.'

'Well, he hasn't arrived.'

She disappeared into the house. The neighbours opposite looked on curiously, over the two-foot-high row of conifers.

Lower down in the tree it was cool and dark like a jungle, full of old spicy dust. But when he climbed higher and the leaves rustled, shards of light splintered down. About halfway up, the branches were closer and easier to mount, but as he stretched upwards he found they grew sparsely, thrusting out at odd angles. At one point he slipped as he pulled up on the creance. He hung on and steadied himself by plonking the soles of his trainers on the bark of the trunk, but the rope had slid in his hands and made their palms bleed. He sat on the branch when he reached it and took a good rest. He was trying very hard not to be frightened. It had been a mistake a moment ago to look down. It reminded him of the awful deep end of the swimming-pool.

This was green, not blue, and leafy, but it was still a terribly long way down. The old drowning feel came back to his throat. *Don't look down*, Dad had said. He took a deep breath and carried on. He knew if he didn't free her, she would hang there and die, her white skeleton swaying in the wind whilst acorns fell and squirrels leapt about her.

Climb by climb he drew nearer. She made small squeezy noises and licked her beak with her pink tongue. She unfurled her right wing into a half-pleated fan as she so often did on the ground. He had one more branch to go, one more heave. The cups of his hands were slippery, wet with sweat and bleeding, but he rubbed them against his torn trousers before reaching up for the final move. He didn't look down but swung up, a monkey stretch, all arms. A moment later, panting, he was sharing her branch.

He now started to inch along. Outwards, away from the safety net of the trunk, away from the swimming-pool rail. Physically it had become easier, mentally much harder. Away from shelter, and the circumference of the branch was narrowing all the time. As he reached her, the bough started to sway, the fulcrum of his body upsetting the balance. He felt terribly faint for a moment and thought he was going to tip forwards. Please Dad, he whispered, save me. Don't look down, he heard his father say which helped him and the dizziness went out of his body, letting him hang on with his left hand whilst, with his right, he fumbled for her leash which was so coiled he knew that, one-handed, he would find it impossible to undo. So he took out his penknife, levered the blade open against his branch and started to cut as near to her jesses as possible. She watched with indifferent curiosity as though it weren't happening to her. The stuff was resistant. He sawed on and sawed on, then suddenly it was severed. 'Go,' he said, 'go, go.' He would have to let her fly free and recall her to the fist only when he was down. But to get down, he would have to look down. He felt shaky, a little bit faint again now the worst bit was over. He folded and pocketed his penknife and began to inch back to the shelter of the trunk.

Claire had followed the same track. She shouted all the way. From the top of the hill she heard Jarvis, who all the while had been guarding the soft option of his grassy patch. She was alarmed to find him alone. 'Where's Sam?' she said clearly and slowly, separating the words as though to a foreign or stupid person, which in his blameless way he was. 'Sam,' she said again. He looked with reluctance towards the track that led into the bracken. 'Go,' she commanded, and he turned and she followed. Dependable in his powers of retrieval, he began to sniff his way down the hill and then up, on track for the tree. From a distance, like an answering songbird on the air, there came the three-pronged whistle and a faint tumbling of chimes.

When she arrived, she saw the two of them united, the boy knuckling her feathers gently, lying exhausted at the foot of the oak. He turned to look at her. His face was changed. It was torn and grimy with a gash on his forehead but it was triumphant. 'I got her,' he said. 'Do you see? I got her. I climbed to the top of the tree. Right up to the top. I got her.' Then he stared at her. 'What's the matter? Why aren't you happy?' He was embarrassed. 'Silly to cry.'

30

They had been talking for two hours. Every time she had gone out of the room, James followed her. She had apparently reduced him to the status of a dog. In the end he had said: 'I feel dreadful. I smell. I must have a bath,' craving the comfort of hot water. After ten minutes he had called her. His voice was so strange, she had come. She found him rocking himself like a baby in the tub. Soap and sponge both untouched. Poor James, she thought. She sat down and stretched out a hand. Poor James.

'The truth is I can't cope without you,' he said.

'You can and you must. Shall I tell you what'll happen? Not immediately, but in due course, you'll get perky and marry again.'

'Never.' He rocked faster in denial.

'Oh yes.'

'No.'

'A sprightly widow. An unlucky divorcée with two kids. A girl looking for a decent set-up.'

'No.'

'It will be silly for it to be too soon. There'll be an interregnum period, of course, between me and the next. Then one day, in a couple of years, say, you'll look round and find you'll have been plonked in the middle of a new house, new room, surrounded by new furniture in the style of the new woman. And you'll like it. You'll think it's nice.'

'Claire, please don't joke.'

She saw he had begun to cry a little. Fully submerged in the water, he was a wrecked ship which had run aground. Yesterday she had remembered only the horrid things about him. Now, a treacherous waft of pity allowed the good memories to return. Family holidays of English shingle and, later, French sand and pine. His solicitude and worry once when she had been ill. 'I still don't understand,' he said. 'I know I've fucked you up, but it's well and truly over. It's in the past, don't you see? There's no question of me being unfaithful again.'

'I know that.'

'Then why? Did you expect me to stand by and let that bugger walk in and smash me up? Jesus, Claire, I've got plenty to forgive too. You let him into my bed.'

He stopped crying and surged from the water, red-faced. The liquid splashed over the edge and trickled in trails to the ground. 'You've had your revenge. I could have killed him and you, and again. Can't we just forgive and forget?'

'You know it's nothing to do with your visit to Ravell. I loathed you but even I didn't expect you to take that lying down.'

'But it can't just be Bella.'

'You took it out on that bird. My bird and Sam's. An eleven-year-old child.'

'She nearly blinded me. Look.' He leant forward to thrust his wound in her face.

'I see it, James, yes. You can take it away now.'

'There was provocation. Any court would say the balance of my mind was disturbed.'

'She would have died. And he could have. He climbed up that tree.'

'But it ended all right.' He was shouting again. 'Why don't you live in the real fucking world?'

She looked down at her hands. They were prematurely old, aged and roughened by outside work. She remembered her father's warning. *Sans teeth, sans eggs, sans husband, sans everything.*

'It's no good. Perhaps if it had been a one-off . . . But it came on top of so many years of lies. The fact is, James, what you want obliterates everyone else. I could forgive you the lot, but not yesterday.'

'Don't you lecture me. "The fact is . . . The trouble is . . ."'

'Perhaps I should have packed it in years ago. Marriage is about service and trust. We had the one, not the other.'

'Claire, half the lonely husbands in London, they all did it, do it.'

'I didn't know it went with the place, with the job. Anyway, it's not that. When I came back from my father yesterday, I was going to stick with you. You know, he's on your side.'

His face lifted at the thought of reinforcements.

'Then you blew it.'

He crumpled. She was more dispassionate now. She thought what a sorry figure he cut in his bath of despond.

'The water's got cool,' she said. 'Your skin's puckered. Either get out or put some more hot in.'

'You haven't thought it through. Where will you go? Not, you say, to Ravell. It doesn't make sense to move out on your own.'

She agreed but didn't say so. Nothing made sense. She was the sort who had a tap-root. Tap-rooted folk don't move. Ravell in contrast was a wanderer. His grandfather, his father, his daughter, all rootless. She could not envisage moving in with him, not at this stage anyway. Never probably. He might never forgive her, not if he had believed James. She had rung him repeatedly last night to deny this perversion of the truth, but he wasn't there. She would get in touch but knew she was on the move alone.

James stood up shakily in the bath and wrapped a towel around his water-putrified skin. 'If you think I'm setting you up in a love-nest, you've got another think coming.'

'Don't worry. I'm moving on my own.'

He thought: with up to half my worldly goods, half my pension, half me, all my children. What am I left with to myself? Mother. 'Christ, I can't believe it.' I'll end up like Dad, he thought. Five years of staring at the Rayburn. Oh God.

'Claire,' he panicked, 'you can't go. I can't cope.'

'Let me quote you back one of your favourite statements. Remember? "I have always thought that one of the great philosophical statements of the twentieth century is *Che sera, sera*."'

She took his hand and helped him from the bath. 'In any case, I'll be your friend. Always, I suppose.'

He remembered the summer afternoon over a year ago. The sparrowhawk seizing the dove in its talons. Its flightpath skimming his hair. He recalled sitting beside the wounded bird in friendship. Awaiting his turn to be plucked.

'Don't we even have a fall-back position?' he pleaded. 'Friendship, but still married.'

'Not really,' she said. 'Fall-down perhaps. Not fall-back.'

She drove to Hereford, too early for her appointment with the solicitor, but then she didn't want to sit waiting at home. The traffic was heavy so she turned off the ring road and into the main inner streets of the city, following the medieval zig-zag of the old grid. Leaving the car here was difficult, so she cut sideways into the alley where Nell Gwynne was born. At the top of the lane, she found a parking place opposite the red sandstone cathedral whose hulk lay on her right. Claire glanced at this sombre edifice, then at her watch and realised she had almost an hour to spare and that a visit might be appropriate. So she walked across its precinct, past the adolescents encamped on the grass and past the exhortatory notices asking them not to go on the grass.

It was welcome to leave the noise and enter this chamber of vast, calm space. There were few other people so she was able to stand still and bask alone in the emptiness. Only the massive elephantine pillars divided its void. Like trees, they marched towards the altar, sprouting their carved roof of fan-branches above her head. Here was Perpendicular England, upreaching and solid, with its all its simple inflexible rules.

Following the visitors' arrows, she walked to the back of the nave, along the end and up the opposite aisle. Past the usual recumbent knight with a dog curled at the feet of his effigy, where she paused to study the inscription. Then as she stared at this veteran of the battle of Poitiers, there came the sound of the organ. She looked up in surprise but it almost immediately stuttered, then ceased abruptly. Silence and a few more chords in search of an anchor, then silence again. She sank down at the end of one of the red clothed pews and waited. These fragments resembled an orchestra tuning up. Surely a piece of greater coherence must ensue. Then, after a short interlude, to draw breath perhaps or even confidence, both player and instrument found marvellous common voice. A rich pure flood of Bach gushed out: 'Jesu, Joy of Man's Desiring'. The notes galloped after each other, a rippling ecstatic outpouring held firm by the base divergent chords. Faithless, a disbeliever, she sat, an unlikely audience of just one, drawing strength from the optimism of the past that surrounded her. Then the glorious sound faded and there was silence again. She sat on in hope, or just reluctant perhaps to move onto less safe ground, but the silence remained unbroken. The organist, it seemed, had spoken once only, then closed down and gone home.

Finally she rose and saw, to the right of where she was standing, an arrow on the wall which pointed to the cathedral's treasure, the Mappa Mundi, the great map of the world made at the end of the thirteenth century, so she walked through the long cool corridor towards the darkened sanctum that was its home.

It was here rather than the church that a small group had assembled. Claire took up a central position beside a man with an earnest Lutheran face and then moved forward to stare at the map's weird calf-skin world. The man beside her started talking in a quiet foreign voice. It was important to realise, he said, that the map-maker had got things wrong. There was a confusion that had arisen from copying. As a result Europe on the left and Africa on the right had been mislabelled. Never mind, he said. Christ sat at the top with his angels on His Day of Judgement and Jerusalem was placed in the centre of the world, in perfect accordance with Christian convention. All secular, all geographical knowledge had been given a divine framework.

She took a step nearer and looked in amazement at the sheer diversity of creation presented in terms of a map. It made you dizzy with detail for everything was happening at once and the more you stared the more became apparent. Past mingled with present and the real with the fabulous. There were salamanders and gryphons and phoenix and dragons. Here you could see the bat-eared people and gold-digging ants; and there a little man with one leg which he used as a parasol against the sun. On the right was India with her 5,000 cities and on the other side, Mount Etna erupting in flames and here, on the left, almost off the map, poor old Britain on the rim of the globe, which, when you thought about it, was a reasonable comment for the late twentieth century. Here was a world so absorbing and varied that it offered refreshment. It was impossible to look at the map and not feel an omnivorous hunger for life in all its various forms.

Then, just when she thought she had finished, she noticed a little drawing on the bottom right, on its own and outside the edge of the curved world. It showed a huntsman with a pair of greyhounds, waving, it seemed, to a man on horseback beside him. He was speaking and she bent to see what he said, but the words were not immediately easy to decipher. 'Passe avant,' said her guide behind her. 'He is waving and saying, "Passe avant." "Go forward."'

She smiled at this kindly stranger and thanked him, then walked out slowly, out of the cathedral and into the town. Out of the old fixed world and into the new which was already shifting. Armed with the words of the huntsman like a slogan she went up Broad Street and turned right, across High Town and eastwards to one of the old lanes in this part of the city. Here she stopped at the door of a brick building and looked at the standard lawyer's brass plaque which was her end and her destination. Ah dear God, she thought. *Passe avant.* Go forward.

31

There seemed more of *passe*-ing *en arrière* in the following
months, than going forward, but at least the terms of the
divorce had been agreed without rancour or wrangling. They
put the house on the market and the estate agents rubbed their
hands, but since it was winter and the offers were inadequate,
Claire agreed with James to hold it over to the spring. Meanwhile
it was dismantled, starting with the bird.

Sam was impatient for the transfer.

'When can I have her?'

'Whenever Wilf moves the cage.'

'Now?'

'Yes.'

'Good.' He edged a bit nearer. 'Is she mine, sort of?'

'You've earned her.'

'You can come and see her,' he said with a grown-up politeness
that was newly acquired.

'Yes.'

'We can hunt together, like we used to. Just sometimes. I
know she's a bit yours.'

'Thank you. That would be very kind.'

She felt a pang at receiving her dismissal but knew that it
marked the achievement of all she had set out to do. It was
worth it, but how achingly she would miss the bird. Perhaps in
the spring she would go to the American deserts and see them
nesting in cactus. Or south to the Gulf and watch the sakers
flying in the Arab sun. These were her consolations but there
were moments when Claire looked at her life and saw more
holes than substance.

She also wrote briefly to Ravell. Stooke told her he'd gone for the winter to America and had left a temporary address. She'd felt she was writing to no one, nowhere, about an episode that had happened long ago. She made several attempts but erased them. Each had the unsavoury flavour of seeking forgiveness. In the end she confined herself to the facts. *James and I are divorcing. I know what he said to you – or at least what he told me he said to you. It wasn't true, or I suppose if I am honest with myself, there was an atom of truth when it started, but not later. I think you must have realised that. I tried to get in touch with you to explain but you'd already gone. Anyway, old events can't be rehashed. One has to draw a line beneath them. If you're ever back, please get in touch. I may be in America myself in the spring.*

Clumsy, she thought, putting it in an envelope, crude, out-of-date, encumbering, but then putting anything on paper was bound to come out all wrong. But nonetheless she would get it off before James arrived for the afternoon as he did once or twice a month. He had indeed at the beginning gone to pieces as predicted but was patching himself together with the help of an adequate substitute who possessed a four-up, three-down, exposed beams house of her own. She had received it as a result of the court's consent to the merry-go-round of her own divorce.

'Is she nice?' asked Claire.

'All right. A bung for the time being anyway.'

'Self-supporting, certainly.'

'At least that.'

'Any regrets, bugger you?'

'Yes.'

'Does she know why we split up?'

'No,' he said, wary of the old quicksands.

'No, I imagine not.' She thought. 'She wouldn't believe it was over a bird, would she?'

He remained silent for a moment, then said: 'Claire. You know I still miss you terribly. I'll try and get used to her, and if she'll do, I'll marry her because I've always been married, but you've only to say about getting back together and—'

'I know,' she said sadly. 'I so wish I could.'

There was a mutual pause, then he asked, 'Have you heard from him?'

'No.'

'Anything else I'm not up to date with?'

'Something Alice told me.'

'What?' He was not sure he wished to know.

'I asked her about the Saintange girl. She said her mother had never died. No car crash at all.'

Finally he said, 'You mean I was taken for a mug on this too?'

'It would seem so. Alice had known her mother when young and didn't keep in touch regularly. But she gathered the girl had been a lot of trouble as a teenager. Clever and hyperactive. It was true she had been upset by her father's philandering.'

He got up. Until this moment he had felt married to her still; but now, for the first time, he felt the stirring of a real desire for a *tabula rasa*. The new world with no mistakes.

'I'll see you next month,' she said.

'Yes.'

They kissed with some of the old affection that had been obliterated in the last few months.

A few weeks later Ravell replied, just a couple of lines. He thanked her for the note. Perhaps he too owed her an apology for leaving abruptly and acting in haste. He would be back in February. Please wait, he said. He would get in touch. At least, she thought, the door had creaked open, the world become a more interesting place. *'Passe avant,'* says the little huntsman. 'Go forward.' The world of 1290 had many marvels, but then so too does the millennium, though you must make your own map.

She went to see Wilf.

'Husband not up to much,' he said slyly.

'Not exactly.'

'Nor the other man?'

She did not answer.

'Come for a bird?'

She smiled.

Later that week the three of them went out together for the first time for months. They went to the foothill valleys of the mountains. In the clear winter light Bella floated above them in leisurely command of her space.

'I've been offered a falcon,' said Wilf. 'A saker. She's special. Would you like her?'

She watched Bella spreading the fringe of her fingertips into the face of the wind. She hung there for a moment then spun across the sky.

'I don't know,' she said. 'I won't know anything till the spring. But it's possible after that. I think yes, after that?'

Passe avant. Go forward.